Outbreak

www.penguin.co.uk

Outbreak

Frank Gardner

BANTAM PRESS

TRANSWORLD PUBLISHERS
Penguin Random House, One Embassy Gardens,
8 Viaduct Gardens, London SW11 7BW
www.penguin.co.uk

Transworld is part of the Penguin Random House group of companies
whose addresses can be found at global.penguinrandomhouse.com

Penguin
Random House
UK

First published in Great Britain in 2021 by Bantam Press
an imprint of Transworld Publishers

A CIP catalogue record for this book
is available from the British Library.

ISBNs 9781787632387 (hb)
9781787630680 (tpb)

Typeset in 11/14.5 pt Palatino LT Std by Jouve (UK), Milton Keynes
Printed and bound in Great Britain by Clays Ltd, Elcograf S.p.A.

The authorized representative in the EEA is Penguin Random House Ireland,
Morrison Chambers, 32 Nassau Street, Dublin D02 YH68.

Penguin Random House is committed to a sustainable
future for our business, our readers and our planet. This book
is made from Forest Stewardship Council® certified paper.

To Lizzie.

Ingen kan tjene to mestere.
Nobody can serve two masters.

NORWEGIAN PROVERB

1

BLINDINGLY WHITE AND bitterly cold, the landscape around them was utterly devoid of life. Bent half double and hunched against the wind, the three muffled figures trudged in single file through the winter afternoon, their snow goggles flecked with tiny crystals of ice. A thin blue nylon cord, tied around their waists, connected the last two to the one in front, their mittened hands steadying their balance as they placed one foot mechanically in front of the other. The blizzard had taken them by surprise. It had come barrelling down the valley, straight from the polar ice cap, eight hundred miles to the north, obliterating the weak yellow disc of the sun within seconds, then tearing and tugging at their thermal protective clothing. Caught out, far from their base camp at Ny-Ålesund, the three environmental scientists from the UK Arctic Research Station had been forced to abandon their field work for the day and make for the nearest shelter.

The hut was tiny, just a distant, solitary blot at the base of a rocky escarpment, its roof obscured beneath a layer of wind-driven snow. No coil of smoke rose from its chimney, no snowmobile lay parked up outside. It seemed no one was home.

'Better not be locked!' Chris Coppinger called to the pair behind

1

him, as they tramped up to the door. But the wind stole his words and swept them away down the valley. Coppinger shrugged. Conversation would have to wait until they were inside. He adjusted the sling of the Mauser 30-06 rifle that hung from his shoulder – mandatory protection against the three thousand carnivorous polar bears that roamed the Svalbard archipelago – and pushed open the door.

The smell hit him the moment he stepped inside. At forty-two, with a PhD in atmospheric chemistry, Coppinger was more than familiar with any number of pollutants harmful to humans and plants. This was not a smell he recognized.

'Bloody hell!' he exclaimed. 'This is rank. Something's gone off in here.' He moved to one side to make room for the others. They stood in the doorway, stamping the snow off their boots and peeling off their goggles and mittens, their eyes adjusting to the gloomy interior. Coppinger hunted through his pockets until he found a torch. In silence he swept the beam across the room methodically, like the scientist he was, from left to right. A stack of wood, an unlit stove, a metal bucket piled high with coal, a wooden chair, toppled over on to the floor. To its right, a large piece of furniture, an old sofa, covered with a blanket, and there was something on it in the corner, a shapeless amorphous mass. And then it moved.

Dr Sheila Mackenzie, the expedition medic, was the first of the three to react.

'It's alive!' she exclaimed, as she snatched the torch and rushed across the cabin to investigate. She stopped just short of the sofa, nearly dropping the torch, as she clamped her hand over her mouth in horror. Lit by the stark white beam, a human figure lay propped against the back of the couch. The man's face was hideously disfigured by livid pustules, some oozing yellow matter that trickled down his cheeks. Twin rivulets of dried blood ran from his nostrils past his lips and over his chin, smeared sideways where he had tried to wipe them away. He was wearing a thick woollen chequered shirt beneath a half-open down jacket. The shirt was caked with what looked like black bile, flecked crimson with splashes of half-dried blood. But her attention was focused on something else: the hideously swollen lymph glands just beneath his earlobes. On both sides of his head she could see them clearly in the torch beam and her medical training told her exactly what they were: buboes, a sign of severe infection.

And now this man's lips were moving – he was trying to say something. Against her better judgement, Dr Mackenzie moved closer to catch his words. His voice was faint and weak, his eyes were closed, but she heard the word clearly. *'Pamageetye.'* She turned to the others behind her for an explanation. *'Pamageetye . . .'* she repeated slowly, for their benefit. 'What does that mean? Anyone know? It doesn't sound Norwegian.'

It happened so quickly after that, no one had time to react. As Dr Mackenzie turned back to face the sick man, without warning he arched his body forward off the back of the couch with surprising speed. His whole torso shook with involuntary convulsions. In that same moment, he coughed violently. His mouth wide open in a rictus gape, he emitted a spray of bile, blood and mucus into the air, his face less than two feet from hers, before collapsing, quivering, on to the wooden floor.

2

Herefordshire, England
Monday, 7 March, 1530hrs GMT

LUKE CARLTON HELD the slim cylindrical suppressor in his left hand and screwed it quickly and expertly on to the SIG Sauer P226 Mk25 pistol held in his right. Fifteen rounds in the magazine. That should cover him. His breathing measured and under control, he rose from a crouch and moved forward slowly, testing each footfall before he placed his full weight. Any noise, any sudden movement, could give away his position.

Ahead of him, less than twenty metres away now, he could see the door to the room. Would it be locked? And what if it was? Okay, sure, he could shoot out the lock, but then the element of surprise would be lost completely. Stealthily, he approached the door from the side, dropped once more to a crouch and reached up with his left hand. His gloved fingers closed around the chrome doorknob and he began to turn it. Covert single entries: always a heart-stopper. There was a soft click and he felt the catch slide out of place. He eased open the door, just wide enough to squeeze himself through the gap, then dashed through it, moving quickly to the side, minimizing the time he would be silhouetted in the space. Good. He hadn't been seen.

Luke found himself at the end of a long corridor, exactly as the floor plan had shown. He knew where he was heading: third door on the left. It was slightly ajar and already he could hear shouts and thuds and screams – the sound of a brutal interrogation under way. He was just in time. Holding the weapon in front of him with both hands, he shouldered open the door, taking in the scene in front of him in a split second. The girl was sitting upright, her hands tied behind her, her arms and legs bound to the chair. Her interrogators were either side of her. Big, well-built men with rolled-up sleeves and black balaclavas. Luke didn't hesitate. He shot the first in the head, then put two rounds into the chest of the other.

As both went down he dropped low, scanning the room for any other threats. There were none. He uncocked his weapon and holstered it, walking swiftly over to the girl on the chair. But she was already up and shaking off the ropes that had 'bound' her.

'Sergeant Louise Kentish. I'm one of the instructors here,' she told him. 'Nice going, but you'll need to be faster through the door next time. The second one might have dropped you.' She walked over to a table and switched off the tape player that had been churning out the sounds of a mock interrogation. The lights were coming on now, illuminating the frighteningly realistic three-dimensional fibreglass dummy targets on springs that Luke had put down with the live fragmentation rounds fired from his SIG. They were inside the Bunker, the purpose-built underground SAS 'Killing House' at Pontrilas, just half a mile from the Welsh border and a short drive from the Regiment's base outside Hereford. As one of a very small handful of serving case officers in the Secret Intelligence Service qualified in close-quarter combat and hostage rescue, Luke Carlton had just passed his annual certification test. Since joining the SIS he had been sent on more courses than he could remember, but this was one of the few mandatory tests he found himself actively looking forward to. It kept him on his toes and that was how he liked it.

'Got time for a brew before you go?' she asked casually, tidying away the last of the exercise's rope coils and stuffing them into a burlap sack. The fact that any one of Luke's shots, if aimed a few degrees to one side, would have ended her life did not seem to faze her in the slightest.

He looked at his watch and winced. 'Christ, no, I'm out of time! I'm supposed to be at an opera in Covent Garden with the girl-friend this evening. Promised her I wouldn't be late.'

The instructor shrugged and turned away with a smile. 'Better not let her down, then, had you?'

3

THE MOMENT DR Sheila Mackenzie felt the liquid droplets hit her unprotected face she knew she was in trouble. Long before the Covid-19 pandemic erupted around the globe she had known all about viral loads and the risks incurred by exposure to an infected person. Yet she didn't panic, she didn't cry out: she did exactly what her years of medical training had taught her. Calmly, and without a word, she bent down and searched inside her day sack until she found what she was looking for: a sealed packet of antibacterial wet wipes. In the grim world of infectious pathogens, she knew this was tantamount to trying to hold off an advancing army with an air rifle, but she had to go through the motions.

The pustules on the man's face, the black bile, the caked blood down his chest, that and the swollen lymph nodes, told her this was no Coronavirus. It was something very different. She had no idea how long the incubation period would last before the horrendous infection struck. But unless she got medical attention, and fast, just one look at the slumped figure at her feet told her all too graphically exactly what the end state would be like.

She could hear one of the scientists behind her calling her name, but she ignored him. She was too busy painstakingly sweeping every last inch of her face with the antibacterial wipes. Blot and rub, just as she had been trained to do. Then, one by one, she dropped the contaminated tissues into a plastic bag and sealed it. She was so focused on her task she barely noticed that outside the wind had picked up and the storm was intensifying. She could hear her name being called above the rising din. 'Sheila!' The voice was ever more insistent. It was Chris Coppinger, still standing just inside the doorway, swirls of wind-driven snow circling around his boots. He was on his phone to the research station back at Ny-Ålesund. 'Are you okay?' he shouted inside the hut. 'They want to talk to you.' He held out his phone and started to move towards her but she put out a hand to stop him. He should have known better.

'Social distancing, Chris!' she rebuked him. 'I'm infected. And, no, of course I'm not okay. What the hell does it look like? I'm contaminated now. It's possible we all are. You can't come near me and I definitely can't touch your phone.' He took a half-step inside the hut, just to catch her words, but no further.

'Right. Of course,' he said. 'So what do I tell them?' Even in the dim light from her torch she could see the fear in his eyes, which she felt just as intensely herself. But she wasn't going to show it.

'Tell them . . .' she began, struggling to keep her voice even. 'Tell them we have a suspected case of a dangerous pathogen. Symptoms resemble bubonic plague. One patient possibly in final stages. One, possibly three, presumed infected. We need a team here now in full PPE gear. Tell them that.'

Dr Sheila Mackenzie cast her eyes down at the slumped figure on the floor and swallowed involuntarily. Would this be her in a few days' time? The hell it would, Sheila. Get a grip on yourself. This is not going to happen to you. You're going to get the best possible medical intervention. So you need to stay calm and get through this.

She glanced across the darkened room at her colleague, still busy on the line to Ny-Ålesund, cupping his hand over the phone. The door of the hut was still open and flurries of snow were blowing in so she couldn't catch everything he was saying. But from the way Coppinger was casting sideways glances at her she caught the gist of their conversation. 'Standing right next to him . . . heavy dose . . . full in the face.'

She looked down at her feet and saw that the sick man had shifted his position slightly. He was still alive, but desperately ill. She did not rate his chances in these conditions.

It was only then that she realized someone was missing. The third member of their team, Victor Skeet, had simply disappeared.

'Chris?' She interrupted his phone call. 'Where the hell has Skeet gone?'

4

Longyearbyen Hospital, Svalbard, Norway
Monday, 7 March, 1617hrs GMT, 1717hrs local

DR JAKOB PEDERSEN was on his tea break in the hospital canteen when the call came through from the Arctic Research Station, far away across the ice and snow in the early sub-zero night. Strictly speaking, it wasn't tea he was drinking from the steaming mug in front of him. It was *gløgg*, a non-alcoholic version of the mulled wine that warmed him on these endlessly long winter nights here on Svalbard. He took a brief sip from his personal mug, emblazoned with his favourite motto that read: *'Null stress'* – Norway's version of 'No worries' – and answered the call.

Pedersen was a famously placid man. His craggy, weather-beaten features rarely betrayed any emotion. But ten seconds into the call, that changed. He hurriedly pushed away the mug to reach for a writing pad and pen. In his twenty-seven years as the resident doctor in Svalbard's main hospital, he had never heard of anything like this before. Broken limbs from a snowmobile accident? Sure. A twisted ankle when someone had slipped on the ice? Frequently. He had even, very occasionally, had to attend to some horrific wounds caused by a marauding polar bear. But this? This was unprecedented. When the world had first gone into lockdown with Coronavirus in the early months of 2020, Svalbard had simply shut its doors to international visitors and not registered a single death. But Dr Jakob Pedersen was far from complacent. He knew immediately that this was more, far more, than anything his remote provincial hospital would be able to cope with.

'A helicopter? Now? At this time?' He was already shaking his head, although there was no one in the room to see it. One glance at the window told him the storm outside had not abated. If anything it was getting worse. He could hear the wind howling from halfway across the canteen and could just make out the snow piling up in the corners of the window frame.

'It's completely out of the question,' Pedersen told the voice at the other end. 'Nobody can fly in this. Not without permission from the *Sysselmann* – the governor – and I can tell you, he is not going to give it. Besides, there is the obvious risk of infection. Surely you can see that. No, I have to follow protocol here.'

Pedersen frowned as he listened to the response. Then his face softened slightly.

'Yes, yes, I realize she could die if it turns out to be what you say it is. But moving her here? To my hospital in Longyearbyen? Don't you see? That could start an epidemic! . . . Tromsø? On the mainland? . . . The University Hospital? That's nearly a thousand kilometres away! . . . Yes, yes, I hear you, but it carries the same risk – the risk of an outbreak. And I will not be responsible for that!'

He paused as a particularly strong gust of wind shook the windowpane, then resumed the conversation. 'Listen, my friend. I will tell you exactly what is going to happen now. I am going to alert the Norwegian Department of Health in Oslo immediately and I will ask them to activate an infectious disease protocol . . .

'What does that mean?' Pedersen sighed, repeating the other man's question back to him. 'It means help is coming, my friend. They have an EMT – an emergency medical team – on permanent standby for just such an eventuality. But I must insist that until then the patients – yes, because that is what they are now – I must insist that nobody goes near them, do you hear me? No one is to be moved or, God help us, this thing will spread out of control.'

11

5

LUKE CARLTON WAS bored to tears. He had nothing against opera per se, but this? No, this Wagner stuff was definitely not for him. He shifted restlessly in his seat and rubbed his eyes with the tips of his fingers. Twelve years in the Royal Marines, the last four spent with Special Forces in the SBS, and now a fully fledged case officer in the Secret Intelligence Service, running covert MI6 agents into dark and dangerous places. And what was he doing this evening? Watching some bearded bloke in a frilly shirt belt out a load of incomprehensible German onstage while the orchestra crashed and thumped in his ears. *Just kill me now*, he thought.

He sneaked a glance at his watch and slumped inwardly. Christ, they were barely forty minutes into Act One and there were another two to come, plus intervals. What had possessed him to say yes to this evening? He looked over at the girl next to him and there, sitting poised and elegant, was his answer. Elise Mayhew, twenty-nine years old, art dealer in Mayfair and his girlfriend of more than three years.

'It'll be fun,' she had suggested brightly, some weeks back. 'It's a marathon performance of Wagner's *Parsifal* at the Royal Opera

House. We can go halfsies on a box with Richard and Sarah and I'll smuggle us in a bottle of champagne and some of those Belgian chocolate truffles you like. Go on, say yes!'

The evening had turned out to be anything but fun. It had got off to a bad start when Luke had turned up hopelessly late, having driven straight from the Killing House on the Welsh borders and then taken ages trying to find somewhere to park. He had kept Elise waiting, alone, nursing a drink at the crowded bar, being bothered by a ruddy-faced man with cigar breath. When he did finally show up, profusely apologetic, they had only just made it to their seats before the curtain went up. Their friends Richard and Sarah had blown them out at the last minute when their babysitter had called in sick. So now here they were, sitting in brooding silence in their half-empty box with two vacant red velvet chairs beside them, the opened bottle of Moët on the floor between them, barely touched. It was as if the gloom of this late-nineteenth-century German opera had somehow managed to wrap itself around the pair of them.

And it was not as if their relationship was exactly firing on all cylinders. More than a year had passed since Luke had returned from a lengthy agent-running op in Iran. The mission had been hailed in Whitehall as a triumph: a kidnapped British minister freed from a remote Gulf island in a daring hostage-rescue operation. Luke and the Service had played a major role in locating him and he had returned to SIS headquarters at Vauxhall Cross to a hero's welcome. But in Elise's and his shared flat in Battersea he had met a somewhat less enthusiastic reception. While Luke had been in Iran and out of contact for days on end, Elise's mother had lost her battle with liver cancer. He had managed to miss the funeral, and for that he had still not been forgiven. When he had finally returned, limbs still aching and the exhaustion showing in the bags beneath his eyes, he had found Elise cold and withdrawn. His absence during the funeral had been unforgivable, she'd told him. She couldn't help looking at him differently now, she said, and it would take her a long time to get over this.

So there was that, and then there was the other matter of

something that had happened while he was in Iran. Something he wasn't proud of at all. Something he hadn't yet decided whether to tell her about. For now, he had parcelled it away in a box in his head and called it 'The Secret'. But sooner or later, Luke knew, he was going to have to do something about it.

Impatient for a distraction, he took out his Service phone, keeping it hidden by his knees. With the tip of his index finger he tapped the print-sensor icon in the top right-hand corner to access S-chat, the MI6 internal messaging and news forum. Hell, anything was more entertaining for him than what they were watching right now. Elise spotted what he was up to, frowned, and wagged an admonishing finger.

'It's on silent,' he whispered.

'I don't care,' she retorted. 'Put it away!'

Just one glance, just one quick glance, to give him something to think about until the interval: that was all he was asking. Luke coded in his personal ID number and pressed the return key. The words he saw next nearly made him drop the phone.

Suspected Plague Outbreak

UNDER NEWS BLACKOUT. Oslo station reports suspected Bubonic Plague outbreak on Norwegian archipelago of Svalbard. Up to four people infected. Possible terrorism link. Norwegian NIS service investigating.

He read it twice, studiously ignoring the death stare he knew he was getting from Elise beside him. And suddenly the phone was vibrating in his hand. Incoming call. From Vauxhall Cross. Luke catapulted himself out of his chair and burst through the swing doors into the empty corridor, where he took the call with his hand cupped over his mouth.

It was Angela Scott, his immediate boss, and she sounded more stressed than usual. 'You've seen the news on S-chat?' she asked him.

'Yes, just now.'

'Listen, Luke, we've got a situation up there.'

There followed one of those awkward pauses he had become all too familiar with. He reckoned she must be thinking how much she could tell him.

'I'm still here,' he prompted her.

'So, someone has gone missing. One of our Arctic scientists, Victor Skeet.'

'And?'

'We think his disappearance is highly suspicious. We need your help in finding him.'

'You mean tracking him down, right?'

'Yes, if you put it like that. But there's something else . . .' Her voice trailed off. Again came the pause. 'Luke, I'm duty-bound to tell you he may be infected with whatever this disease turns out to be. So once you've located him you'll need to keep your distance, do you understand? You'll be working with Norwegian military trackers. When you find him, you call in the medics and they'll take it from there. Is that clear?'

'Crystal. Angela, you do realize I'm not a scientist and I'm not a medic, so—'

She cut him short. 'Save it, Luke. The Chief has already put your name forward. You spent twelve years in the Royal Marines, with God knows how many winters digging snow holes or whatever it is you people do up in the Norwegian Arctic. There's no one else in the Service with your skill-set for this one, so you're in the frame now.'

A girl in a bright scarlet dress was coming towards him down the corridor with a trayful of ice-cream tubs, an eyebrow raised. He waved her away with a forced smile.

'So listen,' Angela continued, 'there's a plane at Northolt waiting to fly you up there and it's being fuelled as we speak. D'you have your passport with you?'

'Always.'

'Good. I told them you would. You'll be met off the plane in Svalbard and fully briefed. The Norgies will give you all the kit and protective gear you need before you set off.'

There were a hundred and one things Luke wanted to ask her, but he had only the one question. 'Small point, Angela, and forgive me for asking. But bubonic plague? You're asking me to go to Norway and track down someone who might be carrying plague, right? Sorry, just wanted to be clear on that.'

'You can cut out the sarcasm, Luke. This is a deadly serious situation. And, yes, you'll be given the full range of protection necessary. They're lining you up for a course of injections the moment you land. Good luck.'

'That sounds joyful. Thanks.'

'Oh, and Luke? Make sure you find him, won't you?' He could hear her anxiety down the line, her sharp intake of breath. 'There's rather a lot riding on this.'

6

Barentsburg, Svalbard
Monday, 7 March, 2015hrs GMT, 2115hrs local

VICTOR SKEET PULLED open the heavy outer door beneath the blinking neon sign that said 'Hostel Pogol' in English and, beneath that, in Cyrillic. He stamped the worst of the snow off his boots on to the frayed and threadbare doormat and opened the inner door into Reception. Immediately he felt a welcome surge of warmth as the central heating swept over him. The elderly woman behind the desk looked up from her novel, adjusted her glasses on a chain as she gave him the once-over, then pushed the register towards him across the desk. She pointed to a sign pinned to the wall: '750 Norwegian krone for a bed for the night. Or 5,000 roubles.' She shrugged. She didn't care, the choice was his. Skeet did not need to see the room to know it was a rip-off. Beggars couldn't be choosers in a place as remote as this and he was in no position to argue, so he handed over the notes without a murmur.

The fact was, he was now in a state of suppressed terror. He had just spent nearly five hours running away from what he was certain was a biological death sentence. Whatever the hell it was back there in that hut, he, for one, was not going to hang around to find out. The whole place had stunk of sickness and

17

death, which was why he'd ventured no further inside than the doorway. One look at that dying man on the sofa with all those pustules and black vomit, and Skeet was out of there. He had probably never moved so fast in his life. Propelled by fear and self-preservation, he had battled his way through the storm, ignoring the plummeting temperatures, the inherent danger of polar-bear attack, and struck out for the nearest settlement, the Russian mining community at Barentsburg.

Head down against the wind as the night closed in, he had concentrated on putting as much distance as possible between himself and that hut. True, he did feel a slight twinge of guilt about abandoning his two colleagues back there, but not for long. If they wanted to stick around in that place and go down with whatever bug that guy had, well, good luck to them, but Victor Skeet was going to look after number one, thank you very much. Skeet was an ice-core engineer by profession, although back home in Cambridge he liked to tell people he was an 'extreme engineer'. Since joining the 145-strong community of scientists and support staff at the UK Arctic Research Station on Svalbard, he had kept largely to himself. When others chose to take their holiday leave in Britain, he had always opted for the shuttle flight down to Oslo. Yet he never spoke about what he got up to there. He knew people probably thought of him as a dark horse, and he didn't care.

And now he had a plan. He would check himself into a discreet hostel in Barentsburg, paying cash, and in the morning he would get himself on to the very first chopper flight down to the international airport at Longyearbyen. If he moved fast he should be able to get off this godforsaken archipelago while the locals were still out searching for him in the snow. From there, he would fly to Oslo, where he could hide up for a few days in Agnetha's flat. Lie low and wait for the fuss to die down. He just had to hope that brute of a husband was still away on the North Sea rigs.

Skeet knew he was almost certainly going to be sacked from the Arctic Research Station for this. Well, fine. Do your worst. Because that surely had to be a whole lot better than dying of convulsions with a slick of black vomit all down your front. There was no question about it, he told himself. He had made the right call. It was only then, as the Russian lady on Reception waddled down the corridor ahead of him, showing him to his dingy room, that he began to feel the first pangs of a real killer of a headache.

7

Longyearbyen Airport, Svalbard,
Tuesday, 8 March, 0643hrs GMT, 0743hrs local

OUT OF A cloudless pink sub-zero dawn, the Royal Norwegian Air Force C130 Super Hercules transport aircraft descended towards the icy runway at Longyearbyen airport. Sitting strapped into one of the red canvas bucket seats that lined the fuselage, Luke Carlton shook himself awake. How many times, he wondered, had he experienced the eerie weightless sensation in the pit of his stomach as the C130 corkscrewed down out of an Afghan sky to dodge any incoming groundfire as they came in to land at some beleaguered outpost? But this was different: now he was up against a very different threat, an unseen biological enemy that no amount of tactics and firepower could bring down.

He'd had to make an unseemly early exit from the Wagner performance at the Royal Opera House in Covent Garden. For Elise, that had been the final straw. Following his late arrival and apparent total lack of interest in the evening, Luke's apologies had cut no ice with her: 'That's the last time I organize something like this,' she'd told him, as he headed off to the black BMW the Service had sent to take him to Northolt. By 10 p.m. he had been airborne, getting his head down for some kip on the five-hour flight up to Tromsø, just north of the Arctic Circle.

He knew it was coming – Angela had forewarned him – but Luke had always loathed injections. So what followed was not exactly happy hour: 4 a.m. and a reception committee of men and women in white coats, 'parachuted' in from the Health Ministry in Oslo, all lined up to pump him full of serums to guard against whatever might be out there. And what was out there sounded horrific.

'Bubonic plague,' he had read en route. 'A highly infectious disease . . . caused by the bacterium *Yersinia pestis* . . . spread by fleas from rats . . . causes swelling, fever and usually death.' Deadly plague! In this age? Surely this was something that belonged back in the Middle Ages. He moved on to symptoms. 'Nausea, fever, vomiting, bleeding and skin turning black with gangrene. Within 7 days of exposure, swollen, tender lymph glands called buboes appear. Onset of symptoms can be sudden.' Now he could appreciate how those military medics must have felt when they'd flown into West Africa to tackle the Ebola outbreak in 2013, an assignment dubbed on social media 'Operation Certain Death'.

But there was little time to dwell on the nature of diseases before it was on to the C130, along with the emergency medical team and two trackers from Norway's FSK Special Forces, for the final ninety-minute hop across the Barents Sea to the most northerly inhabited piece of dry land on Earth.

When the ramp went down, the Arctic air rushed in and suddenly everyone's breath was frosting. 'It's minus twenty-six degrees centigrade below,' remarked Stian, the Norwegian tracker next to him, with a cheery smile. Outside, he could hear the four turboprop engines powering down, but inside the dimly lit fuselage seatbelts were being unbuckled and people were springing into action. Virologists, epidemiologists, nurses and civil protection officers busied themselves checking medical equipment, PPE suits and masks, freeze-dried supplies and cold-weather gear. Luke had been issued with a set of multilayered

Gore-Tex Arctic survival clothing, including thermal underwear, facemask and fur-lined mittens, leaving his redundant London clothes crammed into a day sack at his feet.

Luke already knew that working through the night, with extreme urgency, the Norwegian government had put together Operation Isbjørn, pulling in all the necessary components for a disaster-management team. They were clearly taking no chances. At the forward end of the fuselage he could make out the isolation tent, its clear plastic sides revealing three beds in a row. A pipe connected the tent to a cylinder of oxygen, and he could also see a large, corrugated plastic wastepipe leading from the opposite corner to a metal container. That in turn was connected to a motor. The isolation tent was ready to receive.

Luke had barely had the chance to exchange more than a few brief words with the two Norwegian Special Forces trackers before they all took off from Tromsø. After that, well, the back of a C130 transport plane was just too damned noisy for any attempt at conversation. But now they were out on the runway, moving clear of the gaping cargo door with all the gear being unloaded. They were splitting into two teams: the main body of medics would deploy by helicopter to the hut, the site of the original infection, then evacuate Coppinger and Mackenzie – the suspected casualties – under quarantine conditions. Luke and the trackers would focus on one thing alone: hunting down and isolating the man who had gone rogue, the missing ice-core engineer, Victor Skeet, before he could infect anyone.

Stian, the lead tracker, who held a captain's rank in the FSK, was motioning for Luke to follow him into a snow-blasted prefab cabin on the edge of the airstrip. The moment they went through the door, Luke felt the full blast of the fan heaters inside and he spotted a Thermos of coffee and a stack of white styrofoam cups on a table. A long cardboard box stood open beside it, revealing its blue contents.

'Medical facemasks,' announced a woman, who introduced herself as a police officer from the tiny local contingent in Longyearbyen. 'Please help yourselves. We have plenty to go around.' There was a medic from the hospital too, a young man with a wispy blond moustache on his upper lip. He confessed straight away that, other than Coronavirus, he knew very little about infectious diseases. Someone – the police officer, Luke assumed – had already pinned up a large-scale map of Svalbard on the wall. It was overlaid with a sheet of transparent acetate, marked up with a blue chinagraph pen to indicate distances and timings.

'We start with what we know,' said Stian, when they had all dumped their kit in a corner, peeled off a layer of clothing and filled up on caffeine. He was tapping the map and speaking in English for Luke's benefit. He looked, to Luke, typically Scandinavian. Blond hair, blond eyebrows, pale, piercing ice-blue eyes. Not massively built, like some US Delta Force operator, but still exuding a quiet confidence, giving Luke the impression that he probably knew exactly what he was doing in this sub-polar environment. Almost the only thing that he and Luke had managed to establish in their brief acquaintance so far was that they had both seen operational service in Afghanistan. Stian had done some interesting work in the precipitous, pine-clad gorges of Kunar province, trying to find, fix and eliminate the elusive Al-Qaida cells. With limited success.

'And what we know is this,' continued Stian, in his stilted but near-perfect English. 'At some time close to sixteen forty-five hours local yesterday afternoon, the target departed the hut where the initial infection took place.' Interesting turn of phrase, Luke thought, calling Victor Skeet 'the target'. 'Suspect', 'patient' or even 'victim' might have been more politically correct, but, hey, if that was the direction they were heading, he was fine with it.

'We know he has not returned to the hut. So only two things can have happened. Either our Mr Skeet has tried to survive out in the open or he has found the nearest shelter.' He grimaced. 'Last night I am told the temperature here on Svalbard fell to minus thirty-four.' Now he was looking at Luke. 'Let me ask you, Mr Carlton, does this countryman of yours have the skills to survive in those conditions?' Minus 34°C. Luke knew from bitter personal experience that even if you dug yourself a snow hole and stayed out of the wind you still needed the right kit, the right skills and the right frame of mind to stay alive in those temperatures. He had asked Vauxhall for everything they had on Skeet before he took off from Northolt, so now his answer was unequivocal.

'Can Skeet survive in the open? No. Not a chance. He has no military training, no combat survival skills. He's an ice-core engineer so, yes, he'll be used to low temperatures, but not without back-up and a team behind him. So if he's on his own I'd say he has only one option: to head for the nearest shelter.'

'Exactly.' Stian spoke as if he had already reached that conclusion some time ago. 'And that would be Barentsburg, right here.' He tapped the map again. 'The distance from here to that settlement is just thirty-six kilometres. We have a helo at our disposal. A Super Puma is fuelled up outside and we can be there inside twenty minutes.'

Luke was shaking his head. 'Sorry, Stian, I just don't think that's wise,' he said, putting his coffee down. 'We've got to keep this low-key, remember? Find Skeet, isolate him, get him quarantined and off the island. Those were my orders – unless you guys were told something different?' He looked from one to the other, but nobody said anything. 'So, landing a bloody great chopper on the edge of town is only going to spook him, right?'

There followed a brief exchange in Norwegian before Stian turned back to Luke. 'It's agreed. You are correct. We go by snowmobile. This will take us longer, of course. I estimate one hour. We leave in twenty minutes.'

8

Barentsburg, Svalbard
Tuesday, 8 March, 0704hrs GMT, 0804hrs local

VICTOR SKEET THOUGHT he might be losing his mind. Next to no sleep at all, a thumping headache, sweat pouring off him all night in this overheated Russian-style hotel room. A Coronavirus? Was this SARS-Covid-22? Surely not possible all the way up here in the Arctic. So should he turn himself in? Get himself to a hospital for treatment? That would certainly seem to be the sensible thing to do. But then they'd slap him in isolation for God knows how long and now he had already committed himself. He had gone and texted Agnetha in Oslo and she'd sent him an immediate and enthusiastic response. The coast was clear, she'd told him. Her husband wasn't due back from the North Sea rigs for another nine days, Skeet could come and stay until at least the weekend. And her bed was warm and ready for him . . . Fine. He'd recuperate at her place.

When dawn broke over the snowbound Russian mining colony of Barentsburg, Skeet made up his mind. He would hole up here in the Hostel Pogol for another day until he felt well enough to travel. He reached up and touched his temples with his fingertips. They felt warm, but, no, he definitely wasn't burning up. So this was probably nothing more than a brief bout of winter flu.

25

He'd keep up his fluid intake and sleep it off. Just one more day, then he'd be as right as rain.

Skeet sat in the hostel's near-deserted canteen and toyed distractedly with his breakfast. An undercooked sausage, a plate of cold blinis, a dish of lumpen *syrniki* cottage-cheese pancakes. When the Russian waitress came over to pour him his tea she looked him up and down and tut-tutted. 'You not good,' she pronounced.

'Excuse me?'

'Not well,' she corrected herself. 'You are not well.'

'You're right about that,' Skeet conceded. 'I feel like shit. Do you have any painkillers?'

She looked at him blankly.

'Painkillers,' he repeated impatiently, pointing at his head. 'You know, paracetamol? Nurofen?'

'Ah!' Her face brightened as she understood the question. 'No. We don't have.' Then she held up her finger. 'But I give you *poroshok*.' She came back a few minutes later with a glass of warm brown liquid. 'Drink,' she commanded, and Skeet gulped it down. It tasted foul. But when a human being is under duress the mind will often clutch at straws. Skeet's mind now did exactly that. He was starting to get better, he told himself, no doubt about it. You can't beat a local remedy. He thanked the waitress, put some krones on the table as a tip and pulled himself to his feet. Maybe if he got a few minutes of fresh air it would do him good, just as long as he stayed inconspicuous.

He fetched his jacket from his room and turned the collar up. He put on his black woollen beanie and pulled it down tight over his forehead. He would keep his eyes on the ground and avoid eye contact with anyone. As the first rays of the Arctic sun were lancing across the sparkling, frozen street, Victor Skeet stepped out of the Hostel Pogol into the sub-zero morning. He was unaware that at that exact moment three men with very specialized skill-sets were closing in on him.

9

Near Cambridge Science Park, England
Tuesday, 8 March, 0730hrs GMT

THE MOBILE BESIDE her rang twice before she answered it. 'You're up early!' she said cheerfully, as she reached for her first cigarette of the day.

'Shut up and listen. Something's happened. Up in Norway.'

'Go on.'

'I can't say much. We need to meet.'

'You know that can't happen. Come on, tell me.'

'There's been a . . . there's been an accidental release.'

'What?' she exclaimed, sitting bolt upright and stubbing out the cigarette before she had even taken a drag. 'How many infected?'

'We don't know yet. But Vasiliev's gone, we know that.'

'Gone? What d'you mean, "gone"? Be specific.'

'He's dead! All right? . . . He went down very fast. They had to leave him in the hut.'

'Fuck. Let me think for a moment. Can we shut it down?'

'Nope. It's too late for that.'

'How the hell did it happen? No, wait, don't tell me now. You need to inform Vilnius. And the others. You know what this means, don't you?'

27

'What?'

'We're going to have to bring everything forward. There's no more time now. And, listen, don't call this number again.'

She cut the conversation short, took out the Sim card and walked into the bathroom. She tore off a sheet of toilet paper and wrapped it tightly around the Sim, dropped it carefully into the toilet bowl and pressed the flush, standing over it until it was gone.

10

TO DR SHEILA Mackenzie it felt like the onset of flu. Headache, high temperature, aching joints, chills. But she was under no illusions. This was no winter flu and she didn't think it was respiratory either. The incubation period was way too short for that. She knew that whatever was coursing through her body was of a whole different order. One look at the lifeless figure slumped by the sofa, his torso stained with blood and vomit, told her that. To her shame, she had not even noticed when the last breath had passed his chapped and bleeding lips. He had simply expired, and just after 4 a.m. they had called it in to the research station.

Sheila Mackenzie also knew that if help didn't arrive soon, then whatever had killed the man on the floor was just a glimpse of what was coming down the tracks for her: the horror that would precede her own death. Her medical training made it hard not to think about what was going on inside her body right now. In unpleasantly graphic detail she could envisage the microscopic battles being waged in her bloodstream as the pathogen swarmed through her veins, attacking the healthy cells, then replicating with incredible speed, breaking down more cell walls,

29

invading those neighbouring cells and taking them over. If she was feeling the first symptoms already then this pathogen was virulent; its onset was rapid and severe. She knew she didn't have much time.

'Chris?' she called to her colleague, for the third time in an hour. 'Any word from the base station?'

Chris Coppinger had positioned himself just outside the half-open door, a precaution he had taken on her advice. As an added measure, he had wrapped a scarf across his nose and mouth, which also gave him some protection from the sub-zero blasts that came barrelling down the valley. The Mauser rifle remained slung over his shoulder in case any marauding polar bears should come calling, but, right now, he considered them to be the least of their worries. She saw him glance down at his phone and shake his head.

'Nothing since that last call,' he replied, his voice muffled by the scarf. 'But, Sheila, they're on their way, I promise. The Oslo team will have everything they need to fix this. So just hang in there . . . Okay?'

Sheila Mackenzie didn't answer. She turned away from him and shuffled closer to the stove in the corner, wrapping her arms around herself. Chris had ventured inside the hut just long enough to light it last night, but it had been a rush job and now there was precious little warmth emanating from it. For the second time she removed her gloves to feel beneath her ears, checking for swollen lymph glands, then searched involuntarily for the hideous pustules she had seen on the man on the couch. Nothing. Not yet anyway.

Had she slept at all? She couldn't be sure. No, she definitely hadn't. It is hard to close your eyes and drift off when the temperature is well below zero, there's a man dying on the floor a few feet away, and you can't get it out of your head that you're going to be next. She kicked herself for landing in this situation. Less than three weeks to go before her contract on Svalbard was up and then she would have been back home in London. And now another thought was crowding into her head: Roberta, her niece, her baby niece. Would she ever see that precious child again? If she hadn't been so paralysed with cold and fear she might have allowed herself a tear or two. But something else was distracting her, a noise, coming from outside and from somewhere up above.

It was the sound of approaching rotor blades.

11

Barentsburg, Svalbard
Tuesday, 8 March, 0752hrs GMT, 0852hrs local

LESS THAN FORTY kilometres away, Luke was in position. So, too, were Stian and the other tracker, flanking him on either side, their breath frosting in the still air, spaced thirty metres distant but close enough to see each other's hand signals clearly. They had left the snowmobiles behind them, parked up next to a locked building on the edge of town, and covered the last 500 metres on foot, approaching on snowshoes in near-total silence.

Luke had been busy. In the few short minutes Stian had given them for personal admin before they set off, Luke had spoken to Vauxhall twice. Getting hold of Victor Skeet's personal phone number had been easy: MI6 had had no trouble in procuring it from his employers at the Arctic Research Station. Tracing Skeet's text messages had taken longer and had pulled in the resources of both GCHQ and their transatlantic cousins, the NSA. He had sent only one and they had immediately traced it to a residential apartment in Oslo. That address would soon be getting a visit. The far more urgent question was where Skeet had sent it from. The answer arrived on Luke's phone in a simple set of coordinates:

78.0649 degrees N
14.2337 degrees E

Barentsburg. That was it; it was the confirmation they needed. Skeet was hiding in Barentsburg. His footprints from the day before might have vanished in the snowstorm but his digital footprint was still a dead giveaway. Pinpointing his GPS location from the phone in his pocket had led them to where they were now. Luke took in the scene from his vantage point, squatting at a half-crouch next to a drainpipe that ran down the corner of a building. In front of him: an empty, snowbound street where the Arctic wind came scything down from the mountains. Half a dozen cars of dubious vintage, all parked up and idle, their windscreens half obliterated with snow and ice, a wooden shop sign that swung back and forth in the wind. It was unspeakably bleak.

And there, emerging from the hotel that matched the coordinates he had been given, was Victor Skeet. Luke watched him through a pair of Steiner rubber-coated tactical binoculars after first checking he fitted the photo he'd been sent on his phone. To his right, one of the Norwegian trackers lay flat on his front, squinting down the telescopic sight mounted on a Barrett MRAD sniping rifle, his finger resting lightly on the trigger guard, the barrel supported by a folding bipod. It was a precaution, nothing more. Everyone wanted Skeet alive, in quarantine, and talking. But his behaviour had been nothing short of erratic and there was a serious risk he could be contagious. No one was taking any chances here: all three men were wearing their surgical masks.

And Skeet's behaviour right now was troubling. Watching him through the 10x42mm viewfinder, Luke saw him stumbling around the empty street, missing his footing and clutching his head. It was time to act. Luke signalled to Stian, waited for him to acknowledge, then stood up and walked quickly towards Skeet. He heard a shout from behind him, a warning from Stian that this man was probably infected, but Luke was still several metres off when he called: 'Victor Skeet! I'm unarmed. We're here to help you.'

Skeet stopped abruptly in his tracks. Luke could see that his face was bare, unmasked.

'Who the hell are you?' Skeet yelled hoarsely.

Luke didn't reply. He was now less than twenty metres from his target.

'You need medical help!' Luke called out again. 'You need to stay exactly where you are and we'll bring it to you.'

There are some moments, Luke thought, that can seem like a lifetime: the seconds before he went through the doorway of a mud-walled compound of a high-value target in Afghanistan, a weapons-drawn face-off in the Gulf of Aden with a skiff full of Somali pirates high on narcotic *qat*, the instant before his first kiss with Elise. This, right now, was one of those extended moments. He saw Skeet look him straight in the eyes, he saw him hesitate, and he saw him turn and break into a run, making for the nearest buildings.

'*Stoppe!*' The shout came from behind them, the command sounding identical in Norwegian and English. But Skeet was moving fast now, closing the distance between himself and a row of green-painted buildings. He wasn't stopping for anyone.

The crack, when it came, was deafening, shattering the stillness of the Arctic morning, splitting the air as the bullet broke the sound barrier and slammed into its target. Skeet fell, clutching his right thigh, and groaned once. Luke could see him staring down in consternation at where his blood was spurting out, as if from a garden hose. A crimson pool was rapidly forming on the pristine snow. Everything in Luke's training was telling him to race forward and slap a tourniquet on before the man bled out. He had spent enough time in Afghanistan and Iraq to know Skeet had been hit in his femoral artery by the high-velocity bullet. But Skeet, they all suspected, was carrying the pathogen, and Luke simply couldn't take that risk. He knew that an average adult human has around five litres of blood in their body, but, left unstaunched, a severed major artery will usually be fatal within two minutes. And so it was, on that icy morning in Barentsburg.

Victor Skeet, ice-core engineer, Arctic researcher and resident of Cambridge, England, took 124 seconds to die on that empty, frozen street in Barentsburg. He had, at least, enjoyed a quicker death than the man who had infected him.

12

THE NOISE OF the helicopters approaching the hut was deafening. But to Dr Sheila Mackenzie it was the welcome sound of salvation. The choppers would be bringing in the very people who would save her life. *That's it. Just dose me up with the right antibiotics and I'll get through this in a week or two. Might even write a paper on it for the* British Medical Journal *once I'm over it.*

Oblivious to the icy blast of wind that blew open the door to the hut, ignoring the chills and the beginnings of a fever she could feel pulsing through her body, she waited patiently for the people in protective suits to arrive. But when they did appear, framed in the doorway, it was still a shock. In the clear, sub-zero air of the Arctic morning, she could see six human figures wearing full PPE as they approached the hut, clad in shiny grey chem-bio spacesuits, their faces concealed behind black respirators. Two were carrying assault rifles, a precaution she thought totally unnecessary. Why? What did they think she was going to do to them? Two more had stretchers. Chris Coppinger ventured out a few paces beyond the door of the hut to greet them, but was met immediately by a shouted command in English.

'Get down! Do not move!'

She saw him hesitate, then raise his arms and drop slowly to his knees. One of the men had his weapon trained on her kneeling colleague. This was surely absurd. Then came another shout.

'On the ground! Stay exactly where you are!'

Things happened in a blur after that. Sheila Mackenzie had expected to be treated with care and sensitivity, like the vulnerable patient she was. Instead, she felt more like a captive animal in a lab. Two figures wearing protective suits advanced towards her, ignoring the medical details she was trying to give them, and then they forcefully laid her on a stretcher and bound her arms tightly across her chest. Next, one placed a breathing apparatus over her mouth and nose, covering them completely, with a tube connected to a cylinder that in turn was attached to the stretcher. Her relief quickly gave way to feelings of helplessness and rage as they carried her, half jogging, towards the waiting helicopter. Unable to raise her head, she had no idea what was happening to her colleague, Chris, or to the dead man back in the hut. And why weren't they treating her immediately? Because this headache was rapidly becoming unbearable. Nobody spoke to her.

The flight in the helicopter was loud, claustrophobic and mercifully short. Incapable of movement, she stared up accusingly at the faces that peered down at her, blank and unspeaking, from behind their Perspex masks. Someone, she guessed, had given the daft order that she was not to be spoken to. She heard the pitch of the rotors changing, then a gentle double bump as the wheels set down on a hard surface. Now everyone was up and moving and, once again, she was being carted off like a piece of merchandise. There were a few brief seconds of cold sunlight. Then she saw she was being carried into the cavernous interior of a military transport plane. Still immobile, she fought to contain a surge of panic. Why wasn't anyone telling her what was going on, for God's sake? The stretcher-bearers pushed open the flaps of what looked to her like an isolation tent and set her down on a collapsible hospital gurney. They departed, and now another man appeared, also in full protective gear, but clutching a handwritten note in his neoprene-gloved hand. He held it up close to her face so she could read it.

My name is Dr Eckhardt and you are under my care. I must apologize for the conditions, but we believe you have been infected with a very serious pathogen. You will be treated. You are now on a Norwegian Air Force plane, which will fly you to Brize Norton airbase in England. From there your case will be assessed by the British Defence Scientific Laboratory at Porton Down. I wish you a speedy recovery.

He held up the note until she had read it to the end, then left. Porton Down? Jesus Christ! That was where the government researched some of the deadliest diseases on Earth. So that was it. They were going to keep her alive like a lab rat, long enough for them to find a cure. Sheila Mackenzie felt sick to the bottom of her stomach. Fighting the panic, she tried to twist her body round, but now another masked figure in a protective suit appeared beside her, holding up a hypodermic. With no warning, she felt a sharp jab in her shoulder as the needle slid in. They were injecting her in her deltoid muscle, she could tell, and for a brief moment she felt a painful, burning sensation before her world dissolved into a blur.

13

BLACK, SLEEK AND polished, the Jaguar XF Sportbrake saloon circled London's Parliament Square, then turned left into Whitehall. Matching the number plate with the one on their list, the armed police on the gates to Downing Street signalled for them to be opened and the car waved through to security. Once it moved beyond the heavy black metal barrier, more armed police gave it the once-over before lowering the electronic crash barriers and stepping on to the pavement. Seated in the back and gathering up his papers was Brendan Holmes, the government's CMO – the chief medical officer. His special area of expertise also happened to be microbiology.

Holmes had been alerted by a succession of calls earlier, waking his wife and causing their Burmese cat to leap off their bed in alarm. The calls had come in thick and fast, from both the World Health Organization and America's Centers for Disease Control and Prevention in Atlanta, Georgia. By the time his call had finished he'd learned that Norway had already dispatched an emergency management team to the Arctic. Holmes had scribbled a few notes on a pad he kept by the bed, then rung the health secretary. She didn't hesitate. Holmes was to attend that morning's weekly National Security Council meeting in the Cabinet Room at 0930 and brief everyone present.

Holmes stepped out of the Jaguar on to the rough cobbled parking space between No. 10 Downing Street and the back of the Cabinet Office. It was the unglamorous corner of Whitehall that the public never got to see and it always surprised Holmes how scruffy this back-end of the government power centre actually was. He grunted with irritation as he noticed he now had mud on his polished brogues. He reached into the back seat for his briefcase, then walked quickly around the corner and up the steps to the famous black-painted door of No. 10. He was relieved to see there were no media lined up on the other side of the street today, with their intrusive TV long lenses. More than one career had been torpedoed when someone had been filmed going in clutching clearly visible classified documents.

With the PM away in Berlin, the foreign secretary was in the chair today, yet it was the health secretary, Jay Spelling, who would do most of the talking. Spelling was very much a political appointee and Holmes privately had little time for her. He took his seat next to her and nodded to others around the table. It seemed he was not the only medical professional in the room. There were two of the senior directors from the JBC, the government's Joint Biosecurity Centre, set up in 2020 in response to the Coronavirus pandemic. Here, too, summoned at short notice, was the head of Emergency Response, a woman from the Microbiology Directorate and even someone from 'Health Equity'. A middle-aged man in a graph-paper-check shirt and worsted wool tie introduced himself as from the FCO, and there was that chap Khan from SIS across the river. One look at him told Holmes this meeting was going to be about more than simply public health.

'What I fail to understand,' said the health secretary, as soon as the introductions were over, 'is how we can be seeing an outbreak of bubonic plague in the Arctic, of all places. It's not exactly Madagascar. Surely a pathogen like that can't survive in those freezing temperatures up there, can it? I mean, it's a virus, right?'

Brendan Holmes gave a discreet cough and held up a hand to correct her. 'Strictly speaking, Secretary of State, it's a disease caused by a bacterial strain, not a virus. It's usually transmitted by infected fleas and—'

'Right. Yes. Quite. A bacterial strain. So, as I was saying, how can that possibly survive up there in minus whatever-it-is? I can't believe there are fleas hopping around on the snow in the middle of winter!' Jay Spelling snorted in derision at the very idea of what she had just described. She looked around the table to see if anyone else was sharing her half-joke. There were a few forced grins.

'So, Brendan,' – the health secretary turned to the chief medical officer – 'give us your assessment, if you will. Is this thing containable? Or are we about to have another Covid-19 situation on our hands here – or worse? And don't think I'm being funny, but, if I've got my history right, the Black Death caused around fifty million deaths – about half of Europe – so I'd quite like to know what we're dealing with.'

Brendan Holmes couldn't put his finger on what it was about the health secretary and her mannerisms that intensely irritated him. They just did. He wished they'd left her in Transport, where she could do a lot less damage. He cleared his throat and addressed the NSC.

'Yes. As it stands, this should be completely containable if the Norwegians act quickly, which they are. They're already testing, tracking and tracing on Svalbard and there is no evidence the disease has reached these shores, so I see no cause for alarm.' He tilted his head to one side. 'It's true there is about a ten per cent mortality rate for bubonic plague, but—'

'Treated or untreated?' interrupted the health secretary.

'That's treated, ma'am. Untreated, it's obviously going to be a lot higher, especially if it develops into pneumonic plague and spreads to the lungs. But with modern antibiotics, like gentamicin and so on, I would expect a full recovery. However . . .' Holmes paused and removed his spectacles, blinking, mole-like, as he did so '. . . I should just caution that we don't yet know what this pathogen is. The symptoms described certainly match bubonic plague, but we won't know for certain until we get the full spectrum lab read-out from Porton Down.' Holmes glanced at his watch. 'We expect the patient to be retrieved and quarantined within the hour. We should get the first results back from pathology before the day's out.'

'You're referring to Dr Mackenzie, right?' Jay Spelling again. 'But she's not the only patient, is she, Brendan?'

'Well, we can't be certain at this stage. Of the three UK nationals up there on Svalbard who came into contact with the source of the pathogen in the hut, she is the only one said to be showing symptoms. Her colleague . . . ' he looked down at his notes for the name '. . . her colleague Chris Coppinger reports feeling symptom-free, but, of course, he'll have to be screened thoroughly. We were originally intending to send them to Porton Down for testing, but it's quicker and more convenient to hold them under observation at the Royal Free, here in London. Now, the third scientist, Victor someone – I don't have his surname to hand – has gone AWOL. All we know is that he fled the site of the original infection. I understand the Norwegians are trying to track him down, but, frankly, I don't rate his chances out there in the snow.'

'Director CT?' The foreign secretary turned to the MI6 director of International Counter-Terrorism, standing in for his chief today. 'You wished to add something?'

For a large man, Sid Khan spoke surprisingly softly, but Holmes could see that everyone's attention had now switched to him. Khan was looking up from a tablet he held. 'I have some sad news to report,' he said. 'As of a few minutes ago, Victor Skeet, the third scientist, has indeed perished. I can also tell you that in the last few minutes our Norwegian military intelligence partners, the NIS, have reported that the man they found in the hut is also dead. The Norwegians have labelled him "Patient Zero".'

'Patient Zero?' The health secretary was looking at Khan as she asked this, but it was Holmes who answered.

'Patient Zero, Secretary of State, is the name given to an individual who's deemed to be the original source of an outbreak.'

'Well, let's not call it that just yet,' the health secretary replied. 'Do we have a name for this unfortunate individual?'

'Yes, ma'am,' resumed Khan. 'He's been identified as a Yevgeny Vasiliev.'

'A Russian?'

'Yes. A Russian national. That's not unusual, given the proximity to their mining colony at Barentsburg. But, as you would expect, my Service is working flat out to determine what he was doing there and how he became infected.'

'I think,' interjected the foreign secretary, 'that if this develops we may need an urgent paper from the Joint Intelligence Committee.'

But Jay Spelling, the recently promoted health secretary, was frowning intently. 'Forgive me,' she said archly, addressing the MI6 director, 'but you are the Secret *Intelligence* Service. Shouldn't you be sending someone up there straight away to investigate?'

Sid Khan, a veteran of such meetings, remained unruffled. He tipped his head in mock obedience. 'Absolutely, Secretary of State. We have someone on the case right at this moment.'

14

Barentsburg, Svalbard
Tuesday, 8 March, 1048hrs GMT, 1148hrs local

LUKE CARLTON HAD several abiding memories from his early teenage years, growing up on his uncle's farm on the windswept moors of Northumberland, and not all of them were happy. But one that always made him smile, even all these years later, was watching those old Laurel and Hardy slapstick comedies from the 1930s and 1940s. After yet another clumsy, cack-handed disaster, the larger of the comedy duo – was it Oliver Hardy? – would often complain: 'Well, here's another nice mess you've gotten me into!' This, Luke decided, was exactly how he was feeling at this moment, but he wasn't smiling now.

Luke was standing some distance back from the ice-encrusted window inside a small supermarket on a street in Barentsburg, watching the pandemonium unfold. Helicopters, police, ambulances, cordons being set up and people moving around dressed in full bio-hazard spacesuits. Jesus, what a mess, and it hadn't even been him who'd fired the shot. This was supposed to be a quick and discreet operation, an in-and-out. Find Victor Skeet, isolate him and immediately interrogate him on why he'd chosen to flee from that infected hut straight to a Russian mining colony.

What did Skeet know that the other two unfortunate Arctic scientists didn't?

But Victor Skeet was not going to be giving up any answers now. Instead, Luke was watching a blood-soaked and highly infectious corpse getting double-zipped into a neoprene body bag, loaded into a sealed truck and taken off – probably to be incinerated at high temperature.

'Nice going, Luke. He's not much use to us now, is he?' The words of his line manager, Angela Scott, were still ringing in his ears, her frustration barely concealed. Luke had called it in to Vauxhall, of course, within minutes of the Norwegian marksman felling Skeet with the single fatal gunshot to the thigh. Luke knew he'd probably get a bit of grief from the Service, but he hadn't expected to take the hit for this one.

'You realize there'll be a full investigation now, after this?' Angela had said. 'You've got less than a day before the press get up there. How the hell are you going to make the necessary discreet enquiries in that time?' It was unlike Angela to be so upset: someone in Whitehall must be coming down hard on her. And she hadn't finished yet. 'Honestly, Luke, what is it that we teach you all, down at the Fort? Hmm? Blend in, be the grey man – or woman – and don't attract attention. I'd say this is not exactly the outcome we were looking for here, wouldn't you?'

Luke was used to bollockings. He'd experienced enough of them in the Royal Marines. In fact, as a recruit – a 'nod' – hardly a day had gone by at the Commando Training Centre at Lympstone when he wasn't being bellowed at for some minuscule misdemeanour. But this was different: he was nearly twenty years older and wiser, and the one he'd just received from Angela seemed bang out of order, especially when he had come to trust her better judgement. It was almost as if someone above her had told her what to say.

Words formed in his head. *Sorry, Angela, you're quite right. Once we'd tracked down Skeet I really should have cosied up to him and got myself a full dose of plague. All in the line of duty, right? That was* what he wanted to say, but he didn't. He just took it on the chin. He had followed his orders, helped the Norwegian trackers locate Skeet and stopped him before he could infect half of Barentsburg. 'What can I say, Angela? It's how it happened, that's all.'

'Right. Well, you'll need to sit tight and lie low until the Norwegian service makes contact with you. You've got less than twenty-four hours to find out what you can up there. Then we're pulling you out. Twenty-four hours, Luke. And, for Pete's sake, stay well clear of anyone in the media.'

Right now he was on his own. The two Norwegian trackers had given a statement to the investigating police officer sent by the *Sysselmann*, the governor, then had been swiftly spirited out of there. Probably already on a plane back to Oslo. Luke had duly faded into the background, slipping into a mini-market just as others were coming out on to the street to see what all the fuss was about. He bought himself a packet of fig rolls and half a dozen energy bars, which he would stuff into his pockets after the checkout – he had no idea when or where his next meal would be. Queuing to pay, still wearing his surgical mask, Luke kept one eye out of the window on the building Skeet had emerged from. The Hostel Pogol. That must have been where he spent his last night, poor bastard. He could see a red-and-white police cordon tape, marked 'POLITI', strung up around the entrance. Figures in bio-hazard suits were going in and out, and an ambulance had drawn up alongside. Just then, he felt his phone ping: Vauxhall had sent him the ID for his contact in the NIS, the Norwegian Intelligence Service. He studied the image that came up on his screen: Kristian Berge, a pale face with a square jaw. The phone shook in his hand. Incoming call.

'Luke Carlton? This is Kristian. From NIS.'

'Where are you?'

'Right behind you.'

Luke turned to see a man standing beside the sweet counter waving at him rather obviously, his eyes smiling above his face-mask. He was tall, broad-shouldered and wearing a thick polar jacket. Yet there was something cautious, almost hesitant, about

46

the way he carried himself. Luke took his time before wandering over to join him, then avoided eye contact while pretending to choose a bag of sweets from the display. Basic tradecraft. Even here, you never knew who might be watching.

'Good to meet you, Kristian,' he said, absently examining a packet of jelly babies and studying the price tag. 'So, what do we have on this Patient Zero?'

'Yevgeny Vasiliev?' the Scandinavian replied, keeping his voice low as he looked around him. No one was paying them any attention. 'So very little. But I know a man who may tell us more.'

'Can we talk to him?'

'Yes . . . but he lives out of town.'

'Okay. Let's call him.'

Kristian laughed. 'He has no phone,' he explained. 'We must pay him a visit.'

'Wait,' said Luke, still holding the unwanted packet of jelly babies, 'so this guy is your Barentsburg source, yet he doesn't even own a phone?'

Kristian spread his hands and grinned. 'This is the Arctic, my friend. People talk to each other up here, face to face. There is not much else to do, apart from hunting and fishing. So . . .' Kristian stared out of the window and frowned. It was all still happening out there with the police and the medics. It had started to snow again. 'I have requested transport from my service,' Kristian said, with a sigh, 'so now we must wait until it arrives.'

Luke put a hand inside the breast pocket of his jacket. Yes. It was still there. This wasn't exactly going to be social distancing, but he would have to take his chance. 'Don't worry about transport,' Luke told him, tossing Kristian the ignition key to the snowmobile. 'You can drive because you know the way. I'll jump on the back.'

15

IT HAD TO be said that Kristian Berge was not a good driver. In fact, Luke concluded fairly quickly, this Norwegian spy was quite hopeless at it. 'Mate,' he called to him, just after the Norwegian had managed to steer them straight into the side of a snowdrift, 'I'll tell you what, why don't I drive and you can shout directions?' It wasn't a question, Luke was already back on the snowmobile and taking control of the steering handles.

'Sorry.' Kristian shrugged. 'I am from Bergen on the coast. It rains more than it snows there.'

Luke pulled his facemask back up over the bridge of his nose, adjusted his goggles, wiping the fresh snowflakes off them with his gloves as he did so, then gunned the engine. They set off at speed, gliding smoothly over the fresh snow with Kristian tapping his shoulder to go left or right. Luke was concentrating on keeping them upright, reading the contours of the undulating snowscape beneath the snowmobile's tracks as he drove and making minute adjustments. But he was also taking in the stark beauty of the place, the archipelago historically known as Spitsbergen, a wild, frozen corner of the world, further north than most people will ever travel in their lifetime. 'A pristine environment' was how the Norwegians had described it to him. 'We take nothing away from it,' Stian the tracker had said, 'and we leave nothing behind.' Well, it didn't feel pristine any more, not now it was home to this invisible pathogen.

Bare, bleak mountainsides rose up on either side of them, encrusted with ice but devoid of life. Once, for a few brief seconds, they caught sight of a herd of indigenous reindeer, with their peculiar, stunted antlers, before they vanished over a ridge. Other than that, they didn't see a living soul. Tucked inside his breast pocket and studied on the flight over, Luke's map was marked with the names of long-dead figures from Nordic history. He remembered one in particular: the evocative-sounding 'King Oskar the Second'. But now the snow was coming in harder, not yet a white-out but enough to slow their speed. They had been travelling for just over forty minutes when the house appeared out of nowhere, looming ahead in a swirl of snowflakes. It was small and isolated, built beside a frozen lake. It had red-painted wooden sides and a chimney from which a coil of smoke curled into the leaden sky. Their arrival set off a spate of raucous barking from the Greenland husky tethered to a fence post, followed by a shout of command from inside. Then the front door opened and a slim, sprightly old man stepped out to meet them.

'This is Ivan,' Kristian introduced them. 'He was a friend of my father's, before he moved to Bergen.'

Close-cropped steel-grey hair, tanned, weather-beaten face, a thick, bristly red check shirt, leather trousers held up with braces. Luke put him at a fit sixty.

'His father is from Russia, his mother is from Norway,' Kristian continued, shaking the snow off his jacket and pulling his mask down below his chin.

'It's true,' said Ivan, speaking for the first time. 'I am – how you say? – a mongrel! Come, please, come inside.'

Beside a crackling log fire, cradling a glass of fiery, homemade *akvavit* spirit, Luke felt himself involuntarily relaxing. It was always like this when you came into the warm from the bleak outside: the body just gives a big *aah* and starts to unwind. Well, he wasn't going to let that happen. He was on a mission and he needed to stay focused. The pleasantries over, it was time to ask questions.

'Has anything changed here, in Barentsburg, in the last few weeks?' he began. 'Have you noticed anything different, anything unusual?'

'Sure,' Ivan replied, and Luke leaned closer, eager to catch every word. 'The price of beer has gone up again!'

Both Ivan and Kristian collapsed into laughter. For fuck's sake, Luke thought, is this Nordic humour? But he laughed along with them, forcing himself out of politeness.

'Sorry, what I meant was,' Luke continued, when they had all got over the joke, 'have you come across anyone you didn't recognize in recent days? Seen any activity that made you think, Aha, that's strange?'

'Barentsburg is a small place,' Kristian interjected, answering for him. 'It's just a mining colony, really. Less than five hundred people. So I think Ivan would have told us by now if—'

'Yes.' Ivan cut him short, his lean face now suddenly serious. 'As it happens, I have.'

Luke put down his half-finished glass of *akvavit*. They were past jokes now.

'It was two, maybe three weeks ago,' Ivan continued. 'I was on my rounds on my snowmobile to the east of here.' He gestured out of the window, where the snow was whipping against the glass pane. 'You know, checking my traps, monitoring the reindeer, like I always do. Then I noticed that someone had moved into Karlsen's house, and I thought, That's strange, because the old bastard died two years ago and he still owes me money.'

'When you say "moved in",' Luke asked, frowning, 'how do you mean, exactly?'

'Moving in! Isn't that what you say in English? Yes, they had packing cases, lots of them, and rolls of plastic. So I drove up to the door. There was this guy standing there, and I said, "Hello, I'm Ivan. I'm kind of like your neighbour, you know?" But this guy, he wasn't from here, he wasn't even from Norway. I spoke to him in Russian, he answered me, and he was quite rude actually.'

'What did he say?' Kristian this time. Luke noticed he had downed his shot in one.

'He told me to mind my own business,' Ivan replied. 'He said that they had come here for the nature, for the peace and quiet, and they did not wish to be disturbed.'

'Didn't that . . . um,' Luke said, trying not to sound rude himself, 'didn't that sound a little suspicious? Did you report this to anyone?'

Ivan stretched out his lean frame on the chair and folded his arms behind his head before answering. 'Please understand, Lou—'

'Luke.' Immediately he wished he hadn't said that, because this man was only trying to be helpful. Luke reminded himself that he had just flown through the night from London, driven halfway across Svalbard and watched a man bleed out in front of him. 'Sorry, I interrupted you,' he said.

'Please understand, Luke, that this is Svalbard. If you're not here for coal or fishing, you're here for the nature. It's all we have, mister. So, no, I didn't report it.' Ivan turned to Kristian and said something in Norwegian. Luke watched the two men smiling and sharing a joke before Kristian turned to translate it for his benefit.

'He says the local police chief is a piss-head who couldn't care less anyway.'

Luke could feel his impatience getting the better of him. It would soon be dark, there was work to be done and time was running out. He rose to his feet, his glass of *akvavit* left unfinished on the table. 'So,' he announced, with some finality, 'I think we need to check out this Karlsen's house while there's still light. Ivan, are you able to take us there?'

'What, now?' Ivan shook his head. 'Sorry, mister. I have Ilse coming round with that sick puppy of hers. I said I'd take a look at him for her. But, hey, you can find it easily enough. I'll give Kristian the directions.' He walked over to the window and shook his head. 'But that's quite a snowstorm building out there, just like the one we had yesterday. You sure you want to go ahead in this?'

Luke looked at Kristian, his partner from the Norwegian Intelligence Service, and saw the dubious look on his face. 'Absolutely,' said Luke. 'We're doing this.'

16

High Security Infectious Diseases Unit,
Royal Free Hospital, Hampstead
Tuesday, 8 March, 1440hrs GMT

TWO POLICE OUTRIDERS on motorbikes led the convoy of vehicles racing the seventy miles from RAF Brize Norton in Oxfordshire. They were heading for one of several destinations where patients with a suspected highly dangerous infection were taken. Coming off the A406 at Brent Cross in north London, then turning sharply right into Hendon Way, blue lights flashing, the convoy sped down Finchley Road until it braked to a stop outside a large, eye-wateringly ugly, multi-storey concrete building.

Sandwiched between London Zoo and Hampstead Heath, the Royal Free Hospital has a venerable past. It was awarded its royal title in 1837, the year Queen Victoria ascended the throne, in recognition of all the work it had done with cholera patients. Today it plays a no less vital role. Until Covid-19 came along it was, along with the Royal Victoria High Security Infectious Diseases Unit in Newcastle-upon-Tyne, one of only two hospitals in Britain capable of handling in isolation a patient infected with a deadly pathogen. A few lessons have been learned since then. Back in 2006 the former Russian KGB officer and defector Alexander Litvinenko would have been taken there if only they had known what was wrong with him from the start. By the time the nuclear scientists at Aldermaston's Atomic Weapons Establishment had detected the lethally high levels of radioactive Polonium-210 poison in his urine it was already too late to save him. He died three miles to the south, at University College London Hospital.

If Dr Sheila Mackenzie had been awake and conscious she might have been relieved to see she was being taken straight to a hospital and not, as she had feared, to the experimental labs at Porton Down. But inside the specially adapted ambulance she lay in a medically induced coma, seeing and hearing nothing. Her elaborate transfer from plane to ambulance at Brize Norton had had to be explained away to those watching on the base as 'a snap CBRN exercise', one of many held periodically around the country to test Britain's response to a chemical, biological, radiological or nuclear incident. Which was exactly what this was. Since the advent of Covid-19 the sight of medics in all-encompassing PPE gear raised fewer eyebrows than it used to, but still, the same cover story was given now as Dr Mackenzie was rushed through a side door next to A & E, along a corridor, into a lift and finally up into the isolation chamber. Nurses, doctors and several microbiologists stood at a state of alert, wearing full PPE, ready to receive the patient. As the gurney was brought in, with painstaking care, one of them stepped forward.

'Bring her round,' he ordered. 'We need her awake.'

When Sheila Mackenzie opened her eyes, she initially thought she was still in a dream – or, rather, a nightmare. The mask that had been placed on her face in Svalbard had been removed, but she was still restrained on her bed, like a violent prisoner. She could see there were tubes coming out of her arms, an ECG monitor on her chest, and the glassy, unblinking eye of a closed-circuit camera watching her from directly above the bed. She was in an isolation tent, that much she could see, but there appeared to be no one else around. And something else was absent too: the terrible headache that had been building before they loaded her on to the plane in Svalbard and put her to sleep. That at least had subsided. Then a disembodied voice spoke to her and she struggled to tell where it was coming from.

'Good afternoon, Dr Mackenzie . . . Please nod your head if you can hear me.'

She nodded.

'Good. So you will know by now that you have unfortunately been infected with an unidentified pathogen. As a doctor yourself you will appreciate that we urgently need to establish what that is. That's why in the next few minutes we will need to take live samples from you and expedite them over to Porton Down for diagnostics. In the meantime, until we know its precise structure, we have begun treating you with a broad-spectrum antibiotic.'

Sheila Mackenzie listened to this while a dozen thoughts went through her head. Live samples? This was every bit as bad as she'd feared. What would they show? What were her chances now?

And what about Coppinger and Skeet? Where were they? Had anyone told her family she was here? But all these questions went unanswered, because right now she felt too weak to speak.

'You're probably wondering where you are,' the voice went on. 'You're at the Royal Free in London. I want to assure you that you will be given the best possible treatment while we conduct the necessary tests.'

The voice ended abruptly. No goodbyes, no get-well-soons. Silence filled the isolation tent. Then Sheila Mackenzie felt something on her upper lip, something warm and wet, trickling down to her lips. She flicked out her tongue and tasted it. It was metallic, like licking the back of a spoon, and in her groggy state it took her a few seconds to realize it was blood. Her own blood. It was coming from both her nostrils.

17

THEY STOOD OUTSIDE the front door of Ivan's house as the wind snatched at their clothes and the argument blew back and forth between them.

'This,' pleaded Kristian, 'is sheer madness!' He gestured up at the darkening sky and the snow that fell from it, sticking to their eyelids and lips as they spoke. 'It is better by far we call it in for tomorrow. Then we can go into the house with a full team. I will file my report to Oslo and they can make the arrangements. Yes,' he nodded at the logic of his idea, 'this is best.' He started to pull out his mobile phone, but Luke reached out and gently but firmly restrained him.

'Look, Kristian,' he reasoned, 'in normal times I'd agree with you. And this is your territory, I respect that. But we don't have time to piss around like this. The trail is already going cold. This time tomorrow there could be journalists crawling all over this island. And we both know somebody's been doing something very, very bad up here. Now it's my job – and yours – to find out what the hell is going on and who's behind this outbreak. Can we agree on that?'

From inside the house came the noise of a toilet flushing and for a moment neither spoke. He looked at Kristian's pale, furrowed features and he could see the doubt written all over them.

'All right, look,' said Luke, in what he hoped was a conciliatory tone, 'if you don't fancy coming with me to check out the house, that's okay. I'll get the directions myself, then find my own way there. But don't blame me if MI6 end up taking the credit for solving this and your NIS service doesn't even get a mention . . .'

They rode straight into the wind, Luke in front, Kristian clinging on behind, with the snowmobile's 800cc engine whining in protest as they lurched over the crests and unseen bumps. If the going had been hard before, it was worse now. As the wind-borne snow stung their cheeks, even Luke began to wonder if he had made the right decision. Svalbard felt right now like the remotest place on Earth, and he had known some pretty inhospitable corners of the planet. Hell, at least on the Norwegian mainland they had trees . . .

Once again, the house they sought appeared to rear out of the gloom right at the last minute so that Luke had to brake quite suddenly, causing his passenger to bump up hard against him. They parked up in a spot behind a slight rise and just out of the wind, then dismounted. With the snow swirling and the light fading fast it was hard to tell, but the place certainly looked deserted. Instinctively, Luke patted his right hip and then the side of his thigh, looking for the pistol that wasn't there. Damn. Once more he was finding himself compromised, heading unarmed into an uncertain situation with the clock running against him.

He beckoned Kristian closer and cupped his hand as he spoke into his ear above the noise of the wind. 'Are you carrying?' he asked the Norwegian.

'Again, please?'

Luke removed his glove and held his hand across his chest, finger pointing, thumb cocked. 'I said, are you carrying a weapon? Are you armed?'

Kristian shook his head sadly. 'Only this.' He produced what looked to Luke like a car fob.

'What's that, then?'

'It's a beeper. To contact my office in Oslo. In emergency.' Kristian looked down at the fob. 'But I think it's not working.'

'All right,' Luke said, speaking directly into his ear as they stood against the outside wall, just to one side of the front door. 'We split into two. The light's going, so we'll cover more ground that way. You go in through the front.' Luke pointed at the door. 'I'm going to check out round the back. Then I'll join you inside. Shout if you run into trouble.'

The wind nearly knocked Luke sideways and tiny frozen ice particles stung his cheeks as he moved round the corner of the house and out of its lee. His eyes scanned left and right: a long low wall encircling what looked like a yard with a row of outhouses, or they might have once been stables, at the back. He peered over the wall into the yard. He could see an abandoned fridge, its door hanging open, its shelves bare, and a pile of agricultural pallets. In one easy movement he flipped himself over the wall and into the yard, making a direct line for the outhouses.

Cat-like, he crept up slowly to the door of the first of them. All his senses felt on edge, as if primed for this moment. It was hard to believe that only yesterday afternoon – yesterday! – he had been put through his paces on that hostage-rescue simulation course back in the UK. It just showed you never knew when you were going to need the training to kick in. He slowly turned the handle of the door. It was locked. He looked around for something to wrench it open. Nothing. He tried the second door and this one opened with a rusty rasp. He stepped quickly inside and waited, listening. Was he being watched? He didn't think so. There was nothing but the mournful whistle of the Arctic wind outside.

He took out his phone and pressed the torch function, squinting as he adjusted his eyes to the sudden flood of light. Ahead of him, inside the room, he could see a long steel desk, several chairs scattered around haphazardly and a lamp lying on its side. The place looked as if someone had left in a hurry. Luke walked over to the desk, then opened the first drawer. Empty, except for some unused SIM cards, still in their sealed wrappers. He opened the second drawer: empty, and the third. He was about to leave when he saw something at his feet: a box file, spilling its contents across the floor, clearly dropped by someone in a rush. Luke scooped the papers up and shone the phone torch on them. All in Cyrillic. Russian documents. Well, that didn't prove anything, but he wasn't going to pass them up. He folded them in half and stuffed them into the inner pocket of his jacket for later. It was time to move on and check out the third room.

What he saw when he stepped through the door stopped him dead in his tracks. Everything before him, lit up by his phone torch, was covered with sheets of polythene, from floor to walls to ceiling. In a corner there was a line of blue plastic containers, and a faint chemical smell hung in the air. He decided it was safest to touch nothing and instead he reached for his surgical mask, still folded in his pocket, and placed it over his mouth and nose. Probably a bit late for that, he realized, but he wouldn't hang around. He took in the scene: this had to be some sort of makeshift laboratory. Luke shot a few seconds of video with his phone and was about to take some stills when he thought he heard a shout. He listened again. Yes. There it was: Kristian was calling from inside the main building.

'Luke! Come quick!' He sounded scared.

Outside in the yard it was practically dark now, but Luke snapped off the torch on his phone and blinked several times. He had good night vision, better than most people's: it would just take a few seconds to come back. Moments later, he was across the yard and in through the back door to the house; it was unlocked.

'Kristian?' he called.

No answer.

Luke could see he was in the kitchen, there were pots hanging on the wall, their shiny surfaces reflecting the last vestiges of ambient light from the dying day outside. He froze mid-step. Someone was upstairs, right above him. Someone heavy. He could tell from the tread that it was not Kristian. Luke's entire body went into alert state, wiring itself for danger.

Moving softly now, on the balls of his toes, he went over to the row of utensils above the cooker, searching for a suitable weapon until he found it. A bread knife. Not ideal, he would have preferred something a lot sharper, but its serrated teeth could still do some damage and it would have to do. If his unseen quarry upstairs was armed, Luke would have to be either very quick or very inventive with it, preferably both.

He considered his options. None were good. He could phone for police back-up, but that could take hours and, anyway, he wouldn't know how to begin to direct them to this place. He could sit it out here in the kitchen, waiting for his opponent to come down the stairs, then rush him. But what if he didn't come down? And what if he *did*, and the guy just simply flipped a light switch, saw Luke and shot him? Chances were, whoever was in this house would know their way around it a damn sight better than Luke did. But there was another, more pressing argument propelling him to act now. Kristian could well be lying up there, unconscious or bleeding to death.

One wooden step at a time, Luke made his way up the stairs, painstakingly slowly, dreading each creak that never quite came. Everything about this situation was wrong: he was alone, with no back-up, unarmed and facing an invisible enemy in a darkened house that he would know and Luke didn't. At the top of the stairs he stopped and listened, the bread knife tensed in his hand. From outside came the mournful lament of the wind – and was there something else? It sounded almost like heavy breathing . . .

His eyes were still adjusting to the almost total darkness when suddenly there was a crash and something flew into his face. Luke reacted instinctively, trying to sweep it away with his free arm and dropping into a fighting crouch. But it was just a curtain, flapping wildly in the wind. Someone had opened a window and now the draught was coursing through the entire darkened house.

He saw the body the moment he switched on his phone torch. It was Kristian Berge, lying face up, eyes wide open, legs at an awkward angle, the blunt end of a carpentry screwdriver sticking out of his throat. There was a glistening pool of blood beside him, not yet congealed. Luke swept the room with his torch, checking for movement, then rushed over and knelt beside him, calling his name, his eyes hunting around for something to staunch the blood. He held the tips of two of his fingers to the side of Kristian's neck, feeling desperately for the pulse in the jugular vein. Nothing. He was gone.

Another crash, and Luke whirled round, the knife braced in his right hand. But the room was empty, the killer was gone. The open window was slamming back and forth in the wind. The unseen attacker had jumped through it. Of course he had. It was only a first-floor window and there would be a soft landing on the snow. Luke raced over to the window and heard a mechanical roar erupting from below. The sound of a snowmobile being kicked into life. *Their* snowmobile. Damn! How could they have been so careless as to leave the key in the ignition? The roar swelled and faded, vanishing into the night, as the snow swallowed the retreating sound. The bastard had got away.

He returned to Kristian's side, trying to process what had just happened. A Norwegian intelligence officer had just been murdered on his operation, and now Luke felt sick with guilt and remorse. Who had insisted they came to this evil, godforsaken place today, against Kristian's better judgement? Clutched in the dead officer's hand Luke could see there was a small object. It was the fob, the useless, impotent bleeper that was never going to save him at a critical moment like this. Luke closed his eyes and said a silent prayer. Kristian probably had a wife and family back home in Bergen, he thought, and he, Luke, had never even got around to asking him about them.

18

Porton Down Laboratory, Wiltshire
Tuesday, 8 March, 1655hrs GMT

IF ANYONE HAD been driving along a tiny Wiltshire lane called
Manor Farm Road an hour before sunset on that Tuesday afternoon, they would have been shocked at the speed at which a
blue-and-yellow police car was travelling. It was no ordinary
patrol car. With a top speed of close to 170mph, the Lotus Evora
was the fastest vehicle in use by any police force in Britain. It
needed to be. Inside a locked and sealed medical container resting
on the back seat were three samples, all taken from a live patient
at the Royal Free Hospital in north London: Dr Sheila Mackenzie.
One was blood, one was urine and one was 'exudate' – fluid seeping from the open lesions that had begun to appear on her
forearms. All three samples had been inserted into sealed flasks,
then passed through a 'dunk tank' containing six per cent bleach
to reduce any risk of contamination and infection.

No member of the public witnessed the Lotus Evora screeching up to the entrance gates of the Defence Science and Technology
Laboratory at Porton Down that afternoon. That was because
police patrolmen on motorbikes had already closed off the last
mile of the route, turning away all traffic. Porton Down had been
chosen by Whitehall because it was the only laboratory in the

country capable of identifying the microscopic pathogens teeming and multiplying inside those flasks. And every second counted for this analysis.

The guards outside the gate had been radioed ahead. They lowered their stubby black high-powered Heckler & Koch MP7 carbines and raised the barrier as soon as the Lotus swept up the chestnut-lined drive. 'Response level heightened' read the updated security status on a board displayed beside a chain-link fence that ran the length of the avenue leading up to the entrance. The police Lotus drove on, only slowing down at the last moment for each of the speedbumps. Escorted by two of the on-site patrol cars, it swept into the high-security scientific compound. Past the admin blocks, the neatly mown lawns and the road to the open-air testing range, until they pulled up at the large building containing the BSL4 – the Bio-safety Level 4 laboratory – with its array of silver chimneys belching out their thin plumes of white vapour, all extracted, sanitized and expelled from the labs.

There are four 'suites' within that building and Level 4 is for only the most dangerous organisms on the planet, fatal pathogens such as Ebola or Crimean haemorrhagic fever. The tests that were needed now were about to be conducted in the bio-containment laboratory reserved exclusively for Level 4 agents. Since the work was classed as a national security priority, the job was given to two of the most experienced scientists on the books.

Hannah Blane and Colin Masters lived by one single creed: trust. Working together in close proximity, separated from viral death by mere millimetres of protective clothing, they had come to trust each other completely. So when the order came down from the central building they knew exactly what to do. In the antechamber inside the BSL building they went through the safety checklist with meticulous care. Hannah Blane was the first to remove her watch, placing it, with her pens and anything else that could snag on insulating material, in a locked drawer. Colin Masters watched her do this, then did the same under her watchful eye. Both scientists switched off their mobiles before they went anywhere near the hot zone.

After transitioning through the airlock from Level 3, they crouched low as they approached the workbench, bending their knees, before standing up straight inside their protective suits, their faces and bodies sealed airtight with oxygen supplied through a flexible tube attached to their hoods. As an added precaution, they each wore GSR respirators with two filters, one on either side of the head. When they were ready to begin, Blane and Masters faced the solid, transparent Perspex wall that separated them from the live samples inside the core of the lab and slowly inserted their arms into the polythene arm sockets, flexing their fingers inside two pairs of nitrate gloves that could only be worn for thirty minutes at a time before needing to be changed. As a further safety measure, the lab was kept at negative air pressure from the corridor outside, reducing any possibility of an escape of vapour outside Level 4. Next door, watching proceedings on the closed-circuit TV, several SSAs – senior scientific advisers – and a woman from the Joint Biosecurity Centre stood waiting to report back the findings to Whitehall.

Blane and Masters worked in almost total silence, speaking only when necessary. Their mission was clear: to identify the molecular composition of the pathogen as quickly as possible, just as they had with Novichok, Ebola and SARS-CoV-2. To do this, they needed to analyse the genome sequence by examining the genetic structure of the virus and trying to work out where it had come from. The reported sudden deterioration that afternoon in the condition of their source patient, Sheila Mackenzie, had lent an extra urgency to their work. Word had come from London that she had briefly lapsed into unconsciousness before being given a powerful dose of adrenalin and brought round again. The virulence of the pathogen the scientists were handling was in no doubt: both knew there was no margin for error.

Their first task was to extract the DNA/RNA from the samples rushed over from the Royal Free. Working through the transparent wall, they treated the samples contained in miniature test tubes by adding a number of chemicals. Both scientists were well aware of the terrifying statistics they were dealing with: they knew that each test tube contained between 1 and 10 *billion* infectious doses. Next, they spun them in a centrifuge to separate the DNA and RNA, which, once deactivated, could be couriered immediately around the world, to labs in Geneva, Atlanta and The Hague, for further tests and confirmation. The inert extract would also be examined in Porton Down's own gene-sequence analyser, a process that was likely to take several hours. While that was under way, there was a further stage to be undertaken before the results could be relayed to Whitehall: electron microscopy. This would aim to 'visualize' what the infectious agent looked like under extreme magnification.

For a long moment Blane and Masters peered, unspeaking, at the images displayed on the computer screens linked to the electron microscope. They stood stock-still, mesmerized in horror by what they were seeing. It was Colin Masters who broke the silence.

'Christ al-bloody-mighty!' he exclaimed. 'Are you seeing what I'm seeing?' He looked across at his colleague. Her eyes were wide with fear and she was shaking her head in disbelief.

'What the hell is that?' she replied, her voice quavering. 'I mean, it can't be, it just can't be!'

'But it is,' Masters insisted. 'It's right there on the screen. And we've been barking up the wrong bloody tree all this time. This is a hundred times worse than we thought.' They looked at each other, their faces suddenly drained of colour.

Then he shook his head in disgust. 'This could only have been engineered in a lab,' he said quietly. 'It's been genetically modified. Whoever designed this – this abomination is nothing short of pure evil.'

19

Svalbard
Tuesday, 8 March, 1710hrs GMT, 1810hrs local

ALONE, IN THE dim interior of a traditional wooden house, half-way between mainland Norway and the North Pole, Luke's breath frosted in the sub-zero air. Beside him, the rapidly cooling corpse of Kristian Berge, a grade-six officer in the Norwegian Intelligence Service, lay exactly as he'd found it. Luke had been careful not to move it, or to touch the black plastic haft of the screwdriver that had ended the man's life, just in case there were any prints for the forensics people. He wasn't fazed by being in a room with a dead body. He'd seen plenty from his time on operations in the badlands of Iraq's Anbar province, in the labyrinthine, mud-walled compounds of Kandahar, and in the parts of West Africa he could never talk about. Some of those people he'd never known, some he'd dispatched himself in the heat of battle, and some had been his mates. But that was in war, in combat, and this was supposed to be peacetime. Somehow, Kristian's death felt so much more shocking.

Yet Luke was not going to let himself dwell on it. The inquest, the questions, and maybe the accusations would come later. Right now he needed to focus on the tactical, on his own immediate situation. What if Kristian's killer was not the only human threat inside this sinister building? What if someone else was lurking in the darkness, waiting to catch him off-guard? He looked down at the bread knife still clutched in his hand. It wasn't much of a defence, but it was all he had. Slowly, quietly, room by room, Luke checked the house, bracing himself for violence each time he opened a door or turned a corner, then breathing out slowly. The building was empty.

He sat down in the kitchen, took a deep breath and called it in to Vauxhall. Checking his watch as he was put through, he realized it was less than seven hours since Angela Scott had expressed her intense displeasure on hearing that Victor Skeet had been shot dead in Barentsburg. Now he had another death to report and this time it was someone on the home team. But their conversation, when he got through, was all business. He told her immediately about Kristian and that his killer was now on the loose somewhere on this frozen archipelago. He told her about the makeshift lab he'd found in the outhouse, the polythene covers, the suspicious-looking containers of fluid and the documents he'd snatched up from beneath the desk in the other room.

'Send them over,' Angela said. 'Send us the photos on your phone now and we'll get on to them straight away.' There was a brittleness to her voice, a tension he always noted when an operation was under way. He could hear her clearing her throat. 'Now,' she said, 'about Kristian Berge . . .'

Here it comes, he thought. 'Are you going to tell the Norwegians or am I?' he asked.

'We'll do it,' Angela said. 'It won't be an easy call, but it might be better coming from us. This is looking more and more like Moscow's work. The Chief was planning to keep you up there for longer, to dig around a bit, but that doesn't look like such a good idea now. We definitely don't want you getting bogged down in a Norwegian police inquest.'

'Fine by me. So you have an extraction plan, then?'

Angela hesitated. 'Well, not as such, no. But we'll work one up now. We've got your GPS coordinates from your phone. Keep it switched on and we'll get someone to you as soon as. Are you able to keep warm till then?'

'I'll manage. I'll see you on the other side, Angela.'

Luke ended the call and put away his phone. His eyes were drawn involuntarily to the ceiling above him and he found himself staring up at it. There, he knew, lying one floor above him, was Kristian's corpse, stretched out on the floorboards exactly where he had found him. What had happened, he wondered, between the moment he'd called Luke's name in fear and the moment of his death? What terrors had he faced in those few short awful seconds before his life had ended? And why, for God's sake – why hadn't he, Luke, been there in time to save him?

20

Battersea, London
Wednesday, 9 March, 0736hrs GMT

LUKE'S PHONE WENT off while he was still in the shower. Naked, dripping and yawning, he walked back into the bedroom as he towelled down, his bare feet making dark, damp impressions on the thick beige carpet. He was home, yet somehow he was still mentally in the Arctic.

The extraction from Svalbard had been remarkably swift and efficient. All the more surprising given the horrors he had just witnessed. Exactly twenty-seven minutes after his making the call from that grim house of horrors, he was looking out of the kitchen window at a Norwegian Air Force NH90 helicopter touching down in a swirl of snow outside. Several figures spilled out in chem-bio protective gear, carrying their specialist equipment, while the loadmaster frantically beckoned for him to get aboard. Luke was only too glad to be out of that place. Even as they lifted clear into the sub-zero night he could not stop thinking of Kristian Berge and the fact that his killer had got away. Was this a mission failure? Luke patted the documents he had stashed inside his jacket for reassurance. No, it wasn't. But it had come at a hell of a price.

A quick cross-change at Longyearbyen airport and Luke was

on a flight to London via Tromsø and Oslo. Transiting through Tromsø, the same team of medics who had vaccinated him on the way out had screened him, checked him for fever and cleared him of any contamination. He had given his contact report to the NIS intelligence officer in the lounge and agreed to file a full account from London. And now here he was, back in the Battersea flat that he and Elise shared on the south bank of the Thames; he had even managed to grab a few hours' sleep on the way south.

But now he saw he had three missed calls, all from the office. He looked down at Elise, still asleep, her head buried beneath a pillow and her back turned away from him. Luke picked up the phone from the bedside table and took it into the next room, closing the door behind him and pressing 'call back'. A crisp, no-nonsense voice answered immediately. Angela Scott at SIS headquarters, in Vauxhall Cross, contacting him at this barely respectable hour. He shook his head. Did she ever rest? Apparently not. But over the three years he had known her, Luke had acquired a lot of respect for Angela. Her calm, measured approach had steered them through more than one crisis. And beyond that, she had stuck up for him when others in that building had wanted his scalp, branding him 'a maverick', 'a loose cannon' and, as someone had put it, 'a bloody cowboy'. Truth be told, he probably wouldn't still be working for the Service now if it weren't for her.

'Great. You're up,' she said. 'I was afraid you'd still be asleep. Good flight, I hope?' She didn't wait for him to answer. 'Look, I won't sugar-coat this, Luke. You're about to get a knock on the door, so please don't be alarmed. We got you out of Svalbard in such a rush they didn't have time to give you a full-spec medical screening.'

'Yes, they did. In Tromsø. I got the all-clear.'

'Oh.' She sounded deflated. 'Well, apparently that was a bit cursory and now the Porton Down people need to give you the once-over. You *have* just been in close proximity to a lethal pathogen. Look, I'm sorry, Luke, I know this is probably the last thing you feel like doing right now, but we're still getting to grips with this thing and we can't exactly have you being the super-spreader, so just bear with us, okay?'

'All right, so when can we expect this visit?' he asked.

It was then that the doorbell rang.

'Don't answer it!' he called to Elise in the bedroom, as he dashed into the hallway. He was too late. Elise was already up, wrapped in a dressing-gown and ahead of him, opening the door. He heard her gasp and saw her jump back as two tall figures stood framed in the doorway. Both were wearing full protective suits with purple neoprene gloves, and their faces were hidden behind double-filtered respirators. Even after all the months of seeing and wearing Covid facemasks in public, even after everything he had just witnessed up in Svalbard, Luke was still shocked to see these apparitions turning up on their doorstep, right here in Battersea. He moved quickly to position himself in front of Elise, obscuring them from her view. But once again he felt a pang of guilt. This was his job, his chosen career in the dark world of espionage, and it had brought this nastiness right into their home. Always, he had tried to shield Elise from anything like this and today he had failed.

'Mr Carlton?' He heard a muffled, disembodied voice address him. It seemed to be coming from the taller of the two, but he couldn't be sure. 'We're from the Diagnostics Unit at Porton Down. I'm sorry for the intrusion at this early hour, but we need to screen you. Straight away.'

Luke nodded and asked them to wait outside the door while they got dressed, then followed Elise back into the bedroom. She whirled around to face him, her dressing-gown wrapped even tighter around her shoulders, her knuckles showing white with tension. 'Luke, what the *fuck*?'

He put up his hands, about to explain, but she hadn't finished.

'No, seriously. What the actual fuck? You disappear for two days to God-knows-where – I don't ask because I know you can't tell me – and then you come crashing back into bed at five in the morning, smelling all weird. And now this? You bring two people in spacesuits into our flat and our lives. I'm sorry, Luke, but I really do think I'm owed a bit of an explanation this time.'

He could see that her shoulders were trembling as she said this and he moved to put his arms around her, but she backed away brandishing a warning finger. 'No!' she retorted. 'You don't get to sweet-talk your way out of this one. Not until you've got those horrid people off our doorstep. Now get dressed, finish whatever business it is they want with you and get them out of here. I'm locking myself in the bathroom until they're gone. Is that clear?'

Luke dressed in silence, pulling on his clothes as fast as he could, then let in the pair from Porton Down and brought them into the kitchen. He sat stiffly on a chair, his left sleeve rolled up, watching them unpack their bag of tricks from a medical holdall. He looked straight ahead at the fridge as they checked the temperature on his forehead, studying the reading intently. He glanced away as the needle punctured the flesh on his forearm and they drew out two test tubes full of his blood. One man kept humming the theme tune from *Game of Thrones*, over and over again. Luke said nothing, but it only added to his dark mood. What if he was infected? He thought of that poor bastard Skeet, staggering around on the frozen street at this time yesterday, clutching his forehead in pain. Is this how it ends? he wondered. I get carried off and quarantined, screened from public view in some nameless isolation unit, coughing up blood and bile until I finally throw a seven and check out?

He opened his mouth wide as they swabbed the back of his throat. Finally, he felt their gloved hands probing the glands beneath his ears.

'Checking for buboes?' he asked them.

The humming stopped abruptly.

'I can't comment on that, sir,' one replied.

'I feel fine, by the way,' Luke told them. 'Just in case you're wondering.'

'Right, well, you're all clear for now, Mr Carlton. The tests are showing up negative, but we'll need your contact details.'

'Good.' Luke stood up and rolled down his sleeve. 'I'll see you out.'

'We're not quite done yet, sorry. We need to screen the other occupant in the flat. We understand she's your RCP, yes?'

'My what?'

'Your registered current partner. That's according to Service records.'

Luke looked from one to the other, their faces inscrutable behind their masks. 'Guys. You've just told me I'm in the clear. So how could she possibly be infected if I'm not?'

'Sorry to inconvenience you,' one of them shrugged, 'but it's standard protocol.'

Biting his bottom lip, Luke went and tapped gently on the bathroom door. Elise answered, her voice steadier now. 'Have they gone? Can I come out now?'

'Nearly. They just need to screen you too. Won't take a moment.' He tried to make it sound as casual as possible.

Silence. Then the bathroom door opened. Elise stood frowning up at him, still in her dressing-gown, her face perplexed. Even in that tense moment, Luke couldn't help thinking how lovely she looked, but her words brought him right back to reality.

'Screened?' she said, in a worryingly calm voice. 'Why on earth would *I* need to be screened? Luke, what the hell have you brought into this flat? What are you going to tell me next? That you've brought home a fucking STD?'

Luke stayed silent. He had learned from bitter experience that trying to defend himself in these situations only made matters worse. The trouble was, he knew she was right. Elise had a point and he couldn't blame her for sounding off. He just wanted this episode to be over.

21

King's Cross Station, London
Wednesday, 9 March, 0832hrs GMT

SHE LOOKED JUST like any one of the thousands of others milling around the concourse in one of London's busiest railway stations at that time of the morning. Jeans, trainers, baseball cap pulled down low over her forehead and a canvas tote bag over her shoulder. She walked past WHSmith, past Pret, past the ticket machines and the information desk, stopping just short of the Platform 9¾ shop. She joined others beneath the huge black departures board, squinting up at the flickering columns, appearing to search for her platform number. From high up on the walls above, the Tannoy burst into life.

'Security teams are in twenty-four-hour operation at this station,' crackled the voice. 'CCTV footage is being recorded for your safety.' Noted. 'See it, say it, sorted,' concluded the pre-recorded announcement. She had seen just one uniformed policeman so far, a bobby on the beat, wearing one of those old-style custodian helmets, his bulky, overweight frame crammed inside a yellow hi-vis waistcoat. But she knew there would be others, not necessarily in uniform, plain-clothes officers from British Transport Police, working in pairs. They had warned her about them.

She cast a final glance up at the departures board, made a point of checking her watch, then strolled over to a kiosk selling coffee and croissants. She bought herself a flat white in a take-away cup and took it with her. She walked over to Platform 9¾, past the throng of Harry Potter fans, and took out her phone. Just another tourist taking pictures. She photographed everything: the white station pillars, the black cordon set up to manage the queue, then further off, the Harry Potter shop, the Parcel Yard pub, a Caffè Nero. She checked her watch once more and flinched, as if suddenly realizing she was about to miss her train. Apologizing with a smile, she pushed her way past the fans and out into the concourse, leaving King's Cross station by a different exit from the one she had used to come in.

She had seen what she needed to; every detail was now committed to memory. The reconnaissance was complete.

22

LUKE NOSED HIS battered Land Rover out of the underground car park beneath their Battersea flat and drove eastwards towards the green and sandstone building that had served, since 1994, as the headquarters of Britain's foreign intelligence service, MI6. With Elise's final brittle words still ringing in his ears, he was glad to be heading into work. And there was urgency today. He had been summoned to a briefing with the directors on the third floor. Beside him, on the ripped leather cover of the passenger seat, lay the actual documents he had lifted from the makeshift Arctic lab. He had at least been able to get the pair from Porton Down to screen them for him before they left.

Luke swerved out of the busy traffic on Albert Embankment and pulled up at the heavy steel barrier, waiting for the cameras to swivel towards him. His eyes flicked up to the sad, twisted, leafless branches of wisteria that spread out above the entrance awning, and above that to the pale yellow of the walls and finally the cluster of communications antennae crowded together on the roof. Then the dark green gates slid open, and there was another pause as the black-uniformed security men checked over his vehicle. When they gave him the nod he drove it, ever so slowly, into the ground-floor car park, then used the electronic fob on his lanyard to key himself into the building. He passed the plaque on the wall commemorating the official royal opening and the large SIS emblem in the foyer: the crown, the unicorn, the lion rampant and the motto 'Dieu et mon droit'. He nodded a greeting to some of the night shift as they passed him heading in the opposite direction and checked his watch. Not quite 0855. Was there still time to grab a coffee before he went into the briefing? He certainly needed one. But, no, that might look a bit too casual, given the urgency of the situation. He pressed the lift button and rode up to the third floor. This, he guessed, would be an 'exploratory meeting'. It was the Service's way of deciding what to do about something they simply had not seen coming.

Outside Briefing Room B Luke stopped for a moment, composing himself as he went through exactly what had happened up there in that cold, dark house in Svalbard. The one he had been helicoptered out of just fourteen hours ago. Were they going to haul him over the coals now about Kristian's death? And Skeet's? Probably. He expected nothing less. He could hear the questions already in his head. 'But, Luke, were these actions necessary and proportionate? To whom did you refer for authorization?' He bet it hadn't been like this in his uncle's day, and for a moment he found himself wishing he had been born a generation earlier.

He knocked once, then pushed open the door without waiting for an answer.

'There he is! The man himself!' Sid Khan, MI6's distinctly unconventional director of International Counter-Terrorism, half rose out of his chair to greet Luke. Generously proportioned and deceptively casual, he was wearing one of his trademark cherry-pink polo shirts, his own private two-fingers-up to the Establishment, even though it paid his monthly salary. For a man tasked with helping to keep Britain safe from the next terrorist attack by ISIS, Al-Qaida or some obscure far-right extremist group, Khan always managed to appear remarkably chilled.

'Good morning, Director,' Luke replied, keeping it polite and formal, as he took the empty seat offered. Khan was still standing, beaming down at him even now Luke was seated. Did they know something he didn't? He glanced quickly round the room, nodding in greeting. There were six people at the table in that briefing room and he recognized only two. Khan and Angela Scott, who flashed him a fleeting smile. Her pale, freckled face was drawn and worried, but the other four seemed tense and expectant. One had close-cropped grey stubble and looked almost old enough to have served in his uncle's day in the seventies. The others, two women and a man, he guessed were all in their late thirties, like him.

'Bloody outstanding, Luke,' Khan was saying. Luke felt his boss was gazing down at him rather like a father whose son has just learned how to ride a bicycle. It made him feel distinctly uncomfortable. 'You played an absolute blinder up there!' Khan continued. For one awful moment Luke wondered if this was sarcasm. He had been in the Arctic for less than twenty-four hours, yet in that time two people had been killed on his watch and one was from a friendly intelligence service. The lawyers were going to be all over him for this. Now he could see everyone looking at him, waiting for him to respond.

'Just doing my bit,' Luke said modestly, and flashed a smile.

'Just doing your bit?' Khan mimicked, looking round the room with a huge grin. 'I'd say it's a bit more than that, young man. He's only bloody GRU! You've nailed it for us!'

GRU? Russian military intelligence? Who was he talking about? Luke's mind was racing to keep up here. 'I'm sorry,' he said, 'who are you referring to? Not Victor Skeet, surely.'

'No, not Victor Skeet,' Khan said patiently. 'I'm talking about Yevgeny Vasiliev. The Russian in the hut. Patient Zero!'

Khan had sat down now, but he was still looking at Luke expectantly with eyebrows raised. Everyone seemed to be waiting for some kind of reaction from him, but Luke was at a loss to know what the connection was here. And then he got it. 'Those documents in Cyrillic I sent you last night?'

'Bingo,' said Khan. 'We found Vasiliev's name on one of them, among a lot of other stuff that's still being worked through, and we ran it through the database downstairs. Turns out he works in the chemical and bio-warfare division of the GRU.' Khan looked around the room triumphantly and now Luke could see Angela was regarding him with something approaching professional pride. 'This,' Khan concluded, 'has Russian military intelligence stamped all over it! And it's come just in time for the JIC this afternoon.'

The JIC. The Joint Intelligence Committee, the top-secret Whitehall group that issued all the taskings to Britain's intelligence agencies, made infamous under Tony Blair's premiership for its fatally flawed assessment of Iraq's long-defunct programme to build weapons of mass destruction.

Luke couldn't quite put his finger on exactly why, but right now, somewhere in the back of his head, a voice was urging extreme caution: this was all sounding a bit too simple. 'Can we be a hundred per cent certain on that?' he asked. 'I mean, the GRU got their knuckles rapped over the Salisbury Novichok poisoning, didn't they? Then there was the Navalny affair they thought they could get away with and didn't.'

'What are you saying exactly, Luke?' It was Angela who asked this. She had always encouraged him to question, to argue, to take the contrary view at times, so he knew it wasn't a hostile interruption.

'What I'm saying,' he replied, 'is that it seems a bit implausible they'd try something like this again when they keep getting rumbled. I mean, what if it turns out to be a rogue op?' Luke looked around the table, searching for support.

It was the man with white stubble who answered him. 'I should have introduced myself earlier, Luke. I'm Denys Kovalenko from the Russian section. And, yes, that's a Ukrainian name. My parents both grew up in the Soviet Union before emigrating to the West. So, what do I think?' He spread his hands wide. 'I think there is no such thing as a rogue op in twenty-first-century Russia. Nothing, but nothing, gets done without sign-off from the top.'

'Precisely,' Khan concurred, 'but I do like the way you're thinking, Luke. Intelligence is, as we all know, nearly always an incomplete picture, a case of putting together the pieces and moving them around until they fit. That's why we have the JIC.'

'Right. So we do have other pieces?' Luke tried not to make it sound like a challenge, but that was exactly what it came out as.

'We do.' Khan indicated the ginger-haired young man next to him in a green cardigan, wearing spectacles that Luke thought were just slightly too big for his face. 'Damian here has something I'd like you to hear. He's just joined us on secondment from Cheltenham and is helping process the raw CX intel coming in from all our overseas stations.'

Damian cleared his throat, looked up from a notepad in front of him and glanced nervously at Khan before launching in. 'Right. So, yes, our station chief in Oslo has been in contact with our Norwegian partners, the NIS. They have a SIGINT ship, the *Marjata* – I'm not sure I've pronounced that right. It's on-post just off Svalbard where the outbreak has occurred.' SIGINT. Signals Intelligence. The big ugly rival to HUMINT, human intelligence. The Americans loved it; plenty of people on this side of the Atlantic were wary of it. Luke had already spent long enough in MI6 to know that some in the Service considered it to pose an existential threat to their jobs. Well, the reasoning went, if you could hack into someone's phone or their encrypted comms and steal their secrets, why bother risking someone's life by sending in an agent? There was a good reason why GCHQ's headcount had risen a great deal faster than MI6's had in recent years. But, no, the head honchos in Whitehall had decided there was still a need for solid, old-fashioned human spying: finding, recruiting and exploiting people on the inside with access to the secrets Britain needed. Luke reckoned he might still be in his job for a few more years. That was if he didn't screw it up.

'The *Marjata*,' continued Damian, 'picked up a burst transmission coming out of Barentsburg two days ago.' He stopped there, as if waiting for Luke to catch up. Luke glanced round the room, but was met by knowing stares. Clearly everyone else in the room had already heard this. Now he had the distinct feeling he was arriving late to this party.

'And?' said Luke, thinking, Just get to the point, will you?

'Well, Barentsburg is to all intents and purposes a Russian col-ony on Norwegian-administered territory in the Arctic,' Damian replied defensively, checking his notes as he spoke. 'GCHQ are still working on the transcript, but . . . from what's been decrypted so far, the conclusion is . . .' He paused, as if waiting for a green light to proceed.

Oh, for God's sake, Luke thought, you're not announcing the next winner of *X Factor*, just get on with it.

But it was Sid Khan who finished the sentence for him. MI6's director of International Counter-Terrorism folded his hands, leaned forward on the table and looked Luke straight in the eye. Gone were the habitual bonhomie and the casual slang. He spoke slowly and deliberately.

'Our assessment, Luke, with a high degree of probability, is that Moscow is behind this outbreak. We conclude that the GRU has been secretly testing a new biological weapon up on Svalbard.'

23

THE MEETING WAS held in an attractive converted barn. Red-tiled roof, black wooden slatted walls, a quaint covered porch. True, there was an unpleasant smell of silage outside, wafting over from the adjacent farm, but once doors were shut and the meeting was under way it was soon forgotten. Mobiles were left outside in a box, guarded by one of the trusted members, while another kept watch beside the gate at the end of the drive. This meeting was strictly by invitation only.

When everyone was assembled indoors they sat in a semi-circle on chairs whose metal legs scraped abrasively on the stone flooring. All eyes were on the man who stood facing them. He was large, heavily built, with sideburns and a receding hairline. His paunch protruded unapologetically from behind the flaps of his Barbour jacket. Below that, he wore baggy cargo pants with bulging pockets and a bunch of keys on a chain attached to his belt. A man with important responsibilities. A man of standing. A man with the right connections.

When he spoke, his voice was low and authoritative. It carried the gravitas of an Oxford don or perhaps a lawyer-turned-politician. Yet his words dripped with venom and vitriol as he reminded them of the numerous enemies they faced: the Jews, the Muslims, the freeloading migrants from Africa, the Chinese with their disgusting wet markets . . . The list went on. Heads were nodding vigorously as people turned to each other and smiled in agreement. There were no dissenters here.

And now his voice was rising in pitch as he reminded them of the solution at hand, of the very reason they were all there on that March morning. He raised a nicotine-stained finger in the air and held it there as everyone fell silent, waiting for his next words.

'The wheels of the machine are turning,' he told them enigmatically. 'Deliveries will soon be arriving, and you' – he stopped and jabbed a finger at no one in particular '– you all have a role to play in what is coming. This is your future,' he told them. 'This is your destiny. And *nothing*' – his voice rose now in a crescendo – '*nothing* is going to get in our way!'

24

Paddington Station, London
Wednesday, 9 March, 1215hrs GMT

LUKE CARLTON DRAINED the last of his coffee and tossed the empty cup into the bin. It was time to board the train to Cheltenham. A lot had happened in the few hours since he had walked into that early-morning meeting in Vauxhall Cross. The Svalbard outbreak had now been declared a Level One priority and an entire cross-agency team had been assembled at short notice, pulling in expertise from all three UK intelligence agencies: MI6, MI5 and GCHQ. They were tasked with uncovering everything they could possibly find out about the Moscow connection. For Luke, that meant an urgent visit to the West Country, to GCHQ, the Government Communications Headquarters, to get briefed on the SIGINT and cyber intercepts.

'You'll also be working with someone you know,' Angela had told him breezily, as they filed out of the briefing room.

'Who's that?'

'Jenny Li. From Snuffbox.' Luke smiled at hearing the quaint MI6 slang for their sister agency, MI5, across the river. 'She's their CBRN specialist, remember? She knows more about chemical and biological weapons than anyone else in the agencies. C's happy to let her be in the lead on this one so she's running the show. Learn all you can from her. We need you to get up to speed on this pretty fast. Cabinet Office are demanding answers . . .' She rolled her eyes slightly. 'Like, yesterday.'

Luke remembered Jenny Li all too well from the Colombia op. They had had the shared experience of going into University College London Hospital to interview a man suffering the hideous effects of acute radiation sickness. Jenny, he recalled, could be quite condescending at times, but Luke was the first to admit she knew her subject inside out and was scarily well informed when it came to dangerous substances.

Jenny met him at the ticket barrier, wearing a white silk scarf and a fawn overcoat tied tightly at the waist. Luke could see she was scrolling through her phone messages while periodically looking up and scanning the crowd.

'Good. You're on time,' she said briskly, putting the phone into her pocket. 'Shall we go?'

As the Great Western Railway 12.25 to Cheltenham Spa slid westwards out of Paddington, Jenny folded her hands across the table between them and leaned towards him. Her dark hair was cut short, shorter than he remembered from last time, but it still framed her face, with her soft, hazel eyes, perfectly. Luke noticed a circle of paler skin on her finger where a ring might recently have been removed. He thought better of making any comment. She glanced once behind her, checking that no one else was in earshot, then looked Luke in the eye as she spoke. He had forgotten how intense she could be.

'How much do you know, Luke, about Russia's biological-weapons programmes, past and present?' she asked him.

'Not a lot.'

'I thought so. I need you to listen carefully, because this could have a direct bearing on everything we're going to be working on here.'

If Luke had thought he might use this journey to catch up on his mounting sleep deficit he quickly put that thought aside. For the next two hours Jenny took him on a terrifying journey, starting with how, during the Cold War, Soviet scientists had managed to weaponize smallpox, anthrax and a disease called tularaemia, eventually loading these lethal germs in powder form into the warheads of intercontinental ballistic missiles, all aimed at the most densely populated Western cities, including London.

'Ever heard of a place called Vozrozhdeniya Island?' she asked, as the damp March landscape of Berkshire flashed past the window. He shook his head. 'It means "Rebirth Island". It's an island on the Aral Sea in southern Russia – or at least it was before the Aral Sea practically dried up. It was where they shipped in hundreds of monkeys from Africa, then exploded chemical and biological bombs upwind of them to study the effects.' She stopped. 'Luke, you're frowning?'

'No shit I am. That's horrendous.'

'Well, it gets worse. There were some human casualties too. On one of their programmes a scientist got a fatal needlestick injury. He pricked his thumb while he was working with Marburg. He took three weeks to die. Painfully. Then as recently as 2004 a researcher died in Siberia after pricking herself with Ebola.'

He could see she was looking at him quizzically, studying his face for a reaction.

'You don't know what Marburg is, do you?' she said.

'A virus? Named after a town in Germany.'

'Spot on. Marburg is a particularly nasty haemorrhagic fever, like Ebola. Which means your organs start dissolving and you end up bleeding from every orifice. It's sometimes been described as "human soup".'

Luke grimaced and she noticed.

'I know,' she said. 'Not pretty, right?'

Luke held up his hand to stop her before she continued with her catalogue of horrors. 'Okay, hang on,' he said. 'Let me get this straight. I've read the report from Svalbard and the guy who died up there – Yevgeny – he was bleeding from the mouth and nose. So does that mean—'

'That he was infected with a haemorrhagic fever? No, not necessarily, it could still be other things. But you're thinking on the right lines.' That was the second time today someone had said that to him. Perhaps this was the intelligence community's way of saying, 'Noted, but I disagree with you.'

Jenny sat back in her seat and turned to the window. They had crossed into Gloucestershire now and the River Frome was running parallel to the train line. There were flooded fields on both sides and half-submerged fence posts. Clouds scudded across the sky, threatening more rain.

She turned back. 'Look,' she said, with an air of finality. 'We won't know exactly what we're dealing with until all the lab results come in, but I did make a call to Porton Down yesterday. They've got live samples down there, from the patient brought in from Svalbard.'

'You mean Dr Mackenzie?'

'Yes. She's a medical doctor attached to the Arctic Research Station up there. She must have known the risks, so for this virus to have infected her . . .' Jenny left her sentence unfinished. Instead, she sighed and looked out of the window again. 'Whatever this pathogen turns out to be, it's Dr Mackenzie who holds the clue to the answers. That's if – *if* – they can keep her alive for long enough.'

25

LANYARDS. ALWAYS THE coloured lanyards, thought Luke, with those hard plastic ID tags that indicated you were entering a government building with classified intelligence on the inside. A small reception committee was waiting for him and Jenny as they entered the outer ring of the Doughnut, the name given to the vast, circular, futuristic headquarters of GCHQ, the secret intelligence listening station on the outskirts of Cheltenham. A weak spring sun was doing its best to break through as they strode past the serried ranks of neatly parked cars, CCTV cameras on poles and razor-tipped perimeter wire. This place was huge: the biggest, the most expensive employer in the galaxy of Britain's secret intelligence universe. In pictures taken from the air it looked as if a giant spacecraft had landed on the edge of Cheltenham; from ground level its green, sandstone and steel-grey walls soared into the pale sky of Gloucestershire, like some impregnable digital fortress.

A thin man in a navy-blue pullover and jeans stepped forward in the entrance lobby and introduced himself with the briefest of smiles. 'Welcome, both! I'm Ian. I'm the senior operations officer on all this,' he said, sweeping an arm towards the steel panels that stretched all the way up to the ceiling. 'Let's take you straight to the EMC to get you briefed. The Norwegians have only just got here too.'

'The EMC?' asked Luke. He was well used to a world of acronyms in the military, but in the three years he'd been with MI6 he'd discovered he'd only just turned the first few pages of a whole new lexicon.

'Oh, yes, sorry,' said Pullover. 'It's the Event Management Centre. Our ops room, if you like.'

Luke turned to Jenny as they walked and said quietly, 'You didn't know what EMC stood for either, did you?'

She looked straight ahead, pursing her lips. She didn't reply.

They crossed a short, wind-blown patch of open ground to the main building and entered the busy circular concourse. Luke had been there before, as a serving captain in his SBS days, but it never failed to strike him how impossibly young everyone looked. As they strode along, there was hardly a suit to be seen – in fact, nearly half the people he was looking at were wearing trainers. That's applied mathematicians, linguists and codebreakers for you, he supposed.

'Can we offer you both a coffee? A chai latte, perhaps, or a green tea?' suggested Pullover, steering them towards a Costa Coffee kiosk.

A Costa? At the heart of GCHQ? Over there he could see a Greggs and, beyond that, a Starbucks. To Luke, this place felt more like a Californian campus.

'Luke Carlton! As I live and breathe!' an Ulsterman's voice boomed from somewhere behind them, and he turned to see a broad-shouldered man with a scraggly beard. Luke had no recollection of ever seeing him before.

'Conor Beattie,' he introduced himself. 'We haven't met, but, hey, nice work on that rescue op in Iran!' He looked Luke up and down as if committing his image to memory. 'I was one of those trying to keep track of your movements from here. Have to say, you're a hard man to keep up with. Anyways, must dash. Things are hotting up a bit across the water in the Province.' Luke nodded politely, somewhat embarrassed by this effusive encounter. He wondered how many more unseen people in this building had been quietly tracking his movements every time he went live on an op.

'One of your many fans?' remarked Jenny, with a raised eyebrow, when the Ulsterman had moved out of earshot. It was Luke's turn not to answer.

They rode up in the lift, then went along a narrow walkway, carpeted in red and grey, past rows of men and women working away at their screens. It could have been a call centre, a media newsroom or, at a pinch, a City trading room. Except that these analysts were working on largely classified intelligence, tracking anything from North Korean military hacking centres to proxy servers used by ISIS jihadists, from Chinese cyber hackers to internet troll farms in St Petersburg to American child-porn pedlars hiding in the recesses of the dark web.

A large sign welcomed them to the Events Management Centre. 'GCHQ Never Stops', it read. How original, thought Luke. He wondered if some management consultancy firm had pocketed a small fortune to come up with that one. They met up with the Norwegian team as they clustered around a bank of screens, talking in low voices. As the introductions were made, Luke hoped none of them would make the connection between him and their dead colleague, Kristian Berge; he decided he wouldn't mention the subject unless they did.

Above the Norwegians was a large digital display screen, which, as far as Luke could see, was just a stream of code. Clearly, he had entered a different world here in Cheltenham.

'Yes, we're a twenty-four/seven operation here,' announced Pullover, when they were all gathered in one place. 'We normally operate on a shift system around the clock, but this week is – how can I say it? – somewhat out of the ordinary. A decision was taken at our daily leadership meeting yesterday morning to declare Svalbard "an event". That triggers a certain response, so you'll see a lot of extra bodies in here today.' He swept his arm around the darkened operations room where every chair was occupied.

'So . . . Svalbard . . .' He rubbed his hands together, as if somehow relishing the challenge presented by the horrors that had taken place in the Arctic. 'Well, I can tell you, it didn't come out of the blue. Along with our Norwegian friends . . .' he nodded to the group of smartly dressed visitors '. . . we've been aware of covert Russian activity there for some time. But this event is of a wholly different magnitude. Today we've been asking ourselves: who has the capability to do this? Who was in that vicinity at almost exactly this time two days ago? Well, thanks to some fast work by our friends in Oslo we already knew the name of the victim who died in the hut – Yevgeny Vasiliev. And thanks to Mr Carlton here, we now know his parent organization in Moscow.'

Luke felt everyone's eyes turn towards him and he caught one of the Norwegians squinting and ever so slightly frowning. It was a brief but uncomfortable moment and Luke did what he often did at times like this: he discreetly rubbed the stump of his missing finger where a Taliban bullet had taken it off at the joint.

'Porton Down,' continued Pullover, 'are still working on exactly *what* poisoned him. *Our* task here is to find out *who* poisoned him and why.'

Luke found himself chewing the inside of his cheek in impatience as he listened to this. Nearly an hour had passed since he'd stepped off the train and on to the platform at Cheltenham and so far he hadn't learned a damn thing. Was this session going to be just a long list of rhetorical questions or was this man actually going to provide some answers? Otherwise they might as well get the first train back to London. He admired their thoroughness, of course, but he wished they'd get to the point. He looked across at Jenny to see if she shared his impatience, but, as usual, her expression gave nothing away. Good skills, he had to give her that.

'We have, frankly, hundreds of leads that all have to be discounted,' continued Pullover. 'The current population of Barentsburg settlement is four hundred and ninety-one inhabitants, of whom just twenty-seven are Ukrainians and nearly all the rest are Russians. That gives us nearly five hundred potential selectors with mobile numbers, all routing their comms through

Russian-monitored masts, and all names that we need to run through our own systems.'

Luke noticed that one of the Norwegians was getting twitchy, looking like he wanted to interrupt. But the senior operations officer wasn't done yet.

'So how do we narrow this down?' he asked the group. 'We start by looking at their travel patterns. We can see who's recently arrived and—'

'Excuse, please.' One of the Norwegians had his hand up. 'We should please mention the *Marjata*? Our communications ship offshore?'

'Absolutely,' replied Pullover, cocking his head deferentially to one side. 'I was just coming to that. So, yes, working with your NIS people in Oslo, we've gone back over the intercepts picked up from Svalbard over the past seven days and there's certainly one that sticks out like a sore thumb.'

'Excuse me?' The Norwegian again. 'A sore what?'

'I'm sorry, it's just an expression. I was referring to the burst transmission two days ago.' The Norwegians were nodding knowingly now. 'It was what we call a VOIP, a voice over internet protocol. We traced it to a known GRU number. It's registered to number three Grizodubovoy Street in Moscow. That's the headquarters of Russian military intelligence. They're already on our cyber-threat database as part of what we call APT28. That stands for "advanced persistent threat". And, yes, we immediately alerted our sister agencies.' Now he was looking meaningfully at Luke and Jenny. 'First thing yesterday, just in time for the weekly NSC meeting.' He paused, then grinned, as if imparting a shared joke, before adding, 'Sometimes the heuristics pay off!'

The heuristics? Brilliant, Luke thought. I have a 2:1 degree in international relations from Edinburgh, plus a decade and a half of government service, and I have no effing idea what this guy is on about. 'Sorry,' he interjected. 'Heuristics? You've got me there.'

'Oh . . .' Pullover seemed disappointed that anyone needed the term explaining. 'It just means intuitive shortcuts. We're not all geeks here in Cheltenham, you know! Sometimes we simply have to work on a rule of thumb.'

Luke turned to Jenny again. 'You didn't know that term either, did you?'

Jenny gave him a withering look. 'Luke, I'm a scientist. Of course I know what heuristics means. Now come on, pay attention.'

'There is something else we should share with you,' Pullover was saying. Then he made a sudden movement, pulling up a chair on casters and sitting down on it abruptly. 'We think there's a connection with Lithuania. It wouldn't be surprising. After all, the Baltic states were a part of the Soviet Union for over fifty years and they still have a sizeable population of ethnic Russians. Nearly fifteen per cent of people living in the Lithuanian capital are Russians. So, what is that connection?'

He paused, looking pointedly at two of the Norwegians, who were having a whispered conversation, like two naughty school-boys at the back of the class. 'As I was saying,' he pressed on, 'Lithuania. We've back-traced communications between the Russian individual who died in that hut in Svalbard and an address in a suburb of Vilnius – that's the Lithuanian capital. Sorry, you probably all knew that. The address in question turns out to be a factory . . . a factory that produces industrial chemicals. It's called Matulis ChemExport. And, right now, we're extremely interested in what they're up to.'

26

WHEN A SENIOR Scientific Adviser from the Defence Science and Technology Laboratory at Porton Down requests an urgent meeting it is rarely turned down, even by the prime minister's office. Dr Clarissa Gall, one of just two SSAs with an expertise in genetic modification, requested and got her slot in the PM's diary, with no cut-off time. She drove herself up from Wiltshire in the afternoon, after a morning of intense discussions with her senior team. They needed to be absolutely certain of their diagnosis.

Everyone remembered how the entire UK government machine had been caught off-guard by the elaborate Russian disinformation campaign after the Salisbury Novichok attack in 2018. Surely, argued Russia and its London embassy at the time, it could be no coincidence that the former KGB officer Sergei Skripal and his daughter had been poisoned just eight miles down the road from the Porton Down laboratory. Maybe it was a leak. Or an experiment gone wrong. Whitehall counted at least twenty-eight different explanations put out by Moscow. But in the end much of the world drew its own conclusions and 153 Russian 'diplomats' were expelled from at least twenty countries, thereby dismantling entire networks of intelligence-gathering that had taken Moscow

93

years to build. And more recently, recalled Dr Gall, there had been China's attempt to blame the Pentagon for the Coronavirus outbreak of early 2020. No, they needed to be sure they had the science absolutely right on this, or it could turn very embarrassing.

There were just three of them in the room for the meeting, held upstairs in No. 10 amid the sombre paintings and the terracotta walls: Dr Gall, Lachlan Campbell, the national security adviser, and the PM. The latter was late – last-minute business following a typically bruising session of Prime Minister's Questions in the Commons that afternoon. Dr Gall sat stiffly on the edge of her cushioned chair, while opposite her the national security adviser leaned back in his seat, arms behind his head, legs crossed, highly polished shoes and purple patterned ankle socks on display, in what Dr Gall thought was a completely inappropriate attitude for the gravity of the situation. At least he wasn't manspreading. That was something at least.

'Dr Gall,' said the PM, brightly, as he entered the room, slightly out of breath, and sat down heavily on the chair next to her, 'the floor is yours.' But seconds later his genial smile of welcome faded as he heard what she had to say.

'There's no easy way to say this, Prime Minister,' she began. 'But what just happened in Svalbard could be every bit as serious as Salisbury. Or worse.' Lachlan Campbell did not look so relaxed now. He uncrossed his legs and sat upright in his chair. 'This could have grave implications for public health,' she added. 'We're talking a potential pandemic here.'

For a long moment the PM simply stared at her, saying nothing as the colour seemed to drain from his face. 'Go on,' he said at last.

'We've run the tests on the live samples taken from the infected patient, Sheila Mackenzie – who is still critically ill, by the way.'

'And?' prodded the PM.

'And what she is infected with is an extremely dangerous pathogen. We call it "a chimera".'

'A what? Isn't that a mythical beast?'

'Well, yes,' the Porton Down scientist replied, 'but in our world a chimera is a genetically modified virus. In other words, someone has deliberately inserted the genes of one virus – Marburg – into another virus, one that resembles monkey pox, creating a kind of super-pathogen, if you will. We believe it could carry an extremely high mortality rate.'

'Christ alive,' breathed the PM. 'Don't tell me it spreads by inhalation like Covid?'

'We think it does, yes,' she replied.

'Who would want to do such a thing?' asked the PM.

'This has to be a state actor,' interjected the national security adviser, 'and everything I'm hearing points to Moscow. I should have mentioned, Prime Minister, I took a call from Sir Adam from south of the river a short while ago. They've reached the same conclusion.'

'Which is?'

'That this is another bloody GRU operation. SIS believe the Russians were testing some kind of new biological weapon up there. Something went wrong and whatever it was they were testing leaked out . . . And ended up infecting our nationals at the research station.'

The PM's head sank into his hands, and Dr Gall winced inwardly at the sight. After all the country had been through with Covid-19 – the lockdowns, the lay-offs, the closures, the devastation to the economy and all the mortality on the wards – this was hardly the news she wanted to deliver.

She saw the PM raise his head and come up shaking it in disbelief, his bleary blue eyes fixing the national security adviser with a beady glare. 'No,' he said. 'It just doesn't make sense. Why would they choose Norwegian territory for this when they've got God knows how many Arctic islands of their own to mess around on? If you'd told me this had happened on – what's that place? – Novaya Zemlya, then I could believe it.'

'It's a mystery,' conceded the national security adviser, clearing his throat, 'but the evidence is still compelling. The question now is, how do we respond?'

'Hold on a moment,' said the PM. 'First things first. Right now, today, at this moment, is there a risk of infection to the general population?'

Dr Gall took her time answering. She had not reached the peak of her profession by rushing to conclusions. 'As of this moment, PM,' she said carefully, 'the outbreak is contained. The Arctic scientists who were exposed have been isolated and quarantined. But what's worrying us, and this is why I've asked for this meeting at such short notice, is that we have to assume that someone, a malevolent actor, may possess this virus and the means to release it.'

Once again, the PM lowered his head, as if he were studying the patterns of the carpet intensely before responding. 'You say this second virus was "deliberately inserted" into the first?' he finally asked.

'Yes,' Dr Gall replied. 'That is correct.'

'But how can you – how can we – be so sure?'

Dr Gall was unfazed by his question. 'If you'll permit me, Prime Minister, I'd like to explain how my team came to this conclusion, and, believe me, it's not one we reached lightly.'

He nodded for her to continue.

'Working in our Bio-safety Level 4 laboratory at Porton Down, our scientists extracted the nucleic acids – that's the DNA – from the live patient samples we were sent by the Royal Free. We applied that to an analyser in our Level 3 lab and simultaneously examined the results in the EM.'

'The EM?'

'Sorry, the electron microscope. The results were unequivocal. The genetic sequence we are looking at simply does not occur in nature. This is a synthetic virus, possibly – and I know I'm straying outside my tramlines here – but, yes, it's perfectly plausible that it was created as a biological weapon.'

'Right . . .' The PM was still thinking hard. 'So how do we nail this down? If we're going to respond, we need to be one hundred per cent certain of who's behind it.'

There was a short, weighty silence before the national security adviser responded. 'We think,' he said, 'the answer may lie in

Lithuania. GCHQ have traced a connection to a suspect factory there.'

'Well, what are we waiting for?' The PM looked from one to the other, eyebrows raised. 'Let's get someone over there ASAP. I'll get Cheryl to clear my diary so I can chair the COBRA tomorrow morning.'

27

Kirtimai Industrial District, Vilnius, Lithuania
Thursday, 10 March, 0835hrs GMT, 1135hrs local

GREY, UTILITARIAN AND unspeakably grim. Luke's first impressions of the industrial suburbs of Vilnius were far from favourable. Could this really be the picturesque Baltic capital so beloved of British stag weekends, the place he'd heard so much about? He shrugged. He was here to do a job. And this was definitely a last-minute rushed tasking, with minimal time for prep. He and Jenny Li had still been inside the Doughnut at Cheltenham yesterday when the order came through from Vauxhall. They were both to head back to London immediately, ready to catch the early-morning LOT Airlines flight from City Airport direct to Vilnius. Their cover stories were already being worked up by the security team.

'You'll be going in under official cover,' Angela had told him, on the phone from Vauxhall, as they made their way to Cheltenham railway station. 'You work for the OPCW. That's the Organisation for the Prohibition of Chemical Weapons. They're based in The Hague.'

'I know,' Luke said patiently. 'I worked on the Novichok case in 2018, remember?'

'Yes, of course you did,' she added, in a conciliatory tone.

'Anyway, all of that, plus your biogs and your social-media back stories, will be coming through on your phones in the next few hours.'

'ID? Passports?'

'Already being prepped,' Angela had replied. 'When you get to City Airport go straight to desk thirty-four and someone from Security Branch will be there at check-in and hand them to you in a white A5 envelope. She'll be dressed in a dark blue jacket with a red, white and blue scarf. It's the LOT Airlines uniform.'

'What, no code words?' Luke had replied. 'No "geese flying south in winter" exchange?'

'Don't be facetious, Luke. This is deadly serious.' Her voice sounded stern now and he immediately regretted trying to make light of the situation. 'This tasking,' she said, 'has come direct from Number Ten.'

Luke and Jenny had travelled back to London in almost total silence, with him reading up everything he needed to on his mythical role as a technical inspector at the OPCW, the chemical-weapons watchdog, while Jenny was absorbed in the stream of data coming into her laptop, occasionally muttering cryptically, 'No, no, this is not good.' And now here they were, less than twenty-four hours later, on their way to a chemical factory in an obscure corner of Eastern Europe.

The taxi deposited them almost next to a stark memorial to the victims of Nazi wartime deportations, its grim grey concrete lines framing the plaque that spoke of the horrors of the Holocaust some eight decades earlier. Luke regretted not reading up more about the history of this little-visited country on the eastern edge of Europe, but his head was already overflowing with a bewildering array of facts and figures on chemical weapons and how the world was trying to stop them falling into the wrong hands.

They walked the last few yards to the gates of Matulis Chem-Export. A chill wind from across the Belarus border to the east blew swirls of dead leaves around their feet and flurries of dust and grit into their faces. He looked across at Jenny and they exchanged grins; this was not pleasant. She was wearing a dark blue Puffa jacket, which she now zipped up to her throat as they trudged past grey stone Soviet-era apartment blocks and bare winter trees.

The entrance to Matulis ChemExport had seen better days. Someone had clearly collided with the wrought-iron railings at some stage, denting and buckling them out of shape. A drunk driver? A disgruntled employee? Who knew? Luke pressed the buzzer while Jenny stood next to him, hunched against the wind in her Puffa, shoulders raised. The first time he buzzed nobody answered. And the second. But then he heard a click and the gate began sliding uncertainly to one side, opened by an unseen hand somewhere inside the building that now stood in front of them. Dingy red-brick walls, trucks in the courtyard, some with their engines idling, belching clouds of blue exhaust. But then, somewhat incongruously, a large turquoise hoarding depicted a sunlit beach somewhere, captioned with some words in Lithuanian he couldn't decipher, all ending with an exclamation mark.

An unsmiling man in a suit met them in the courtyard and took them up a flight of stairs to a waiting room, where he introduced them to a middle-aged woman sitting behind a bulky computer. The sales director's PA eyed them suspiciously, her cat eye spectacles reminded Luke of the bossy clerk in the cartoon film *Monsters Inc.* For ten minutes, Luke and Jenny sat waiting in silence, still bleary-eyed from their early start, waiting for their hastily arranged appointment with a Mr Sergei Kadunov, the sales director. Luke glanced around him at the swirly patterned carpet, the sundial clock on the wall and the half-filled ashtray on the cracked Formica-top table. He felt like he had just stepped back into the 1970s.

A steel box on the PA's desk buzzed into life and she spoke briskly into a microphone, in Russian, Luke guessed, then gestured for them to go in. 'Gentlemen,' said the sales director in a thick accent, ignoring the fact that Jenny was, very obviously, not one. 'This is quite unorthodox, but we are happy to help. What can we do for you?' No tea or coffee was offered, they noted, as they took their seats. In fact, the burly Mr Kadunov did not even rise from his chair behind his metal frame desk. He looked as if he had once been a wrestler, Luke reckoned, or a bodybuilder, or both. Can't say I blame him for being grumpy, he thought. A snap visit at almost zero notice from two OPCW inspectors to this chemical factory would not be the best news he'd had all week. Behind him, and slightly to one side, stood another man, younger, in his late thirties, Luke guessed, but prematurely balding.

Kadunov waved him forward. 'Let me introduce my assistant here,' he said. 'This is Darius Janulis. He is – how you say? – our legals officer.'

Interesting, Luke thought, as the younger man gave an exaggerated bow. With a name like Kadunov, the boss of this sales division must be an ethnic Russian. But his assistant, Janulis, must be an ethnic Lithuanian. One of the few statistics Luke had had time to learn about this country on the way over was that just under five per cent of the population was ethnic Russian and they were viewed with suspicion by some ethnic Lithuanians. He wondered how Janulis felt, reporting to a Russian in a position of seniority. Was there something he could exploit here?

'We'll keep this as brief as possible,' Jenny was saying, 'and then we'll be out of your hair. We'd like to take a look at your sales records of all exports to Scandinavian countries, starting with Norway, going back for the past three months. And we'll need the names of everyone who signed off on each shipment and—'

She was cut short by a burst of throaty laughter. It came from the sales director and it was a mirthless, cynical sound. 'Lady, please . . .' He raised his hand. 'You cannot just come marching in here and expect us to open our books like this!' He thrust out his jaw aggressively, then turned towards Luke with a patronizing smile. 'Please, mister. You can explain this to your Chinese friend?'

Your Chinese friend? Luke could hardly believe what he was hearing, but this naked display of misogyny and racism had him up on his feet and facing down the sales director. 'Let me stop you right there,' Luke said, adding a menacing edge to his voice.

'Because guess what? This is exactly what we *can* do and it's what we *are* doing,' he told the startled man behind his desk. 'Let me remind you, Mr Kadunov, that your government signed up to the Biological Weapons Convention in 1998 and the Chemical Weapons Convention in 2004.'

Luke and Jenny had come prepared, expecting there might well be some pushback, and now Luke pulled out a document from his inside jacket pocket. He made sure he had the man's full attention before he read it out loud to him.

'This is a statement from the recent CWC conference,' he told him. 'Lithuania, it says, "condemns in the strongest terms all use of chemical and biological weapons by state or non-state actors anywhere in the world. Lithuania welcomes—" '

'Yes, yes, yes.' Kadunov waved a hand dismissively. 'We know all of this.'

But Luke placed the document in front of him on his desk. 'Well, you now have two OPCW officials in front of you, so we would appreciate your full cooperation.' Luke stood back and folded his arms. 'Or do I need to make a call to our head office in The Hague?'

For several seconds the two men stared at each other. Luke had taken an instant dislike to Kadunov and suspected the feeling was mutual. But then the sales director appeared to recover his composure. He assumed an air of being the blameless victim, extending his hands palm upwards and shrugging his shoulders in a gesture of helplessness. 'But this is crazy, mister! You are talking about chemical weapons! Like this is Syria or something. And this, my friend,' he gestured towards the door they had just come through, 'this is just a factory that produces agricultural compounds for the farming industry. My assistant can show you around if you like.'

'Good,' said Luke. 'Then you'll have nothing to hide. So, if we could just take a look at those sales records to Scandinavian importers . . .'

Kadunov held up his hand, as if refusing a request from an unruly child, and turned to his lawyer. They spoke rapidly in

Russian, their voices rising and falling, before the sales director faced his visitors with an unctuous smile. 'We would of course be happy to provide you with what you ask for. But you must understand this will take a little time. In the meantime you must excuse me.' Kadunov rose from his seat for the first time. 'My assistant will see you out. I do hope you enjoy Vilnius. It really has so much to offer.' He handed Luke a business card. 'For example, I can recommend you some excellent gentlemen's clubs. Just call me on this number and I can arrange.' He threw a dismissive glance towards Jenny Li. 'But I would suggest you should leave your Chinese companion behind in her hotel.'

28

Whitehall, London
Thursday, 10 March, 0850hrs GMT

AJAY CHAKRABARTI WAS exhausted. As the most recent civil servant to join Britain's National Security Secretariat he was used to being handed long and complex tasks at very short notice, usually at about 6 p.m., just as he was heading out of the door. But nothing could have prepared him for this.

'National security adviser wants to see you. Now,' he was told. That had been early the previous evening. Fifteen minutes later he had emerged from his boss's inner office in a state of mild shock. He had had to ring his fiancée on his personal mobile to give her the bad news. 'Best cancel our table at Hakkasan. Really sorry. This is going to be a late one.' That had turned out to be a serious understatement.

All through Wednesday night and on into the early morning, Chakrabarti had led the Cabinet Office staff team as they worked feverishly to prepare the report ordered by the prime minister in readiness for the next morning's 0900 COBRA crisis meeting, called as a direct result of the shocking findings made by the laboratory at Porton Down.

At 0600 there had been a preliminary virtual meeting of senior officials from Health, Defence, Home Office and the intelligence agencies, all conducted remotely using Artemis, the government's encrypted version of Zoom. It was now 0850 and Chakrabarti was casting a final nervous glance over his team's handiwork. The product of their overnight labours was a document known as a 'commonly recognized information picture'. It was a pull-together of all the latest situation reports from every relevant government department. The opening one-page executive summary was given a Strap-level secret classification and read through by the PM next door in No. 10, just ahead of the COBRA meeting.

It started late. When the prime minister took his seat at the head of the table in that windowless, subterranean room, the conversation died. This was the first prime ministerial COBRA since the outbreak in Svalbard at the beginning of the week. Ajay Chakrabarti was not present at the meeting, but before it had begun he had gone downstairs and personally checked that there was a numbered and bound copy of the CRIP printed out and laid neatly on the table for every minister and official attending.

'This meeting,' the PM told those present, 'is to establish what we know about this outbreak, who we think is behind it, and what we need to do to prepare for the worst-case scenario, should that develop.'

Jay Spelling, the health secretary, seated on his right, was nodding vigorously.

'Dr Gall,' the PM said, 'will you give us your findings, please.'

The Porton Down scientist took a deep breath, placed her spectacles on the table in front of her, then shared with them the full horror of what her team in Wiltshire had discovered.

'Marburg,' she said, 'is a filovirus. It's one of a group of haemorrhagic viruses, like Ebola, that can result in uncontrolled bleeding from every orifice. You may recall the Ebola outbreak in West Africa in 2014?' Several nods around the table. 'Well, that killed over eleven thousand people across six countries. The more recent outbreak in the DRC killed at least fifteen hundred people in just the first ten months.' She stopped as a hand went up. It was the defence secretary, an ex-RAF Typhoon pilot and another recent appointee to his post.

105

'I'm sorry,' he said, 'but I'm not quite getting this. I'm not playing down those numbers, Clarissa, they're bad enough. But, come on, they're dwarfed by the death toll from Covid-19. The world saw, what, nearly two million deaths, I think it was, from Coronavirus in 2020 alone. This Marburg thing doesn't sound like it's anywhere near that level. Or am I missing something here?'

The expression on Dr Gall's face said it all: *Yes, you're completely missing the point and you also cut me off before I'd finished.* She smiled at him patiently before continuing in a calm, measured tone: 'There are two reasons why we need to worry, Secretary of State. One is that, unlike Covid-19, which was naturally occurring in the animal population, this virus has been deliberately genetically engineered. The second is that this isn't just one pathogen we're looking at here, it's two.'

The PM's head hung low as he listened, passing a hand across his face, as if trying to wipe away what he was hearing. When he said nothing Dr Gall continued, 'Some of you may be familiar with monkey pox. It's related to smallpox, but it hasn't been eradicated. It's been cropping up in Nigeria and—'

'Symptoms?' interrupted the PM, looking up abruptly.

'Oh, fever, exhaustion, a rash across the face . . . swollen lymph nodes. That would probably explain the early misdiagnosis in Svalbard as bubonic plague.' She took a moment to look around the whole room before sharing her team's deduction. 'Taken together,' she concluded, 'there's no knowing just what damage these pathogens could inflict on a human population when combined into a single unit.'

At the head of the table the PM now removed his jacket, undid the cuffs on his shirt sleeves and rolled them halfway up his forearms before turning back to the Porton Down scientist. 'All right,' he said. 'Then give us the bottom line here. We can come up with an antidote for this, right? There'll be a cure for it, yes?'

Dr Gall exchanged a hurried glance with Brendan Holmes, the chief medical officer. 'In time, yes,' she replied cautiously. 'I would hope there'll be a vaccine of sorts. But this is very early days, Prime Minister, and we've only just mapped the sequence. We're still trying to understand exactly what we're dealing with here.'

There was silence in the room, then a hand went up. It was Brendan Holmes. 'If I could just add a codicil to what Dr Gall is saying, Prime Minister? We are working closely with the CDC in Atlanta – that's the Centers for Disease Control and Prevention. They are the world's leading authority on pox viruses. They have the absolute latest research. I've had an hour-long teleconference with them already this morning. We've sent them over a deactivated sample for cross-checking. It left RAF Northolt last night and should be with them shortly. I should add,' he said, looking up and down the long table, 'that our own Joint Biosecurity Centre, the JBC, is recommending that everyone who came into contact with the infected patient be tested, as a matter of urgency. Test, track and trace; we have to do this without delay.'

The PM had his eyes shut as he nodded in agreement. 'So tell me, Brendan,' he said, his eyes still closed as he spoke, 'worst-case scenario. If someone chose to release this virus here, in Britain, could the health system cope?'

Brendan Holmes's cheeks flushed visibly and he had to clear his throat twice, noisily, before answering, rather quietly, 'Prime Minister, this is a complex and particularly lethal pathogen we're talking about here, potentially many times more contagious and more deadly than Covid-19.'

'I hear you,' the PM replied, 'but I'll repeat my question. Could we cope?'

'No,' conceded the chief medical officer, 'probably not.'

'Probably not,' the PM repeated. 'I'd say definitely not, wouldn't you? So let's not waste any more time. We have to prepare for the worst.'

29

'WELL, THAT WAS a complete bloody waste of time, wasn't it?' Luke pushed away the plate of half-eaten sausages and folded his arms, biting his bottom lip. 'That man Kadunov was a total knob,' he added. He glanced across the café table at Jenny Li for her reaction, but she was still eating, looking down as she chased a morsel around her plate, and, at first, she didn't answer him. ' "Explain this to your Chinese friend," ' Luke mimicked the sales director sarcastically. 'Jesus! I felt like putting him up against the wall and sorting him out.'

They had taken refuge in the first café down the street from the Matulis ChemExport factory. The Café Baltika was basic and functional, with all the frills and fancy trimmings you would expect from an unreconstructed Soviet establishment that had somehow staggered on into the era of Lithuania's independence and membership of the EU. Jenny had ordered mushroom cookies and pickled cucumber; Luke had chosen sausages. Neither choice could be described as an unqualified success. Luke's coiled sausages bore a disturbing similarity to something left on a pavement.

In a move that surprised him for its tenderness, he saw her reach out and squeeze his arm.

'Luke,' she told him, 'your chivalry is much appreciated, really, but trust me, I've had to put up with a great deal worse. And yes, Mr Kadunov is, as you so delicately put it, "a total knob".' She smiled at him for a moment. 'But given what Porton Down have come up with, this mission of ours – right here and now – it's more important than ever. So the fact is, we still need to access those Scandinavian sales records or we're not going to get to the bottom of the connection between Matulis ChemExport and what's broken out on Svalbard.'

Luke considered this for a moment, nodding in agreement. 'Leaving aside our personal distaste for the man,' he said, 'I got the definite sense that he had something to hide, didn't you?'

'Without question,' she replied, spearing a pickled cucumber with her fork, examining it for a second and deciding to leave it on her plate.

'So how should we take this forward?' Luke asked, thinking out loud as he contemplated having a second stab at his sausages and likewise deciding against it. 'Do we get GCHQ to simply hack into their archives? It could save us a lot of time.'

Jenny laid her cutlery neatly to one side, pushed her plate a fraction further away and gave Luke her full attention. 'Human intelligence,' she reminded him, 'is the bedrock of what you do at SIS, you know that, Luke. There is only so much anyone can do in cyberspace. At the end of the day you have to get close with the enemy, up close and personal. Case officers are like the infantry of espionage. There really is no substitute for—' She stopped abruptly as Luke held up his index finger, his eyes on the door of the café.

'Sorry to interrupt,' he said quietly, 'and don't turn around, but I think the guy who's just walked in is the lawyer who was sitting in Kadunov's office.'

He watched as Jenny took out her phone. For a moment he thought she was taking a selfie as she held it casually in front of her face. Then he noticed she was subtly angling it so she could see exactly what was going on behind her. Good skills, he thought. I must remember that trick.

'You're right,' she said, in a low whisper, 'it is the lawyer. Janulis. He's coming over now.'

Luke looked up and feigned surprise as Darius Janulis approached their table with a smile. 'May I please join you?' he asked, helping himself to a chair before waiting for an answer. Already Luke suspected Janulis's being there was no coincidence.

'Please do,' Luke replied. 'I guess this is your local?'

The 'legals officer' for Matulis ChemExport didn't answer straight away. He signalled to the waitress, who broke off from texting on her phone to give him a radiant smile, recognizing him immediately. They spoke briefly in Lithuanian, and then he turned to face them.

'This,' he said, gesturing expansively towards the street behind him, 'this is Kirtimai district. Of all the beautiful places you could have come to in my country, you choose this place for lunch? It is an industrial zone, my friend. It is . . . how you say it? . . . a shit hole. Yes. We only have two cafés in this street. One is closed, this is the other.' He looked around despairingly at the decrepit décor, the faded and unframed posters of Swiss mountains, and an ageing photo of the Russian tennis star Maria Sharapova.

'Still, here we are,' Luke replied pleasantly. 'Can we get you something to drink?'

The Lithuanian ignored the offer. Instead he sat down and lowered his voice, looking quickly over his shoulder and adopting a conspiratorial tone. 'That meeting did not go so well for you back there in the office, did it?'

Luke was surprised at his abruptness, but he shrugged, turning to Jenny, who seemed to be studying the man. Somehow, even in these chilly Eastern European spring temperatures, the lawyer had managed to acquire a sheen of sweat across his forehead. 'I mean,' he continued, a sly smile spreading across his face, 'you can play it cool and British if you like. But let us be honest, you did not get what you came for, am I right?'

'Maybe,' Luke said non-committally. Now he was certain: it was definitely no coincidence running into Janulis in here. Luke was intrigued.

Janulis leaned forward again, lowering his voice even further, forcing them to draw closer to his shiny face. 'So . . .' he paused, drawing it out for dramatic effect '. . . it is possible that I have the thing you came for.' Luke flashed a look at Jenny, but her face was impassive, giving nothing away.

'Okay. Can you be a bit more specific?' said Luke.

'Be more what?'

'I said, "be more specific",' Luke replied. 'What is it you're offering, exactly?' Suddenly he found himself experiencing an uncomfortable flashback. He was a rookie trainee at the Fort on Britain's south coast, going through his paces on the SIS agent-running course. A course in which, during one exercise, he, Luke, had completely blown it on his first attempt to recruit 'an agent'. The man posing as the agent had asked Luke to spell out exactly what he wanted him to steal from state archives. It was a trap and Luke had fallen right into it, showing his hand much too soon and finding himself slammed up against the wall by a couple of goons. It didn't matter a damn to Luke that at least half the others on that course had made exactly the same mistake. He had never got over the failure. Which was just the lesson his instructors had wanted him to learn.

'I can offer you . . .' Janulis was looking slowly around the café now, even though no one was paying them the slightest attention '. . . I can offer you everything you came for. Sales records, names, shipment dates, everything. All on a single flash drive. And I don't ask any questions.'

Luke regarded him with an even stare. He guessed that the man in front of him probably had little love for his boss, and for good reason, but Darius Janulis did not look the kind of individual to drop a gift like this into their laps for nothing. There would be a price to pay, and he guessed they were about to learn what it was.

'All I ask in return,' Janulis continued, with a smile, 'is just fifty

111

thousand euros, in cash.' He said this casually, as if it were a day-to-day commonplace exchange. 'I am sure this amount is small change for your organization.'

Several things went through Luke's mind as he heard these words. Bingo. This is exactly what we came here for. If we can get this transaction completed quickly, we can rush the data back to London and push forward the investigation. And at the same time another part of his brain was telling him to slow down, to think this through. In practice, MI6 would have no qualms about signing off on several thousand euros in exchange for this data, provided it was genuine, but there were their cover identities to consider. He and Jenny were supposed to be officials sent out from the OPCW and, as with any bonafide multinational organization, they would be subject to strict rules on bribery and corruption.

'Mr Janulis,' Luke began, 'I think you're forgetting something here. We are the OPCW. We can sequester this information through our own lawyers. Now, we've tried to be reasonable—' He stopped as Janulis was wagging his finger and shaking his head. He seemed very sure of himself.

'We both know that will take a long time,' said the Lithuanian. 'And I am guessing you are in a hurry or else you would not be here, right?' They stared at each other, Luke holding the other man's gaze.

'Twenty thousand.' It was Jenny who spoke up. She had been silent all this time, but evidently she was thinking the same as he was: let's get this done and get back to London.

Janulis sighed, as if exhausted already by the tedious business of bargaining. He moved to get up. 'Fifty thousand. Take it or leave it,' he said wearily. He did indeed look ready to leave.

'Okay,' said Jenny, calmly. 'You have a deal. But we'll need to see the flash drive.' She held out her hand expectantly.

Janulis laughed and shook his head once more. 'Not so fast, lady. I have a lot of work to do first to get you this information. It will take some time and I must – how you say? – cover my tracks.'

'Fine,' Luke said. 'We can meet next to our hotel. There's a place called—'

'No, no, no.' Janulis had dropped any pretence at unctuous charm: he was all business now. 'We do this my way. You are in Lithuania now. You will bring the money this afternoon to the Gediminas Tower. Here, I will write it down for you.' He took out a biro, reached across the table, grabbed a napkin and scribbled down a name. 'There is a railway – it goes almost to the top. The last journey is at four p.m. You take that. I meet you at the top. It's agreed?'

Luke looked across to Jenny and she nodded.

'It's agreed,' Luke said.

'Then good.' Janulis got up and left without saying goodbye.

30

BARNS BUILT OF pale limestone, sloping roofs of black slate, all ringed by a succession of dry-stone walls that encircled its wind-swept fields. This was a traditional hill-country farm of the high Peak District in the English county of Derbyshire. Half hidden as it was by a line of ash trees, set well back from the road and any prying eyes, you would have to go to some trouble to find Abbot's Farm. You could walk for miles up here and not meet a soul.

Which was exactly why they had chosen it, purchasing it at a rock-bottom price some months earlier after the owner had died, leaving it in a shocking state of disrepair. The contractors had been chosen carefully, because this was rather more than simple remedial work. There were cellars to be excavated, trenches to be dug and, to anyone with more than a passing curiosity, some measures that looked as if they were possibly constructed more for fortification than for comfort.

On this wet morning in March, a lone figure was carrying out a meticulous tour of inspection. Lotti James was oblivious to the rain that swept across the bleak fields and trickled down the fence posts, collecting in pools at her feet. She could see that the contractors' work was all but done: the refrigerated units were up and running, the accommodation was ready, and there were food supplies to last at least three months. True, there had been some delay in getting the high-voltage fences installed, the specially adapted ones brought in from the Continent with a charge so powerful they would knock a man six feet backwards and paralyse the part of his brain that controls his breathing. But the infrared intruder alarm system was operational and the armoury was in place, the weapons checked, oiled and ready, the ammunition all stashed to hand in carefully labelled boxes with quick-release catches.

Yes. Lotti James was more than satisfied with what she saw. The Farm was ready for what was coming.

31

Old Town, Vilnius, Lithuania
Thursday, 10 March, 1250hrs GMT, 1550hrs local

THE CONTRAST COULD not have been more dramatic. After the grim, grey industrial suburb of that morning, Luke now found himself in another world: a world of pretty cobbled medieval backstreets, elegant baroque churches, leafy courtyards and cosy cafés. No wonder the Old Town of Vilnius had been declared a UNESCO World Heritage site.

Luke used the Google Maps navigator on his phone to check his route, then walked briskly down Bernardinu Street towards the cathedral square. Two boys on e-scooters overtook him, oblivious to his presence as they listened to music through their AirPods. Other than that, the street was empty on that late-winter weekday afternoon. Luke paused halfway down the street, pretending to examine a painted teapot that someone had embedded in the ochre-coloured wall, so that he could discreetly glance up and down in both directions, making quite sure he wasn't being followed. He wasn't.

Was he being over-cautious, he wondered, paranoid even? After all, Lithuania was supposed to be friendly territory. He knew it was a loyal NATO member with a small, largely symbolic, multinational battlegroup deployed to hold up the massed divisions of the Russian Army for about four and a half minutes, should Moscow ever decide to do a Crimea and reoccupy its former territory. But fieldcraft doesn't stop at borders and Luke felt – both he and Jenny felt – there was something distinctly sinister about the burly sales director back in the factory. Jenny, they agreed, would stay in the hotel, working up her analysis on the stream of data coming in from Porton Down. As one of the agencies' foremost authorities on chemical and biological weapons, there was no chance London was going to leave her in peace, especially on a job like this. Luke, it was decided, would meet the contact alone.

'Two euros.' The white-haired man in the ticket kiosk held up two fingers, then took Luke's cash before letting him in through a turnstile. The doors hissed open to the tiny funicular railway cabin, empty save for a discarded fast-food carton lying on the floor.

The wind hit him the moment he stepped outside at the top. The magnificence of the view over the Old Town was largely lost on him as he shivered inside his jacket, his eyes watering with the cold. From far below came the distant hum of traffic. Luke stood with his back to the Old Town and quartered the ramparts and paving stones with his eyes, searching for his contact.

Of Janulis there was no sign, only a lonesome couple posing for a selfie, leaning against the stone walls of the Gediminas Tower, with fixed grins and an arm outstretched, the grand sweep of the Baltic capital laid out beneath them. A shaft of pale sunlight, low on the horizon, broke through the clouds, briefly illuminating the red-tile roofs and sparkling off the River Neris that coiled through the city, separating the Old Town from the modern high-rises to the north.

When he heard the crunch of a footstep on gravel behind him he whirled round. How had he missed that? Was he losing his edge? This person had come out of nowhere, catching him off-guard.

'You are here for Janulis?' She was a child, barely into her teens, her face half hidden by a frayed grey hoodie, but her voice was strong, with little trace of an accent.

'Yes,' Luke replied. 'Is he with you?'

'He couldn't come,' she said flatly. Luke frowned, making no attempt to hide his annoyance. He didn't like this. It was starting to look like Janulis was playing games. And why send a child? She should not be mixed up in this. 'He sent me instead,' the girl said, 'because he's still getting you what you want.'

'You're his daughter?'

She shook her head, and handed him a piece of paper, her pale, frail hand gripping it tightly so it didn't blow away in the wind. 'He is my uncle. He says to meet him here, at this place, tonight. At ten fifteen. He will be there this time, he promises.'

Luke peered at the note. Ten Commandments Bar, it said, on Vilniaus g.39. He looked up to thank her, but the girl was already gone.

32

Royal Free Hospital, London
Thursday, 10 March, 1813hrs GMT

DR SHEILA MACKENZIE was feeling a whole lot better. She was still in the isolation tent at the Royal Free Hospital in north London, but now she was sitting up in bed, propped on pillows, the oxygen mask removed from her face. The broad-spectrum antibiotic they had pumped into her veins over the last few hours must be doing the trick, she reckoned, she was feeling better and the bleeding from her nose had stopped. A TV had been installed in her room and it was showing a news programme about a worsening shortfall in nurses recruited from the EU. She smiled to herself: this was a topic close to her heart.

Later, as her mood improved further, she thought of asking her own nursing team about possible visitors. She would request a full set of her medical notes when this was all over. As a patient who was on track to beat the mystery infection on Svalbard she must surely be making medical history. Briefly, she indulged herself with a future projection, an image of her delivering a ground-breaking lecture to a packed and attentive audience of the best and brightest of her profession at the Royal College of Physicians overlooking Regent's Park. There would be talk-show interviews, maybe even a book deal . . .

It was only a short while later that her condition started to change, and it all happened with terrifying speed. Dr Sheila Mackenzie began to feel hot and unwell. Using the voice communicator beside her bed, she asked the nurses to turn down the temperature in the room. It was 19°C. When the tremors set in she could feel her body starting to ache all over, especially in the joints and muscles. Her heart was racing, she could tell, and her face was slick with sweat. By the time she heard a worried nurse tell her that her body temperature had risen to 40.7°C, or just over 105° Fahrenheit, and they were going to step up the dose of antibiotics, Dr Mackenzie was barely listening because the nausea was becoming unbearable. When she vomited, twice in quick succession, it did little to relieve the pain. Looking down at the front of her now-saturated hospital gown, she could see streaks of blood among the effluent. And she noticed something else. Where her arm had been punctured earlier to take samples for analysis at Porton Down, droplets of blood were forming, seeping from her skin and dripping slowly on to the sheet.

She was vaguely aware of several figures standing on the other side of the isolation tent, watching her with worried expressions, one holding a clipboard and pen. And they smelt terrible. Yes, there was a really disgusting smell in here. It took Sheila Mackenzie a few moments to realize that the smell wasn't coming from them, not from the people at her bedside, it was coming from her. She had lost control of her bowels. Seventeen minutes later she was gripped by uncontrollable convulsions and then, finally, a catastrophic seizure.

At 7.12 p.m. on the evening of Thursday, 10 March, three days after entering an Arctic hut on the archipelago of Svalbard as a fit and healthy researcher, Dr Sheila Mackenzie died.

33

Ten Commandments Bar, Vilnius, Lithuania
Thursday, 10 March, 1915hrs GMT, 2215hrs local

OLD, OVERDRESSED AND out of place. That was pretty much how Luke felt as, shortly after 10 p.m., he and Jenny walked down the rain-splashed cobbles of Vilnius Street in the Old Town and approached the bar calling itself Ten Commandments. It was a young crowd out in the party district of the Lithuanian capital tonight, students mainly, oblivious to the falling temperatures and the spasmodic drizzle. They were standing around in noisy groups on the pavement, making little attempt at social distancing.

Luke was surprised to find himself feeling self-conscious. He was still in his thirties, just, but he felt almost old enough to be these students' father. He was wearing a dark blazer, black polo neck and dark skinny jeans. Jenny had procured herself a stylish black cocktail dress, the result of a last-minute dash to a department store just before it closed for the day. In the event, they had had some heated words.

'Oh, for God's sake,' Luke had protested, as she tried to steer him towards a green suit and shiny black shirt ensemble. 'I'm not dressing up like Borat!'

Jenny had fixed him with a steely gaze. 'Listen, Luke,' she had reminded him, and not for the first time, 'someone in Europe's got their hands on a deadly new pathogen and we still don't know who. I've got Thames House calling me for answers practically every hour and you're quibbling about what to wear tonight? Get some perspective, Luke. Just wear whatever it takes to get this done. We go in, we find Janulis, we hand over the money and we leave with the flash drive. End of.'

They had settled on the polo neck, which was exactly what the man on the door was wearing. Blond, massive, tattooed and earringed, the club's bouncer didn't give them a second glance: he looked right past Luke and waved them inside. Purple lighting, the sweet smoke of shisha pipes and young, happy-looking people. Those were Luke's first impressions as they stepped through the door. This wasn't flashy downtown Moscow, it was Vilnius, relaxed, low-budget, informal. The club had a dark, smoky vibe, with an illuminated blue neon waterfall effect on the wall. A pair of ash-blonde girls sat up at the bar, twirling on their stools and sucking at shisha pipes, their manicured fingers gripping the corrugated stems of the waterpipes as they inhaled the scented smoke. One smiled up at Luke as he and Jenny went past, then tilted her head back and blew smoke rings up at the ceiling. A huge screen above the bar was playing Billie Eilish's 'Bad Guy' music video from 2019 as her song thumped out from giant speakers mounted on the walls.

'I'm going to check out the rest of this place,' said Luke. 'See if I can find him.' He waved towards a padded leather sofa in the corner. 'D'you want to grab that spot before anyone else does?' He moved past the bar, behind which a girl in a black leather minidress was expertly spinning a bottle of vodka in the air as she mixed the drinks. Luke wasn't watching her: he was noting the exits and scoping the clientele. He needed to be sure they had an escape plan if this all went pear-shaped and it turned out to be a set-up. It wasn't the authorities here he was worried about, it was the underworld Mafia that had sprung up in the Baltics ever since independence in the 1990s. He had read up about it in the pre-mission briefing. Former Soviet Spetznaz Special Forces operatives, who had reinvented themselves as they spread their tentacles into organized crime. They had a reputation for violence that made the Italian Mafia sound mild.

Luke moved on, turning a corner into the washrooms, where two girls were waiting patiently for their turn, both head down, scrolling intently through their phones, ignoring each other. No sign of Janulis yet. Luke turned on his heels to go back the way he had come and found his path blocked by a giant of a man in a tight black T-shirt, bald, bearded, muscled. Instantly on alert, Luke mentally measured him up. They were the same height, but, if it came to it, Luke wasn't sure he could take him down. The man smiled and politely moved aside to let him pass. False alarm.

Luke rejoined Jenny on the sofa. 'There's no bloody sign of him,' he said, raising his voice to be heard above the music.

'What?' She turned her face towards him. 'I can't hear you, Luke.' He repeated it and noticed she had got them drinks that sat on the smoked-glass table next to her knees. He took a sip, a weak G&T, and kept scanning the club. The place was starting to fill now and a couple was dancing annoyingly close to them, interrupting their field of vision.

'Oh, shit!' Jenny exclaimed, nudging him suddenly in the ribs with her elbow as she stared at what was on her phone. She handed it to him without a word. It was a brief text from her contact at the Royal Free in London.

Agent X patient Dr Sheila Mackenzie dead. NOT public yet it read. She looked at him long and hard and he wondered what was going through her mind, this quietly brilliant expert on biological warfare with her head crammed full of data on viral loads and mortality ratios. Well, the stakes had just been raised, that much was clear.

'This is bad,' she said at last. That sounded to Luke like an understatement. 'This thing is even more virulent than we feared.'

Luke was about to reply when something caught his eye that

didn't look right, something out of place. Just beyond the couple in front of them he could see a man in a leather jacket, older than most of those around him. He was staring right at Luke and he was taking out his phone. Now why would he be doing that in a noisy place like this? Luke couldn't be sure, but it looked like the man was trying to take his photo. Not good. Luke twisted his body away from him, turning towards Jenny, bringing his face so close to hers that she recoiled. When he turned back the man was gone, vanished into the crowd. And now someone on Luke's other side was tapping his shoulder. It was a girl in a blue dress with a sash tied round the middle, smiling down at him with perfect white teeth and a gold nose ring.

'May I sit?' she asked, pointing to the space next to him. Before Luke had a chance to answer she had already sat down, sweeping the hem of her dress beneath her knees. She leaned closer to him as if about to confide a great secret. 'You want something special?' she said, into his ear. She gestured to her handbag. 'I have MDMA, ketamine, White Knight. What you like?'

Luke was no stranger to being offered drugs in clubs. It used to happen to him and his mates all the time in Plymouth, back in his days with the Royal Marines, although he had never partaken. But this, right now, felt altogether more dangerous. He wanted the girl to leave them alone, to get out of their space as quickly as possible. This was an annoying distraction when they just needed to get on with the exchange with Janulis and be gone.

'We're all good, thanks,' he told her firmly, edging slightly away from her. The girl shrugged, then gave him an odd look as she was getting up. To Luke, it seemed almost like pity.

'What was that about?' Jenny asked, still scanning the crowd for their absent contact.

'Just someone offering us drugs,' he replied. 'She's gone.'

'Right. I'm going to the Ladies,' Jenny announced, getting up and straightening her dress. 'Keep watching. I won't be long.'

Sitting alone on the sofa, Luke leaned forward, arms folded, resting them on his knees as his eyes kept scanning the faces in front of him. As the place grew busier and more people came in he was starting to get jostled. A girl spilled some of her drink on his shoulder and apologized profusely. The DJ, sitting above them in his tiny booth, had jacked up the volume and now the music was irritating him. In hindsight, Luke realized, this had been a mistake, coming to this noisy, crowded place for the hand-over. Why the hell couldn't Janulis have agreed to meet at that discreet little café by their hotel?

The music was thumping louder than ever when Luke saw the crowd part to make way for a pair of large, grim-faced men in black leather jackets, accompanied by a uniformed police officer in a dark blue tunic. Girls were staggering backwards on high heels, clutching their drinks, as the men pushed rudely past. Someone, he guessed, was about to get arrested. Perhaps it was the pusher in the blue dress. With a jolt, Luke realized they were coming straight towards him. In the moment they spotted him they surged forward, elbowing the last few people out of the way. Luke rose half up and out of his seat just as two of them grabbed his arms from either side, pinning them behind his back. Another was straight in, searching his pockets, while the uniformed officer addressed him sternly, shouting at him above the music: '*Policija*. Organized Crime Investigation Unit.'

Luke kept his cool. Something had clearly gone wrong here, but he would be polite and cooperative and this would all be smoothed over. 'You have the wrong person!' he shouted back, so as to be heard. 'I'm British,' he added, as they hauled him to his feet. The officer didn't reply. He turned instead to the plain-clothes officer who had just searched Luke's jacket pockets and nodded. The man held out his open hand. Resting on the palm were three small polythene sachets, each containing a white powder. No, no, no! This cannot be happening, Luke thought, shaking his head in vigorous denial. I'm being set up here.

'These are not mine!' he protested. 'Someone has put them there.'

The uniformed police officer ignored him. Instead, he very deliberately picked up one of the three sachets and waved it in front of Luke's face with one hand, wagging an admonishing finger with the other. Even while this was going on, Luke was aware that a crowd had formed around them. People were pointing. Some even had their hands over their mouths in surprise at the drama unfolding before them. It all felt utterly surreal, as if he were playing the lead part in some hammy drama with an all-too-predictable ending. Yet this was real, this was happening. Where the hell was Jenny when he needed her?

Luke saw the uniformed policeman signal to the others and a moment later he felt his shoulders being jerked backwards and the cold metal embrace of handcuffs being snapped into place. Still the music was thumping, a hideous soundtrack to his staged arrest, and now everything seemed to be moving in slow motion. He was aware of the crowd parting as the policemen frog-marched him out of the club. He saw people nudging their friends as he passed. Some had their mobile phones out and were videoing, thrusting their phones into his face. And all the while he was aware of the metal cuffs digging painfully into his wrists. The one thing he could not see was any sign of Jenny Li.

34

Vilnius, Lithuania
Thursday, 10 March, 2010hrs GMT, 2310hrs local

SLEET WAS FALLING in cold wet splashes when the doors of the blacked-out van were yanked open and strong arms reached inside to manhandle Luke out on to the street. Within seconds his hair was soaking wet and he could feel the icy water starting to trickle down his back. They had been driving for a while, but stuck in the back in the dark as he was, he had absolutely no idea where they had taken him. His phone, passport and wallet had all been removed. Not that he could have reached for them anyway: the cuffs were still in place and now his wrists were worryingly numb where the metal restraints had dug in. This was not a good situation to be in.

The building that loomed above him had just one distinguishing feature – a green neon sign that simply said 'Policija'. Other than that, it was a bleak, blank façade. And there, dimly visible above the neon through the falling sleet, was another detail he noticed that worried him: CCTV cameras, all turned away to one side instead of covering the entrance doorway. So there would be no record, he realized, of who was being brought into the building at this hour of the night.

Luke winced silently as they marched him up the steps into

the rear of the building, forcing his arms into a painful position. To take his mind off the pain, he ran through a rapid checklist in his head. Who could have set him up like this? Who had they encountered so far? Who, apart from a select few people in the agencies in London, even knew they were in the country and what they were up to? It came down to a shortlist of two: that Neanderthal sales director at the factory this morning and his unctuous in-house lawyer, Darius Janulis. Whoever it was, someone clearly didn't want them here in Lithuania.

It was an old Soviet-era building, with peeling interior walls painted an institutional shade of green. A large gilt-edged portrait of a square-jawed, unsmiling man in braided uniform with purple lapels hung high on the wall, but other than that the entrance hall was devoid of decoration. In silence they led Luke down a corridor before they stopped abruptly at a closed door. One of the police escorts knocked twice, a gruff voice answered, and Luke, flanked by the same leather-jacketed officers who had arrested him in the club, went in.

It looked to Luke like some kind of office, which was vaguely reassuring – for a while back there he had wondered if they might be heading for the woods. He could see there was only one other person in the room and he was sitting behind a large desk, his bulky frame half turned away from them as he spoke on the phone. The man, evidently someone in authority, twisted round in his chair to squint up at them, just long enough for Luke to see a heavily lined face with thinning hair, then turned back to finish his call. There was a full ashtray in front of him, Luke noted, which would account for the lingering presence of cigarette smoke in the room, and a framed photograph of someone in a camouflage jacket holding up a large fish.

When the man eventually hung up, he leaned back in his swivel chair, which creaked each time he moved. He regarded Luke for a long moment without saying anything, just occasionally tapping the end of a biro on the desk, never taking his eyes off Luke's. Mind games, he reminded himself. The guy's playing mind games. And for a moment Luke's mind dredged up an

128

uncomfortable memory: tactical questioning – TQ – the part of UK Special Forces Selection he would much prefer to forget. The long hours of being made to stand in stress positions, hands behind his head, eyes blindfolded, white noise blaring constantly in his ears, no sleep for three days, then the abuse screamed at him from so close his cheeks were wet with spittle. And then the questions, on and on and on they went, as his mind and body cried out for rest. Luke hadn't cracked on that course, but he'd seen men a lot bigger than him come out whimpering like babies and getting RTUd – Returned to Unit. After all that, Luke reckoned, he could probably handle what this overweight Lithuanian police chief had to throw at him.

'Strip.' It was a single-word command, spoken in English by the man behind the desk, and it caught Luke off-guard.

'Excuse me?' he replied. Perhaps he'd misheard him.

'Strip,' repeated the officer, louder and more menacing this time. 'Take off your clothes. Everything. Or you want us to do it for you?'

35

Near Braintree, Essex
Thursday, 10 March, 2022hrs GMT

THURSDAY NIGHTS WERE always busy at the Rose and Crown pub in the north Essex village of Collier's Green and tonight was no exception. The car park was full, the regulars were at the bar and a good-natured argument was just kicking off over the comparative merits of East Anglia's real-ale industry. Like countless other venues across the country, the Rose and Crown had taken a hit during the months of Covid, struggling to stay afloat as it poured away unsold beer by the gallon when the restrictions kicked in. But it was back in business, and to the regulars all that seemed like a bad dream now.

Upstairs, behind the white mock-Tudor walls and in a room whose door had an old-fashioned sliding lock, bolted firmly shut, sat four men and one woman around a table. Spread on its surface were maps, colour-coded, schematic diagrams and timetables. The planning committee was in session.

From downstairs came the sound of laughter and the occasional cheer, but in that locked room the atmosphere was far from jovial. Doubts were being voiced, even at this late stage in the planning, as to the targeting. There was a simplicity, they all agreed, as to the choice of location. Railway stations were good: they meant a lot of people crowded into a confined space. And railway stations had one major selling point: they didn't have airport-style security checks. You could walk in off the street, buy a ticket, get on to a train and nobody would stop you. But then the dissenters round the table, and there were two, had their objections. Was the cure for the disease too painful for the patient? Were they going to end up hurting the wrong people? Should they not be hitting somewhere more focused, somewhere less open to the general public?

They spoke in low voices and took notes. At irregular intervals one would get up from the table and walk ever so quietly to the locked door, silently slide back the bolt and yank it open, just in case anyone should care to be listening on the other side. They weren't.

The planning committee had another problem. Not an insurmountable one, but a problem nonetheless. The closer they got to the time of delivery, the greater the risk of disruption by the police or MI5. What they needed, they all agreed, was an expert, a specialist in counter-surveillance. Someone with military or security experience who believed in the cause. Someone they could count on to identify the threats on the final journey to the target and help to circumvent them. So much had gone into this, so much time, money and effort invested, so much was at stake, that they could not afford a last-minute slip-up. The future of society, they all agreed, depended on it.

And they had thought they had the perfect man, until a few days ago. Sean Jennings had served with the Royal Signals: he had the right skills, and he was committed to the cause. At least they'd thought he was. Until he had announced he was pulling out and going off to live the quiet life in Somerset with his new girlfriend. She was devastated when it happened: a dreadful accident caused by the brakes failing on his car, such a sad end to the life they'd planned to live together.

Now time was running short, but they would keep looking for the right person. Everyone in that room knew there could be no second chances when the day came.

They left before closing, departing at different times, going off in different cars by different routes. No one had brought a phone or any electronic device.

36

FOR SEVERAL SECONDS Luke did nothing, said nothing, as he sized up the situation in the police chief's office. Could he, should he, make a run for it? What was it that those British Army instructors used to hammer into them, over and over again, on the escape-and-evasion course? *Do not get caught. Whatever you do, do not get caught.* Well, it was a bit late for that now. He could see the odds were heavily stacked against him. There were four of them in the room, some armed, and he was still handcuffed. He wouldn't even make it to the door, let alone down the corridor or out into the car park. There was only one person who could get him out of this and that was Jenny Li. And she, inexplicably, had disappeared.

The police chief gave a theatrical sigh, shook his head and opened a drawer. Luke watched as he took out a pair of blue rubber gloves and threw them at one of the leather-jacketed policemen, who failed to catch them in time. He nodded at Luke. 'Cavity search,' he explained.

Okay, definitely not great, but also not worth getting shot for. He was aware of someone removing the handcuffs behind his back, then he briskly took off his clothes and laid them at his feet.

It was over quickly – he reckoned this was more about showing him who was boss than anything else. Then they all watched him as he got dressed again. One of the policemen kept gesturing at the stump of his missing finger and asked him something in Lithuanian.

'Afghanistan,' he replied simply. He doubted that would make any difference to his predicament, but now was the time to make his point.

'I want to call my embassy, the British Embassy,' Luke said to the chief at his desk. 'These drugs are not mine, this is a false arrest.' He stood his ground as one of the officers began nudging him towards the door. The police chief smiled for the first time, as if he had just had to listen to a quite ridiculous suggestion, and shook his head.

'Tomorrow,' he said, 'you will appear before the judge. But tonight, you stay with us.' He waved Luke towards the door. He was done with this 'drug pedlar'.

Down the corridor, a sharp right turn, then down a flight of steps. Another corridor, darker this time and dingier. Where the hell was Jenny Li? She'd better be working on his release or this was starting to look very grim. Hell, she wouldn't even know where they'd taken him. Luke detected the damp, rotting smell of mildew and the pungent, ammoniac tang of stale urine. They turned left and stopped. In front of them was a row of steel bars, floor to ceiling: a holding cell, impossibly brightly lit by a neon striplight on the ceiling. It already had several occupants – as the guards got out their keys, Luke counted five men, all dirty and dishevelled. Two sat slumped and dozing in a corner. But the other three sprang up at his arrival, exchanging expectant glances.

The guards gave Luke a final shove, then locked the door behind him with an elaborate clanking of keys and left. Great. So he was now sharing a cell with a bunch of petty criminals, people so far down the pecking order they didn't even have the Mafia connections to get themselves out. And meanwhile no one had read him his rights – no one had even read him the charges. No phone call, no lawyer. Bloody hell. Lithuania was supposed to be a simple, straightforward mission to map the links between the Svalbard outbreak and a suspect chemical company in Eastern Europe. But something had gone very, very wrong. He'd been set up and he had absolutely nothing to show for it.

In the silence that followed the guards' departure, Luke's new cellmates looked at him and he looked at them, sizing each other up. One said something in Lithuanian and Luke froze. While he didn't understand a word of their language there had been one in that sentence he did recognize: 'Svalbard'.

'Sig-ret?' The largest of the three facing him took a step towards him, his lips curling into a smile, and made a smoking gesture with his thumb and forefinger. His blond hair was shaved down the sides, there was a lightning tattoo on one side of his bull-like neck and his pink, bloodshot eyes regarded Luke with a deadpan expression. This wasn't an offer to share: it was a demand to hand over what he had, and the man held out his left hand. For a split second Luke was distracted as he glanced down at it. Too late he realized the mistake. It was a deliberate decoy and Luke had fallen for it. The man brought his other hand up fast, balled into a tight fist, hitting Luke hard, just below his left eye, before he had time to dodge it. Pain ricocheted around his skull and Luke reeled from the blow, staggering backwards and almost losing his balance, but he was still standing. *Don't go down. Do NOT go down*, a voice in his head was telling him. *You hit the floor and they'll have you.*

Luke fought to clear his senses and recover his balance. He was aware of someone else sneaking behind him and suddenly a man had his hands around his waist and was scrabbling to undo the buckle of Luke's belt. This time he didn't need to look down. He could sense exactly where the man was, his head just behind and below Luke's elbow. Keeping his eyes trained on the first man, who had adopted a boxer's stance and looked poised to deliver a second blow, Luke cupped his right fist inside his left hand then slammed his elbow vertically down on to the back of the other man's neck. A couple of centimetres further to one side and he could have severed his spinal cord. As it was, the man let out a howl of pain and dropped to the floor. One down. The next blow came in fast and Luke just had time to deflect it, twisting his left forearm up and to the side in a classic martial-arts block, before stepping in and headbutting the large man between the eyes. But instead of going down as Luke had expected him to, the man shook his head clear, laughed, and said something in Lithuanian. At the same moment Luke sustained a crippling blow to his left kidney. Christ, that hurt. Had he been stabbed? It felt like it. The pain was so explosive it was almost overwhelming, threatening to rob him of all his strength when he needed it most. He could see the blow had come from the third man in the cell and now Luke caught a glint of metal in his hand. It wasn't a blade, he realized, but a knuckle-duster, the curved metal brackets ringing the man's clenched fist. He was about to take a second swing with it, this time aiming for Luke's jaw. A fleeting thought flashed through his head: How had these thugs managed to smuggle a knuckle-duster into this cell? The answer was obvious. It would have been supplied by one of the guards. No point calling out to them. Even if they could hear him down here in this dangerous cell they wouldn't come to his aid. No, he decided, the guards were part of the problem.

The two assailants were facing him square-on now, lurching and shifting as they readied themselves to deliver the next strike. Yet Luke felt strangely in control. Up there in the police chief's office, handcuffed and flanked by armed men, he had been helpless, trapped with no means to fight back. But down here in this grubby cell he was back in the game and in with a chance. Luke knew exactly what he had to do. He would exploit the momentum of their coming attack against them. It was what he had been trained for. When he saw the arm with the knuckle-duster come shooting out towards him he didn't parry it away. He stepped back and grabbed it with both hands. In the same moment he twisted his body round and yanked the man's arm so hard he forced it behind his back. The man's cry of pain was surprisingly high-pitched, but Luke was already pressing home his advantage. He had the man in an armlock now, and as he wrenched it upwards he pushed his captive hard against the larger man, upsetting his balance. 'Fuck you,' he grunted, as he gave him a final, powerful shove.

Luke was still working out what his next move should be – the big guy wasn't going to go down easily and he almost looked like he was enjoying this – when he heard shouts from the corridor. The guards had rushed back and he could see them frantically juggling with keys in the lock. Luke had no idea what they were shouting in Lithuanian but they seemed very angry. Had things not gone the way they had planned?

He released his grip on the man with the knuckle-duster. The largest prisoner backed away, trying to look all defensive, pointing down at the third man still groaning on the floor, then back at Luke. The remaining two prisoners, who'd been fast asleep when this all kicked off, clung to each other, staring in bewilderment. The guards had got the door unlocked now and they poured into the cell, still shouting at everyone. Luke saw them coming straight for him. He didn't resist when they grabbed his arm and pulled him out of there, pushing him roughly down the corridor.

'Now – extra charges,' one said to him grimly, as they shoved him into a cell of his own.

Alone at last, in the silence of the cell, Luke took stock of his injuries. His left side hurt like hell: that would be where they'd hit him in his kidney with that knuckle-duster. He ran his fingertips over his ribs and pressed gently. Good. Nothing broken there. His face still ached, where he'd been hit below his left eye, but again, nothing broken, he reckoned. All in all, he had got away lightly, considering the odds. So far. But the harsh truth was that it was now past midnight and he was still stuck in a Lithuanian police cell on a trumped-up charge and facing a judge in the morning. Would they come for him again in the middle of the night? Possibly. He'd have to be ready for them if they did.

Luke pulled his knees up to his chin as he sat in the far corner of the cell, eyes on the door, ears tuned to the sound of any approaching footsteps. He was asleep within a minute.

37

Whitehall, London
Friday, 11 March, 0900hrs GMT

'SO WE'RE ALL agreed, then. This is Moscow's work.' It wasn't a
question, it was a statement of fact. She said it with finality, her
eyes sweeping around the faces at the long table at the morning
COBRA meeting. 'We've concluded that is the *only* logical explanation. It has to be. The documentation recovered from Svalbard
proves it. And meanwhile a patient – a UK citizen – has died as a
result of their actions. Now the question is: what action should *we*
be taking in response?'

The foreign secretary, newly appointed in the latest cabinet
reshuffle, had been in the job for just four weeks after coming
from a junior minister's post in Work and Pensions. This was her
first ministerial COBRA.

'The mistake our previous government made,' she continued,
her eyes shining with conviction, 'was that after the Russians
poisoned Alexander Litvinenko right here in London with radioactive polonium in 2008—' She broke off. Someone was tentatively
putting their hand up.

'Um, forgive me, Secretary of State,' said a civil servant, somewhere quite far down the table, 'but it was 2006. Litvinenko was
poisoned in 2006.'

She gave him a piercing look, then carried on. 'Yes. Quite. So, as I was saying, the government at the time simply didn't react in a timely way. It took years, didn't it, for a police investigation and a public inquiry to conclude that, yes, in all probability the Kremlin had carried out a state-sponsored assassination on British soil. And meanwhile the killers were long gone, safely back in Russia and beyond our reach. The net result? Moscow must have reckoned they'd pretty much got away with it.'

There was some brief tut-tutting and nodding around the table before she resumed her piece.

'Fast-forward to 2018 and the Novichok poisoning in Salisbury and look at the difference. Over a hundred and fifty Russians expelled from embassies around the world! No ifs, no buts. Just instant retribution. That's the only language Moscow understands.'

She was on a roll now, nodding to herself, as if listening to someone else's words and agreeing with everything being said.

'So I think our response has to be equally robust and proportionate, does it not? Moscow has been a signatory to the Biological Weapons Convention since 1972, yet what they've been up to on Svalbard . . . well, it shows they're in clear violation of that treaty. Therefore' – she placed the palm of her hand down on the table for emphasis – 'we intend to introduce the following measures.'

She turned to the special adviser sitting beside her, put on her spectacles and glanced quickly through the document being passed to her, eyebrows arched, frowning slightly, then putting it back on the table.

'First, I am instructing our ambassador to the UN in New York to call for an emergency session of the Security Council this afternoon. We will demand a full and frank account of Russia's current biological research programmes, both declared and covert. That's number one.' She looked up, eyebrows raised once more, as if waiting for someone, anyone, in the room to challenge her. No one did.

'Second, I will shortly be summoning the Russian ambassador to the Foreign Office to register our strong objections to this flagrant contravention of an international treaty. Third . . .' she paused to check the list in front of her '. . . third, my department will be working closely with the Treasury to draw up a draft sanctions list of Russian nationals with business interests in this country who are known to be close to the Kremlin leadership—'

She broke off, seeing a hand up again, halfway down the table. Someone from the Treasury. 'Yes, Simon? You had a question?'

'I'm sorry to butt in, Secretary of State, but can the country really afford that? Isn't it rather self-defeating to our economy? I mean, there are over a quarter of a million Russians living here in London and their money literally underpins the property market. After all the trauma we've gone through with Brexit and the pandemic . . .' he hesitated, as if the obvious didn't need to be stated '. . . can we really afford to lose so much Russian investment in this country?'

The foreign secretary swept the spectacles off her face as if she were swatting away some biting insect. 'I thank you for pointing that out, Simon.' She gave the junior Treasury minister an over-sweet smile. 'But I can assure you the PM and I have already gone over this ground. I'm sorry, but a stand simply has to be made. We must stick with our principles. So now, moving on . . .' She threw him a stern look. 'Let's discuss the list of possible sanctions in more detail.'

All this time her special adviser was discreetly trying to get her attention. When she finally succeeded, she handed the foreign secretary a tablet with a screenshot displayed. The minister put her spectacles back on and paused to read it. Suddenly her shoulders slumped and all the energy and verve seemed to vanish from her voice. 'Oh, bloody hell,' she said quietly.

38

Vilnius, Lithuania
Friday, 11 March, 0904hrs GMT, 1204hrs local

'AH, THANK GOD!' Luke sprang up from the chair in his solitary cell with such force that it fell backwards on to the stone floor with a metallic clatter. Framed in the open doorway, Jenny Li was accompanied by a guard with a bunch of jangling keys, and to Luke she had never looked lovelier. He felt like giving her a massive hug, but instead he just stood there, feeling a wave of immense tiredness wash over him.

'Sorry it took a while,' she said, jerking her head ever so slightly towards the man with the keys. 'This took quite a bit of sorting out, I can tell you. I've been up half the night. Had to get the ambassador to wake up the interior minister in the end.' She went up to Luke and inspected his bruised face, placing the soft palm of her hand on his cheek. It was the kindest, gentlest thing he had ever known her to do.

'Looks like you've really been through it,' Jenny said. 'Here.' She handed him a bulging black bin bag. 'There's a set of clean clothes in there, plus your phone, wallet and passport. You can change at the safe house.'

'We have a safe house?' he asked. There were a dozen other

things he wanted to ask her, but they could wait until they got well clear of the police station.

'We do now. I'll fill you in on the way.'

The British Embassy car took them northwards, through dark woods on the edge of the capital where the weak March sun flickered through the bare branches as they sped towards the Old Town centre of Vilnius. Sitting in the back, Luke leaned forward and started to wrestle himself out of his jacket.

'Here,' she said, 'let me give you a hand with that.' Again, he was surprised at her compassion. This was an altogether different Jenny Li from the one he'd been working with up until now.

'All right,' he said, turning to face her. 'How much can you tell me?' He tilted his head questioningly towards their driver up front. Jenny understood what it meant.

'Yes, he's been developed vetted,' she said. 'Been with the embassy almost since independence. Look, I'll give you the full version when we're indoors, but here's the gist of it. You won't be surprised to hear it's your friend Kadunov behind this.'

'That fuckwit sales director back at the factory?'

'That one.'

Luke looked away, out of the window, and sucked in his cheeks before turning back to her. He could feel the anger boiling up inside him and he began massaging the stump of his missing finger. 'D'you think he knew?' he asked.

'Knew what?'

'Who we really work for. Do you think he had us "made"?'

Jenny made a pouting face as she thought about this. 'Possibly. But I'm not sure it makes much difference. Kadunov would consider both the OPCW and the Service to be a threat. What matters is he's got underworld connections and people high up in the police. Which was how he set you up with that drugs bust.'

Luke nodded thoughtfully. None of this surprised him, but he still had a lot of unanswered questions ricocheting around in his head.

'Okay,' he said, 'so let's just rewind for a moment, Jenny. The last time I saw you, you were heading off to the Ladies in that club. Just before I got framed and lifted. Then what?'

'Our man Janulis showed up. I found him hiding next to a store cupboard behind the bar. He was in quite a state.' Jenny winced slightly as she recalled the moment. 'He grabbed my arm and said he thought his phone had been compromised and he'd been followed—'

'Well, he was right about that.'

'Exactly. Which was about the time I saw those goons moving in on you.'

'Wait.' Luke sat bolt upright in the back seat of the car and peered intently at her. 'You watched all that go down and did nothing?' He shook his head in mock disbelief. Luke knew Jenny well enough by now to grasp that there would have been a good reason behind it, but after what he had just been through he wanted a full explanation.

She put up her hands in a defensive gesture. 'Slow down, Luke. Trust me, it was time well spent.'

Luke shuffled round on the rear car seat and watched as she reached inside her jacket to take something out. He looked down at the small black oblong object that lay in her palm, a smile breaking over his face. 'Is that what I think it is?' he asked.

'Yes,' replied Jenny, sitting back in her seat and looking quite triumphant. 'We made the exchange. We got the flash drive.'

39

Whitehall, London
Friday, 11 March, 0937hrs GMT

THE WORDS STARED out from the tablet screen in her hands, taunting the foreign secretary with their bold, black font and their damning accusations.

'COLD WAR COVER-UP!' exclaimed the online tabloid's lead story. One look at the byline beneath the headline was enough to ring alarm bells in her head. No less than three of the paper's top investigative reporters had collaborated on this story. They must have worked fast – Svalbard had only happened on Monday so, clearly, they must have thrown everything at it. She skimmed down the page, sifting swiftly through the words that followed, and swore quietly again.

'Britain drops its guard' . . . 'Germ war Armageddon' . . . 'NHS woefully under-prepared' . . . 'Intelligence failure' . . . 'Supine government' . . .

The list went on. How had they got hold of all this so quickly? Was somebody in the Cabinet Office leaking? She had to speak to the cabinet secretary about it. Quite possibly this would need a full investigation, get the Met detectives in from Counter-Terrorism Command, open up everyone's emails, their digital diaries and all their WhatsApp messages to scrutiny. But that would have to wait. Right now she had other, more pressing priorities. Most importantly, she must be seen to be doing something. Something strong and decisive, a bold gesture that would stamp her mark as the new no-nonsense foreign secretary. It was still going to need the PM's sign-off, obviously, but she didn't expect any pushback from that quarter. No, this was her time, her moment. She put down the tablet, waved away her special adviser and called the meeting to order.

'This,' she announced, with what she hoped was a suitable degree of gravity, 'is a time for concerted action. We want to – no, we *must* – send a message to Russia that their actions are completely unacceptable!' As she said this she again placed both hands palms down on the table for emphasis. 'They cannot be allowed to get away with what they've done on Svalbard with impunity. Therefore, in addition to the measures I have already announced today, I will be making a recommendation to the National Security Council. As from Monday next week we will restrict the regular Aeroflot service between London and Moscow to just one flight a week.'

A hand went up, halfway down the table. Someone from Trade this time.

'Forgive me, Foreign Secretary, but is this really prudent? Surely they'll do the same to BA.'

She peered at the speaker for a moment. She was getting tired of having to deal with all these waverers. 'Then we'll have to cross that bridge when we come to it, won't we?' she told him. 'But I haven't finished yet. As a further measure, I will be recommending that we close Russia's consulate in Edinburgh. It is imperative . . .' she looked around the table, then repeated '. . . it is imperative that we draw a line in the sand against what is nothing short of reckless, state-sponsored, biological terrorism.'

40

Epsom, Surrey
Friday, 11 March, 1117hrs GMT

DR CHRIS COPPINGER considered himself a lucky man. Out of the three scientists who had set out from the Arctic Research Station on Svalbard four days previously, he was the only one still alive. This, they had told him, just before they released him from quarantine, was because he'd had the foresight to stay outside the hut where that poor Russian was spewing lethal germs into the room. Clever man, they said to him, after the tests came back negative. Good sense of self-preservation. A natural survivor. He decided not to mention that he had, albeit briefly, dashed inside the hut to light the fire for Dr Mackenzie.

The news that she, his fellow researcher, had died the previous day had come as a terrible shock to Chris Coppinger. He had really thought they would be able to save her. So much had been learned from dealing with the Ebola and Coronavirus outbreaks, surely critical care in developed countries like Britain was supposed to be on top of these things. So now, released from quarantine and given a week's leave, Coppinger was on his way to Epsom to see Sheila's next of kin. It was not a journey he relished, but in her dying hours in the Royal Free, Sheila Mackenzie had made this special request, that he should visit her baby niece,

Roberta. So, naturally, that was exactly what he would do. Chris Coppinger, devoted to his research work in atmospheric chemistry and still unmarried at forty-two, had no idea what sort of a present you gave to an eighteen-month-old girl. So he simply went into the nearest toy shop and bought the first thing that caught his eye: a soft pink dinosaur. 'Tyranno', it said on the label attached to its floppy tail.

Just before Chessington he turned off the A3 and drove his hire car towards the sedate Surrey market town of Epsom. He had keyed the family's address into the satnav, he had Classic FM playing on the car stereo, and now that the sun was starting to emerge from behind the clouds it almost felt like spring. It wasn't until the next turn-off that he started to feel a headache pounding behind his temples. Thinking he could simply be dehydrated, he pulled over at the next corner shop and bought himself two bottles of Highland Spring mineral water. Sitting in the car with the door open, he drank them both in one go. Yet he still felt increasingly unwell. He undid a button on his shirt and checked himself in the mirror above the driver's seat. Not good. He saw something approaching desperation in the face that stared back at him, and noticed it was shiny with sweat. In March. Something was wrong here.

Dr Chris Coppinger was a cautious man. It was what everyone said had saved him outside that Arctic hut in Svalbard. And now his caution kicked in again. When he noticed a sign across the street for Epsom General Hospital he didn't hesitate. He started the engine, lurched the car into gear and drove himself straight towards A & E.

41

Vilnius, Lithuania
Friday, 11 March, 1122hrs GMT, 1422hrs local

THE SAFE HOUSE in Vilnius was not what Luke had expected. In training, on the eight-week agent-running induction course down at the Fort, he had been taught the art of discreetly slipping unseen on to a housing estate in Cosham or Fareham on the outskirts of Portsmouth. Or letting himself in through the back door of some rundown Hampshire farmhouse. But training was over long ago and what he was looking at now was a rather smart tourist hotel.

'Really?' he remarked to Jenny, as they clambered out of the back of the car, Luke still nursing his bruised left side. 'The Shakespeare Hotel? It's a bit obvious, isn't it? I mean, we might as well be wearing a couple of Union Jacks on our backs.'

Jenny allowed herself a faint smile as she turned to Luke after dismissing the embassy driver and looking up and down the street, checking they were not being observed. Her heels were making loud clicking noises on the cobbles, but he wouldn't have been surprised if she magicked up a pair of trainers from nowhere.

'Has anyone ever told you, Luke,' she said, leading him through

a terracotta archway into a tidy cobbled courtyard, 'that sometimes you need to think outside the box?'

'Frequently.'

She paused in front of the short flight of steps that led up to
the hotel's reception area. 'Well, now would be a good time to
use your imagination,' she continued. 'Security Branch chose
this place for us precisely because it's a boutique tourist hotel.
Couples come in and out of here the whole time, all year round.'

'Couples?'

'Yes, Luke, couples.' She threw him a coy look. 'It's all right,
there's no need to freak out. They've booked us a twin room. Separate beds. The Service is very proper about things like that.'

'I'm sure they are.' Luke didn't give a damn what the Service
thought. He was worrying as to what Elise would have to say
about this cosy little arrangement. And whether he should tell
her now, later or never.

Their room key was one of the old-fashioned ones, complete
with a clunky wooden toggle, just in case anyone thought of
walking off with it. The young man from Reception insisted on
showing them up to their top-floor room and he threw open the
door with a flourish. 'Please,' he gestured, 'your superior twin
room, the Charles Dickens.' He bowed and disappeared down
the stairs.

The room was delightful. Low, sloping ceiling with two dormer windows, traditional wooden carvings on the walls, soft
discreet lighting and a richly patterned crimson rug on the floor.
It was the sort of place Elise would have loved to stay and once
again he felt a stab of guilt. There was then a brief, awkward
moment as he and Jenny tried to move past each other to get into
the room at the same time and he suddenly found himself pressed
against her in the narrow space between the wall and the bathroom. Their faces were so close that, for an instant, he detected
the faint waft of her scent.

'Sorry.' He blushed, stepping backwards. 'You go first.'

They dumped their bags on their respective beds and Jenny
immediately disappeared into the bathroom. He heard the lock

turn the moment she closed the door behind her. Luke went to the nearest of the two dormer windows and looked down on to the quiet street below. He was, he realized, deeply, desperately tired – and injured. All he wanted to do right now was shower, crawl into bed and sleep for twelve hours. He knew that was out of the question: their mission in Lithuania had yet to be completed and his aching head still buzzed with troubling, unanswered questions. What was the link between Kadunov in the factory and the people in the abandoned house in Svalbard? And why had one of those thugs in the police cell last night mentioned Svalbard? Luke rubbed the palms of his hands over his face, as if trying to erase the unpleasant experience he had just been through. Maybe he had misheard him. It was possible, he supposed. And perhaps what was on the flash drive would give them the answers. Impatient now, he wished Jenny would hurry up and get out of the bathroom so they could go through what was on it and report their findings to London.

'All yours.' Jenny emerged, her hair pinned back, wearing a tight grey T-shirt and jeans. She smelt wonderfully clean and fresh.

'I'm all good, thanks,' he said. 'Let's get started on that flash drive. The clock is ticking.'

Jenny sat on her bed, putting on her watch as she did so, and regarded him.

'Yes, the clock is ticking,' she replied, 'and I don't know how to put this politely, Luke, so I won't. You smell pretty rank after your night in the cells. So, please, for my sake, go in there,' she pointed towards the bathroom, 'have a decent wash, and I'll have coffees ordered up by the time you come out. Deal?'

'Deal.' Luke gave her a smile of thanks. He could find Jenny bloody annoying at times, but he was definitely warming to her. God knew what she must think of him.

Inside the tiny bathroom he switched on his personal phone. Just one missed call: Elise. He scrolled through the settings function to double-check he had location services switched off so no one could casually trace his whereabouts. He sent her a holding text, then switched his phone off again. In front of the mirror, still partially steamed up from Jenny's shower, he peeled off his clothes and examined the livid purple bruise that had spread down the whole of his left side. His face was a mess, too, with some purpling beneath his left eye. He would have to stay out of trouble for now – he was in no condition to get into any more fights.

Luke turned the water temperature as hot as he could bear it, then stood beneath the shower with his head back and his eyes shut, savouring the cleansing, scalding stream of water as it washed away the grime and corruption of that police cell. He had only just turned off the shower and was standing there, steam coming off his shoulders and towelling himself dry, when there was a knock on the bathroom door. He realized he hadn't bothered to lock it.

42

DR CHRIS COPPINGER never made it to A & E at Epsom General Hospital. In fact, he chose not to. When he paused at the traffic lights he reached up to his neck and touched lightly beneath his ears. It confirmed all his worst fears. Buboes. Swellings. One on either side. It told him all he needed to know. In that precise moment he knew that he was infected with the virus. He felt sadness and a strange calm. Forty-two years old and there was so much he had left unfinished, so much he had still wanted to achieve. His thesis on atmospheric chemistry in the Arctic, his anthology of amateur poetry, his hopes and plans to start a family one day. None of that was going to happen now.

His mind flashed back to the horrific scene in the Arctic hut on Svalbard, to the living corpse on the sofa, his face distorted with pustules, the blood and black vomit down his chest. No way. He wasn't going out like that. And what of his colleague Sheila Mackenzie? They had given her the best care possible at the Royal Free, but it had turned out to be nothing more than palliative – she had died anyway; nastily, he'd heard. And so much for the clean bill of health they'd given him. This virus must be more agile than they realized: it was clearly capable of hiding itself and lying dormant before re-emerging to ravage its host. No, his time was up, there was no way of ducking it, so now he was going to take control. Chris Coppinger was also a decent man and he knew that if he turned up at A & E he'd infect everyone he came into contact with: doctors, patients, porters and nurses. And he didn't want that on his conscience.

He knew what he had to do.

He parked up beside the road, took out his phone, his hands shaking slightly, and dialled the number of an old friend who worked at the Marsden in London. They had both studied biochemistry at university, then gone their separate ways, Chris into atmospheric chemistry, his friend Mike into oncology medicine. Mike answered on the second ring.

'Chris! Good, I heard you were back. You jammy bugger, you dodged a bullet there, didn't you? Poor old Sheila Mackenzie, though. What a way to go, eh? Let's hope they sort this virus out before we all get put into lockdown again. I don't think my marriage could take it!' He broke off to laugh, part of the gallows humour that surfaces at the sharp end of the medical profession. Chris Coppinger waited for him to finish. He decided he would spare him the full truth, just tell him what needed to be known.

'Listen, Mike . . .'

'Yes. Lunch. Is that what you were going to say? Because we're long overdue. There's a new place down the Fulham Road you'll love—'

'No. Listen. This virus . . . It's . . . it's even more dangerous than they thought. It hides itself. It's not showing up on any of the tests. So, look, I need you to speak to the crisis team at the Royal Free and also to the National Institute for Health Protection. Joint Biosecurity Centre will need to know about this. Tell them they need to double-screen – no, triple-screen – everyone who might have come into contact with it.'

His friend at the Marsden laughed, but this time it was a nervous laugh. 'What are you saying exactly, Chris? And shouldn't *you* be making these calls?'

'Yes, Mike, I should, but I'm afraid I have to be somewhere right now. I'm sorry, I have to run.'

Chris Coppinger ended the call and switched off his phone, knowing Mike would ring back for answers he wasn't prepared to give. He rubbed his temples with the heels of his hands. His head was pounding and his hands came away slick with sweat. He knew he shouldn't be driving, he had to get off the road, but his mind was made up. He was thinking now about a place not far from here, on the way to Malden Rushett, a place with a lake. On a Friday lunchtime in March he doubted there would be anyone around. Twelve minutes later he found the spot he was looking for and it was deserted. From the top of the slight rise he could see there was a clear run straight down to the water. He closed his eyes, said a silent prayer, then lowered all four of the car's windows, checked his seatbelt was fastened, put the car into gear and accelerated towards the inky blackness of the water.

43

GRU Headquarters, Moscow
Friday, 11 March, 1248hrs GMT, 1548hrs local

THE HEADQUARTERS OF the GRU, the main directorate of Russia's Armed Forces, is a modern, plate-glass-and-steel building at No. 3 Grizodubovoy Street in Moscow. The nine-billion-rouble edifice has a state-of-the-art shooting range, a gym, a pool, a café and even a winter garden with its own fountain. Vladimir Putin once famously landed on its roof by helicopter to begin his tour of inspection, pacing over the GRU's sinister black bat emblem on the floor. It is not a building that welcomes outsiders.

Colonel Arkady Petrov was no outsider. A clinical virologist by training, he had been 'encouraged' to transfer his skills at an early stage of his career from civilian medical research into the branch of the military that oversaw Russia's vast chemical and biological warfare stockpiles, inherited in the 1990s from the now-defunct Soviet Union. Inside this man's head there were countless dark secrets. Among the many qualifications that had propelled him to the senior ranks of the GRU was a surprisingly detailed knowledge of what went on inside Britain's top-secret laboratory at Porton Down. He had gleaned it in large part from the GRU's own network of agents in Britain before they were unceremoniously expelled in the wake of the Salisbury Novichok attack in 2018.

And today Colonel Petrov was a worried man. He found himself facing a problem he did not know how to fix. At lunchtime he had been ordered to an unscheduled meeting across town at the Kremlin. He had expected it to be about the forthcoming annual military manoeuvres in southern Russia. But instead he had been asked to explain what exactly his department was up to in the Norwegian Arctic, and why he had not informed his superiors through the proper channels about the testing of a new biological weapon. It seemed the Russian ambassador to London had been summoned to the Foreign Office that very morning and been forced to issue a blanket denial. The ambassador had then got straight on the phone to Moscow to seek an explanation. Yet Colonel Petrov was at a loss to explain events in the Norwegian Arctic. And now the British were claiming a phone number had been traced from the scene in Svalbard back to his headquarters. Well, that proved nothing. It could have been made by a third party using a proxy dial-in. The British might have made a mistake – they could be making it up. Hell, there were any number of explanations for that.

But now, as he returned to his office in the dying light of the late afternoon, stepping past the piles of dirty grey slush that spelled the tail-end of a Moscow winter, Petrov had a gnawing feeling of anxiety in the pit of his stomach. What if it were true? What if a rogue actor was indeed operating from within his own command? He knew only too well what was coming if he didn't get to the bottom of this in double-quick time. Those goons from the FSB – the Federal Security Service, the successors to the KGB – would be crawling all over his department, going into their computers, hauling his people in for questioning, making life impossible. No. He couldn't have that. Not on his watch. Colonel Arkady Petrov had to move fast if he was to have any hope of saving his career.

44

IN THE SPRAWLING high-security government science complex outside Salisbury, the news of Sheila Mackenzie's death from the pathogen they were calling 'Agent X' had come as a real blow. Not totally unexpected, but still a setback. The Defence Science and Technology Laboratory had had little more than forty-eight hours to work on the samples rushed over from the Royal Free, but already the pressure was intense. Big Pharma would combine forces to take on the task of trying to find a vaccine, just as they had with Coronavirus. It was a process expected to take months. Porton Down's mission was to ascertain the origin of the virus and to come up with an early and effective therapy.

On the director's orders, a large digital clock had been installed on the wall of the lobby in the main administration block, counting the minutes and hours since the virus had first erupted in Svalbard, just to keep everyone on their toes. To add to the pressure, TV crews and reporters had started to turn up outside the main entrance. RT, Russia's Kremlin-backed satellite news channel, was taking a particularly keen interest.

In a side room on the second floor an emergency meeting was under way. The SSAs – the senior scientific advisers – sat hunched

156

over their laptops alongside experts drafted in from around the country, a delegate from Norway and another from the WHO in Geneva. Hannah Blane and Colin Masters, the two virologists who had identified the genome sequence, were resting upstairs, after working straight fifteen-hour shifts. With Dr Clarissa Gall still up in London, it was left to her fellow scientist Gareth Banks to bring everyone up to speed.

'In just under an hour,' he told them, 'this is going to be declared a "public health event of international concern" – something we all know as a PHEIC. What does that mean for us?' He was standing up to address them, but resting the knuckles of his hands on the surface of the table, like a brooding silverback mountain gorilla, as he gazed around the room. 'It means that whatever we discover here, in our own laboratories, we're going to have to share it. Not just with our Five Eyes partners – the US, Canada and so on – but also with the GHSI, the Global Health Security Initiative.'

'Hang on,' interrupted one of the senior scientists, a notoriously prickly individual. 'You mean we're now sharing our findings with the *Mexicans*? Along with half the world? That means it'll be with Moscow inside a day!'

'We don't know that, do we, Kevin?' admonished Banks. 'And we can only follow protocol here. These are international health regulations and that Health Security Initiative has been up and running since just after the 9/11 attacks and the anthrax packages in 2001. So I think we should give them some credit, don't you? Given that they've spent the best part of twenty years working on responses to just such an outbreak as this.'

But the prickly scientist wasn't giving up. 'Right,' he replied sarcastically, looking around the room for support. 'So what this is really all about is testing our bureaucracy to see if it works, isn't it? You don't think it's a bit late for that?'

He didn't find the support he was after. In fact, a number of people were tut-tutting.

'Kevin, if you continue down this line,' Banks retorted, 'then I'm going to have to ask you to leave the room – as well as this task force. These interventions of yours are simply not helpful and I need everyone fully onboard here.' The two men glared at each other in silence until the more junior of the two backed down and looked towards the window, muttering something unrepeatable under his breath.

'Now,' resumed Gareth Banks, 'we need to address the priority matter of the therapy. As we have established, this virus is a chimera – a fusion of Marburg haemorrhagic fever with an unidentified form of monkey pox. Normally, when searching for an antidote, we would expect to start where others have left off. But this is hardly a normal situation we're facing, is it?' He stood up straight and began to pace around the room as he spoke.

'We do have stocks – right here on-site – of cross-immunity vaccines for smallpox. Obviously, the NHS freezers are holding a great deal more. A company in Europe has tested them for monkey pox and they were found to be in large part effective.'

'Well, isn't that the way forward, then?' interjected the official from the WHO. 'We hold stocks of smallpox vaccine ourselves.'

'I wish it were that simple,' said Banks, grimacing as he spoke. 'It takes between five and seven days for the *Vaccinia* antidote to take effect – *if* it works – and, of course, now, tragically, we no longer have a live patient to work with, since Sheila Mackenzie is . . . is . . .' For the first time Gareth Banks seemed to lose his momentum and he stumbled over his words. 'Since she is no longer with us. Which means we're going to have to fall back on our laboratory substitutes, with – I have to say it – unpredictable results.'

'And Marburg? The haemorrhagic element?' It was the delegate from Norway, and his pale features bore a look of suspended shock, as if he were still trying to digest what had just happened in his country.

Gareth Banks stopped pacing to address his question. 'Yes, thank you.' He acknowledged him with a nod. 'Again, we have to start where others have got to. There are new experimental vaccines under study right now for haemorrhagic fevers in central Africa, in the DRC. We've worked on some of them here at Porton

Down. Will they work for Agent X? That I can't tell you yet, but—'
He put up his index finger. 'Excuse me. Yes?'

He'd broken off as a young man had entered the room without knocking and come straight up to whisper something in his ear. Banks stared at him.

'You're certain?' he asked. The man nodded. Gareth Banks turned to the rest of the room.

'I have some bad news,' he announced grimly. 'There has been another infection.' He waited a moment to let this sink in. 'It's a Norwegian policeman up on Svalbard. Confirmed infected with Agent X. This has an immediate consequence for us here in Britain. From this moment on, we can give no assurances to Whitehall that this outbreak can be contained.'

45

NAKED AND STEAMING from his shower, Luke stood rooted to
the spot as he heard the gentle knock on the bathroom door.
Instinctively, his eyes flicked to the handle, visualizing it slowly
opening and then ... Then what? Had he given off the wrong
signals here? Was he reading the situation in completely the
wrong way? They were supposed to be gathering vital national
intelligence in Lithuania, not playing suggestive mind games in
a boutique hotel room.

'Luke?' Jenny knocked again, sharper this time. 'You need to
come and have a look at what's on the laptop. Are you nearly
done in there?'

So it was business. That was all. Luke scolded himself for his
presumption. What was he thinking? Idiot. Of course she wasn't
interested in him in *that* way. It was a relief. They could get on
with the task in hand.

He emerged from the bathroom, fully clothed now and feeling
like a new person. He saw that Jenny had reorganized the room,
turning their twin bedroom into something resembling a makeshift office. She had pulled a small circular table into the centre of
the space and was sitting behind it with her laptop open, phone

on charge in the corner, her half-drunk cup of coffee next to her. Despite her casual grey T-shirt, she somehow managed to look crisply professional. Luke blushed inwardly that he had ever imagined her in any other way.

'Feeling better?' She didn't wait for him to answer. She gestured to the empty chair on the other side of the table. 'Have a seat, Luke. Coffee might have gone a bit cold now, but I can order you another, if you like.'

'It's fine. Let's just crack on with this.' He sat down opposite her, took one sip of his cold coffee and regretted it.

'Good,' Jenny said briskly. 'So we'll start with our man Darius Janulis, the so-called "legals officer"' – she threw him a wry smile at the description – 'since he's our entry point into Matulis ChemExport. I got Cheltenham to take a deep dive into his online activity, starting with his public persona, his social-media postings, friends, likes, places he's been and so on. Then moving on to all the stuff he doesn't want the world to see. I had to pull a few strings to get them to make it a priority tasking, but GCHQ stepped up to the plate and this is what they came back with.' Jenny swivelled her laptop round so it faced him, then sat back in her chair and looked out of the window. 'Seems like he has quite a colourful private life,' she added.

It was the aspect of intelligence work Luke often felt most uncomfortable with: peering into other people's personal lives like this, metaphorically leaning over someone's shoulder to see what they'd been up to, both on- and offline. He preferred to meet his targets face to face, even if that meant at 2 a.m. in a dark alley – that was still better than all this snoopy stuff, which he was quite happy to leave to others. He scanned through GCHQ's executive brief on Janulis, then scrolled down to the next page.

The photograph had been taken indoors and the flash had bleached out some of the detail, but the face was instantly recognizable. It was definitely Darius Janulis and he was wearing nothing but a crimson thong, with a studded leather choker around his neck attached to a leash held by someone who was half out of shot. He scrolled down again and there was more of the same: gimp masks, golf-ball mouth restraints, chains, piercings. Luke shrugged, and pushed the laptop back towards Jenny.

'So?' he said, slightly irritated. 'Janulis is into the S & M scene. I'm not sure that proves anything, does it?' He gave her a curious look. 'I'm sorry, Jenny, I'm not getting this. There's supposed to be a deadly pathogen on the loose in Svalbard, we've flown a thousand miles out here to probe the connection with a Lithuanian chemical company and what are we doing? We're sitting in a fancy hotel bedroom looking at someone's private stash of S & M selfies. So what exactly is the connection here?'

Jenny squeezed her eyes shut and massaged between her eyebrows with her fingertips for a second or two. Was this a sign of exasperation with him? Was he being a bit dim?

'All right, I'm sorry, Luke.' He saw her hazel eyes blink open and she flashed him the sweetest smile. 'That wasn't fair. I should have given you more info before showing you that.' She closed the lid of her laptop with a snap. 'Let's start again. So, what we're looking at here is a network. London certainly think Janulis is our way in. In fact, they've given him a designated codename, so we'd better start using that from now on.'

'Which is?' said Luke.

'It's Earl Grey. Like the tea.'

'Nice one.' Luke laughed. 'I'm liking the irony there. Who chose it?'

'The computer did, at VX,' she replied, using the Service abbreviation for Vauxhall Cross. 'Come on, you know that's how it works. So, what's making our bosses think he's our way into the network? Because of what he told me, back at the Ten Commandments Bar, last night. We had very little time to talk and he seemed extremely nervous. But he did tell me he's involved with two underground societies very much at odds with each other.'

'What kind of societies?' Luke asked. 'You mean cults?'

Jenny folded her bare arms across her chest and glanced towards the window, thinking and frowning. 'Not exactly, no, I wouldn't call them that. But here's the thing. Janulis has a split persona. There's his private life.' She gestured at the closed laptop. 'You saw a slice of it in there. And then there's something else, some kind of network he's part of, something altogether more sinister. And whatever that network is, he's not happy being part of it. He wants out, he told me. Janulis's English isn't perfect, but he made it pretty clear he thinks they're too extreme.'

'Too extreme? Meaning what?'

Jenny's eyebrows knitted as she thought. 'I'm trying to remember his exact words. Something like: "They've done things to people, really bad things." Yes, that was it.'

Luke got up from the table and went over to the hotel phone on the dressing-table. 'Do you know what?' he said, dialling Reception as he spoke. 'I do need that coffee after all. Can I get you one too?'

'Please.'

'I have to admit,' Luke said, sitting down at the little circular table, 'I'm struggling to join the dots here. How is Janulis our entry point into this "extreme" network that he's in such a hurry to get out of?'

Jenny leaned forward, her slim bare arms resting on the polished surface of the table, and spoke in almost a whisper: 'Because, Luke, it was this "network" that organized the shipment of chemicals from Matulis ChemExport to Svalbard.'

'Bloody hell!' he exclaimed. 'That's massive. And you found all this out in one conversation in the club last night? While I was busy being fitted up with some planted drugs?'

'No.' She smiled. 'If only it was as simple as that. After I'd handed over the money, Janulis gave me the reference code for the network's shipping orders. London have already matched them up with what's on the flash drive I sent them this morning. See?' She smiled at him again. 'This is why I needed you out of the shower and fully focused.'

Luke didn't feel fully focused at all. If anything, he felt he was playing catch-up every step of the way. Was it exhaustion that was slowing him down? He admired Jenny's intelligence, and her clinical efficiency, and he was glad they were on the same team. But at the same time he was starting to feel like a fifth wheel. 'Jenny, this is brilliant,' he began. 'You've done a fantastic job here.'

'*We*'ve done a fantastic job,' she corrected him. 'And it's not over yet so let's hold off on the congratulations.'

'Right. But I'm not sure you actually need me from here on in, do you?'

'Um, nice try, Luke,' she replied briskly. 'But I'm afraid it doesn't work like that. You need to get yourself in front of Earl Grey and exploit what he knows since he's going to be our HP into this network.'

'Our HP?'

'Our human portal. Our entry man. Come on, Luke, keep up. Didn't they teach you anything on that agent-running course?'

'Fine,' Luke said. 'Do you have his number? Because then we can ping him a WhatsApp and fix up a meeting. Preferably somewhere I'm not going to get framed for a bogus drug deal.'

'Actually, you've got his number,' Jenny replied. 'I sent it to your phone while you were in the shower. But don't call it yet. Our Vilnius station's sending you a facilitator, someone to work alongside you, someone who knows a way in, someone you can trust.'

Luke couldn't help noticing she'd said 'you', not 'us'. 'What's with the "you"? Why? Where are you going?'

'London. Sorry, Luke, not my choice, but I'm being pulled back.' She glanced down at her watch. 'I fly back this evening. They only just told me.'

He looked beyond her to her still-untouched bed and her opened suitcase. He noticed she hadn't unpacked a thing. 'Apparently,' she added, getting up from her chair, 'there's been another fatality from this horrible virus and they need all hands on deck back home. It's over to you now, Luke. This is your show, here in Vilnius.'

She strolled over to the window for the last time. Music was starting to spill out from a bar across the street as she turned back towards him. 'Earl Grey is keen, Luke. He wants our money and I think he's ready to dish the dirt on this network. He's ripe for the plucking.' She gave him a smile of encouragement. 'So get in there and milk him for everything he's got. Because right now he's the best lead – the *only* lead – we've got.'

46

Near Braintree, Essex
Friday, 11 March, 1441hrs GMT

THE DISUSED CONCRETE bunker in north Essex was a dismal hangover from the days of the Cold War. When nuclear Armageddon sometimes seemed only a hair-trigger away, Britain's Ministry of Defence ran a nationwide network of monitoring posts – small underground bunkers from which to observe and assess the after-effects of a Soviet nuclear attack. The men – and it was almost entirely men – who were to staff this doomsday galaxy of dystopian outposts were drawn from the Royal Observer Corps. Wound down after 1991, now long since disbanded, its members pensioned off, many of its bunkers remain, gathering moss and mould, their dark recesses either locked and empty or scattered with crumpled beer cans and soggy cigarette butts. Foxes love them.

On this bleak March afternoon, winter seemed to have returned to the hedgerows and ploughed fields north of Braintree. A flock of gulls wheeled and mewed in the chill wind that blew off the North Sea, and the still-bare trees bent their branches and clashed together with every gust. Unnoticed by anyone, three figures made their way along the edge of a field, out of sight from the nearest road. One carried a rucksack on his back while two others hefted a large box between them. The box was covered with an old brown blanket, and they carried it by rope handles at either end. Every now and then, when one missed his footing on the squelching mud, a faint cry could be heard from inside the box, but otherwise the party moved along in silence.

They stopped some distance from the bunker and set their cargo down. One moved forward, cautiously, to make quite sure they were still alone. He picked his feet over the cloying mud at the edge of the field, staying close to a sheltering hawthorn hedge, stopping to scan the fields for any unwelcome observers, before proceeding to check the bunker. Ten minutes later he was back and noiselessly waving them forward.

Down the grey moss-covered steps they went, through the heavy metal door on its rusty hinges, and into the first room. The remains of a pigeon lay in the corner, picked clean by foxes, and the room smelt of damp and decay. An old mattress, stained black with age and mildew, was half propped against one wall. But the place was empty and that was all that mattered. They moved through the first room, changing hands on the rope handles now as they carried their burden the final few yards, and went into the inner chamber, the monitoring room. A row of ancient sockets ran along one wall where once field telephones would have been plugged in, relaying practice messages back to Whitehall for the day when the unthinkable happened.

They set down the box on the damp floor and removed the blanket. The man with the rucksack crouched, placing it at his feet, and undid its straps. Ever so carefully and slowly, he removed a canister attached to a timer. He walked over to the far corner and placed the canister and timer on top of a pile of rubbish. He made some last-minute adjustments to the device and stood up, hands on hips, to admire his work. Satisfied that everything was in place he nodded to the others. They unfastened the lock at the top of the box and opened the lid. Immediately there were shrieks of excitement and a small face peered up at them. Dark eyes, pink ears, flared nostrils and a mouth slightly agape. Tenderly, they lifted the rhesus macaque monkey out of the box and attached a chain to a collar around its neck. Then they fastened the other end to the only hard point in the room: a metal table leg from a long-disused workbench. They placed a plate of seeds and dried fruit within the creature's reach, along with a bowl of water. They checked their watches and, one by one, they filed out of the bunker, pulling the heavy iron door shut behind them.

The final test was about to begin.

47

Vilnius, Lithuania
Friday, 11 March, 1539hrs GMT, 1839hrs local

LUKE ROLLED OVER in bed and killed the buzzing alarm, his badly needed power nap already over after less than an hour. He padded into the bathroom, splashed some cold water on his face and regarded his reflection with disapproval. He looked haggard and bruised. The strain of flying up to the Arctic and back, then heading straight to the Baltic and fending off that attack in the cell, must be catching up with him. He had been on the go non-stop since that call had come through while he was at the Royal Opera House. And that had been barely four days ago. How many times, in all those years in the Royal Marines, had he pushed himself through the pain barrier, carrying on when every sinew in his body was begging him to stop? But he had to face facts: he was a lot closer to forty than thirty now, and if he went on at this pace, sooner or later his body was going to let him down when he needed it most.

Jenny's parting act, before disappearing off to the airport and a flight back to London, was to fix up his meeting with the facilitator, the local contact provided by Vilnius station. Her name was Lina, Jenny told him. She'd be wearing a green US Army-style jacket with a red scarf and they were to meet in Lekutis café at

168

the end of their street at 7 p.m. That was it. When Jenny closed the door of the hotel room behind her, trundling her small, compact suitcase down the corridor, Luke was suddenly aware that the mission here was now down to him, and him alone. Orphaned at the age of ten when his parents had died in a car crash in Colombia, he knew that deep down he probably had latent abandonment issues. For twelve years he had immersed himself in his surrogate family: 'the Corps'. The Royal Marines had been his home, whether it was in barracks or out on operations in the badlands of Helmand province. Yet now, waking up alone after dark in this fancy hotel, he was experiencing something completely unfamiliar and, briefly, it rattled him. Luke felt a pang of loneliness.

He dressed, checked his phone for messages and got to the rendezvous point early. He positioned himself in a corner of the café so he could watch the door while he sipped a cappuccino and pretended to scroll through his phone. Funny, he thought, you fly a thousand miles east, to practically the edge of Europe, yet this could be almost any upmarket café in London, Manchester or Edinburgh. A young, well-dressed clientele, mainstream music, mainstream drinks. And here, bang on time at 6.59 p.m., came his contact.

Lina was tall, with wire-framed glasses and mouse-brown hair, and she carried a canvas tote bag. As promised, she wore a red scarf around her neck, but it was so voluminous it was practically a shawl. She looked to Luke like a PhD student who had just stepped off campus; he put her at about twenty-eight. She pulled up a chair, sitting so close to him anyone watching would have thought they were old friends, or even lovers. She must be a regular here, he reckoned, as he didn't notice her order anything yet moments later the waiter brought her a bottle of Salaus Alus beer, which he poured with a flourish, dark and foaming, into a tulip-shaped glass. She took a long swig before she spoke.

'Your first time?' Her eyes, he noticed, were pale blue behind those wire-framed glasses.

'In Lithuania? Yes.' Was this going to be small talk? He didn't really have time for that.

'I heard what happened,' she said abruptly. 'In the police station.' She shook her head. At the mention of the police station Luke moved his hand unconsciously to touch his face, just below his left eye. 'Yes, I can see,' she said. 'That Kadunov is a bastard. You must have pissed him off. He definitely wants you out of the country. Be careful.' She wagged an admonishing finger at him and took another swig of her beer.

'You don't say.'

'Excuse me?'

'Sorry, it's just an expression. So, Lina,' Luke said, placing his hands on the table, 'we need to meet up with this guy Darius Janulis. He's the in-house lawyer at Matulis ChemExport.'

'I know this.' Another swig. She had practically finished her beer while he was still toying with his lukewarm cappuccino. 'I have already made contact with him.'

'You have? Great!' Luke said. 'Where do we meet him?'

'Are you tired?' She stared at him appraisingly, her expression hard to read.

'No,' he lied. 'Why?' What an odd question, he thought.

'That's good, because it will be very late tonight. I have the address. We will go together. It is . . . a special kind of venue. I hope you can be . . . let's just say, open-minded.'

48

Moscow
Friday, 11 March, 1613hrs GMT, 1913hrs local

IN THE BRITISH ambassador's office the lights were still on, long after darkness had descended on the Russian capital. At this hour on a Friday evening, when most of his staff had packed up their work and left for the weekend, Jeremy Houghton was still at his desk and his PA was still at work in the connecting outer office. The PA took the call at 7.13 p.m., trying not to register his surprise, and patched it through to the ambassador. Exactly nine minutes later Her Majesty's Ambassador to Moscow was downstairs, climbing into his official car, flanked by his close-protection team. As they drove out into the Moscow night, the regular FSB tail moved neatly into place behind them, making no attempt to disguise their presence. Squat and ugly, the black Mercedes Geländewagen stayed close, even jumping the lights at one point so as not to get left behind. Other members of Britain's diplomatic mission were being followed in more subtle ways.

The Ministry of Foreign Affairs of the Russian Federation on Smolenskaya-Sennaya Square is an imposing building – some would say Orwellian in its towering, sinister appearance. As one of seven Stalin-era skyscrapers in Moscow, its daunting 'wedding cake' architecture soars 172 metres above the city. It was to here

171

that Jeremy Houghton was summoned that evening, his car pulling up amid the grey-brown slush of old snow in the forecourt, where he was greeted curtly and escorted by broad-chested men in black suits with earpieces and bulges beneath their jackets.

It was what is commonly known in diplomatic parlance as 'an interview without coffee'. The ambassador was told, via the interpreter who sat in the room, that Britain's recent 'neo-imperialist' lobbying at the United Nations was totally unacceptable. The British government's allegations of Russian activity in the sphere of biological warfare were completely without foundation. What had occurred on Svalbard was of international concern, including to Russia. The Russian Federation abided by all its international treaty obligations and any suggestion to the contrary, he was informed, would be met by Russia taking appropriate measures that Britain would come to regret.

Jeremy Houghton left the building tight-lipped, ears ringing, feeling as if he had just stepped down from a boxing ring. He would need to call London now from the SSR, the secure speech room, back inside the embassy – the electronically secure construction more commonly known as the Box. On the journey back his driver turned up the volume on Vesti FM, the Russian-language news channel that was preset on the car's radio. It was a lengthy item all about Britain's history of espionage against Russia. Even today, it said, Britain's 'arrogant and colonialist actions around the world proved conclusively its malign intentions. Every single British expatriate in Russia should be considered a potential spy. From now on,' concluded the broadcast, 'they should all be viewed with the utmost suspicion.'

49

LINA PICKED HIM up from his hotel just before 11 p.m., her arm outstretched, holding open the back door of the cab as the engine quietly belched exhaust into the chill night air. At first Luke simply didn't recognize her. Gone was the casual, dressed-down student look, the red scarf and the glasses. The girl budging up for him now on the back seat was transformed. Scarlet lip gloss, heavy mascara, hair pulled tightly back, black fishnet stockings and stilettos beneath a short black leather skirt.

She gave him a brief, appraising look and Luke, as usual, felt underdressed. He was wearing the same jeans he had been arrested in, no time to get them cleaned, and now, in the confined space at the back of the cab, he thought he could still smell the police cell. His mind flashed back a few years to a hot and humid night in Colombia, on his first ever mission for the Service, when he'd had to spend an evening in some dodgy nightclub in the company of a corrupt police officer on the take from the narcos. How did he keep ending up in these situations?

Lina spoke briefly to the driver and they moved off in silence, bouncing over the cobbles on the narrow backstreets in Vilnius's historic Old Town. Despite the cold, people were sitting out at bars on Bernardinu Street, clustering around outdoor heaters or wrapping borrowed blankets around their shoulders. It would be 8 p.m. back home and Luke wondered what Elise would be up to now. After-work drinks with her friends from the art gallery? Or being wined and dined by that smoothie ex-Goldman Sachs banker Hugo, who seemed to pop up every time Luke was away on a mission? He sincerely hoped not. This was where the job, and the Service, took its toll on any relationship. Luke wasn't complaining – they'd warned him about it during Induction – but, still, it nagged at him, prompting the unspoken question between them. How many more months could their relationship sustain this?

Outside the window the scene had changed. They had left behind the quaint, UNESCO-designated historic centre and now they were in some industrial no man's land beside the river. Lina, who had so far stayed silent, after pointing towards the driver up front and holding a varnished nail to her lips, announced they were nearly there. Involuntarily, Luke found himself tensing for action. His left side still ached from the fight in the cell, and if things kicked off out here, he was a long way from being fighting fit.

It looked like a warehouse from the outside. Not quite derelict, but it had definitely seen better days. This was all starting to look needlessly cloak-and-dagger.

'What the hell is this place, Lina?' he asked, as they got out and the cab drove off into the night. She was standing in the cold, holding up a little pocket mirror to her face and checking her lipstick, even though there was almost no light to see by. 'Could we really not have met Janulis in town?' he added.

'No.' Lina was nothing if not direct. 'He says it must be here. He feels safe here.' She snapped her compact shut and put it away. 'Come, it's this way.'

She led him along the side of the warehouse until they reached a doorway, lit by a single sodium light. Two men stood outside, hands in pockets, hunched against the cold. Lina spoke to them and nodded towards Luke. They gestured for him to raise his arms and patted him down politely, before opening the door for them both.

They went down a corridor, dimly lit, where the thump of techno grew louder with every step, and suddenly emerged into a cavernous dance space where music seemed to pulse from the very walls and purple lasers criss-crossed the sweating throng like frantic searchlights. Was there a theme here? It was hard to tell. Some people were wearing carnival masks, others surgical masks, whether for health protection or out of irony he couldn't tell. Either way, it was an uncomfortable reminder of all those months of Coronavirus lockdowns.

Luke caught sight of some tanned and muscled young men dancing together in a group, naked from the waist up, and beyond them, up on a pedestal, a girl was suggestively licking what looked like whipped cream off another girl, who was slowly pirouetting in a bikini and high heels. There was a time, Luke thought, when he and his mates would have revelled in coming to a club like this. Now he just felt old and out of place.

Lina reached out, grabbed Luke's sleeve and pulled him along behind her as she forged a path through the crowd. She seemed to have a plan, seemed to know exactly where she was going. Good. He just wished she could have shared it with him before they'd got this far. Now she was swerving left, away from the dance floor and down another passageway, music still reverberating off the walls. God, he really couldn't stand this techno din. Several people were lounging against the side of the corridor, passing joints to each other, ignoring Luke and Lina as they squeezed past. Then another turning, and Lina stopped in front of a closed door. She knocked three times and waited for it to open.

When it did, the figure that stood behind it was a shock for the eyes. He was tall, taller than both of them, wearing white tights, towering block heels, a short red skirt and a matador's embroidered jacket over a bare, hairy chest. On his shoulders was a life-size pig's head, dripping blood from the snout. Luke couldn't tell if either the pig's head or the blood was real. It didn't matter.

175

The effect was hideous. The grotesque figure seemed to recognize Lina and made an elaborate welcoming gesture, ushering them in and closing the door behind them. Instantly the thump of techno became muted. A small mercy, Luke thought, as they made their way over to a long couch in the corner, although oscillating psychedelic lights were still criss-crossing the room and someone was shining a handheld laser at them.

Two figures were sitting bolt upright on the sofa, dressed head to toe in all-encompassing black leather gimp suits, like something out of a medieval torture scene. Across their mouths were closed zips and the tiny slits for their eyes were fringed with sparkling glitter. The smaller of the two wore a studded silver chain around his neck, which the other held, posing like some country laird with his faithful retriever by his side. What, thought Luke, have I just walked into?

Lina appeared to have no such doubts. She strode confidently to the couch, sat down at one end and patted the space next to her, beckoning Luke to join her. 'So, Luke,' she commanded, in a matter-of-fact voice, 'sit, please.' She placed her hand on the leather-clad knee of the smaller of the two gimp figures next to her. 'This,' she announced, 'is the man you have come to see. This is Darius Janulis.'

50

Moscow
Friday, 11 March, 2033hrs GMT, 2333hrs local

COLONEL ARKADY PETROV was not someone to waste time. Just under eight hours had elapsed since he had been summoned to the Kremlin that afternoon for the deeply unsatisfactory meeting. A rogue operation, being run from within his own organization, his own cadre? This could be career-ending. He knew he had to move fast and he had done just that. To his office inside the GRU headquarters on Grizodubovoy Street he had summoned the three people he trusted most, all graduates of the gruelling three-year training course at 'the Conservatory', the GRU Military Academy at No. 50 Narodnoe Opolchenie Street in Moscow.

'If you want to call it a witch-hunt,' he'd told them, 'then fine, call it that, I don't care. Just find me the treacherous bastards who've been carrying out these biological tests on Svalbard without my authorization. And do it quickly and quietly. This has to be contained, do you understand?'

Now, despite the late hour, he was still poring over the initial findings. His people had started with the obvious: the digital trail, mining everything from emails to friends-only postings on VK, Russia's answer to Facebook. They needed no warrants, no special clearance: Colonel Petrov's orders were sufficient. Sure enough, there were all the usual revelations he was expecting: the phone sex lines being dialled up from work when someone thought no one was listening, the suspect payments for luxury items on government expense accounts, the guilty proof of visits to an upmarket sauna by someone claiming to be nursing a cold at home. These he could live with: he was after bigger fish, and so far he wasn't landing one. Not a single clue leading to Svalbard, no hint of the betrayal he was so determined to find. Someone must be covering their tracks extremely well. But he would find them, of that he was in no doubt.

51

Vilnius, Lithuania
Saturday, 12 March, 2128hrs GMT, 0028hrs local

OF ALL THE scenarios they had trained him for, Luke had never expected to end up in a situation like this. Past midnight in a pop-up nightclub on the outskirts of a Baltic capital, and he had to try to hold a serious conversation with a man zipped up inside a leather gimp suit, whose face he couldn't even see. From beyond the walls came the rhythmic, monotonous thump of techno music, and the man with the pig's head on his shoulders was still standing by the door, watching him – or, at least, Luke assumed he must be, although it was hard to tell. There were nearly a dozen other people scattered around the room, some on sofas, some standing huddled in a corner clutching drinks. Luke had the feeling that a lot of eyes were fixed on him, the outsider, the intruder into this closed world. How ironic that he should be the one to feel self-conscious.

'Mr Janulis,' he began.

'Mr Carlton.'

The formality of the exchange on the sofa seemed completely absurd to Luke, given the circumstances, but he put that swiftly to one side because right now he was intensely focused on getting what he had come for. Janulis had already delivered last night – for a price – and handing over that flash drive to Jenny meant their mission here in Lithuania was already technically a success. But Luke had now spent enough years in the intelligence world to know that raw intel alone was not enough: you needed to fill in the missing pieces of the jigsaw. He needed to exploit what they had and the next few minutes could determine the real success or failure of this entire part of the mission.

And he didn't think he could do that with Janulis still zipped up inside the black hood, let alone chained to someone else. Luke turned to Lina, and whispered in her ear. She listened, concentrating, then nodded. She spoke rapidly in Lithuanian and a minute later Luke was alone on the sofa with the in-house lawyer from Matulis ChemExport, now unmasked. It was time to get to work.

'I heard about you in prison,' Janulis said, with a wry smile. His thin hair was plastered to his scalp with sweat from the hood.

Luke didn't trust him for one second, but he was going to try very hard not to show it. 'It wasn't prison exactly,' he replied, 'it was a police cell, but, yes, not fun.'

Janulis smiled again, although it was more of a smirk, Luke thought, as if he were laughing at some private joke. 'You know it was my boss, Mr Kadunov, who arranged for you to be arrested?'

'So I hear. And why?'

'Why?' Janulis repeated Luke's question in a mocking tone and spread his hands wide. 'Why do you think? You were asking much too many questions, that's why. He wanted to keep you out of things he didn't want you to see.'

'Such as?' Here we go, nice and gentle, just a little probe to find out what he knows.

But Janulis was on to him. He tapped his nose knowingly. 'Not so fast, my friend. We will talk money later.'

Now it was Luke's turn to smile. He didn't mind that Janulis seemed to be almost entirely motivated by money: that kept things a lot simpler. Everything has its price. It was just a question of how much the Service was prepared to fork out. And the Service wasn't infallible in that department. Like in 2010, before his time, when the newspapers broke the story of how MI6 had paid tens of thousands of dollars to an impostor who pretended he was a top-level Taliban commander. He had turned out to be a very canny Pakistani shopkeeper from Quetta.

'Is there a reason,' Luke asked gently, 'why we needed to meet all the way out here in this, um . . .' he gestured around him '. . . this venue of yours?' He was relieved to see that people were no longer looking at him.

Janulis took a deep breath before answering. 'Are you a racist, Mr Carlton?'

'No. Why do you ask?'

'Do you hate gay people?'

'Not at all.'

'Do you have a problem with Jewish people?'

'No. I'm none of these things,' Luke replied. 'Come on, Janulis, where are you going with this?'

'Please, call me Darius. We start to know each other now.' Janulis was looking intently at him. 'Because I am not these things either. And as you can see . . .' he swept his arm at the room behind him '. . . I have different tastes. But some of the people I know here in Vilnius, they are not very accepting of others, shall we say?'

'Go on.'

'Do you mind?' Janulis reached across Luke's lap and retrieved a packet of Winston cigarettes and a lighter from beneath a cushion. He lit one, offered it to Luke, who declined, then took a drag, tipping his head back and blowing a plume of smoke up into the room.

'So, when I joined the company,' he said at last, 'that is, Matulis ChemExport, I was "encouraged" – yes, I think that is the word – I was encouraged to join a certain society, a secret group, if you like.' Janulis looked at his feet, then up abruptly. 'Do you know about WaffenKrieg90?' he added, fixing Luke with an intense stare once more.

'Do I know about WaffenKrieg90?' Luke repeated, giving himself a moment to think. The name sounded familiar from briefings he'd attended at Vauxhall, but somehow not quite right. 'You

181

mean Atomwaffen Division,' he corrected him. 'That far-right outfit in the southern USA?'

'No,' Janulis replied. 'I do not mean them. I said WaffenKrieg-90.' Luke had to admire the directness of East Europeans sometimes. They didn't beat about the bush, they told you exactly what they were thinking. 'WaffenKrieg90 is an organization here in Europe. It has connections everywhere. Here in Vilnius, in the police, in the government, in America, in England . . .'

'In Norway?'

'Yes! In Norway too.' Janulis suddenly gripped Luke's arm, his sweat-shiny face moving close to his. 'These are bad people, Mr Carlton. They do terrible things. They hate so many people: Jewish, Muslim, African, Arabs, even gay and lesbian. They hate . . . they hate anyone who is different.' He looked deflated and his shoulders slumped perceptibly.

'What d'you mean, "they do terrible things"?' Luke prompted him. He remembered Jenny saying Janulis had told her the same thing in the Ten Commandments Bar.

'You want me to go into detail?' Janulis's eyes were wide open now, his eyebrows arched. 'I am talking about sulphuric acid thrown into people's faces, people burned alive inside their homes, brakes changed on someone's car so they crash and end up a broken person for the rest of their life.' He shook his head. 'Shall I go on?'

Disturbing as this was, it wasn't getting Luke anywhere. He needed to pin down the link to Svalbard, if there was one. 'Can you tell me about their international connections?' he asked.

'You remember Christchurch?' Janulis said. 'The shootings in New Zealand at those mosques in 2019? So, they are saying that it was one of their "brothers" who did it. Yes, that's what they call them. "Brothers".'

Luke had reached the conclusion some time ago that Janulis must know that he, Luke, represented something rather more than the OPCW in The Hague. Otherwise he wouldn't be telling him all this.

'All right, Janulis, let's talk money.' Luke leaned forward and clasped his hands together. 'What information can you actually give me and how much do you want for it?'

Janulis took a final drag of his cigarette and stubbed it out on the side of the packet. He waved away the smoke, and looked around the room. He spoke in barely more than a whisper. For the first time Luke could see the fear in his eyes.

'I will tell you this. WaffenKrieg90 are planning something very big,' he said, 'and they have help . . . They have someone on the inside. Someone inside the system – in your country. Someone who works for your intelligence people.'

52

IT WAS A boy who noticed it. First weekend out after his birthday and he could hardly wait to sail his new radio-controlled toy yacht across the lake. And it was everything he had hoped for. Shane Collins was only in year six at school, but when it came to gadgets he left his parents behind. Deftly, he manoeuvred the miniature yacht, *Endeavour*, so it tacked neatly across the surface of the lake, while his father looked on admiringly. But five minutes in, something caught his attention.

'Dad?'

'Yes?'

'Look over there. What's that?' He pointed. His father could see nothing. 'There!' He pointed again. 'It looks like someone's driven a car into the lake!'

'Don't be silly, son. Nobody would do that.'

'They have! Look! It's underwater. It's got its boot sticking up.'

And for a moment his father could see it too. A car, submerged, but only just. Then the wind picked up, ruffling the surface of the lake.

'D'you think there's anyone in it?' asked the boy, excitedly.

'Now you're just being daft, Shane. Of course there won't be

184

anyone in it. They'd have drowned, wouldn't they? No, it'll just be someone who wanted to dump their old banger and they must have rolled it down the hill. Honestly, some people. I'll phone the council on Monday and let them know. Now, come on, show me what you can do with that yacht.'

And for the next thirty minutes Shane Collins raced his toy yacht to and fro across the water, just above the slowly decomposing body of a man riddled with one of the most lethal pathogens ever to threaten the human race.

53

Vilnius, Lithuania
Sunday, 13 March, 0919hrs GMT, 1219hrs local

IT WAS HIS third meeting with his source, Earl Grey, in under forty-eight hours. The man was spilling secrets and the Service was haemorrhaging cash – Luke had twice had to contact London to get pre-authorization for money transfers to Janulis's nominated bank in Helsinki. But, so far, the feedback from Vauxhall was encouraging. The raw intel, the so-called 'CX', that Luke was sending back was getting fast-tracked to the reports officers for cross-checking. They liked what they were reading, Luke was told, but they had one concern. The Service placed a huge amount of trust in its agent runners, but Earl Grey's greed was just starting to raise suspicions. Could he be embellishing what he was delivering in the hopes of earning more of the filthy lucre?

People defect or become agents, betraying secrets, for any number of reasons. It can be personal: a growing, festering grudge against the state or a colleague. It can be ideological: a sometimes starry-eyed belief that Britain, or wherever, is some kind of utopian paradise compared to the flawed purgatory they are living in. It can be hideous disillusionment: the belated discovery that life in whatever country or organization the agent is in is not what they thought, and they want out. But often, more often than people realize, it comes down to plain old money. And Darius Janulis, 'legals officer' at Matulis ChemExport, and designated SIS human informant, wanted lots of it.

They sat on a bench in Bernardine Park, between the banks of the River Vilnia and the ochre walls of Vilnius's Old Town. It was a spot Luke had chosen where it would be exceptionally hard for anyone to overhear them. Janulis appeared to have overcome his earlier nervousness, perhaps soothed by the thought of all the cash flowing into his numbered account in Finland. In return, Luke was extracting from him every last item of intelligence on WaffenKrieg90, its twisted worldview and, crucially, what his US military counterparts in Afghanistan would have called its TTPs – its tactics, techniques and procedures.

They parted at lunchtime, just as the park was filling with mothers with prams taking advantage of the sudden mild early-spring weather. By agreement, Luke left first, then Janulis ten minutes after that, each departing in a different direction. Luke chose a circuitous route back to the safe house: it was a habit drilled into him by his years of military service that he never returned the same way he'd set out. At the corner of two streets he stopped by a shop window, using its reflection to check behind him that there was no tail. Just standard counter-surveillance. There was no tail. Vilnius's Old Town was the largest-surviving medieval quarter in Eastern Europe, a quaint step back in time, interspersed with boutiques doing a brisk trade selling amber jewellery and Lithuanian cheese and wine. But these delights were lost on Luke as he started to compose in his head the contact report he would need to send to Vauxhall based on what he had just learned from Earl Grey. Perhaps because he was so focused on this, it didn't trouble him that when he turned left, down a narrow, cobbled street flanked by low, crumbling, terracotta-coloured walls, he found he was suddenly alone. This street was deserted.

He heard it before he saw it. The deep-throated roar of a car engine being gunned into overdrive. Luke whirled round to see a black Mercedes A-Class, with tinted windows, accelerating down the street in his direction. For a brief, fleeting moment he thought he was being over-cautious. A half-second later the vehicle had mounted the kerb and was on the same pavement he was. Too late, he realized he had entered a street where there was no barrier between road and pavement, nothing to shield him from the oncoming Mercedes that was closing on him with terrifying speed. This was no Sunday-afternoon joyride, this was a targeted hit. On him, Luke Carlton. The Mercedes was being driven so close to the wall next to him its sides were practically scraping against it. There was absolutely nowhere to run to. And not a soul to witness what was about to happen to him.

In desperation, he glanced around for an escape. Anything. An alcove, an open doorway, a flight of steps. Nothing. The sides of this cobbled backstreet offered him no way out, only blank walls and closed doors. Luke braced himself for the seemingly inevitable, bone-splintering impact as 1,500 kilograms of unyielding metal crushed his body against the wall.

And then he spotted it. The thin black iron bar was protruding horizontally from the wall just above and a few metres beyond him. At one time it must have held some sort of a sign. Right now Luke knew it was his only chance of salvation if he could reach it in time. With the deafening roar of the Mercedes-Benz 2-litre engine filling his ears, Luke exploded into action, launching himself into the air, his hands reaching out until they locked around the bar. Oh, God, please let it hold. Using the momentum of his jump, Luke swung his legs up and clear, feeling the rush of the saloon car as it roared past beneath him, missing him by centimetres. There was a hideous scraping noise as the side of the vehicle careered into the wall and, for a moment, the driver nearly lost control. Then the car righted itself and accelerated down the centre of the narrow street and was gone. It was all over in less than five seconds, and Luke cursed himself. He should never have dropped his guard like that, and he had never had a chance to catch sight of the registration number.

Luke let himself fall to the ground, remaining in a crouch for a moment, poised to break into a sprint if the Mercedes returned for a second run at him. Then he doubled back down the street the way he had come, heart still pounding. Things were getting out of control here in Vilnius. Someone was trying to kill him – that much was obvious. Turning left on to a street full of shops, he ducked into a doorway, got out his phone while scanning the road left and right. Accessing the secure line, he typed in a single word: *CRUCIBLE*. Then he waited.

Seconds later, the reply came back: *CHANDOS*.

Luke put away the phone. He knew what he had to do now. He had just activated the emergency abort signal and the coded response from Vauxhall Cross had been immediate. It meant: 'Acknowledged. Abort the mission and get out.' He moved to the corner of the pavement and ignored the first taxi that passed, and the second, in case they were somehow in on the act – another piece of tradecraft learned in basic training back at the Fort. Then he flagged down the third. 'Airport,' he told the driver. 'And take the highway – no backstreets.'

54

Peredelkino, Moscow Oblast
Sunday, 13 March, 1550hrs GMT, 1850hrs local

COLONEL ARKADY PETROV was at his family dacha just west of Moscow when he took the call. Like so many Muscovites he liked to be out of the capital at weekends, get back to nature in this pretty wooded village where Boris Pasternak was said to have written *Dr Zhivago*. When Coronavirus had rampaged through Moscow, carrying off so many of his countrymen and -women, this was where he had sat it out with his family, a loaded hunting rifle always at the ready in case any unwanted and infected intruders should venture too close.

Now his phone was ringing in his pocket just as he was turning over the skewers of *shashlyk* on the patio grill, the scent of aromatic spices coiling up from the kebabs into the chill evening air. Colonel Petrov did not like to be disturbed on a weekend. He gave the skewers a final turn, wiped his hands on his apron and took the call, his brow furrowing in concentration as he listened to the voice of his subordinate at the other end. It was a long call and the news was promising. Their investigations had turned up a suspect, who was in their custody now and was currently having 'an introductory conversation' with his interrogators downstairs. Would the colonel like to come and take over the questioning in person? He looked at his watch. The timing was inconvenient, but he knew he must do this. He would have to drive all the way back into Moscow and take charge. Colonel Petrov ended the call, cast a brief, longing look at the half-cooked *shashlyki* and tipped them into the bin.

Forty-five minutes later he pulled up at the address they had given him. It was in Cheryomushki district, in the south of the city, nowhere near GRU headquarters. His men were not stupid: this whole investigation needed to be off the books and out of sight. Officially it did not even exist. The building looked like any one of a hundred other uniform tenement blocks in this former dormitory of the Soviet Union's military-scientific community: tall, faceless, somewhat dilapidated. Colonel Petrov stepped over the small mound of wind-blown litter that had piled up beside the concrete entrance awning and nodded to the man on the other side of the glass door: one of his own. The door opened. Petrov stepped inside and followed the man down the steps to the laundry room. A well-built man in jeans, white T-shirt and black anorak stood guard at the top of the stairs, making sure no one followed: another of his own.

To most people it would have been a shocking sight: the half-naked figure tied to the chair, one eye purpled and swollen shut, blood dripping from his battered nose and lips. This was interrogation 1.0: crude, basic, occasionally effective. Colonel Petrov showed no emotion when he walked into the room. He barely glanced at the prisoner before reading through the sheet that was handed to him. There was the man's name, Konstantin Makarov, originally from the city of Magnitogorsk, his current address, his job specification within the CBRN division: biomedical supply assistant. A junior position, then, but still one with access to controlled materials. So far, the notes said, he had failed to give a satisfactory explanation as to why he had placed calls from inside the GRU building in Moscow to a number on the Norwegian archipelago of Svalbard.

'Research?' Colonel Petrov addressed him from across the

floor of the laundry room. 'What kind of research needs contact with a NATO country? Who authorized this?'

Silence. The man's head hung low on his chest. Colonel Petrov walked over and lifted Makarov's head with his hand. No reaction. Petrov turned to the others in the room and issued a stream of orders.

'Bring him round. Work on him until you get all the answers. Go to his home, search it from top to bottom. Laptops, phones, USB sticks, everything. Then bring his wife in here and start on her. Keep him conscious for that. When you have all the answers . . .' Colonel Petrov walked to the bottom of the flight of stairs that led up to the ground floor and turned back towards his team of investigators '. . . and only then, I want you to call me.' He gave them a mirthless smile. 'Keep up the good work.'

55

Battersea, London
Sunday, 13 March, 1955hrs GMT

DODGING DEATH WAS nothing new to Luke. He'd done it for years in uniform and then gone on to have some narrow escapes while on assignment for SIS in Colombia, Armenia and Iran, but what had happened today in that backstreet in Vilnius had left him more shaken than he'd want to admit. Was he getting careless? Forgetting the vital drills that had kept him alive? Or was it that he'd been on his own, operating solo with no recourse to close support on the ground and without the back-up team the Service normally provided? Either way, he had to sharpen up from now on.

Taking no more chances, he had headed straight for Vilnius airport, arriving a full four hours before his flight and having the few personal effects he'd left at the Shakespeare Hotel couriered over to him in the terminal. Its clean, modern interior and smiling Baltic charm had done little to reassure him. Someone in this country had just tried to kill him and he'd thought seriously about getting an earlier connecting flight via Warsaw. Instead, he had found a quiet corner of the departure lounge and held a long, encrypted conversation on the phone to Angela. At this time on a Sunday, despite the fears over the Svalbard outbreak, there were only weekend on-call staff working in Whitehall. But across the river in Vauxhall Cross a lot of staff had been drafted in to work through the weekend on the Moscow angle. Angela was one of them. If anything, she was even more rattled than he was by what had just happened to him. But when he told her what he had gleaned from Earl Grey she had listened intently. Everything he told her would now be relayed immediately to the cross-agency taskforce working around the clock. 'Stick with the direct flight to London,' she told him. 'The Chief will want to be briefed by you in person first thing tomorrow.'

The cab from London City Airport dropped him right outside the block where he and Elise lived. He should have been happy to be home. Yet he found his finger hovering over the door buzzer at street level and something, he wasn't sure what, was stopping him pressing it. In the almost four days he had been away on the Vilnius mission Luke had received just one curt WhatsApp message from her. Already, these days, he could feel himself growing inexorably more distant from her, as if a rip tide were pulling him away from the shore. He had wanted to ask her how her training was going for the London Marathon, how things were at the art gallery where she worked, whether she was still concerned about her old dad coping in that Buckinghamshire cottage on his own. All the normal, mundane things that had absolutely nothing to do with a lethal, genetically engineered, contagious disease threatening to break out into the general population. And yet he had asked her none of these things. He had simply swung himself into work mode and focused all his energies on the mission. Switching his personal phone back on after the flight from Vilnius, he had thought about sending her a text from the airport to say he was on his way home. But in the end he hadn't. Luke had never found it easy to express himself in text form, and since joining MI6 what little ability he'd had in that department seemed to have evaporated altogether.

Now, riding up in the lift to their flat, he wondered why he'd chosen not to announce his arrival from downstairs. He closed his eyes for a second. He couldn't say why. A naturally suspicious mind, maybe. Well, now it sounded like it was justified. Standing on the landing outside the door to their flat, he could hear the giggles even before he opened the door. Luke silently inserted his key into the lock, eased open the door and strode into the living room.

'Babes – you're back!' Elise sprang up from the sofa and threw her arms around his neck, kissing him as he dumped his bag on the carpet and squeezed her tight. After the squalor of that Eastern European police cell and the processed fug of a four-hour flight this girl just smelt so good. So good, in fact, that for a moment he forgot about everything else and began nudging them both towards the bedroom. And that was the moment when the spell was broken.

A figure appeared from the kitchen, framed in the doorway, two full glasses of wine in his hands. A figure that was all too familiar to Luke. A short, stocky figure with a thick monobrow, a pink Swiss cotton shirt monogrammed with his initials, 'HSS', and double-cuffed sleeves fastened with a pair of personalized gold cufflinks.

'Oh, sorry,' Elise said breezily, disentangling herself from Luke. 'I should have mentioned. Hugo's come over. We were just watching *Love Island, The Sequel.'*

Hugo. Bastard. St. John. Squires. His perpetually tedious nemesis. How was it that this irritatingly successful finance type kept turning up at Elise's side every time Luke was away on a mission?

The buzzer went from downstairs.

'That will be Deliveroo,' she said cheerfully. 'We've ordered Thai.' She buzzed the deliveryman in, telling him to come up in the lift, and waited by the front door for him, leaving Luke and Hugo facing each other awkwardly.

'Hugo.' Luke held out his hand and gave him a particularly forceful handshake, gripping him for perhaps a little longer than was necessary as he looked him in the eyes. Elise held open the front door, tipping the driver as he handed over the warm bags of food, and then returned, placing them on the dining table and

195

lifting out their contents. 'Luke, I hope you'll join us. Huge – can you fetch another place setting?'

'Huge'? 'Hope you'll join us'? What the hell was this? Luke made no attempt to hide the scowl on his face as he stood there, taking this in. This was all sounding way too familiar for his liking.

'I thought you were engaged?' he said to Hugo. 'To someone else,' he added icily, as they sat down and Elise divvied up the dinner for two between the three of them. 'Did that not work out?'

He caught Hugo throwing a knowing glance at Elise.

'Well,' Hugo began amiably, 'after I left the bank and set up a small boutique outfit with a couple of friends we rather went our separate ways. Oh, look, you haven't got any wine. Let me fetch you some.' And off he went into the kitchen, Luke and Elise's kitchen, seemingly oblivious to the hostile vibes Luke was giving off, leaving him and Elise alone together, sitting in silence over the Thai green chicken and fast congealing jasmine rice.

Luke realized he had nothing to say to her.

56

IT WAS STILL dark when they brought her in. Shiny with perspiration. Feverish. Contagious. Samantha Bradley – 'Sam' – had started working at the children's toy shop in Epsom at the beginning of the year. The pay was minimal, the hours weren't great, but it was only ever intended to be a means to an end, nothing more, just a way of saving up enough cash for her big South East Asia trip in the summer with her mates. Angkor Wat, Luang Prabang, Hue, they would visit them all. But Sam's plans were holed below the waterline the moment an off-duty Arctic scientist had walked into that shop and handed her a pink toy dinosaur at the till. When Chris Coppinger tapped his debit card against the contactless machine on that Friday morning, it didn't register, so instead she took his card to try it on a different machine. And that was when his hand brushed hers and minutes later she touched her face to wipe away a lock of hair. Sam Bradley's fate was sealed.

She was brought into the Royal Free visibly trembling. Using a special entrance, they transferred her straight upstairs to the High Security Infectious Diseases Unit. She had seen the news, she had heard about the Svalbard outbreak, and she knew that someone had come back here, to this very hospital, and died of the virus. When she thought she might have the symptoms, she went straight to A & E at Epsom General, unlike Chris Coppinger. And that was when they started treating her like a dangerous alien species.

In ordinary times it's quite possible they might have overlooked it, missed it for what it was. But the alert had gone out to every NHS trust in the country: people were on the lookout for the danger signs, and when Sam presented herself the protocols had kicked in immediately. In the ambulance, on the way up to the Royal Free in north London, a woman had asked her questions from behind her Perspex visor and mask, which Sam found almost as unnerving as the thought of what might be taking over her body right at that moment. Where had she been in the last forty-eight hours? Who had she been in contact with? Did anyone she'd encountered look ill?

In a quiet, frightened voice she had recounted how, yes, on the Friday morning, a man had bought a pink toy dinosaur from the shop where she worked and, no, he hadn't looked very well at all. The woman had made her repeat this and Sam did as she was told, all the while touching the lumps she could feel swelling beneath her ears.

When they installed her in 'the tent', in the heart of the Infectious Diseases Unit, the hospital director came to see her personally. He asked her the same questions, promised they would take good care of her, and left. He went straight to his office and phoned Brendan Holmes. Britain now had another patient infected with Agent X. Everyone she had been in contact with had to be traced, isolated and tested. Now it was definite: they were going to need extra beds on standby.

57

MI6 Headquarters, Vauxhall Cross
Monday, 14 March, 0748hrs GMT

LUKE HAD NOT slept well. To say that Hugo Squires had out-
stayed his welcome last night would have been an understatement.
Luke thought he would never leave and even Elise seemed quite
embarrassed by the end. He had drunk his way single-handed
through a whole bottle of claret and was making noises about
opening another, his face growing shinier with each glass. Christ,
the man was as thick-skinned as a rhino – could he not take a
hint? Squires had also started making obnoxious, sweeping gen-
eralizations about the state of the country, the people in it and
what needed to be done to put things right. Finally, it took Luke
standing up and clapping his hands together to draw the evening to a close, and call a cab for their guest. ·

Alone together beneath the duvet, Elise had announced she was
all in and turned her back on him, seemingly fast asleep in seconds.
Luke's eyes were still wide open, staring at the beautiful curve of
her neck that he had kissed so often, and he was left wondering
what had gone wrong between them.

When his alarm went off a few hours later he was glad of the
excuse to get up and out of there into work. And now here he
was, suited and booted, standing outside the door of the Chief's

outer office, waiting to be summoned in. Angela had gone over several heads to request this urgent meeting for Luke to present his findings in person and it was a mark of how much confidence the Chief had in him that he had got his 0745 appointment. Some eyebrows would be raised at this in the 0900 directors' meeting. But now, as the minutes ticked by, Luke began to question whether he should have done this differently. What he was about to tell the head of MI6 was going to have major diplomatic and political consequences. Should he have run it by Sid Khan first? Or the Counter-Proliferation people? No. Luke trusted Angela to spare him from getting all bogged down by Service protocol.

'Would you like to come in? He's ready for you now.' The Chief's PA: an indomitable battleaxe of a woman who had seen a succession of Cs come and go in her time. Grey hair cut short, spectacles on a chain and a dress sense that made few concessions to the twenty-first century. Brenda was something of a legend within the Service. What secrets have you been privy to? Luke thought, as he followed her through to the Chief's office. The first thing he saw was that the Chief was not alone. Sitting demurely on the couch, ankles crossed, hands on her lap, was Jenny Li. Luke was not surprised to see her – Lithuania had been their joint deployment – but this was no place for an effusive greeting. Next to her sat Angela. Both women gave him warm smiles, but kept silent. Sir Adam Keeling was still sitting behind his desk, reading something intently, and at first he didn't look up. This was his last year in the job, everybody here knew that. Retirement from government service beckoned, along with a generous pension and probably a comfortable non-executive directorship at one of the big City firms in Canary Wharf where they would expect to take full advantage of his trusted contacts. Sir Adam would hardly want to rock the boat at this stage of his life. Which made Luke's task doubly tricky.

'Come.' The Chief gestured to the chair nearest his desk, but still he didn't look up. Luke watched him sign something in the famous green ink. There are many things about the Secret Intelligence Service, MI6, that have changed beyond recognition as it drags itself into the twenty-first-century world of cyber, ISIS and lawyers needing to be in on the ground floor of every operation. But some things haven't changed. The head of the Service is still called 'the Chief', or simply 'C', and he still signs letters – yes, letters – in green ink.

Sir Adam Keeling put down his pen, looked up sharply and gave them his full attention. 'So,' he began, folding his hands and looking from one to another across his desk. 'You're both back from Lithuania. That was good work, you and Jenny getting the flash drive. It's brought us a valuable piece of the jigsaw.' Even as he was saying this, Luke suspected that any congratulations would be short-lived. And he was right.

'But I have to say,' Sir Adam continued, 'that I'm deeply concerned by what you, Luke, have relayed to Angela.' He paused, frowning, looking down for a moment. This didn't seem to Luke to be a good moment to interrupt.

'All our analysis,' the Chief went on, looking directly at Luke, 'points to Moscow being behind the Svalbard outbreak. And by Moscow, I mean the Kremlin. So I'd like to hear, in your own words, Luke, how exactly you think Earl Grey's product fits into that analysis?'

Luke adjusted his position on the chair and returned the Chief's stare. He knew this was a make-or-break moment for him. Get this wrong and his career at MI6 might never recover. But he didn't hesitate. He was ready for this. 'That's just the point, C. It isn't the Kremlin per se.'

'What d'you mean, "it isn't the Kremlin"?' Sir Adam's voice bore a distinct note of irritation as he said this. 'Every single lead on this case goes back to Moscow. Everything we've been pulling in, from our Oslo and Moscow station heads, from GCHQ, from Norway's NIS, it all points clearly and unequivocally to this being a GRU operation. That's what we've given the Joint Intelligence Committee and that's what the data supports. And you're now asking me to throw all that out of the window and tell them there's a non-state actor to blame?'

Luke felt the change in the atmosphere of the room even as the

Chief was speaking. He started to answer when Angela cut in, speaking from the couch to his left, over by the window. 'C, I think what Luke is trying to say is that this may not be quite as straightforward as we thought.'

Thanks, Angela, I knew I could count on you for support, Luke thought, but I'd best mount my own defence here. 'I know it *looks* like GRU,' he said. 'That's what they want everyone to think. But this is a false-flag operation made to appear as if the Russian state is behind it. And based on everything Earl Grey has divulged, this doesn't point to the Kremlin.'

'So who in heaven's name do you suppose it is, then?' Sir Adam exclaimed. He was leaning forward in his chair now, eyes glaring at Luke from behind his huge desk. Luke knew there was absolutely no time for hesitation.

'It's far-right extremists. It's this group calling themselves WaffenKrieg90. They've got the resources, they've got the contacts and, most importantly . . .' Luke paused for emphasis, hoping to ram home his point '. . . they've got the scientific know-how to produce a bio-weapon, and they're planning to release it, right here, in the UK. Think neo-Nazi ideology grafted on to a state-level capacity in bio-terrorism.'

For a long moment the Chief said nothing. He just stared at Luke, eyes still blazing. Inside his head, Luke counted to ten. By the time I finish counting, he thought, I will either be believed or I'll be looking for a new job.

Then, very quietly, the Chief spoke. 'I take it you've done the source validation on Earl Grey?'

'We have, C.' This time it was Jenny who spoke. She had been silent till now. 'I can concur with what Luke has just said.'

Sir Adam sat back in his chair, then buzzed his intercom and spoke to his PA. 'Cancel my eight-fifteen, reschedule my call with Riyadh station. In fact, hold all my calls, will you? And get Sid Khan in here immediately.'

The Chief seemed suddenly to have aged about ten years.

58

Braintree, Essex
Monday, 14 March, 0821hrs GMT

THEY LEFT IT nearly three days before they returned to the bunker to check on the results. Not without taking full precautions, of course. In addition to the original three who had gone there on the Friday, two more men carried a large bundle between them, containing full chemical PPE. Before Covid they might have had some difficulty in accessing that sort of specialized protective gear without raising suspicions. Now they had had no difficulty at all.

In the limited shelter of the hawthorn hedge, staying well clear of the sharp thorns, two of the group pulled on their PPE, checking each other's fastenings and seals, making sure the respirators were fully functioning. A third went forward, as last time, to check the coast was clear. When he gave them the thumbs-up they trudged forward, moving like astronauts on the surface of the moon, their rubber overboots making heavy progress in the cloying Essex soil.

It had been agreed which of them would open the heavy door to the bunker. They all knew that what they were about to see was not going to be pretty. But they had all accepted that this was just a necessary stepping stone on the path to progress. It was simply a job that had to be done. With a grinding scrape of its rusty hinges, the door heaved open and first one, then the other, stepped gingerly inside. The man in front had come prepared. He carried a camera and a torch, which he now shone ahead of him as he made his way through the first room. Even though he was in full protective gear he subconsciously held his breath as he stepped into the inner chamber. Silence greeted him. Well, that was to be expected. He played the torch beam from one side of the room to the other and then froze. There was the chain, still attached at one end to the table leg, just as they had left it on Friday. But at the other end there was nothing.

The rhesus macaque had vanished.

59

MI6 Headquarters, Vauxhall Cross
Monday, 14 March, 0908hrs GMT

'LET ME SPELL this out so we're all crystal clear where we stand,' said the Chief, his voice as deep and as grave as Luke had ever heard it. 'We aren't just talking about a distant outbreak of an unknown pathogen in some distant Arctic archipelago. No. This threat is, right here and right now, in this country.' He jabbed the index finger of his right hand vertically downwards, several times, on to the table-top for emphasis. 'We are talking about an extremist, transnational terrorist organization with sociopathic intent. An organization previously unknown to us and one we have almost no chance of getting anybody upstream inside within the time frame.'

Luke looked around him. They were in the Crisis Room on the ground floor. On his left sat the D-GRAT, the director of Global Risks and Threats, the rather grandiose title of the MI6 division that dealt with serious threats from Russia and China. To his right was Sid Khan, director of International Counter-Terrorism, across the table was the Chief and next to him was the director of Internal Security. Beside him was some tech wizard from Counter-Proliferation, a tall, sharp-faced woman with red-rimmed glasses, whom Luke had seen before, scurrying around the building, always in a hurry, always clutching some file or

205

other. The soft blue-upholstered armchairs reserved for more informal occasions had been pushed to one side. Everyone was sitting bolt upright on stiff-backed functional chairs. Last to arrive, slightly out of breath, was Jenny Li, bearing a laptop which she took out from a slim black leather case.

Luke had found himself this morning right inside the beating heart of Britain's Secret Intelligence Service and it was all down to what he and Jenny had discovered in Vilnius. It was quite possible, he realized, that there would be some people upstairs – ambitious middle-rankers, people who had joined the Service a good few years before him – who were not going to like him for this. There were men and women in this building, loyal servants of the Crown, Luke knew, who would spend their entire careers working their way up through its ranks, and never even come close to being invited to attend a directors' 0900. Yet here he was, a field operative, an agent runner, a relative junior with less than five years on the books, still cutting his teeth in some people's eyes – and now he was sitting at the top table.

'Obviously,' Sir Adam was saying, 'we still need to find corroborating sources on all this, to support what Luke and Jenny have uncovered. Security Service will be working all their contacts over here. Cheltenham will be working the data. But, as I see it, we could be looking at a triple threat. There's the bio-weapon itself – this pox, this virus, whatever the hell it is these people have cooked up on Svalbard. Containing it is not our problem. Finding out who's got it, that *is*. That's the task now facing all of us in the intelligence community, here in this building, across the river at Thames House and over in Cheltenham.' Sir Adam ran his hand through his thinning hair and frowned. In fact, Luke wasn't sure that he'd stopped frowning for the last hour.

'Second,' continued the Chief, nodding in the vague direction of Whitehall, 'before the hour is out I'll have to go across the river to Number Ten to tell the prime minister in person that – guess what? – we might have got this one wrong, and it looks like it isn't the Kremlin behind this outbreak after all.' He took a deep breath, pursed his lips and shook his head.

'And as if that isn't bad enough,' he stopped to give an ironic smile, 'there are indications, again based on the raw CX from Vilnius, that somewhere inside the intelligence community there could be a leak. In other words, a mole.' The Chief winced as he enunciated the dreaded word. The taboo term hung in the air like a bad smell. A traitor. An Insider Threat. The Enemy Within. It was every intelligence agency's worst nightmare. And everyone in the room knew what it meant. It meant triggering an internal investigation, a witch-hunt, by Security Branch, and that was now going to make everyone's job a whole lot harder.

'So, Luke.' The Chief waved a hand towards him. 'I'd like you to repeat for everyone here what you told me earlier, just so we're all up to speed.'

Luke had no notes – he didn't need any. He had gone over everything Janulis had told him again and again in his head on the flight back from Vilnius. Over the next fifteen minutes he took them through what he had gleaned about WaffenKrieg90, its far-right extremist ideology, the tentacles of its international network and its deeply unhealthy interest in what used to be termed 'weapons of mass destruction', more accurately known now as 'weapons of mass effect'. When he finished he sat down and glanced around the room. Right now, he really, really needed a coffee. He could see a steaming silver pot just sitting on the table in front of them, beside seven cups on a tray, yet such was the tension in the room that no one had budged to pour it.

'Jenny?' Sir Adam turned to Jenny Li, her face half hidden by her opened laptop. 'Does this tally with your findings?'

'I'm afraid it does, C, yes.' Jenny wasn't even looking up from her laptop as she said this. 'The contents of the flash drive we acquired from Earl Grey are still being assessed by the joint team downstairs. They're cross-matching it with the data-sets my team are providing on known illicit exports from former Soviet Union states.' And now she looked up from her notes. 'But can I give you my own frank assessment – the heuristics, as it were?'

'Please do.' The Chief nodded.

'The indications are that someone high up at Matulis Chem-

Export was authorizing the export of a growth medium that would be ideally suited for the cultivation and production of a biological weapon like this one.'

Sir Adam's brow furrowed further as he considered this. 'And your evidence for that?' he said, resting his chin on his hand as he faced her.

'There are substances appearing on their sales records, C, that we would definitely take issue with in this country under the government's current counter-proliferation strategy. I can give you their chemical breakdowns, if you like?'

The Chief waved a hand to stall her. 'Not right now, but thank you, Jenny.' He glanced up at the clock on the wall. 'Right. I'm going to bring in Moscow station now.' He looked over his shoulder at the woman standing some distance behind him. 'Miranda, can we get the VTC up and running?'

The large TV screen on the wall flickered into life and there, rather too close to the camera, was the face of the Moscow station head. Close enough, Luke noted, to see his wispy, receding hairline and the network of spider veins across his cheeks. Luke could also just make out the walls of the Box behind him, the secure fibreglass cage in Britain's Moscow embassy where the most sensitive conversations were conducted inside an electro-magnetic shell, impervious to penetration by hostile intelligence agencies. No preambles, he launched straight in. Yet the man's lips were moving noiselessly: there was no sound.

'Miranda?' Sir Adam swivelled in his chair. 'Can you fix the audio, please?'

Flustered and clearly embarrassed, she moved quickly to her laptop and a moment later sound filled the room, as clear and as sharp as if the Moscow station head were sitting among them.

'Our sources here have informed me,' he began again, 'that on Friday afternoon – that would be four days after the Svalbard outbreak – a certain Colonel Arkady Petrov was summoned to the Kremlin. Petrov, as some of you know, is the GRU's senior serving scientist on their chem-bio research projects.' A long pause. 'Which was one of the contributing factors towards our belief that Moscow was behind this.'

'And your conclusion now?' The Chief spoke into a desk mike.

'We don't have *de visu* reporting on who was in that meeting or what was discussed. But . . .' Another long pause.

Luke leaned over to the director on his left and whispered a question. '*De visu*? What does that mean?'

'It means "eyes-on", as you military types would call it.'

'But what?' The Chief was prompting the Moscow station head.

'But we're hearing from an additional source that this Colonel Petrov may be in difficulty with his bosses. It looks like he may have a rogue operator on his hands.'

60

11,000m above Siberia
Monday, 14 March, 1000hrs GMT, 1300hrs local

COLONEL ARKADY PETROV twisted around in his cramped seat
and stared out of the frost-encrusted window of the Ilyushin Il-
96 airliner as it lumbered eastwards across the skies over Siberia.
Far, far below, in the sub-zero air, unobscured by any cloud, lay
the vast white expanse of the endless Siberian taiga. Mile after
mile of frozen forest: it had been nearly an hour since they had
flown over anything even resembling human habitation. Colonel
Petrov was not someone to spend a lot of time dwelling on the
man they had pegged out in the cellar of that apartment block
back in Moscow's Cheryomushki district. What was his name?
Konstantin Makarov? Yes, that was it. Well, they had what they
needed from him and the man had already been temporarily
reassigned – once they released him from the GRU's own sana-
torium – to a penal colony north of the Arctic Circle and just east
of Archangelsk. Konstantin Makarov had eventually proved
most forthcoming with information, once they had used the
industrial bleach on him.

Information was power and Colonel Petrov had wasted no time.
Using his GRU credentials, he had boarded the first official flight
available from Moscow to the city of Novosibirsk, four time zones

to the east, close to the Mongolian border and deep in the heart of Siberia. He was heading for the State Research Institute of Virology and Biotechnology, better known as VECTOR, a place infamous during the Cold War for its work on the Soviet bio-warfare programme, Biopreparat. Today it was one of only two places in the world – along with the CDC in Atlanta in the US – with declared stocks of the smallpox *variola* virus, and it was regularly inspected by the WHO as part of Russia's accession to the Bioweapons Convention. All was not well at the VECTOR facility in the suburb of Koltsovo. That much Petrov knew. In late 2019 there had been a mysterious explosion on the fifth floor, in the decontamination room where scientists changed out of their protective suits. Windows were blown open, a fire had taken hold, and there were fears at the time of a possible global viral outbreak. Petrov, and many of his fellow officers in military intelligence, suspected then, and still did, that the explosion was a deliberate act of sabotage.

The temperature was minus 13°C when the GRU colonel stepped out of the arrivals building at Novosibirsk's Tolmachevo airport. His breath frosted in the still air and his eyes stung from the pollution that still belched from the nearby factories, along the River Ob. The car was exactly where they had told him it would be, unmarked, discreet, a vetted driver in front, personal security in the back. This was to be a low-key, fact-finding visit, not an official inspection. The drive across town to the wooded suburb of Koltsovo was short, the conversation minimal. When they pulled up at the identical dormitory-like research buildings on the edge of town, Colonel Petrov knew exactly where to go: this was hardly his first visit to VECTOR.

The meeting was held in the empty conference room, the projector lying silent, the chairs empty, the windows caked with geometrically shaped particles of ice. It was just the two of them, Colonel Petrov and a man called Aleksei, the head of security for the entire facility. They had met before, on a training course back at the Academy, and Petrov had taken an instant dislike to him. Petrov had no interest in niceties today: he had hard questions to ask and he expected immediate answers.

'How many vials of live pox virus left this facility under escort on January the seventeenth to go to the Ivanovsky Institute of Virology in Moscow?'

The other man looked confused. He stared back at Petrov. 'I couldn't tell you right now,' he replied. 'I would have to check.'

'Then I will tell you,' said Petrov. 'It was four.'

'Four?' Aleksei repeated.

'And how many arrived in Moscow?'

'Four?' The head of security was looking distinctly uncomfortable now.

'Try again.'

'Look,' said the VECTOR security man, 'I run security here at Koltsovo. What happens here is my business, my problem. And I can tell you, we have everything accounted for – you can check that with the WHO. They carry out regular inspections, you should know this.' He wagged a finger at Petrov. 'But what happens in Moscow, my friend . . .' He shrugged. 'Well, that is not my problem, is it?'

'Normally, no,' Colonel Petrov replied evenly. 'Except that only three vials of smallpox arrived in Moscow. And it is your name at the bottom of the transfer order.'

61

THE MOMENT THE silver Mercedes turned left off Whitehall and drew up at the entrance to King Charles Street, the retractable steel crash columns slid swiftly into the ground. Its rather obvious registration number – RUS 1 – was already logged with the elderly commissionaires on the gate. Once they had validated IDs they waved it through towards the inner courtyard with a courteous nod. The Russian ambassador had arrived at the Foreign and Commonwealth Office.

Greeted and escorted up the purple-carpeted staircase with its grandiose balustrade, the ambassador and his assistant were ushered into the foreign secretary's office. There, beneath the ceiling-high windows looking out on to St James's Park, and their lavish crimson curtains, the two Russians took their seats on the overstuffed red leather armchairs. Tea was brought in and set down on the polished mahogany table: strong and black, the way the Russians liked it. Yet it was to be the most awkward of meetings for both sides.

'If you will allow me,' the foreign secretary began, dipping her head slightly as she peered over her glasses at her guests, 'I would like to come straight to the point.'

'Please.' The Russian ambassador gestured for her to continue.

'On behalf of the British government I would like to offer my apologies. It seems that we were – how can I say it? – a little hasty in our conclusions earlier. We now believe that a transnational criminal organization is behind this viral outbreak, rather than the Russian government.'

The ambassador stirred his tea, and said nothing.

'And therefore,' she continued, 'we will be withdrawing the measures we announced on Friday. I am relieved that we have been able to reach this point before they were put into effect.' The foreign secretary smiled bravely and looked from one to the other before the ambassador eventually spoke.

'It is indeed a great shame that your government has chosen to portray my country in this way. You should know that Russia has only peaceful intentions in this world. We tried to explain this to you after the unfortunate death of Alexander Litvinenko and again after the Skripals were poisoned in Salisbury by that leak from your own laboratories at Porton Down. And yet, again and again, the British government chooses this path of needless confrontation.' The ambassador regarded his host with a mixture of sadness and condescension.

'Well,' the foreign secretary began, somewhat taken aback by this defiant riposte, 'I can only say that we extend our sincerest regrets at the earlier misunderstanding. In fairness, I should point out that there are still worrying indications that one or more individuals in your country's security agencies may have been in some way involved so—' She stopped: the Russian ambassador already had his hand up, palm facing her.

'I regret to inform you, Madame Secretary, that the time for such empty apologies has passed. The damage has now been done.'

'Well, I was actually offering you our regrets, Mr Ambassador,' the foreign secretary said. 'The important thing now is that we move on and look to future relations between our two countries.'

The Russian ambassador gave a heavy sigh and shook his head sadly. 'I have been instructed by my government to inform you,' he said, 'that we are currently reviewing the number of your diplomatic personnel at your embassy in Moscow. I should also inform you that the operations of British Petroleum in the Russian Federation are also under critical review.' He stood up, followed by his assistant. 'We thank you for the tea, Madame Secretary of State.'

62

Essex
Monday, 14 March, 1128hrs GMT

'WHAT THE FUCK d'you mean, "it's gone"? You're not trying to tell me it's just vanished into thin air, are you?'

Behind the doors of the haulage company's office the two men stared at each other, one contrite and reticent, the other red-faced and furious. He answered his own question. 'No. Of course it bloody hasn't. So find the sodding monkey. Find out who's taken it and finish it off. We can't have this all kicking off before we're ready.' He waved a nicotine-stained finger in the other man's face. 'You told me no one ever goes into that bunker. I should never have listened to you.'

'They don't, normally,' offered the other man.

'Shut up, wanker. I'm doing the talking.' He turned and walked towards the old metal filing cabinet, a hangover from the company's pre-digital days. He placed his hands on its corners and hung his head in thought. Just outside the window someone was reversing a forklift truck and the constant beeping seemed to invade the whole room. It did little to ease the tension between them.

'All right,' he said at last. 'I'll need to let Moscow know what's happened. They're not going to be happy about this. Not happy at all.' He stood up straight, turned and gripped the other man around the back of his neck. 'So you get out there,' he breathed, 'and deal with that bleeding animal – now.'

63

FOR EVERYONE IN the room on that Monday morning there was a sickening sense of déjà vu. We've been here before, they were all thinking, when Covid-19 hit in 2020. Because the projection on the screen was chilling, no doubt about that. The axis along the bottom showed the timeline in days; the vertical axis showed the notional increase in infections if Agent X made the leap into the general population and could not be contained. The incline was exponential, the graph line soaring like a ski jump, a seriously steep one. Standing next to it was Brendan Holmes, the chief medical officer, and arranged on chairs in front of him were some of Britain's foremost experts in disease control, all summoned to the headquarters of the National Institute for Health Protection. The group known as SAGE – the Government's Scientific Advisory Group for Emergencies – was in session.

'As of this moment,' Holmes told them, 'Norway is reporting six cases of Agent X infection, all on Svalbard. We've had four confirmed cases in this country and so far – *so far* – we have managed to isolate the cases before the infection spreads to the general population. But the incubation rate seems to vary wildly and we are still a very long way from any effective vaccine or cure.' He looked from one face to another, as if expecting somehow to find the answers there. 'Dr Mackenzie died within a couple of days of being brought back here. Her colleague Chris . . .' He looked down at his notes. 'Chris Coppinger is now known to have taken his own life by drowning himself in a lake in Surrey. That's caused the entire area surrounding it to be cordoned off, quarantined and declared an area of high public risk. The third patient, Samantha Bradley, is currently in critical care at the Royal Free, and we honestly don't know yet if she's going to make a recovery.'

He moved away from the screen and sat down heavily at the head of the table. 'I have to say that the fourth patient is a worry. She was one of the A & E staff on duty at Epsom General on the day they took in Ms Bradley. We've had to transfer her to the High Consequence Infectious Disease Centre at Guy's. And obviously we are now having to trace and test every single person who might have come into contact with her, as well as everyone who came anywhere near Ms Bradley since the moment she sold that stuffed toy to the late Chris Coppinger.' He shook his head at the thought of how such a benign, mundane action could have had such terrible repercussions.

'If the numbers turn up anything close to our worst expectations,' he said, waving to the chart on the screen, 'then we're looking at another Nightingale situation: a secure quarantine unit with enough beds, full twenty-four-hour care and enough PPE to see us through.'

Strained, worried faces stared back at him. There was a long silence before eventually someone broke it. It was one of the mathematical modellers who had helped draw up the chart on the screen.

'And lockdown? Are you suggesting the country will have to go back into lockdown?'

Brendan Holmes put his hands out in front of him, as if holding back an imaginary crowd. 'Look,' he replied, 'this is still very early days and we can't be certain of the R number, the infection rate, of this virus. Remember, as long as that stays below 1.0 – that's one new individual infected for every human already infected – then we should be able to bring this thing under control. But if it's higher . . .' He paused, as if uncertain whether to voice his fears out loud. 'Well, if it's higher, yes, we could be facing a national emergency. So, Clarissa.' He brightened as he turned to the Senior Scientific Adviser from Porton Down Defence Laboratory. 'Give us some good news, if you will. What progress on the cure?'

'Well, this isn't going to be straightforward,' Dr Clarissa Gall replied. 'If we were just dealing with a variation of smallpox, that would be bad enough but manageable – we could always have rushed in stocks from the States and probably shut this thing down overnight. No, I'm afraid this is something much more complex and sinister. Why? Because of the Marburg filovirus it's been combined with. We're pulling in expertise from the WHO, and from Atlanta, but we're still a long way off coming up with a cure.'

The chief medical officer grimaced. 'So one of the biggest challenges for us now,' he told the room, 'is how we sufficiently inform the public without triggering a panic.' He picked up a sheet of paper that he'd been toying with while Dr Gall spoke. 'My team have drawn up a communiqué that I'm going to recommend we put up on the website this afternoon.' He began to read it out.

'As a precautionary measure, UK scientists are working closely with international experts to implement rapid infection-control procedures for this new virus, provisionally designated as Agent X. These will include, where necessary, tracing, contacting and isolating those people who may have come into contact with infected individuals.'

'If you don't mind my saying,' interjected one of the epidemiologists from Imperial College, 'that all sounds a bit bland, doesn't it? I mean, we're not exactly telling them anything new there, are we? The fact is that Agent X is a man-made, genetically modified pathogen. It hasn't jumped species in a Chinese wet market. This thing has been deliberately cooked up in a lab with malign intent. I think we owe it to the public to give them a bit more info, don't you?'

'Well, I was coming to that,' replied Brendan Holmes, looking rather piqued. He read out the rest of the communiqué.

'Initial symptoms of monkey pox include fever, headache, muscle aches, swollen lymph nodes, chills and exhaustion. A rash can develop, often beginning on the face, then spreading to other parts of the body. The rash finally forms a scab, which later falls off.'

He stopped abruptly.
'That's it?' asked the epidemiologist.
'That's it.'
'I'm sorry, but I think the public will say we're taking them for fools. Have any of you looked at Twitter today? This is all over it. Here . . .' Dr Gall got out her phone, thumbed the app and scrolled down. 'Have a look at hashtag-virus, hashtag-pox, hashtag-disease. Wherever you look people are talking about it. The Sunday papers were all across it yesterday – the *Sunday Times* even got somebody on to Svalbard. No.' The scientist shook her head decisively. 'I don't think you can keep people in the dark about this. I, for one, feel strongly that we need to level with people on what the true nature of this pathogen is and, more importantly, what precautions we're putting in place if Agent X takes off.' She looked at Holmes across the table in silent challenge.

He held her gaze for just a second, then turned away. He felt distinctly uncomfortable. 'I'm not sure we're ready,' he said quietly, 'to announce our precautions. Because we haven't taken any yet.'

64

LUKE PUSHED HIS chair away from the screen and blinked several times. There was only so much scrolling through texts and transcripts and images he could take before he started to feel like a caged beast. If someone had said to him before he joined MI6 he'd be spending half his life in front of a computer screen he might have had second thoughts. But then again, just thinking about that near-miss from the speeding Mercedes that had tried to wipe him out in a backstreet of Vilnius was more than enough to get his adrenalin flowing.

He stood up and walked over to the narrow, bulletproof window of his office. This place was such a fortress he sometimes felt like he was looking out from some medieval castle with arrow slits for windows. The view from this south-facing side was a lot less inspiring than the one northward across the river. Two floors above him and on the other side of the building, the Chief and the directors had the glorious picture-window views over the Thames and Vauxhall Bridge; he got to look down on a petrol station, a spa called Chariots and the rush-hour traffic dribbling out of London.

On this early Monday evening he could see 'normal people' – civilians, as he still thought of them – all heading home from work. Despite the current crisis Luke knew that most of Whitehall would have emptied out by now – it was worse on a Friday, when places like the MoD main building were practically ghost towns after 5 p.m. And what exactly did he, Luke Carlton, have to look forward to? Another awkward evening with Elise and all those unanswered questions about what Hugo Squires was doing, getting so cosy in their flat. They had made no plans for this week, mostly because Luke could give her no guarantee he wasn't going to be working late into the night. Or jumping on to a plane to somewhere cold and dangerous. Elise had already told him she would be staying on for drinks with friends after work this evening. That was fine by him. He'd go to the gym, give himself a beasting on the free weights, cook up some carbs and get in an early night.

'Knock knock.' He turned to see Jenny Li standing in the open door, her hand resting on the frame.

'Oh, hi,' he said warily. What now? This was the second case he had worked on with Jenny and it had only increased his professional respect for her and her encyclopaedic knowledge of CBRN. But, my God, the woman was a machine: she never stopped working. Was she about to inform him they were going to have to pull an all-nighter?

'So . . .' She flashed him a smile. 'I just came to see how you were holding up. You know, given everything that happened in Lithuania.'

His hand went instinctively to his left side, where he'd sustained that heavy blow in the Lithuanian police cell. It still hurt to the touch, but he was getting used to it. 'I'm in shock!' Luke joked. 'She cares!'

'Don't push it, Luke Carlton,' she replied, with another smile. 'We both know I've done you a favour and kept most of that stuff in the police station out of my contact report. Otherwise you can bet your pension that HR would have you spending the next ten days on some psych-evaluation programme.'

223

'And we wouldn't want that,' Luke said emphatically. He was enjoying this exchange, some light relief at last after the unrelenting tension, both at work and at home.

'No, we would not. So . . .' she glanced at her feet '. . . I think we could both do with a drink, don't you?' She looked up, questioningly. 'Unless, of course, you have plans?'

Luke gave her an appraising look, noticing for the first time the curve of her figure beneath her navy-blue jacket and skirt. Mentally, he shook himself. Stay professional, Carlton. 'No,' he replied, quickly adding, 'I mean yes. Absolutely. No, I don't have plans and, yes, we should do that. Go for a drink.' Hardly smooth. What was the matter with him? 'Vauxhall Tavern?'

She raised a quizzical eyebrow. 'You're being ironic, right, Luke?' He wasn't. 'No one from this place goes there. It's just too obvious. Think about it, it's the closest bloody pub to SIS headquarters! No, I'm thinking that new wine bar on the river by Battersea Power Station. Caravan or something.'

'Works for me.'

'Good,' she said briskly. 'I'll just go and grab my coat. Looks like it's still drizzling outside.'

They didn't get past the foyer on the ground floor.

'Jenny Li, Luke Carlton? I'm from the Chief's office. I've been sent by Brenda to fetch you.' It was an eager young man, rather out of breath, as if he had just run down several flights of stairs instead of taking the lift. 'C wants to see you both now. In his office.' As an afterthought, he added apologetically, 'Sorry to interrupt your evening.'

Sir Adam Keeling had presided over some notable successes in his time – getting agents 'upstream' into ISIS, cultivating a handful of human informants inside Iran's suspect nuclear industry. But today, Luke knew, would have been an exceptionally awkward one for the Chief. Having to tell the PM, the foreign secretary and half the cabinet that contrary to the way the situation had looked, contrary to all the snippets of raw intel pointing towards the Kremlin, this deliberate release of a deadly pathogen was quite possibly not the work of the Russian government after all. So now Luke was concerned. What did it mean to be summoned to the Chief's office at the end of the day? It wasn't going to be an invitation to cocktails, that was for certain.

They were ushered down the corridor, past the framed photographs of royal visits, into the carpeted inner sanctum, with its paintings on the walls and all those souvenirs from foreign intelligence agencies: a carpet, a curved dagger, an incense burner and, bizarrely, a carved seagull.

'Welcome, both. This is art,' announced the Chief, abruptly, the moment they walked in.

Luke had only one thought going through his mind: Is the Chief losing his marbles? Has he summoned us up here at the end of a long day just to show off his idea of an art collection? Maybe it really was time for Sir Adam to move on. But, no, he was now indicating a man sitting opposite him, tanned, with short black hair and a lot of product worked into it, wearing a button-down Brooks Brothers white shirt and a well-tailored suit. This man had 'Langley' written all over him, Luke thought.

'This is Art Krantz,' the Chief repeated, 'one of our senior colleagues from Langley. Our friends at the CIA have made a disturbing discovery, which they have been kind enough to share with us. Art?'

The man from Virginia cleared his throat, looking first at Jenny, then at Luke as he spoke. 'Well, it's really the folks at the NSA who did the heavy lifting on this one, but I guess I'm the guy who's bringing you the bad news.' He looked across at the Chief, who nodded. 'We've run the deep-trawl analysis on the intel you've sent us and, guess what?' Luke and Jenny looked at him with blank expressions, waiting for the punchline.

'We have a mole. Or, more precisely, *you* have a mole . . .' Again, he looked from one to the other. 'Someone inside UK intel is leaking. There's classified intel from here popping up on far-right extremist forums on our side of the Pond.'

Luke exchanged a meaningful glance with the Chief. This was further corroboration that Earl Grey had been telling the truth. It was the Lithuanian lawyer who had first alerted Luke to this fact, back in the nightclub in Vilnius, and Luke had passed it on to Vauxhall immediately. But he felt no sense of triumph on seeing his work vindicated. If anything, this could end up being deeply embarrassing for the Service. Sure, the Americans had had their share of disasters in this department – the FBI's Robert Hanssen passed secrets to the Soviets and Russians for twenty-two years; the CIA's Aldrich Ames turned out to be a highly valued KGB double agent. Yet it had taken years for US intelligence to get over its sheer horror at the extent of the damage done by Britain's 'Cambridge Spy Ring': the decades-long betrayals to Moscow carried out by the likes of Kim Philby, Guy Burgess and Donald Maclean. The most damaging of all the double agents, George Blake, whose treachery sent hundreds to their deaths, lived on in Russia until 2020, celebrated there as a hero till the end.

As the lead partner in the so-called 'Five Eyes' intelligence-sharing arrangement between the US, UK, Canada, Australia and New Zealand, Washington was understandably cautious about exactly what it chose to share with its allies. And now here they were again, facing the possibility that somebody inside MI6, MI5 or GCHQ was leaking intel, not to the Russians this time but to a transnational group of far-right extremists.

'So we're going to tackle this on two fronts,' announced the Chief. He was on his feet now and pacing the room. Art Krantz remained seated, but Luke could see his eyes following Sir Adam around the room, tracking him like a hawk. 'Security Branch will run their official investigation in conjunction with SO15 at the Met. That will take its natural course.' He turned to face Luke and Jenny. 'But I want you two to work in parallel on this – for me. MI5 are putting together a crisis team to deal with the UK extremist end of the Agent X bio threat. I want both of you on it. Luke, you'll be attached to the agent-running team. Jenny, you'll be on the investigative team. You'll report to Thames House at 0845 tomorrow morning.' The Chief stepped forward a pace and placed a hand on each of their shoulders, as if he were a priest giving them a sacred blessing. 'I'm counting on you both,' he said quietly. 'Help us find that mole.'

65

THE RAIN WAS sweeping in horizontal skeins across a landscape drained of colour. The team on the ground fanned out in pairs across the fields, while the tech team scanned the internet and even the dark web for any hints, any clues. Whoever had gone into that disused military bunker in north Essex and freed the chained-up macaque could surely not have gone far. They also, clearly, had no idea of the danger they had exposed themselves to. If the Cambridge people – the scientists – were right, the assumption went, then the virus should already have taken effect, the monkey would be contagious – whether it was alive or dead.

The tech team had been busy for the last twenty-four hours, since the moment of discovery on Monday morning when they learned that their research primate had vanished. They started with the obvious – the National Anti-Vivisection Society, People for the Ethical Treatment of Animals (PETA) and the Captive Animal Protection Agency. If the monkey was in their hands, someone somewhere would surely have been unable to resist talking about it online. But the trawl had drawn a blank. Either it wasn't them, or their opsec – their operational security – was better than people gave them credit for.

It was just past 8 a.m. when two of the field team spotted something at the edge of the road: it looked like a pile of old brown clothes at first, the sort of thing a casual fly-tipper couldn't be bothered to take to the municipal dump. But as they approached they could make out furry limbs, an outstretched hand, almost human, and a small face, constricted into a rictus smile, teeth bared, lips pared back over gums discoloured with dried blood.

'Found 'im.' The older of the pair called it in, turning his back to the wind as he spoke into his phone. There was a brief exchange and when it ended he straightened up. He could not believe what he was seeing. 'Oi!' he shouted. 'Get the hell away from it! Don't be a twat! Put it down!'

The younger man had walked up to the dead monkey, picked up the loose chain around its neck in one hand, a slender, lifeless limb with another, and taken a grinning selfie with his phone.

66

SHOWERED, SHAVED AND dressed in casual rig, as his mates in the Royal Marines would have called it, Luke parked his Land Rover behind Tate Britain on the north bank of the Thames. He then walked briskly down Millbank for the last few hundred metres to the MI5 headquarters building at Thames House.

When he and Jenny had filed out of the Chief's office the previous evening nothing had needed to be said. There was no more talk of going for that drink: they both knew the moment had passed. Luke had gone home and done exactly what he'd always planned to: he'd given himself a serious workout down in the gym, pushing himself until his muscles screamed and the wooden floor beneath him was splashed with his sweat. When he came up to the flat, still glowing with exertion, he found Elise was back from her work drinks and, after a brief, strained exchange, they had ended up arguing about Hugo Squires.

'He's harmless, you know,' she'd told him, as she started emptying the dishwasher and putting plates in a cupboard. 'And he's a great comfort to me when you're away.'

'I'm sure his intentions are entirely honourable,' Luke said, and immediately regretted it.

Elise sighed in exasperation. 'I wouldn't have expected you to understand, Luke. Sometimes I think you have the EQ of a hedgehog.'

'EQ?'

'Yes. Your emotional quotient. You're just simply not tuned into how other people feel, are you?'

Ouch. That stung. She might have a point there, he conceded. He considered mentioning that Hugo Squires's EQ seemed to be focused entirely on getting Elise into bed and that he was quite prepared to flash enough cash around to achieve his aim. But, no, Luke realized that was probably a low blow, so he'd grunted something non-committal and disappeared into the bedroom. He hated arguing with Elise. He just didn't know how to fix whatever had gone wrong between them. For a moment, he stood there, staring at the bedside table, lost in thought, questioning if it was even possible to hold down this difficult job and still be with Elise. The two things seemed to be becoming ever less compatible.

In the morning, once again, he'd found it a relief to be getting out of the flat and into work. He noticed that, for the second time in five years, Thames House was cocooned in scaffolding and tarpaulins, like some monstrous chrysalis, as people worked to give its grimy walls a facelift. Unattractive as it was to look at, he bet this suited the men and women who worked there just fine, allowing them to turn discreetly off the Millbank pavement and up the steps into Britain's domestic intelligence agency, unseen now by the traffic nosing past into Westminster.

He went through the tubular *Star Trek*-style security doors and into the largely featureless foyer, where TV screens on the walls ran twenty-four-hour-news channels around the clock.

'Luke?' He turned. He knew that voice and his spirits sank. It was John Friend, one of the small army of the Service's in-house legal advisers. Everything had to be signed off by them these days, right from the initial conversations, long before an operation went live. Luke knew these things were needed, after the fiasco of Libya and Britain's involvement in extraordinary rendition to Gaddafi's prisons. Yet he couldn't help seeing Friend as a human 'fun-detector', a killjoy out to mess up the missions of people at the sharp end like him.

'Just passing through, John?' he said hopefully, as they greeted each other awkwardly.

'No, no,' Friend replied cheerfully. 'I've been assigned to this one. The Agent X outbreak. Making sure there's no legal come-back when it's all done and dusted. We'll be working together again. I'll rather enjoy that. And, look, here comes our escort.'

Luke turned to see a young woman walking towards them, her ID badge swaying on its lanyard. She introduced herself, then led them down a corridor and through MI5's Knowledge and Information Centre, its in-house library of open source material. Luke felt his spirits sink lower still. The bald fact was he knew next to nothing about far-right extremism. He sensed that a world of warrants and digital paperwork beckoned, and now he was about to have this lawyer peering over his shoulder every minute of the day. Christ, he actually missed Afghanistan.

67

No. 10 Downing Street
Tuesday, 15 March, 0901hrs GMT

BRENDAN HOLMES HAD requested an urgent meeting with the PM and he had got it. As the government's chief medical officer, it was his duty, along with the chief scientific adviser, to keep his prime minister appraised of every possible development in the threat from Agent X, and this, he thought, could not wait.

With his vehicle registration details phoned through in advance, he was swiftly cleared through the armed police cordon that ringed the historic home of Britain's prime ministers since 1735. Let in through the back entrance facing St James's Park, he made his way up the staircase lined with photographs of past prime ministers. A butler took his coat and offered him tea or coffee while he waited. He declined. Ten minutes later he was shown into a room where the PM sat at his desk, scribbling away with a fountain pen. He could see a cup of tea steaming beside him on the desk, a soggy slice of lemon resting on its saucer.

'Brendan.' The PM looked up and gave him a tired smile. 'Take a pew, will you? I'll just be a tick.'

'Prime Minister.' As chief medical officer, Holmes had had plenty of occasions to get to know the PM, but the two men had never been close. Their conversations often began like this.

'Well? Let's have it,' the PM said briskly, putting away his fountain pen and regarding Holmes across the desk. 'Do we have this outbreak thing under control yet or not?'

Holmes looked down at the patterned carpet and briefly studied its weft and weave before replying. 'No, I'm afraid we don't. So far, this pathogen has infected four of our own citizens that we know of. That's our two Arctic researchers – they have both sadly succumbed – plus a shop assistant from Surrey and an A & E nurse from Epsom General. They're both in intensive care right now.'

'Right.' The PM seemed distracted as he allowed himself a quick glance at his watch. 'I think I already knew this, Brendan. Was there anything else? Because I've got the EU trade commissioner coming in twelve minutes. Not that I wouldn't rather listen to you, believe me.'

'Yes, there is.' Holmes inched his chair a little closer to the prime minister, trying to keep him focused. He found it hard to understand how anyone, especially the PM, couldn't see that this was more important than any other matters of state. 'Chris Coppinger,' he said. 'Does that name ring a bell?'

'Nope.' The PM studied him with a blank expression. 'Should it?'

'Well, Coppinger is – or, rather, was – the second Arctic scientist to fall ill with the virus.'

'Awful. Just awful.' The PM looked at him wearily. The minutes were ticking by. 'I think I read that somewhere in the brief. Tragic.'

'Well, the point is this, Prime Minister. Coppinger took his own life, but right before he did that he placed a call to a medical colleague at the Marsden. He knew he was infected and he wanted people to know that this virus, this Agent X as we're calling it, is a lot more virulent than we thought. You see, Coppinger had actually *been* tested and he came up negative. The antibodies simply didn't show up. The virus had hidden itself.'

'Oh, Christ. This is worse than Covid.'

'Exactly,' Holmes concurred. 'And there's another thing.'

'Which is?'

Holmes could see he had the PM's full attention now, but the man was still giving him a wary look. 'The CFR rate is off the scale.' He shook his head. 'We've never seen anything like it.'

The PM made no attempt to hide his exasperation. 'Brendan! I've told you before, I don't do science. Please stop throwing acronyms at me. What on earth is a CFR when it's at home?'

'Oh, yes, sorry. It's what we call the case fatality rate. It's the percentage of deaths per number of cases of infection. So, if we take the WHO report on monkey pox in the Democratic Republic of Congo in 2020, for example, the CFR was just two per cent for the whole country. But this chimera, this Agent X, seems to have a near-hundred per cent mortality rate. Basically, whoever gets it dies. We haven't seen anyone survive it yet.'

For a long moment the PM just stared at him as he took this in. 'So what's your conclusion?'

'I've discussed this with Joint Biosecurity and with Porton Down. There's only one conclusion we can reach.'

'And that is?'

He saw that the PM had loosened his tie and was rolling up his sleeves. Probably a good sign that he was taking this seriously. 'And that is, PM, that whoever engineered this synthetic virus deliberately built in a symbel.'

'A what?'

'A symbel. It's an old Saxon word for "feast", but in this case it's a technical term for deliberately unpredictable diagnostics. Meaning that the normal screening procedures simply don't work. To quote our former home secretary John Reid, they're not "fit for purpose". A negative result can show up positive, and vice versa. It's specifically designed to confuse.'

'Christ . . . Well, this doesn't sound like the work of amateurs. I've only just written a letter of apology to the Russian foreign minister. I hope you're not about to tell me this was made in one of the Kremlin's labs after all?'

'We actually need the Russians in on this one. Yes, they are part of the problem, but if we play this right they can also be part of the solution. Patient Zero came from *their* colony at Barents-burg on the Svalbard archipelago. Plus they know an awful lot more about biological warfare than they're letting on.'

The PM regarded him with one eyebrow slightly raised.

'You see, Prime Minister, we're not talking about a couple of incompetent thugs smearing Novichok nerve agent on a door handle in Salisbury here. This is a sophisticated pathogen – a people killer. If this thing got into the Russian population . . . well, with their crumbling health system they'd be in a far worse spot than we are right now. They could barely cope with Covid-19, let alone something like this. And the modellers think we're only at the bottom of the upward curve. Which could mean we're about to see a massive spike in cases.'

'I see.' The PM tapped his fingernails repeatedly on the surface of his desk while he thought for a moment. 'So, Brendan, I'm sure you haven't come here to tell me this in isolation. Are you about to recommend what we do about it?'

Brendan Holmes took a deep breath before answering: he knew this was a long shot. 'What I'm going to suggest, Prime Minister, might sound counterintuitive, but I think it's the only way forward. We're going to have to ask Moscow for their help.'

68

Thames House, London
Tuesday, 15 March, 0917hrs GMT

'CHRISTCHURCH ... EL PASO ... CHARLESTON ... Finsbury Park ... Hanau in Germany. The list of far-right extremist – or what we tend to call FRE – attacks around the world is growing. Exponentially.'

The woman addressing the packed room that morning could have come from any one of a hundred different professions. Her ash-blonde hair was neatly tied back, and her clothes were smart but not overly dressy. She wore only the faintest hint of make-up. There was nothing about her, other than her ID card on its lanyard, that announced to the world that this person, Louise Band, was a spook, a senior intelligence officer in the Security Service.

'So what unifies them, these far-right extremists?' she asked the room. 'I'll tell you. It's an ideology of hatred, founded in fascism, racism, anti-immigration, nationalism or xenophobia. And sometimes all of the above.'

They were ten minutes into the briefing at Thames House, MI5's London headquarters. No preliminaries, just the swiftest of introductions so everyone on the teams knew the parameters of the operation. In MI5 investigations the agent runners, the men and women at the sharp end who run the covert human informants, are kept separate from investigating officers. The firewall between them is so strict that the investigating officer on a case does not even have access to the database of agents involved; she or he is expected to make their own independent judgements. So, that morning, Luke and Jenny were sitting deliberately apart, on different sides of the briefing room. He found himself next to a Norwegian intelligence officer seconded from the NIS in Oslo; Jenny was beside a data analyst from GCHQ.

'Since we're all going to be working on this together,' said Louise Band, 'I need to bring you up to speed on what we know about FREs. And, believe me, we've been on a steep learning curve ourselves since we took this over from the Met, back in 2019. Most of us here in the Security Service have transferred from G Branch where we've been covering international counter-terrorism. Some of the methodologies we've been using there are equally applicable in dealing with far-right terrorism. Others have not worked so well.'

Luke was close enough to the front to see her purse her lips at this point. Was she remembering, perhaps, some of the early assumptions about this home-grown ideology that had turned out to be wrong?

'But I can tell you,' she continued, 'that today FRE terrorism has become the fastest-growing domestic threat we face here in the UK. In 2018, the year we started to really notice the uptick, we saw a thirty-seven per cent spike in far-right referrals to government and by the end of 2019, we had as many subjects of interest from the far right being referred to deradicalization programmes as we did jihadists. Now . . .' she removed a small ball of white fluff that had attached itself to the sleeve of her jacket '. . . what's happened on Svalbard has taken us into a whole new arena and, frankly, we're still sprinting to catch up. Until now FRE attack planning in this country has been pretty basic, what I would call "Terrorism 1.0". Crude pipe bombs, knives, the odd bit of arson targeting a mosque. Not that I'd want for a moment,' she spread her hands in a placatory gesture, 'anyone in this room to think I'm playing it down, because I'm not. These groups have been busy. We know they've been studying the tactics of ISIS and reading their manuals online. But this? A departure into bio-terrorism? This is a whole new ball game and it is, if you'll pardon my French, serious shit.'

Louise Band paused to take a sip from a cup of water, a green, reusable eco-cup, Luke noticed. He reminded himself to hurry up and get one before someone reprimanded him for not using one.

'Okay,' she continued, wiping her lips with a paper tissue. 'So what exactly, you might ask, is this extremist ideology of theirs based on?' She looked around the room, then answered her own question before anyone else had a chance to. 'You know, with ISIS, it was relatively simple. It was all about reviving the Caliph-ate in some form or other, punishing anyone who got in their way, then putting those punishments online as a warning to others.' She started to pace up and down at the front of the room. There was really not much to relieve the eye in this place, Luke noted. Just a single massive TV screen at one end, a clock, a long, horseshoe-shaped table around which they all sat, and a row of barred, shaded windows. The bland, functional business of counter-terrorism.

'But these guys,' Louise Band continued, 'the right-wing extremists? Well, they're big on conspiracy theories. Who here has heard of the great replacement theory?'

A few hands went up. She scanned the room, nodding in appreciation. 'Good,' she said. 'Okay, that's a good start. So this is one of their core beliefs. It's the idea that Europe's white Western Christian population is being systematically replaced across Europe – at a cultural level – by Muslims from the Middle East and sub-Saharan Africans crossing the Mediterranean on rafts. Yes, ma'am, you have a question?'

It was the data analyst from GCHQ. A slim woman with thin lips and no jewellery that Luke could see. He put her age at about thirty-five.

'Well . . .' She hesitated. Luke wondered if she already regret-ted speaking up. 'They do have a point there, don't they?' Silence in the room as all eyes turned towards her. 'I mean,' she pressed on, 'Germany did let in one and a half million migrants – sorry, refugees – from Syria in 2015. That's surely changed the character of a whole nation and—'

'Okay, let me stop you there.' Louise Band took a few paces towards her and she was wagging her finger. 'This is a question for another time,' she said briskly. 'We are here this morning to address an urgent terrorist threat. A threat from the sort of mind-set inhabited by people like Anders Breivik, the man who shot dead dozens of young people on a Norwegian island in 2011. So, if there are no further questions let's continue.'

That was an odd intervention, Luke thought. He exchanged a discreet glance with Jenny, then took a long look at the data analyst. He noticed she was staring at her notebook and blushing.

'Right, so, on top of the great replacement theory,' continued the MI5 briefer, 'you've got the white genocide theory. This was something the neo-Nazis in the US got exercised about, back in the seventies. They reckoned there was an actual plot to wipe out white people through racial integration. I know, I know,' she put up her hands theatrically, 'sounds crazy, right? But these ideas *are* coming back and they're being propagated daily through online manifestos. Who in here has heard of 8Chan?'

Everyone nodded, including the Norwegian intelligence officer sitting next to Luke.

'All of you? Good. So before it got closed down, 8Chan was the web forum where a lot of people shared their extreme ideas and even posted manifestos. And here there are definite commonalities with ISIS in the way they put out their propaganda. They create content – extremist material, if you will – and they put it out on social-media platforms.'

Luke noticed Jenny was busy scribbling everything down while he was trying his best to commit all this to memory. He was certain she would have come top of every class at school, a sort of latterday Hermione Granger. And there, sitting quietly on the opposite side of the horseshoe table, was John Friend, the Service lawyer, also scribbling diligently away and constantly looking something up in a pamphlet he kept retrieving from his inside jacket pocket.

'When people comment on this material on social media,' the briefer was saying, 'that's when they try to lure them on to the encrypted apps. And *that* is where the conversations take on a more violent turn – you know, people talking about what they'd like to do to others.'

It was Luke's turn to put up his hand. 'Sorry,' he said, and now all eyes swivelled towards him. 'Can you be a bit more specific about who you mean by "they"?'

'Ah.' Louise Band pointed a finger straight at him. 'Good question. Right, so, yes, there is no single cohesive group. We're basically talking about a lot of disconnected splinter groups with different grievances but all united by hate. I can tell you, some of the stuff they talk about online is nothing short of sick. Torture, Satanic snuff rituals and so on. Fortunately nearly all of it never gets beyond the aspiration stage. It's fantasy rather than actual operational planning.'

'And WaffenKrieg90?' Luke asked.

The silence lasted several seconds. He wondered if maybe he had mispronounced the group's name. He looked across at Jenny, who gave him a supportive shrug. Louise Band looked surprised. 'We haven't released that name yet,' she said, sounding somewhat flustered. 'Right now, as of this moment, we have almost no information on WaffenKrieg90. We're starting from a blank page.'

69

Novosibirsk, Russia
Tuesday, 15 March, 0934hrs GMT, 1634hrs local

DAPPLED, DIFFUSED AND filtered through the snow-laden branches of the Siberian forest firs, the weak sun cast jagged shadows on the path before them. Colonel Arkady Petrov's boots made a crisp, crunching sound as he walked. He was not a man to make rash, sudden decisions. He had spent the morning mulling over the courses open to him. Neither was attractive.

'So we can do this in one of two ways,' he said, stooping to remove a fallen branch that blocked their path. The man beside him rushed to help, but was just too late. Colonel Petrov threw him a glance and straightened up. He knew he had this man exactly where he wanted him. All he had to do now was press home his advantage.

'Aleksei . . .' He threw a paternal arm around his shoulders, the python enveloping its prey. In the brief twenty-four hours since he had landed in Siberia their relationship had changed, perceptibly for the better, as far as he was concerned. Gone was the bristling, defensive hostility from the resident head of security at this remote, secretive biological research establishment. Aleksei was now indebted to him, the GRU man from Moscow. That much was evident, because the understanding was there between them. The colonel was making it very clear that it would take just one phone call from him and Aleksei would find himself in a whole world of pain. He had him by the balls.

'So listen,' Petrov continued, brushing a sprinkle of freshly fallen snow off his jacket, 'I can call it in, yes? And what would I tell them in Moscow? Hmm?' He turned towards the man beside him, noting the vein pulsing in his temple. 'That it was your signature – yes, *your* signature alone – on that transfer document for the smallpox vials. And I think we both know how this would go from there, don't we?'

Aleksei didn't answer, his face blank as he looked straight ahead while they continued their walk through the woods. Petrov decided he would take this silence to mean agreement.

'You would be arrested, obviously,' went on Petrov, walking more slowly now. He didn't want this local security man to miss a word. 'You would be . . . questioned, extensively . . . by my people, among others. In fact, I think there would be a queue. Then comes the trial, the sentencing, the transfer to a prison colony on an island in the Arctic. You will lose your career, your pension, your freedom. Your family will be disgraced and ostracized and your daughter – her name is Olga, I believe – would have to move schools, but, believe me, the scandal would follow her wherever she goes.'

Petrov stopped and faced him. He could see the vein in Aleksei's temple pulsing ever more rapidly now. His cheeks were sucked in and his lips were pursed.

'Or . . .' The GRU man lightened his tone as he brushed the snow off the stump of a fallen tree, sat down on it and took out a packet of Ziganov cigarettes. 'Or we do this a different way,' he told Aleksei.

'I'm listening,' Aleksei said at last, almost the first words he had spoken since they'd begun their walk in the woods. Petrov was in no hurry to reply – he was starting to enjoy this. There was a long pause as the colonel took off his gloves and flicked his lighter several times until the flame caught, the cigarette was lit and he took a long drag, without offering any to the other man.

Petrov regarded him, squinting through the blue cloud of cigarette smoke that hung in the chill, sub-zero air before drifting away into the pine woods that encircled them. Aleksei's bulky stature and pugnacious boxer's demeanour didn't count for much now. He was outgunned and outwitted by Petrov, who carried the weight and the menace of the GRU First Directorate with him.

Petrov had spent a busy morning logging on to the GRU files, finding out what he needed to know. Being a colonel in Russian Military Intelligence had its benefits and its privileges, as well as its sacrifices. All that secrecy and double-talk, so tedious at times, but so worth it. And, of course, he was serving Mother Russia. His country that he loved so dearly, his country that had been so badly treated and humiliated by the treacherous and imperialist West. All the grovelling and sucking-up to Washington by that shameless drunkard Yeltsin in the 1990s while greedy Western capitalists flew in and plundered his country's natural resources. *Ublyudki!* Bastards! God, it made him sick. And to think that we let their scientific inspectors into our secret biological programmes at Biopreparat? It was nothing short of treason. Well, thank heaven the rot had been stopped. Now the West and its plans had been unmasked. It was plain for all to see that everything it did, every foreign policy move, every NATO exercise, it was all designed to damage Russia, to humiliate and subjugate its citizens. That was why Russia needed a GRU. And that was why the GRU needed him, Arkady Petrov, accomplished expert in the art of chemical, biological, radiological and nuclear warfare.

He stubbed out his cigarette on the side of the tree stump, flicking it into the snow, then stood up abruptly. 'I'm giving you three days,' Petrov told him. 'I want the names, all of them. I want the dates, the details, the quantities right down to the last millilitre. I want nothing left out. You will find out exactly what happened to that missing smallpox vial and where it is now.' He studied the other man's face, watching for his reaction. There was none.

'And then?' Aleksei replied at last.

'And then I will decide what to do with your case. The more information you provide now, the easier it will go for you. But remember, three days, that's all.' Petrov rolled back the sleeve of his jacket and peered at his watch. 'And the clock starts now,' he added.

70

Near Braintree, Essex
Tuesday, 15 March, 0952hrs GMT

THE LARGE MAN in the Barbour jacket drove fast along the lanes as soon as he got the phone call. So his people had found the missing monkey. That was a relief. The fact that the animal appeared to have died of its infection was also a validation: the pathogen that had invaded its cells was clearly every bit as virulent as the Cambridge team had said it was. It still didn't explain who had cut the chain around its neck and released it, but now they had a more immediate problem: the lad who had picked it up and handled it had become an immediate potential health hazard to all of them. It was a problem that was going to have to be fixed with some urgency.

He pulled up in a lay-by and walked the last two hundred metres, hunched against the drizzle with the long beige canvas bag slung over his shoulder. He found them all standing around in a huddle, some distance from the solitary figure and the pathetic mound of dead fur on the ground beside it. They had been waiting for instructions.

'Anyone come past yet?' he asked.

'No, boss.'

'And no one's phoned for an ambulance?'

'No, boss. You told us not to.'

'That's right.' He patted the nearest man on the shoulder. 'Good boy.' He looked beyond him, selected two others and sent them down the road to make sure no traffic was coming. Couldn't afford to have anyone see what was about to happen. Then he picked out one more, a man in his late twenties with a goatee and a faded tattoo on his neck, and whispered instructions in his ear. The man nodded and went off to address the rest of the group. Within minutes they had all dispersed, moving back some two hundred metres and out of sight behind a hedge. Now there was just the beleaguered lad, still standing over the dead macaque some distance away, and him, the big man with the long canvas bag. The lad had his back to him.

He chose his position carefully – had to get this right first time, couldn't afford any more cock-ups. With a grunt he got down on his belly just behind a damp tussock of grass, reached beside him and carefully unsheathed the hunting rifle, a Remington 700 with a scratched-off serial number and a folding bipod beneath the stock. Designed to take down a stag at a range of half a mile, it was rather more powerful than was needed today, but still, it would do the job. The big man didn't know the lad who had got himself into this mess but, frankly, it wouldn't have made any difference if he had. He chambered a round, brought the butt up into the shoulder, closed one eye and steadied his breathing. The lad still had his back to him, just standing there in the drizzle, smoking a cigarette. He was pleased to see that, because he had no reason to want to make him suffer: this was strictly business, nothing personal.

'Cheerio, old son,' the big man said to himself, as his right index finger very gently increased its pressure on the trigger. There was a single crack as the 7mm projectile left the barrel, flying through the air at 756 metres a second. At a range of just 150 metres he was hardly going to miss. He watched through the telescopic sight as the young man pitched violently forward, as if punched from behind by a giant invisible hand. He waited a full thirty seconds, watching for any movement. There was none.

The problem had been dealt with; Cambridge could be notified. Everything was back on track.

247

71

Thames House, London
Tuesday, 15 March, 1110hrs GMT

INSIDE MI5'S LONDON headquarters Operation Methuen was ramping up into fifth gear. Two teams were being deployed, one upstairs on the third floor, one at ground level. In the final minutes before they went off on their separate ways the overall mission statement was read out to them in the Central Briefing Room – twice – by the authorizing officer, the final reminder, as if anyone needed it, of the extreme urgency of what they needed to do.

'Our job,' he reminded them, 'is to acquire the timely intelligence needed to prevent WaffenKrieg90 from releasing the viral pathogen Agent X in the UK. Everything you do, every minute of every day from now until this is over, should be given over to that task. I want each and every one of you to eat, sleep and breathe this mission as if nothing else matters. Any questions?'

Listening to this in the briefing room, Luke was momentarily transported back to another instant like this, another time, in a place thousands of miles away from the hushed corridors of Whitehall. His final pre-mission briefing in Kandahar, Afghanistan, before a Taliban bullet ripped his middle finger off at the joint. Luke had been fortunate that day – it could have been a whole lot worse – and, knowing that his luck was not going to hold much longer, he had quit the SBS and hung up his boots. But was his life now really any safer? Only two days ago someone had very nearly succeeded in killing him in that quiet street in Vilnius. He shook himself back to the present. The authorizing officer had said his piece and was heading out of the door. Luke, as an agent runner, was automatically assigned to the ground-floor team. Jenny Li, with her scientific and analytical background, was dispatched to the investigative team up on the third floor. Luke grunted as he noticed that John Friend, the SIS Service lawyer, was remaining close by, down here with him on the ground floor.

'Staying to keep an eye on me, John?' he asked him.

'Not at all,' the lawyer replied, snapping shut his laptop. 'We're all on the same team, aren't we? We're all friends here.'

Brilliant, Luke thought. We're racing to track down a team of sociopaths planning to release an apocalyptic bio-weapon on the streets of Britain and I'm saddled with some box-ticking lawyer. But then he reminded himself that if things went wrong, and in his experience they usually did, he'd need the legal top cover provided by someone like Friend. And he had to admit he was still trying to get his head round the different way the Security Service did things from what he was used to on an SIS operation. To Luke, the hierarchy of this investigation seemed laborious, even needlessly bureaucratic. As he returned to his seat and fired up his laptop he ran through the structure in his head. At the top was the authorizing officer, the man who had just delivered them the mission statement and sent them all on their way. If Operation Methuen went belly-up for any reason, the buck stopped with him.

So, who came next? He had to think for a second or two. The controller, that was it. This was the manager who had to make the judgement call on what measures were 'necessary and proportionate', a phrase that seemed positively to bounce off the walls everywhere he went inside MI5's Thames House. The controller, Luke reminded himself, was also the person that he, as an agent runner, was now directly reporting to when meeting and debriefing informants.

But there were yet more layers to this human pyramid, he

remembered. On the next rung down were the investigative officers or 'desk officers' (such a dreary-sounding name for such a vitally important job, he thought). This was the big team sitting out of sight, upstairs in the situation room, analysing and assessing the material that he and others were bringing in from the sharp end. They must already have been going through the information he'd brought back from Lithuania.

So that left the most important elements of all: the agent, the case, the source. Everyone here at MI5 seemed to refer to them as 'the CHIS' – the covert human intelligence source. And this had become his world, his domain, ever since he'd been selected for the MI6 agent-running course down at the Fort. With the ground-floor room in Thames House now half emptied, Luke moved to a seat closer to the front. One of the controllers was addressing the agent runners who remained.

'It's important,' he was saying, 'to baseline why we're doing this. Operation Methuen is a Tier One national priority. We are reacting well past our comfort zone here. You'll all be working your cases hard to generate penetrative insight into this network's mindset and physical locations. And you're not alone,' the controller continued. 'The Met are working with us on this from the get-go to find the best evidential package that will deliver successful prosecutions. And let's not forget the lawyers.' That'll be the day, Luke thought. 'Our legal advisers will be keeping a careful eye on our ethical obligations to our agents throughout this case. I realize some of the people you'll be dealing with are, to put it mildly, somewhat unsavoury, but we still have a duty of care to them.'

The controller looked up towards the ceiling and closed his eyes, as if remembering a past operation that had not gone to plan. 'We all know,' he said, looking back at the room again, 'that agent reporting can generate intelligence we can't get through technical means. Only an agent can reveal the attack planning that's not visible through surveillance. But that doesn't mean . . .' he stopped and made a theatrical gesture with his hand towards the frosted glass panes '. . . that we can simply throw our agents' rights out of the window when it suits us. Now . . . I'm going to leave you to talk through your cases with your OPSYs. We meet back here at five.'

Luke scanned the room. He hadn't yet met his operational security adviser. The person who sits outside the official hierarchy of an investigation so he or she can focus on the security of the agent and the public. 'Have a think,' someone had once said to Luke, 'what it would mean for your agent if everyone in your target network got arrested except for him. Their cover would be totally blown, wouldn't it? You'd have to rehouse him or her and then you've lost your source. So your OPSY is there to stop you making a mistake like that.'

Luke spotted her as she made her way over to him. Young, early thirties, with a nose ring.

'Luke? Michaela Norton.' She flashed him a smile as she introduced herself. Was there a slight trace of a northern accent?

'I'm afraid you might have drawn the short straw here,' Luke said.

'And why's that?'

'Well, I work across the river, which I'm sure you know, so . . . my agent isn't in this country, he's overseas.'

'You're talking about Earl Grey?' she replied brightly. 'Yes, I've read the file, Luke. That was nice work in Lithuania.' Michaela cocked her head to one side for a moment. 'But I'm afraid the fact he's over there doesn't mean you can get rid of me quite that easily. As your OPSY on this case, I'm still going to be hovering over your shoulder regardless of whether your man is in Timbuktu or Tooting.'

'Understood.' Luke nodded. He liked her. She may have been a few years younger than him but she exuded a quiet, no-nonsense professionalism. Rather like his line manager, Angela, but with smiles.

'Relax, I don't bite,' she said. 'Let me get you a coffee and we can discuss how we're going to keep Earl Grey one step ahead of the people he's betraying.'

251

72

Cambridge Science Park, England
Tuesday, 15 March, 1321hrs GMT

LOTTI JAMES HAD finished work early for the day. She walked up to her car, looked quickly around her, then got in and drove slowly out of Cambridge Science Park, sticking carefully to the speed limit. Her nerves were on edge. There was still so much that could go wrong. Like that business with the monkey. Well, at least that problem was solved now – this morning's phone call had come as a relief. But, still, she had to do something about the pent-up tension – maybe pop something from the bathroom cabinet when she got home.

And where had all the anger come from? It was a question she often asked herself and she thought about it now as she turned the corner by the Tesco Express and drove slowly past the mosque, the community centre and the newsagent on the next corner. A straight-A student with a flair for science and a gift for modern languages, Lotti James had never been in any kind of trouble at school. At least, not until the time she was accused of writing something unrepeatable about Jews, Muslims and the 'N-word' on the door of the girls' toilet in the school gym. She denied it, of course, and they were never quite able to pin it on her, but from then on she knew she needed to be a lot more careful.

It's possible, she admitted to herself, that her rock-solid belief in her own racial superiority – and the contempt and hatred that came with it – would have quietly faded away had she not gone to study in Germany. But the prospect of enrolling for an MSc in molecular biology at Tübingen University, one of the foremost in its field, was just too good to pass up. And it was there, in her first year at the Interfaculty Institute of Microbiology and Infection Medicine, that she had met the man who would change her life. Professor Schultze was a brilliant scientist, revered by his students, and he had taken a special interest in the English girl who had chosen his course. Long after the lectures had ended she would stay on and listen to him for hours, hanging on his every word, their conversations migrating first from the lab to the campus canteen, then on to cafés in town and finally to his antique, hand-crafted bed.

It was after the third time they'd slept together that he invited her to come to a meeting. It was not about science, he warned her, it was about something else, something he believed would intrigue her, but he was cryptic about just what it was. She was surprised at first to find herself being frisked at the door by a big man with bulging biceps and close-cropped blond hair. 'What are you looking for?' she had asked.

'Microphones, recording devices, anything that shows you are a journalist or an "unwanted person",' had been the reply.

She was even more surprised by what followed. When the doors were closed behind them and the meeting began, everyone stood stiffly to attention and threw out a Nazi salute while martial music blared from the speakers on the wall.

'It's the "Horst Wessel",' explained her professor, after the last chorus of 'Die Fahne Hoch' had faded and everyone had taken their seats. 'It was the anthem of the Nazi Party until 1945,' he said, giving her hand a squeeze. 'For all of us here it speaks of a better time, a time when Germany was racially pure, before we got infected by all these Turks and Syrians and people from Africa.'

Lotti James was shocked initially – was all this really

permitted in this day and age? Apparently so, if you were with the right people. And she knew, right there in that moment, that these were the right people for her. After that her professor took her to other meetings in other towns, and in the university holidays they attended rallies in eastern Germany, the part of the country that had previously been behind the Iron Curtain and governed by the Communists. She met people from all over Europe and even the US, people who shared the same ideals but often disagreed on the best ways to achieve them. When her course at Tübingen ended she graduated close to the top of her class and it was then that Professor Schultze introduced her to a select group of microbiologists, men and women from Britain, Norway, Germany, Russia and Lithuania, all working in secret on a very specialized project.

With her proven skills in the laboratory, and an endorsement from Professor Schultze, Lotti James was warmly welcomed into their circle. Three months later she was admitted into the group calling itself WaffenKrieg90. And now, as she drove home from her place of work and her cover job in Cambridge Science Park, she felt a shiver of excitement that everything they were working towards, all the ideals and dreams they held so dear, was drawing close to fruition.

73

BLINIS. HE ABSOLUTELY loved his blinis. Couldn't have enough of them. Not that anyone could ever make them like his mother used to, but, still, it was one of life's little luxuries that Colonel Arkady Petrov could never do without. And he was getting impatient for them now. How long had he been sitting in this empty hotel cafeteria, waiting for the kitchen to bring him exactly what he had ordered? Warm, they must be warm, and topped with cream cheese, mashed potato and sour cream. Preferably a sprinkling of caviar, too, but he didn't trust them to deliver on that all the way out here in Siberia.

Petrov took a swig from the vodka glass and nodded to himself. Yes, this afternoon's conversation in the woods had gone well. He had been right to make this trip. When his phone rang he could see it was a Moscow number, but not one he recognized. He thought about letting it ring. He had kept to a minimum the number of people in the directorate who knew of this visit to VECTOR, out here in the frozen east. Tomorrow he would be flying back to Moscow anyway so, really, could it not wait? Irritated now, he picked up his glass, tossed his head back, draining the last of the vodka, and took the call.

Seconds later there was a tinkling sound as the vodka glass shattered on the linoleum floor beneath his feet. A waiter came running over, but Colonel Petrov waved him away and turned his back on him. When the phone call ended the GRU colonel let out a groan of exasperation and rage.

'*Verolomstvo!*' he said out loud. 'Treachery!' He had just been ordered to do something he had never, in his entire career, thought remotely possible. And the very idea sickened him. But orders were orders and Colonel Arkady Petrov, Russian patriot to the core of his soul and foremost expert on chemical and biological warfare in the GRU, had just been given his.

At the direction of the Kremlin, he was to cooperate with a British-led investigation into the pathogen outbreak on the Arctic archipelago of Svalbard.

74

Thames House, London
Wednesday, 16 March, 0852hrs GMT

'MR CARLTON? THE DG would like to see you.' An eager young
graduate, intercepting him in the foyer, just past security. 'Oh, and
your colleague Ms Li is already up there.' Of course she is. Probably reported for duty at 0600.

The director-general of MI5, the Security Service, had a
pedigree stretching back over three decades. Margaret Stratton,
known as 'Marge', but never to her face, had spent four years running International Counter-Terrorism. Before that, seven years in
Counter-Espionage, trying to stop the Russians and the Chinese
nicking Britain's secrets. Before that, several years at the sharp
end, running informants into extremist groups, and a stint across
the water in Northern Ireland. Agent runners didn't normally
make it all the way to the top in MI5 so Marge was something of
a mould-breaker. She had only screwed up once, making a wrong
call on an agent who turned out to be working for the other side.
Deeply embarrassing at the time and she had duly offered her
resignation, which had been refused. Thereafter it had been a
steady ascent to the top.

Luke was 'delivered' upstairs to the spacious outer office,
where he stood making pointless small talk with the boss's PA

until he was buzzed in. Despite its size, the place seemed sparser than her MI6 equivalent's across the river, somehow more functional, less exotic. He remembered his uncle telling him how rude MI6 officers used to be about their Security Service colleagues in the old days, calling them 'glorified coppers'. Well, those days were long gone now. The two agencies worked hand-in-glove on countless cases.

The director-general came out from behind her desk and welcomed him. Black trousers, white top beneath a striking leopard-print jacket with a gold crocodile pinned to the lapel; she had a surprisingly warm smile for someone in her position. Luke and Jenny nodded to each other.

'We're sending you both to Moscow,' announced Margaret Stratton, abruptly, the moment they were seated. Luke looked across at Jenny, but her features remained impassive; she didn't turn to him. Which he took to mean she must already have been told this.

'The PM's decided we're going to have to work with the Russians on this one. They have as much to lose from this outbreak as we do and they know things we need to know.' 'Marge' was perched on the edge of her chair facing them as she said this, looking from one to the other. The light glinted on her gold brooch each time she moved. 'Between the pair of you,' she continued, 'I have complete confidence that you have the appropriate skill-sets for this job.' She used the word 'job' like it was something mundane and ordinary. 'You'll be going in declared. Moscow already knows who you work for. But I'm afraid that means the Russians will gather and store all your biometrics. Now, we've cleared this with Security Branch at VX, but if either of you has any personal objections, then now is the time to raise them.' Again, the disarming smile. This time it was Jenny who gave Luke a look, raising one sculpted eyebrow at him. He shrugged. If it was already cleared with his bosses at Vauxhall, who was he to object?

'No, ma'am,' he said.

'Good. I thought not. So . . .'

The director-general got up from her chair and started to pace around the room. 'This mission would be sensitive at any time – sending in two of our intelligence officers declared like this – but there is an added factor here. Russia has an indigenous far-right extremist community of its own and we believe some of them have covert links to the Russian government. There's an individual in St Petersburg, for example, who's on the FBI wanted list. He's sitting there beyond their reach in Russia, wearing an "I love Putin" T-shirt and directing a whole damn online network in the States with the Kremlin watching his back for him. Which means you're going to have to watch *your* backs and be ultra-careful who you talk to.'

'Understood, ma'am.' Luke didn't want to show it, but he was getting increasingly impatient to know the mission. This preamble was going on too long for his liking.

Just as he was thinking this the DG walked back to her desk, returning with a sheaf of A4-size documents. 'I want you to get into bed with a certain GRU colonel,' she said, dividing the documents into two and handing them to him and Jenny. 'Not literally, obviously,' she continued, 'but I want you to get close to him. You'll be working with this man.' She leaned forward and tapped the documents she had just handed him. 'He's Colonel Arkady Petrov, their principal authority on CBRN and, by all accounts, a nasty piece of work. But right now we need him. We need to know everything he knows about covert bio-warfare programmes getting into the wrong hands and who in this country might be on the receiving end. There's only so much we can glean through SIGINT intercepts. In the end, we need to send in real people and that's where you both come in.'

Luke cleared his throat to interrupt her.

'Yes, Luke?'

'Forgive me if this is a dumb question,' he began, 'but surely we represent the enemy to this guy. Aren't we everything he's spent his whole career working against? Why would he—'

Margaret Stratton held up her hand to stop him mid-sentence. 'I hear you, Luke. You don't need to say any more. It's a perfectly reasonable question. But as I was telling Jenny just before you came in, this has already been signed off at a political level. Above my pay grade, if you catch my drift.' Her eyes flicked momentarily to her left, in the direction of Whitehall.

'I see,' Luke replied. 'Timings?'

Instinctively, she looked up at the clock on the wall. 'Well, you won't make the ten-fifteen BA flight,' she said. 'Which is just as well as Q Branch south of the river want a piece of you for the next few hours. They need to take you through how you're going to manage secure comms without our Russian friends listening in to every single word.'

She said it with such a bright, radiant smile it almost came across as a joke, when everyone in that room knew exactly how serious this was. Russian signals surveillance and penetration were formidable. Already lives had been lost in Syria and Ukraine from conversations overheard that were never supposed to be.

'So you leave tonight,' she said. 'My PA will give you all the details on your way out, but I believe we've booked you on the twenty-one thirty-five BA flight into Domodedovo. It's a direct flight, now that the PM has rescinded that scale-back. But I'm afraid you still get into Moscow at some ungodly hour of the morning. Sorry about that, but I expect you're used to it.' She stood up, pulling at the hem of her jacket to straighten the creases. The meeting was over. 'Oh, and one last thing. I know I don't need to say this, but I'm going to say it anyway. Don't go getting yourselves into any compromising situations, will you?' She's trying not to look at me, Luke thought. Why do I feel this is being said for my benefit? 'Because the FSB will be watching every single thing you do from the second you step off that plane. They're still the KGB by another name.'

Luke and Jenny travelled down in the lift together, absorbed in their thoughts on the mission ahead. She had remained remarkably quiet all through that extended send-off and he wondered what was on her mind. He turned to her in the lift. 'First time in Russia?' he asked.

'Yep.'

'Same.' And for a fleeting moment he thought he saw her face soften. 'Are you nervous? That's natural if you are because—'

'Luke!' She cut him off. 'Please, spare me this . . . Thank you.'

When they reached the ground-floor lobby they encountered a familiar figure. It was John Friend, the Service lawyer from Vauxhall, and he seemed agitated. 'Ah, Carlton, thank God I've found you. I've been trying to track you down all morning.' A bit of an exaggeration, Luke thought, given that it was not yet 9.30 a.m. 'Look, um, I gather you're off to Moscow.'

'Word travels fast. Yes.'

'I'm terribly sorry, Luke, but I don't think you can go.'

'Why's that?'

'Well, you still haven't done your unconscious-bias course, have you? It's mandatory, you know, for all our staff. No exceptions.'

'Can't it wait until I'm back?'

'I don't think it can!' Friend looked genuinely distressed at the prospect. 'That would be breaking protocol.'

Luke put his hand on the lawyer's shoulder and gave it a friendly squeeze. 'Goodbye, John,' he told him, then walked on towards the exit. Out of the corner of his eye he could just see Jenny struggling not to smirk.

'Wait!' Friend protested, following after him. 'I'll have to report this, you know.'

'You do that, John,' Luke called back over his shoulder. 'I've got a plane to catch.'

75

Cambridge Science Park
Wednesday, 16 March, 0927hrs GMT

LOTTI JAMES PLACED the burner phone on the car seat beside her, a notepad balanced on her lap. She had it on speaker, which she knew was a risk of sorts, in the unlikely event that MI5 had the car bugged. But then so was almost any conversation she had anywhere at this juncture and Lotti James was very careful indeed with her choice of words. Every term she used sounded innocuous, bland enough, in fact, to stand up to scrutiny by the prosecution in any trial, yet each had a hidden meaning. Besides, she was confident that if her name had come up on anyone's radar by now their source on the inside would have tipped them off. Yes, the source was that well placed.

'We need to talk about "marketing",' she said.

'Marketing?' the disembodied voice at the other end of the line asked.

'Yes, marketing. The "sales brochure". We need to get the timing and distribution just right.'

'Agreed.'

'Because when this . . . product goes on sale to the public we need to be sure the market is ready for it. We want buyers prepped for maximum impact.'

'Oh, it'll do that, all right.'

'Good. I like your confidence. So what are we talking?'

'It's nearly ready for publication. Then it'll go out online. The page will go live just ahead of product launch for maximum effect.'

'Anything else? Projected sales figures?'

'Sorry, I would have thought that's more your department. All right, since you ask, we're aiming for at least five thousand units in the first week.'

'Here's hoping. See you at the Farm, then.'

Lotti James ended the call, carefully removed the SIM card from her phone, opened the door of her parked car and flicked it into the ditch, then started the engine. By the time anyone found it this would all be over.

She had heard exactly what she needed to hear. WaffenKrieg-90's manifesto was nearly ready to go online. The number of people projected to be lethally infected in the first week after the release in London was five thousand plus.

76

'PHOTONS . . .' THE MAN from Q Branch looked from Luke to Jenny and back again. 'Can either of you tell me what photons are?'

Luke stared back at him. He had absolutely no idea what photons were. They hadn't played a big part in his degree course in international relations.

'Aren't they particles of light?' Jenny said.

'Very good,' said the instructor. 'To be precise, they are polarized light particles, encrypted using a secret, random key, and they are crucial to what I'm about to tell you.'

Luke looked at her with admiration. It was easy to forget on jobs like this that Jenny had been a scientist long before she became an intelligence officer. They were down in the basement, two floors underneath the lobby of the Vauxhall Cross headquarters of the Secret Intelligence Service, visiting the mysterious part of MI6 that did the gadgets and tech. Luke remembered his uncle telling him that Q Branch had not always been called that. It used to be known as 'TOS', short for Technical Operational Services, until its boss complained that his team were fed up with being called 'Tossers'.

Now, with the Moscow mission looming within hours, a decision had been taken at the highest level to give Luke and Jenny a crash course in the very latest advances in encrypted communications.

'Quantum key distribution is a lot to take in so I'll try to keep this simple,' the man from Q Branch pressed on.

Please do, Luke thought, as he sensed he'd be well out of his depth in the next few minutes.

'So,' continued the boffin, warming to his subject now, 'even though you'll be working in tandem with our Russian "friends", make no mistake. They're going to be all over your comms like a rash. We can expect all three of their intelligence agencies – the GRU, the FSB and the SVR – to be doing their damnedest to get inside your devices and intercept every byte of data you send back. So how should you communicate securely? I'm going to show you.'

He took a couple of paces over to the white workbench next to him and picked up a smooth, flat object. 'Looks just like an ordinary smartphone, right?' He answered his own question with a knowing shake of his head and a waggle of his finger. 'Well, it isn't. This beauty is your transmitter. Not long ago it would have been about the size of a traditional stereo music amplifier, the sort of thing we had in our bedsits when I was growing up. But now, with a bit of input from the private sector, we've been making great strides in miniaturization these days. And this little baby will send—'

'An encrypted beam of photons?' Jenny cut in.

'Exactly! And they can only be decrypted by the receiver, which we operate.'

'But doesn't that require a fibre-optic cable?' Jenny said. 'You're not going to tell me we're using the Russian grid?'

The man from Q Branch gave a great belly-laugh, as if this was the best joke he'd heard in ages. 'No, that wouldn't be wise. Instead,' he held up a finger, pointing towards the ceiling, 'we use a low-orbiting satellite. The beam of photons will go straight up from your device into space, where it's picked up and bounced back to Earth, where our people then decode it using the same random key.'

'You've tested this in the field?' Luke asked.

'We have. Although I must admit, I think this is the first time we've used it in Russia. You'll need to keep it sheathed in one of these.' He picked up another object, a flat, black pouch with a Velcro fastening.

'A Faraday glove?' said Luke.

'Exactly. I'm sure you've used these on assignments. It stops anyone trying to remotely suck the data out of it using a stand-off device. So . . .' he rubbed his hands together '. . . let's run you through the operating manual, shall we?'

Luke glanced at his watch. If he could get through this tutorial inside two hours he reckoned he could just about squeeze in an hour or two with Elise before he left for the airport. He knew the timing was tight, but he was determined to try to set things on an even keel between them before he left. If he was going into Russia, the last thing he needed was to be worrying about whether he'd still have a girlfriend when he got home.

77

Peak District, Derbyshire
Wednesday, 16 March, 1615hrs GMT

UNSEEN BY THE motorists who sped, unknowing, along the
nearby A6 between the towns of Stockport, Buxton and Derby,
preparations were nearly complete at Abbot's Farm. Almost a
week had passed since Lotti James had carried out her tour of
inspection. A week in which much had changed. Thanks to the
accidental release up in Svalbard, the world now knew about
the hideous symptoms of the virus. The horror effect was just as
she had predicted: the newspapers had seen to that. But this was
just a little hors d'oeuvre, an *amuse bouche*, a teasing foretaste of
what they had planned. The number of those infected was still
minuscule and the health authorities – in Norway and in Britain –
had reacted with commendable speed. This limited outbreak was
probably something the authorities thought they had under
control.

Well, that was about to change.

At Abbot's Farm, the beds were now made up. Every 'chosen
survivor' of the biological apocalypse to come had been allocated
a bed space and a number. There were rosters for sentry duties,
specified times for patrolling the perimeter, individuals tasked

with checking on everything from the array of generators in the outhouse to the motion-sensor cameras on the gates.

And today a special package had arrived from Cambridge, driven up in person by a trusted member of WaffenKrieg90; it was far too sensitive to be consigned to the post. It was a last-minute precaution, something only to be handed out to everyone at the Farm if it all went wrong.

The package contained the goodnight pills.

78

LUKE'S SMALL CASE was packed and zipped up next to him as he sat waiting for Elise in the café on Duke Street, just south of Oxford Street. The place was popular with a clientele from the Gulf, and two young Arab women were poring excitedly over a message on their phones, cupping their freshly hennaed hands over their mouths as they shared a joke. The door swung open and Elise breezed in, earrings twinkling, and gave him a radiant smile. She was wearing a low-cut, dark-green dress, a thin gold chain around her slender neck. She was slightly flushed, perhaps because she was late, but to Luke she was as gorgeous in that moment as she had been the very first time he'd met her.

'I'm starving,' she announced as she settled into the chair opposite him and fixed her hair with a hair tie. 'It must be all these long hours I've been doing. Hey!' She squeezed his arm. 'How's you? I feel like I've hardly seen you.' Before he could answer a waiter appeared at their table, pen and notepad poised.

'I know exactly what I'll have,' Elise announced. 'Avocado on rye toast with smoked salmon.' Odd choice for the time of day, Luke thought, but he didn't comment on it.

'I'm good,' he told the waiter. 'Just a glass of tap water, please.'

Elise frowned and reached out to touch his cheek. 'So, come on, babes, what's bothering you these days? I'm glad you got me out of the gallery. I'd like to get things out in the open between us. You know we've always been honest with each other.'

Honest. The word stung him. Because he hadn't been honest with her, had he? Not about what had happened on that mission in Iran. And it was as if the awful secret of what he had done there had kept burning into his conscience ever since. So now his mind was made up. It was time to tell.

'So, Lise,' he began. 'You remember when I was away in Iran, back when I was working on that hostage case?'

'How could I forget?' she said, raising an admonishing eyebrow. 'You missed my mother's funeral.' He could see her good mood evaporating and already he regretted broaching the subject. Yet there was no going back now. He had to do this.

'I know, I know.' He looked down at his hands. They were clasped tightly together. 'And I still feel bad about that, you know I do. But there's something else I need to tell you.'

Elise sat back in her chair and gave him a coy look. 'Go on.'

'I'm afraid something happened over there,' he said. 'Something I'm not proud of at all and—'

'Luke, if this is about you finishing somebody off in cold blood I really don't want to know. It might be just part of the job for you, but I'd rather you spared me the details.' She tucked into her avocado on toast and ate it noisily while glancing around distractedly.

There. She had just offered him an off-ramp right there. He could take it with both hands and she'd be none the wiser. But, no, he loved her, and he wanted to make a clean breast of it: this bloody secret kept gnawing away at his conscience and he felt he owed her the truth.

'No, Lise, I'm afraid it's something else. Something a bit more personal than that. Something that affects us both.' Come on, Carlton, spit it out. You're only prolonging the agony here for both of you. 'Look, I'm really sorry,' he said, 'but the fact is . . . the fact is I slept with someone over there.' Total silence. 'In Iran,' he added pointlessly.

Slept with someone? There hadn't been any sleeping involved as he remembered it. It had been a moment of pure carnal lust between him and Tannaz, the twenty-three-year-old daughter of a senior Iranian Revolutionary Guard officer, someone he was supposed to have been protecting. They had needed each other that morning in the Bandar Abbas safe house, but he knew full well that that didn't wash. What he had done that day was inexcusable. The fact that Tannaz hadn't survived the ensuing firefight a few days later made their brief union in that hot Gulf bedroom all the more poignant. But he chose to spare Elise that particular detail.

He waited. Her reaction, when it came, was not what Luke was expecting.

Elise didn't blink. She reached out an arm and Luke braced himself for the stinging slap across the face that he knew he deserved. But instead she stroked his cheek once more. Wow. He hadn't seen that coming.

'It's okay, Luke. I guessed something like that must have happened.'

'You did? But you never said anything.' How come women are so good at knowing these things, and us guys are just crap? he thought.

'Call it a girl's intuition, I don't know,' she said mildly, looking away towards the window for a moment. 'Anyway . . .' she wiped her lips with a napkin '. . . that was delish,' she pronounced. 'And I have some news of my own.'

'You do?' Elise's behaviour was unnerving him: she was taking this suspiciously calmly. Luke, on the other hand, was finding it hard to hide his anxiety. He began rubbing the missing-finger joint beneath the table, as he so often did in moments of stress.

'Yes, Luke, I do.' Elise folded the napkin neatly into a triangle and laid it on the table between them before she looked him straight in the eyes. 'I think you should know,' she said quietly, 'that I'm pregnant.'

79

Domodedovo Airport, Moscow
Thursday, 17 March, 0130hrs GMT, 0430hrs local

NOT A WINK. Not one minute of sleep on that overnight flight
from London. Jesus, he was tired now. Usually Luke had no problem sleeping on planes. Learning to grab a few minutes' kip
whenever you could was a skill he'd had to learn as a recruit
going through basic training down at the Commando Training
Centre at Lympstone. Yet all night, as he flew eastwards across a
darkened Europe, his mind was wired and buzzing as it tried to
process this news.

Pregnant. Elise was pregnant. He kept running the words
over and over in his head. What did that mean for them now?
Well, for a start, he was to become a father. Part of him felt elated
about that. He could see himself on a Saturday morning in years
to come, kicking a ball around the park with his son, teaching
him to swim underwater, taking him rock-climbing, doing stuff
together – that it might be a girl wasn't really on his radar. And at
the same time he also had his nagging doubts. This could hardly
have come at a worse time. He and Jenny were right on the front
line of an ongoing national crisis: he couldn't afford to let himself be distracted. But what would happen when he returned
from the mission? Should they get married? Did people still *get*

married? Lots of his military mates had gone down the aisle and then he'd watched their marriages fall apart. Too much time away on operations, too hard to relate to normal life when they got back. And where should they live? Did this mean moving out of town into somewhere bigger with a garden? That might just have to wait a while, given his not-overgenerous MI6 salary and her modest pay packet at the Stratford Gallery in Mayfair.

No. On balance, Luke felt deeply uncomfortable about this news. Worse than that, he felt ashamed that he was not more excited about it. But the fact was Elise had delivered this bombshell just as he was leaving for one of the most sensitive and vital missions of his career. And this was no time to be thinking about what colour to paint the nursery.

'Ready for this?' Jenny flashed him a smile as they wheeled their cases along the arrivals concourse. He had decided not to share his news with her so she probably thought he was absorbed with the coming mission. Which was what he should have been thinking about. This was hostile territory they were heading into now and neither of them could afford any slip-ups. The man they would be working with, Colonel Petrov, was with GRU, Russian military intelligence. But it was the FSB who would be on their tail, day and night. The FSB, Federal State Security, were the true successors to the infamous KGB, and recent history had shown that old habits died hard. Alexei Navalny, the Kremlin's most outspoken critic and anti-corruption campaigner, had apparently been poisoned twice with Novichok nerve agent by FSB agents in 2020. Luke and Jenny would be wiping down a lot of surfaces on this trip.

Domodedovo airport was like almost any other major airport in the world: vast, modern and cavernous. But Luke and Jenny were no ordinary passengers stepping off flight BA237 from Heathrow. By the time they reached the passport kiosk they had already been photographed nine times. The phones in their pockets – 'clean phones', carefully prepped by the security team at Vauxhall Cross – had been remotely scanned using a hidden 'grabber' device installed in the arrivals terminal. Their

IMSI – international mobile subscriber identity – numbers were now logged in the FSB's computer system. Those numbers in turn were already being cross-checked electronically with several databases, many linked to FSB out-stations in embassies around the world. And all before they had even been asked to produce their passports.

The man who stepped out from behind the counter was unremarkable to look at. In fact, he could have passed for any government official in almost any country in Europe. He approached them with a curt nod and produced a small purple leather wallet, which he held out to show them. It was stamped with gold Cyrillic lettering and a twin-headed imperial eagle, with a sword and shield. An FSB identity badge. Luke noticed he did not bother to ask them for their own ID. With a thin attempt at a smile, the FSB man waved them past Passport Control and Customs and out into the darkness of the pre-dawn. It was a mild minus 1°C.

'You are sleepy,' he announced, making it sound almost like an order. 'So. You will be taken to your hotel now.' He gestured towards the open rear door of a black Mercedes limo that already had its engine running. 'Later this morning we will collect you from your hotel. Colonel Petrov will meet you in his office.' He waited until Luke and Jenny were installed in the back seat, then closed the door after them, issuing a quick instruction to the driver.

Through the darkened Moscow suburb of Voyevodino they sped along the A105 highway, past tree-shielded dachas and empty parks. Conversation between them was pointless. The driver would have been told to record every word they said and, besides, they were craving sleep.

The Red Square Guesthouse on Serafimovicha Street was exactly what Luke had expected. It looked absolutely nothing like a guesthouse. Instead, they pulled up outside a vast, imposing building on the banks of the River Moskva, with expensive blue lighting in every window and an elaborate colonnaded façade. Once inside, they were escorted straight up in the lift to the fourth floor where a man in a suit sprang up from his seat in the corridor and showed them to their rooms. Luke noticed he had a discreet earpiece.

'Try to get some sleep,' Jenny said to him, as they parted in the corridor.

'You too,' he answered. 'See you in a few hours.'

Exhausted, Luke could not be bothered to go hunting around the room for the inevitable listening devices he knew would have been placed there. The room would be monitored, that was a given. On one wall at right angles to the corridor he noted a large, unobstructed mirror. That, he was pretty sure, would be two-way, with some creepy guy in a booth probably observing him right at this minute. Luke got undressed, hopped into the shower, towelled off, then slid naked into bed. It was only then, as he laid his head on the pillow, that he saw the cheaply mounted photograph someone had placed on the bedside table, directly facing him. The colour drained from his face.

It was a framed photograph of Elise.

80

Moscow
Thursday, 17 March, 0812hrs GMT, 1112hrs local

THE PHONE CALLS were infuriating. Twice in the early morning the phone beside his bed had gone off. A wrong number, apologized the receptionist. Sure. Luke knew exactly what this was. Someone in the FSB had told her to make sure he was deprived of sleep. Gaddafi's people had played the same game, he recalled, when British detectives had gone to Libya to try to find the culprits for the murder of PC Yvonne Fletcher years earlier.

But now it was ringing persistently and he could see it was mid-morning already. The voice on the line told him he needed to be downstairs in fifteen minutes: the car was ready to take them to meet Colonel Petrov. Fine. Fifteen minutes. He could do that, although it meant no time to grab a bite downstairs. But Luke was still seething about the photograph at his bedside. This was old-style, unreconstructed KGB tradecraft that had somehow lingered on into the twenty-first century. Show your opponent something that unnerves them. Keep them guessing how much you know about them. Throw them off-balance at every turn. For Pete's sake, Luke thought, we're supposed to be on the same bloody side for this one, aren't we?

He recognized the photograph as one Elise had posted on her

Facebook page, so it wasn't exactly rocket science for them to have got hold of it. She and Luke had already had the conversation about never posting any photos of him on there, though, which made him wonder just how they had connected her to him. Worrying. And annoying. But he would have to let it slide for now if they were going to make any kind of success of this fragile, new-found Anglo-Russian cooperation. Had they done something similar to Jenny? He made a note to ask her the next time they were somewhere they couldn't be overheard.

Luke closed the door to his room behind him and nodded to the goon in the corridor, who sprang up and – quite unnecessarily – raced across the carpet to press the lift button for him. He was still thinking about the photo of Elise as the lift doors pinged open at the lobby floor. He was damned if he was going to let this rattle him, but he worried about other tricks they might have planned.

'The route is approximately eleven kilometres and the journey will take us twenty-eight minutes.' Their GRU escort had twisted round in his seat next to the driver to address them in the back of the car as they moved off. He was young, probably not yet out of his twenties, Luke reckoned, and looked like he spent a fair bit of time in the gym. Smart suit, dark tie, cutaway collar and yet another discreet earpiece. Luke had already studied the city map of Moscow so he and Jenny would have some idea of where they were being taken and by which route. He figured they would either follow the edge of Gorky Park and head south-west or go straight through the centre of Moscow with all its traffic.

'Eleven k', he said to Jenny. 'That means we're taking the scenic route past the Kremlin.'

Within minutes they were crossing the Bolshoy Kamenny Bridge with the majestic expanse of the River Moskva flowing beneath them, lit by the glint of a weak winter sun. Luke had predicted correctly. There, out of the right-hand window, were the impressive walls and towers of the Kremlin, adorned with those enigmatic gold onion domes and fairy-tale red spires. This was the picture-postcard Moscow of travel brochures, but the traffic was light at this time of day and soon they were turning west, leaving the Kremlin walls behind as they sped down New Arbat Avenue past modern skyscrapers and expensive-looking shops. The pedestrians they passed seemed affluent, cosmopolitan, modern. They might have been 2,500 kilometres east of London, but this could have been the heart of almost any capital in Europe.

'Not what you expected?' Luke remarked to Jenny.

She shrugged, said nothing and continued looking outside the window. They were crossing the city's ring road now and a massive piece of Stalinist wedding-cake architecture was looming up on their right.

'There's an underground station below that,' Luke said, monitoring their route on his phone. 'It's called Krasnopresnenskaya according to this.'

'Da . . . da . . .' the escort in the front was saying, clearly having a conversation with his bosses. He kept turning to check on them, as if Luke and Jenny might suddenly have done a runner at the lights. They were in the western outskirts of Moscow now, travelling at speed down a broad six-lane highway with very little other traffic. Soaring, faceless, pink and white tenement blocks rose up on both sides. There did not seem to be any pedestrians around.

And then, suddenly, they had arrived. 'We are here,' announced their escort as they pulled up at the outer wall surrounding the GRU headquarters on Grizodubovoy Street. Luke glanced up at the imposing three-metre-high wall, built, so he'd read, to withstand being rammed by a main battle tank. At the entrance gate, guards checked their ID and briefly inspected their vehicle, then it was through to a forecourt where men, some in military uniform, others in suits, were getting in and out of cars. A shiny round building, around five storeys high, towered above them, like a miniature version of GCHQ's Doughnut in Cheltenham. Beyond that, Luke could see several taller, white-fronted buildings.

'Well, this isn't weird at all,' he said to Jenny, as they stepped out of the car.

'You're telling me,' she replied. For two serving British intelligence officers to be here, in 'the belly of the beast', was an extraordinary moment for both of them. The GRU, Russia's hugely powerful military intelligence arm, was the *bête noire* of just about every NATO country's intelligence service. In recent years its operatives had been very busy on the world stage. The Crimea invasion of 2014, the infiltration of eastern Ukraine by the mysterious 'little green men' – the GRU's Spetznaz special forces dressed unconvincingly in civilian clothing – Moscow's surprisingly successful deployment into Syria, the Salisbury Novichok poisoning: all these operations would have been planned and executed from right inside this building, Luke was thinking, as he appraised the shiny steel structure above them.

'Luke Carlton? Jennifer Li?' Three men were walking up to them, wearing the pale grey double-breasted tunics of GRU officers. Black tie, white shirt, and in the case of the taller of the three, walking in front, gold epaulettes denoting a colonel's rank. 'Welcome,' he said, in a thick accent and without so much as a trace of a smile, 'to the Main Intelligence Directorate of the Russian General Staff.'

81

Moscow
Thursday, 17 March, 0901hrs GMT, 1201hrs local

LUKE RECOGNIZED HIM immediately. God knew he'd studied the man's file for long enough. And you wouldn't forget that face. High cheekbones, intense dark eyes with sagging bags of loose skin beneath them, a lifelong smoker's upper lip, betrayed by all those tiny vertical lines between his nostrils and his mouth, and a long aquiline nose.

'Colonel Petrov,' he returned the GRU officer's greeting. *You piece of shit, Colonel Petrov, placing a photograph of my girlfriend beside my bed like that.* 'Good to meet you,' he added, through gritted teeth. *Stay professional, get the job done.* The Russian nodded curtly, looking him and Jenny up and down, then said something in Russian and waited. A young man in glasses rushed up, exchanged a few words with the colonel and then, slightly out of breath, translated his words in a pronounced American accent.

'The colonel welcomes you to Moscow,' said the interpreter. 'He apologizes that he does not speak much English. Please, if you could follow this way for the briefing.' He pointed towards the round steel building.

In silence they were led through the entrance and into the atrium, with its giant bat emblem on the marble floor, the GRU's answer to the CIA's iconic seal at Langley, with its bald eagle and sixteen-point compass. Guards stood stiffly to attention, staring straight ahead and saluting as their party went past. For Luke and Jenny there were no formalities: everyone in the building seemed to know who they were and why they were there. Luke watched as barriers were lifted and men stood aside. Then it was through a glass door and along a corridor where every door was firmly closed except the last.

'Pozhaluysta,' said Colonel Petrov, gesturing for them to walk through it. 'Please.' It was the first word he had spoken since the car park. In single file they went into a lecture room that looked like any other in the world, but for one thing: the large blue circular emblem on the wall, emblazoned with the sinister black silhouette of the bat. Beneath that was a motto, in Russian and in English: 'Выше только звезды!' 'Only Stars are Above Us!' Luke and Jenny took their seats at the large, central table, as instructed, while an orderly came in bearing a tray of steaming glasses of tea and a plate piled with some sort of ring-shaped biscuit.

'Sushki,' explained the interpreter. 'Russian biscuits. Please to try.' Luke suddenly remembered how hungry he was. He picked up one, took a bite and nearly broke his teeth on it. It was rock hard. Was this a test? He put it down and raised his glass of tea to his lips, then stopped. This was how the former KGB officer and defector Litvinenko had died, drinking tea laced with radioactive polonium-210. He waited to see if the colonel was going to drink his, but Luke's hesitation had not escaped his notice. The Russian muttered something to the young interpreter, who again translated: 'Do not be afraid, the colonel says. There is no polonium in the tea.'

So this was dark Russian humour, then. Luke smiled and took a sip of the hot liquid just as the colonel began a long speech in Russian.

'The colonel would like to make it clear from the outset,' the interpreter said, looking from Jenny to Luke and back to his boss, 'that the outbreak of this virus did not come from Russia. Absolutely not. In fact it occurred on the territory of a NATO member,

281

Norway, yes? So the Russian people were deeply upset by the accusation of your government that we could possibly have been in any way responsible.'

Luke groaned inwardly. They had been expecting something like this. He just hoped they could move on quickly.

'But,' the interpreter continued, in the same flat transatlantic monotone, 'we are meeting today as professionals, as experts in our fields. We shall put aside our differences in the spirit of international cooperation.' He waited for a reaction and now it was Jenny who spoke up.

'We fully appreciate your cooperation,' she said diplomatically, 'and I'm glad that we can put the past behind us. Now, I have two requests.' She folded her arms and regarded the colonel as she spoke. 'First, we're hoping you can update us on your own investigations, given that . . .' Luke could see she was looking Petrov straight in the eye now '. . . phone calls were made at the time of the outbreak between the suspect area on Svalbard and this very building.' She let that hang in the air while it was translated. Luke flashed her a knowing look. He had always had a profound respect for her encyclopaedic knowledge of biological and chemical weapons, but now he felt a secret surge of pride in her. Jenny clearly wasn't daunted by their surroundings, nor their current situation: she had cut straight to the chase.

The interpreter was starting to look uncomfortable, but Colonel Petrov did not react. His face remained blank and expressionless yet Luke sensed an immediate chill in the atmosphere.

'Second,' Jenny continued, her voice clear and crisp, showing no trace of the tiredness he was feeling, 'I would like to visit your Ivanovsky Institute of Virology, here in Moscow.' Silence. 'At number sixteen Gamalaya Street,' she added.

The colonel spread his hands wide in an expression of hurt disbelief, reminiscent of the sort of denial they had encountered from Mr Kadunov back in the Lithuanian chemical factory. He gave Luke a brief, bemused look, which he took to mean *Help me out here. Surely you can see this is unreasonable.* Luke said nothing.

'Do you have a special interest in chlamydia and venereal disease, Miss Li?' retorted the colonel. 'Because that is what we study there. Or maybe you would like to know more about the incidence of influenza among the birds of western Siberia? Because that is also one of the research programmes at the Ivanovsky Institute.'

It was Jenny's turn not to blink when this was translated to them. Luke was pleased to see she wasn't backing down. If anything she looked as if she was just getting into her stride, moving her chair closer to the table and leaning forward towards Petrov.

'I have no doubt,' she replied coolly, holding his gaze, 'that those are all very valuable research programmes for the Russian Federation. But then so is the one into the Genome Structure of Haemorrhagic Fever. And the study of viruses with variable genomes. Both of which apply, I think, to the current outbreak on Svalbard.'

Once more she paused to let the translator do his work. When he'd finished Luke noticed something he hadn't seen before: a vein was standing out on the colonel's face and visibly pulsing. Bullseye, he thought.

'Colonel Petrov,' Jenny continued, 'this is a synthetic manufactured virus we're dealing with. We both know our governments urgently need to find out who has produced it and how it got into the wrong hands. That's why we're here today in your headquarters. And . . . and . . .' she was raising her voice for emphasis now '. . . we need to do this before anyone else gets infected, here in Russia or anywhere else. Because we would not like to imagine what this virus could do, for example, to people on the Moscow Metro.' Jenny folded her hands. 'Otherwise we might as well catch the first flight back to London.'

Luke strongly suspected that this GRU colonel would like nothing better than to see the back of him and Jenny, but, clearly, he had his orders from above. He turned to one of his two subordinates in the room and spoke rapidly to him in Russian. It was some time before the translation was forthcoming and when it did it rang immediate alarm bells in Luke's head.

'The colonel says,' announced the interpreter, 'that we will accept your request. Miss Li will be taken from here this afternoon to the Ivanovsky Institute. We must ask her to please follow all instructions and to wear protective clothing at all times.' He turned to Luke. 'You, Mr Carlton, will accompany Colonel Petrov to an address in Moscow where we will share with you the progress we have made in our investigations. Do you have any questions?'

Luke could see that the colonel and his entourage looked like they were preparing to leave the room, but what they were suggesting broke every security protocol he'd ever been trained to follow. Split the two of them up? On a deployment like this in Moscow? Absolutely not. This was not going to happen, not on his watch.

'Just hold on a minute,' he said, putting his hand up.

But Jenny reached over and held his arm. She was sitting bolt upright, her face set in determination. 'Luke . . . Luke . . . It's all right. I've got this. We can do this.' For several seconds they looked at each other. This was really a discussion they needed to have out of earshot of their hosts, but that was hardly going to happen in this building. Inside his head a debate was raging. Together they were a team; separated, they were potentially exposed, vulnerable. Splitting them up was unequivocally against the rules and Luke knew they should be referring this back to Vauxhall for clearance. But weighing against that was time. Every hour counted if they were going to stop this horrific attack by WaffenKrieg90. Their mission here was to get Moscow's cooperation and Petrov was giving them just that. Still . . .

'Jenny, are you absolutely—'

'Yes. I'm absolutely sure. We need this. I'll be fine. I'll see you back at the hotel this evening.'

Luke breathed out loudly through his nose, lips pursed.

He did not have a good feeling about this.

82

COLONEL ARKADY PETROV closed the door to his office, sat down behind his desk and frowned as he loosened his tie. 'Where is Carlton now?' he asked the young captain standing stiffly to attention.

'He's in the canteen, Colonel, with the others, having lunch. The transport is ready.'

'And the downloads?' He lifted his head, eyebrows raised. 'What have we found on their phones?'

The captain looked down at the printout in his hand. 'Not so much. Just their flight details, some apps, no *Kompromat*. We have nothing on them. They're using burner phones.'

'Calls to London? To their embassy here?'

'None so far.'

Colonel Petrov frowned again.

'Then find out how they're communicating with London. They haven't been to their embassy so they must have some other means. Find an excuse to take them to the second floor and make sure they walk past the screens, then bring me the images. What have the hotel team found?'

The captain swallowed and looked straight ahead, his face expressionless. 'Again, nothing useful, Colonel. They have completed the search, but the British brought very little with them. These are intelligence people.'

This was to be expected. 'No matter,' Petrov continued. 'The devices are attached to their cases now, yes? And properly concealed?'

'They are, Colonel.'

'And the operation at the institute for Miss Li? They are ready for her?'

'Almost. They are working on it now. Everything will be in place by four p.m.'

The GRU colonel nodded solemnly. 'No mistakes, mind. Or it will be your career on the line. Do I make myself clear?'

'Perfectly, Colonel.'

Colonel Petrov dismissed him with a wave of his hand. So, things were working out better than he had expected. After his initial fury at being told to cooperate with two intelligence officers from that despised country, Britain, matters had now played nicely into his hands. With some of his most trusted people, they had worked fast to produce a dynamic plan to turn this visit to their advantage. And so far it was going exactly to plan. He leaned back in his chair and contemplated the bronze bust of Vladimir Ilyich Lenin that he kept on his desk. Yes. He, Arkady, was the spider. He needed only to sit tight now, and watch the flies come into his web.

83

Thursday, 17 March, 1052hrs GMT, 1352hrs local

PRACTICALLY IDENTICAL. EVERY street, every bus stop, every tenement apartment block they passed looked exactly the same to Luke. Of course this city held plenty of cultural gems, he knew that. They'd driven past a few this very morning on the journey from their Red Square hotel. But the place they were driving through now? This 'workers' paradise' of the suburbs? No, this was another world, still seemingly trapped in a post-Soviet dystopia of unending grey steel and cheap concrete.

They were in convoy, a line of three black Mercedes jeeps, one of the hallmarks of the GRU, dominating the road and at one point jumping a red light as traffic lurched to a stop to let them past. Sitting on the back seat, a taciturn Colonel Petrov beside him, and bracing himself against the door as they took the corners at speed, Luke was following their progress via the sat-map on his phone. He could see they were making a wide sweep in an arc to the south-west of the centre, but his request to be told where they were going had been met with a gruff 'You will see.'

Luke felt a gnawing pang of worry. Not on his account, but on Jenny's. Splitting up their team had definitely not been in the plan and it was far from ideal. By deliberate design, he suspected, they had been given no opportunity to check in with London via the QKD transmitters – they certainly weren't going to risk a burst transmission from a locked toilet cubicle right inside GRU headquarters. Instead, they had just had to take a command decision on their own and go with it. But now he was having second thoughts. Jenny was his senior and he knew she could more than take care of herself, but if anything happened to her out here . . . well, he couldn't help feeling personally responsible.

Thirty minutes after leaving GRU headquarters they passed another towering example of 1950s Stalinist wedding-cake architecture. A hypertext link on Luke's map showed it to be Moscow State University, 'the tallest educational establishment in the world'. Was he being taken to meet an academic? Maybe a professor of bio-medicine? But, no, the convoy drove on, leaving the university behind, and the sleet that had begun falling when they set off was now turning to snow. They had entered a strange suburban wasteland of endless red garages and lockups, devoid of normal habitation. Every single person they passed was male, mostly hanging around in groups, hunched against the cold, seemingly waiting for something or someone. Others were working on dilapidated cars and glanced up with worried faces as the convoy passed by. Everyone in Moscow knew that three black Mercedes jeeps meant only one thing: military intelligence.

Sitting up front, the interpreter asked the colonel a question in Russian and he nodded his assent. He then turned to Luke. 'This place,' he said, 'is called Garage Valley. Also we call it Shanghai.'

'Garage' he got – they were surrounded by them – but Shanghai?

'Why Shanghai?' Luke asked. The interpreter looked questioningly at his boss, who shook his head. The interpreter shrugged and turned back to face the front.

They had slowed to a crawl now, moving slowly along an unpaved road between two lines of lockups, their wheels slithering through shallow troughs of wet slush. A man in a baseball cap, bomber jacket, boots and cargo trousers appeared, looming close to the windscreen, cradling an automatic carbine. Even from his seat in the back Luke had a good enough view of him to recognize the weapon in his hands: an AKS-74U, a short, stubby version of the Kalashnikov, perfect for close-quarter encounters and part of the chosen armoury of the GRU's Spetznaz Special Forces.

They stopped.

'Wait here,' Colonel Petrov said, in English, before getting out and closing the door behind him. Luke watched him walk off, his greatcoat reaching almost to his ankles, then talk to the man with the carbine. Twice they turned and looked at him as he sat in the back of the car, feeling caged and tense. When Petrov returned he held open the car door for Luke to get out.

'Okay, you come now,' he said in English, which made Luke think he understood a lot more of it than he made out. They picked their way through the wet slush, Petrov leading, as the snow fell around them in fat, wet flakes. He turned a corner to see several more GRU men guarding the door to a garage, weapons held in their gloved hands, all eyes watching him. Petrov gestured for him to go in, but for a second Luke hesitated. If this is where I get whacked on the back of the head, he thought, Vauxhall Cross will at least know my location from the GPS tracker in my phone. And that's a fat lot of use to me right at this moment. But there was no turning back now: he had to see this one through. Luke stepped through the doorway and into the dim interior of the lockup, his eyes adjusting quickly to the gloom. The place smelt awful, damp, musty, decrepit, and there was something else here that he couldn't quite put his finger on. Was it fear? Despair? This certainly felt like the kind of place where someone could disappear without a trace.

And there, in the middle of the room, was the reason. Stripped to the waist, his beltless trousers half falling off his skinny frame, his arms pinned behind his back and attached to a chain that went up to a pulley on the ceiling. Luke could see that, suspended like that, the prisoner was struggling to stand upright on the tips of his toes, in an effort to avoid the agonizing pressure on his shoulder blades. Luke stood stock-still, shocked at what he was seeing. This was like Afghanistan all over again, going into a police station with his patrol and finding some chained-up prisoner half beaten to death in a back room. Luke knew what it was like to be tortured – he'd experienced it first-hand in Colombia – and the sight of this wretched individual, guilty or not, sent shivers right through his body. And this wasn't just wrong, this was dangerous – for him, career-wise. The Service had strict rules about this sort of thing nowadays. If you witnessed torture you had to leave the scene. No exceptions.

So why wasn't he turning on his heel and walking straight out? There were other men in the room, bulky figures moving around in the shadows, and he sensed everyone was waiting to see his reaction. Calmly and without emotion, he addressed Colonel Petrov. 'Let him down, please.'

The colonel was standing with his arms folded across his greatcoat, his legs slightly apart. On hearing Luke's request he turned towards him with his customary blank expression. 'You are not in charge here, Mr Carlton,' he said in English. 'This is our investigation and you are in Moscow now.' For several seconds they stared at each other. This was a make-or-break moment in the investigation and both men knew it. Walk out of here and Luke would return to London with mission failure, having learned absolutely nothing. Stay put, cooperate with these thugs, and he might get somewhere, while at the same time leaving his conscience in the gutter.

It was Petrov who broke the silence. He issued a command to a large man in overalls sitting in the corner with his hands on a pulley chain attached to the ceiling. The prisoner was lowered a few centimetres, just enough to stand on the soles of his bare feet. He raised his head, his dank hair plastered over his forehead. He looked up imploringly at Luke, saying nothing.

'This,' said Colonel Petrov, indicating the prisoner as if he were just some sort of inanimate object, 'is our gift to you. This man is a member of Cherny Nozh. You understand what that means?'

'No.'

'Cherny Nozh, Mr Carlton, means "Black Knife". It is an

extremist organization here in Russia. We caught him only a few days ago. He is in contact with "extreme people" in your country, in UK, people who are planning something big. How do we know this?' For the first time Luke saw Colonel Petrov smile. To him, it looked more like a wolf baring its teeth.

'We know this,' Petrov continued, 'because we have been monitoring his communications. And so . . .' He stopped speaking as he strolled over to a wooden table and chair placed in the corner of the lockup, beckoning Luke to follow him. Petrov moved casually, like a man who had all the time in the world. There was a laptop on the table and he opened it now, plugging in what looked like a USB device. He entered a series of rapid keystrokes, then issued a command to those behind him, not even bothering to turn round. Luke heard, *'Razvyazhitye yevo,'* which meant nothing to him, but now there was a flurry of activity around the prisoner. For a moment he thought they were going to start on him again and this time he braced himself to intervene. But instead he saw two guards untie the man's wrists then put their arms around him to half carry him to the chair, sitting him down in front of the laptop. His head sagged and he kept murmuring something in Russian, but he stopped as Petrov spoke to him at length.

Listening to the Russian, unable to understand a single word, Luke wondered why on earth the Service couldn't have sent a Russian speaker for this mission. Once more his conscience was stirring. He had been a teenager when Al-Qaida flew those planes into the World Trade Center on 11 September 2001. But he knew that in the panicked aftermath Washington was so convinced another catastrophic attack was coming they went to extreme lengths to uncover any plot, real or imagined. It was a morally dark period of illegal snatching of suspects, who were then transported, cuffed and blindfolded, across the world to secret CIA 'black sites', where they were subjected to what was euphemistically called 'enhanced interrogation'. One man, Khalid Sheikh Mohammed, was subjected to waterboarding – simulated drowning – at a black site in Poland 183 times. Again, Luke felt a strong urge to get up and leave, and again he stayed. The prisoner in the chair was shaking his head and repeating '*Pozha-luysta*' over and over again. This, at least Luke knew, meant 'please'.

'This man,' explained Petrov, 'would like very much to help you.' Luke gazed at the sorry figure slumped in front of the laptop. He didn't look like he wanted to do anything of the kind. No, Luke thought, enough of this. He should extricate himself from this whole situation now and bug out back to London without delay. He started to say something, but the colonel cut him off.

'He has access to the encrypted forum for the people who run WaffenKrieg90. I think you know of this group. As a gesture of brotherly cooperation, we will let you use his identity to contact them. But we expect you to share everything you find with us.'

Colonel Petrov took a pace backwards and for the second time his face showed a trace of a smile. 'Unless, of course, you disapprove of our methods.' He shrugged, pulled out a cigarette, lit it and turned his back on Luke. 'The choice is yours, Luke Carlton,' he said, facing the bare walls of the lockup. 'But I can tell you this, you don't have much time.'

84

ANGELA SCOTT WAS not usually one to dodge protocol. A vicar's daughter who'd won a scholarship from St Paul's Girls' School to Newnham College, Cambridge, she had always played by the rules. Now, after years as a career case officer in MI6, she knew full well you didn't go barging into the Chief's office whenever you felt like it. You rang ahead, you spoke to his PA, you booked an appointment in his overfull diary and, if you were lucky, he might see you for a few minutes the following week. Yet today she did exactly that. She stood outside the outer door of his office, straightened her skirt, adjusted her hair, took a deep breath, then marched straight through into his carpeted office, just as Sir Adam was finishing a phone call. He looked up in surprise.

'I'm so sorry to barge in, C,' she began, 'but I thought you ought to know this.' She hoped he wouldn't notice how tense she was, standing there, balling the fingers of one hand inside the other. Well, if he had noticed, he wasn't commenting on it: instead he gestured politely for her to take a seat.

'We've had word from Luke Carlton in Moscow,' she

continued. 'He's back at his hotel and he's sent a burst transmission using the quantum key.'

'And?' The Chief showed neither irritation nor pleasure at this unscheduled interruption. His years of playing 'the grey man' as a junior case officer had clearly stayed with him right through to where he was now, in his late fifties, at the pinnacle of his profession.

Angela shifted her position slightly and tucked a wisp of hair behind her ear. 'Luke says he's been offered an entrée into WaffenKrieg90. Right into their command circle. Using an adopted alias. The Russians do seem to be playing ball on this one. They're ready to help us. For once.'

Sir Adam sat back in his chair, pressing his fingers together in a steeple, staring at her with a concentrated gaze. My God, he looks tired, she thought.

'Is it genuine?' he asked her at last.

'I'm sorry?'

'Do you think they're being sincere, the Russians? I know this has all been signed off at a political level, but still . . .' He breathed out hard and shook his head. 'Maybe I spent too much of my career on the Moscow beat. But if there's one thing it taught me, it's never to take anything from that lot at face value. Believe me, Angela, when it comes to the Russians, there is always a hidden game plan. You just have to look for it in the right place.' He stood up, pushed away his chair and walked over to the window. 'All right, so go on, tell me, because I'd value your opinion. What's *your* evaluation?'

She was ready for this. Angela Scott did not go into meetings unprepared. But still she swallowed slightly before she replied. 'We've red-teamed it, C. We've looked at what they might have to gain from taking us down a wrong path.'

'And?'

'And our assessment is that, on balance, they have more to gain from working with us than against us on this one. Agent X is a threat to both our nations' populations. Biological pathogens don't stop at borders.' She waited for him to say something, but he kept regarding her in silence so she pressed on: 'Look, I'm not saying Moscow doesn't have secrets they want to keep from us on the bio front. Of course they do. Washington slapped sanctions on some of those biological research units in 2020. And let's not forget there is something of a grey area between state and non-state activities in this sphere. So, I suppose I'm saying yes, it's a genuine offer, but with caveats.'

Sir Adam nodded, still deep in thought. He frowned as he spoke. 'I get that. So let me ask you a delicate question.'

She caught herself biting her lip. This sounded like something she hadn't prepared herself for.

'I hope you can reassure me, Angela, that this access you say Luke is being offered into WaffenKrieg90 has not been extracted under some kind of duress. Because I don't need to remind you that the Service cannot afford another scandal like Libya.'

She hesitated for just a second. Luke hadn't mentioned anything about that, but then again she hadn't asked him, and Angela knew she should have double-checked. Maybe she had simply been too busy trying to help head off Britain's first full-scale biological attack in modern history.

'No. I think we're clean, C. Luke would have mentioned if that were the case, I'm sure of it.'

The Chief walked over to her. For a moment she thought he was about to lay a hand on her shoulder, a gesture she had always resented as deeply patronizing. But he stood at a respectable distance, facing her as he gave her the green light to go ahead.

'Good. Well, that's settled, then. Speak to Thames and get everyone working on Luke's legend and keep me closely informed. Good work, Angela. Now, if you'll excuse me . . .'

Angela had never cared much for lunch in the Service canteen and today, she quickly decided, there was far too much at stake to waste time with something as trivial as eating. After making a couple of calls to Thames House she intercepted the senior liaison officer from MI5 just as he was heading out of his office for lunch and turned him around. By 2.45 p.m. they had pulled together the team, and an hour later, with the help of some of the data mining provided by Cheltenham, they had sketched out a rough outline of the alias Luke would adopt online. He would become 'Steve Keane', an imaginary former member of the SRR, the British Army's secretive Special Reconnaissance Regiment, disgraced and court-martialled the year before for repeatedly racially abusing one of his subordinates. The case had supposedly been hushed up – it had never made it into the public domain – and the mythical 'Steve Keane' had disappeared quietly into anonymity in an Oxfordshire village.

Angela knew the next step would be extremely challenging, given the impossibly short time frame. Using the contact details and passwords supplied to Luke by Petrov's prisoner in Moscow, they now had to get Luke inserted into WaffenKrieg90's inner circle under his Steve Keane alias. Under normal circumstances this would need months of painstaking work, with no sudden moves that might spook the target. But time was a luxury they didn't have. Every hour that ticked by brought closer the possibility of what they feared was coming: a deliberate and catastrophic release of Agent X into the general population.

85

Near Braintree, Essex
Thursday, 17 March, 1427hrs GMT

THE BOXES HAD arrived from Cambridge. Stacked in the corner of the room and labelled 'Garden Supplies', they contained the last remaining components for what was to come. The big man checked them over himself, taking out a box-cutter knife and carefully slicing open the seals. They were all there, exactly as ordered: the white chem-bio protective suits, the respirators, the masks. Everything needed for the final preparation before the release.

The plan wasn't perfect, despite all the months of preparation, he'd be the first to admit that. In an ideal world none of them would ever need to be exposed to the agent. There was enough space for all of them up at the Farm in Derbyshire. But volunteers were still needed to drive to the target with what had to be delivered. Lots had been drawn, names had been chosen, Cambridge and Vilnius had been informed, and those who were assigned knew exactly what was expected of them when the day came.

He stood up, hitched up his trousers and breathed out heavily. He smiled to himself. That day, he knew, was coming soon. And the people who ran this country were not going to know what had hit them.

86

Moscow
Thursday, 17 March, 1555hrs GMT, 1855hrs local

NIGHTFALL, AND LUKE was now seriously worried. He had already had a conversation with Petrov's office, accepting the colonel's offer of help with the prisoner's leads into Waffen-Krieg90, and had been told that a flash drive would be dropped off at his hotel. But nearly three hours had passed since they had brought him back and Jenny had still not returned from the Ivanovsky Institute. No answer from her phone, no answer from her room when he knocked. He went down to the lobby and asked at Reception if anyone had seen her come in or go out. No one had. Luke had returned to his room and sent off a burst transmission to Vauxhall, using the quantum key, giving a status update, but had decided not to mention her missing status just yet. He would look a fool when she suddenly showed up.

He called Colonel Petrov's office again, twice, only to be met with platitudes. 'She is in a secure location,' they assured him. 'She will meet you back at your hotel.' Pacing around his room, grazing unhealthily on packet snacks from the minibar, he kept checking his watch. Jenny had missed the agreed check-in time by phone. That was unlike her. Jenny did not miss appointments.

When the knock on the door came, he answered it immediately, striding quickly across to open it. It was not Jenny. Instead, standing in the doorway was a slender, dark-haired girl in a black, low-cut dress. Silently, she handed him a package. His fingers felt the outline of the contents through the padded envelope. It was the USB from Petrov's people.

Luke thanked her and began to close the door on her, but she reached out and caught it with her hand. 'Massage,' she announced, a trace of a smile playing around her lips.

He thought he might have misheard. 'Sorry. What?'

'You order massage.'

She made it sound like a statement of fact rather than a question, but either way, Luke was having none of it. He shook his head. 'Another time,' he said firmly, and gently closed the door on her.

Yet another of Petrov's mind games, he thought, as he put the chain on the door. Or a blatantly transparent attempt to gain some *Kompromat* on me. Did these people never give up?

He looked down at the package in his hand and gently opened it. The black USB stick fell into his palm. All those names, aliases, passwords that they needed, contained in just this tiny gadget. It would need to be quarantined and screened before anyone could access its contents. Luke had received enough briefings on offensive Russian cyber ops to know it would almost certainly be loaded with the latest most sophisticated malware. But, still, he had got what he had come to Moscow for and he should be feeling a sense of achievement that at last, after all this time in Svalbard, Vilnius and here in Moscow, he was finally making real headway. But if he couldn't track down Jenny very soon, this whole mission would be called into doubt. He contemplated getting into a taxi and going in person to the Ivanovsky Institute to push for answers, but decided against it.

When the phone rang beside the bed twenty minutes later the voice on the other end was brisk and stern. 'Come down to Reception,' the man said. He didn't sound like somebody who worked for the hotel.

Three of them were waiting for him at the far end of the reception desk, all stockily built men in dark suits; one wore an earpiece. They introduced themselves as working for Colonel Petrov and the oldest flashed his ID badge.

'Come, please,' they told him. 'We go to GRU headquarters.'

Despite this being his first, and most probably last, visit to Russia, this was exactly how Luke had imagined it would be in his dealings with Russia's shadowy security apparatus. His uncle had spent long hours telling him tales of Soviet life in the seventies and early eighties, when he'd been posted undercover to the British Embassy during the dark days of Leonid Brezhnev. It occurred to Luke now that when it came to state security nothing much had changed since those times.

Sitting once more in the back of the car, being driven across Moscow at night and past the floodlit red walls of the Kremlin, Luke pressed again for an answer. 'I would like to speak to my colleague, Miss Li,' he said, leaning forward to address the man in the front passenger seat. 'Her phone is switched off and she is with your people at the Ivanovsky Institute.'

He waited while a hurried conversation in Russian flowed back and forth between his three GRU escorts. Finally, the man in front replied: 'I have some news. Miss Li has met with an accident. We are sorry.'

'What?' The news hit Luke like a blow to the head. They had stopped at a busy intersection and the lights of the vehicles were flashing past like a kaleidoscope, the roads glistening with a light dusting of snow. There was silence in the car, just the drone of the traffic outside the windows in the freezing night.

'What do you mean, "Miss Li has met with an accident"?' Luke demanded.

For the first time he could see the man in front looking uncomfortable as he stared hard at him. The officer held up his hand as he took out his phone, pressed a key, then spoke to someone on the other end. Luke could see his brow furrowing. When he put the phone away the officer said simply, 'The colonel will see you in his office.'

They pulled up in the forecourt of the GRU building on Grizodubovoy Street with a squeal of tyres. Car doors opened and slammed shut. Men were running into the building and shouting. For a brief moment Luke found himself completely alone in the back of the vehicle, frantically rubbing the joint of his missing finger with anxiety as he thought of Jenny Li. Something had definitely happened and he needed to find out what.

The three GRU men escorted him into the vast, cavernous lobby, past the portrait of the President on the wall, down a corridor, cramming themselves into a lift, then riding up in silence to Petrov's office on the second floor. The door was open and they stopped just short of it, gesturing for Luke to go in.

The colonel was standing in the middle of the room, his posture braced and upright, hands clasped behind his back. But it wasn't the sight of Colonel Petrov that caught Luke's attention. It was the fact that he was flanked by two medical orderlies in white coats.

Of Jenny Li there was no sign.

87

Vauxhall Cross, London
Thursday, 17 March, 1738hrs GMT, 2038hrs Moscow

FOR ANGELA SCOTT, the news brought a dreadful sense of déjà vu. It seemed like only yesterday that the night duty officer had taken that early-morning call from Bogotá informing them that their Colombia station chief had been found murdered in the jungle. Angela had been part of the team that had deployed Luke Carlton to go out there to investigate, with painful consequences for him. Now, less than five years on, Carlton was once more 'at reach and at risk', as their partners in the SAS were fond of saying. He was in Moscow and the apparent success of his mission had come at a terrible cost. Angela took a deep breath before knocking on the Chief's door.

'Something has happened to Jenny Li,' she told him, with no preamble, as she stood on the carpet facing him. 'She's been infected with a virus. In Moscow. It's possibly deliberate, we don't know yet. The Russians are keeping her in isolation.'

Sir Adam Keeling looked up sharply. He was wearing a dark blue pinstripe suit and a pale blue Cambridge tie tucked into the top of his waistcoat. Impeccably smart at all times, his demeanour seemed frayed, the strain of the last few days definitely showing.

'What virus?' he replied hoarsely. 'You mean Agent X? And how the hell did this happen? Has Carlton got it too?' He got up from his chair and came round to her side of the desk, offering her a chair, but Angela remained standing. Somehow it didn't seem right to her to be delivering this news sitting down.

'They split up to save time,' she told him, folding her arms across her chest. 'Jenny went to interview the virologists at the Ivanovsky Institute while Luke went to—'

'Wait a moment,' the Chief interrupted. 'Who authorized that?'

She couldn't help herself – she knew it was a cliché, but Angela swallowed before replying. This had happened on her watch. 'No one authorized it, C. They took an on-the-spot decision. Luke says there was no chance to refer it back to us.'

Sir Adam waved a hand dismissively. 'All right. So what's her condition now? And how did this happen?'

Angela bit her lower lip. She had been in the Service long enough to know the one thing chiefs and directors disliked more than anything was being given an incomplete set of information. 'From what Luke has told us,' she said, 'it seems there was some kind of accidental release in their BioLevel3 lab – at least, that's what they're telling him. And, no, it's not Agent X, thank God. But Jenny is in an induced coma while they keep her in isolation.'

The Chief began pacing the room as he often did. He stopped, removed his suit jacket and threw it over the back of a chair. 'This stinks,' he said. 'I smell a rat here, don't you?' Angela nodded. 'Jenny Li is our foremost expert on CBRN. I know that, you know that, they know that. We always knew it would be a calculated risk sending her over there, but I didn't think they'd try something like this. Oh, this is rich.' He shook his head. 'Moscow will be trying to pump her for information the moment she comes round. I wouldn't put it past them to use their experimental truth serums on her. Right . . .' He thought for a moment, wiping the palms of his hands over his face and momentarily closing his eyes. 'Get someone from our embassy over to wherever she's being treated, have them stick as close as they safely can, and get Luke Carlton back here as fast as.'

303

'It's already done, C. He's on his way to Domodedovo now. He's got the flash drive with the WaffenKrieg90 contacts. I've got a bike meeting his flight into Gatwick the moment he touches down. We'll get it screened the second it comes into the building.'

The Chief nodded, still thinking. 'Good. We need him operational on this as soon as he gets back here. And someone needs to call Jenny's next of kin. And, Angela?'

'They'd better prepare them for the worst.'

88

Gatwick Airport, England
Friday, 18 March, 0840hrs GMT

SVALBARD . . . VILNIUS . . . MOSCOW . . . Vauxhall Cross. For
Luke, the last few days had passed in a blizzard of flights, briefings and missions. So much so that now, groggy with sleep, as
the overnight Air Baltic flight 651 from Moscow via Riga touched
down at Gatwick Airport, he briefly struggled to remember
where he was. But the moment he opened his eyes, blinking at
the rain-spattered plane window beside him, the awful truth
returned: he had left behind a virus-stricken Jenny Li in Moscow.
God knew he hadn't wanted to. Right up to the last minute,
almost missing his flight, he had argued with Vauxhall Cross
that he should stay and see her safely home. But the order had
come direct from Sid Khan, the director of International Counter-
Terrorism, and it had left no room for manoeuvre. *Return home
ASAP*, it read. *Embassy will look after JL.*

Now the Airbus A220-300 had taxied to a halt next to an air
bridge at North Terminal, but the captain was asking everyone to
remain in their seats. A tall blonde Latvian flight attendant in a
dark blue tunic and yellow scarf approached Luke's seat and bent
over him to whisper, 'The captain asks if you could come up to
the flight deck, please.'

Luke was expecting this. As he got up from his seat, feeling the other passengers all watching him, he discreetly reached his hand inside his jacket pocket to check that the package was still there, feeling with his fingertips for the familiar outline of Petrov's USB stick. The engines were still running as they unlocked the door to reveal the Service courier sent from Vauxhall, standing alone on the air-bridge ramp, helmet under his arm. He removed his gloves, produced his ID for Luke to check, then took the package and was gone.

Seventeen minutes later Luke was through Immigration and waiting on the platform for the Gatwick Express to Victoria. Glancing at the other passengers, he almost envied them. None of them know, he thought, of the horror that could be unleashed on the population if we don't succeed in stopping this in time. Then, as the train pulled up and the doors hissed open, another thought struck him. He was going home as a father-to-be. So much had happened in the short time since he had left for Moscow and he had been so focused on the mission that he had pushed this to the back of his mind. But now he was back and it was real and he was going to have to sit down with Elise and discuss their future. The prospect left him feeling both excited and exhausted.

It was 10.30 a.m. when he entered the flat, walked into the living room and was surprised to see Elise still there. Instead of having left for work she was sitting upright at the breakfast table, wearing a fawn cashmere cardigan, and reading a book, the grey morning light coming through the window, a cushion resting on her lap.

'Hey, you're still here!' he said, dumping his bag and going over to kiss her.

Elise flashed him the briefest of smiles, as if he had just popped down to the shops for some milk instead of spending the last two days in Moscow. He immediately sensed something was wrong. She barely returned his kiss – there was no warm embrace, no 'Welcome home, Luke.' He sat down next to her and reached out to squeeze her hand, but to his dismay she recoiled. Elise moved her chair back from the table, as if trying to put some distance between them. She looked at him with a deadly serious expression.

'What's wrong, Lise?' he asked tenderly. 'Is someone in trouble?'

'Luke . . .' she began, then stopped.

'Are you okay?' he asked again.

'I'm fine,' she replied, rather too quickly, glancing out of the window at nothing. 'Look . . . there's something you need to know.' She was intertwining the fingers of her hands now, writhing them together, like mating snakes.

He had never seen her so nervous. Even her voice sounded different, somehow brittle and alien. 'Go on,' he said gently.

She was looking down at her hands now, unwilling to meet his eyes. 'Luke, it's time you knew. I've been looking back at the calendar. I've looked at the dates, at when you were here and when you were away and, well, I've got some bad news. It's not . . . I'm afraid it's not yours.' She blurted out the last words in a rush, her face flushed.

'What isn't?' and he could hear the lameness in his words even as he spoke them. Because he already knew the answer.

'Oh, come on, Luke, for God's sake!' she snapped. 'Don't make this harder than it needs to be. The baby, Luke! It's not yours. Do I have to spell it out for you?' Then, softening her tone, she added, 'Look, I'm sorry, but that's all there is to it.' Elise pursed her lips and looked at him for a reaction.

The sadness was so overwhelming he thought he might drown. Two days ago she had told him he was going to be a father. That meant they would be a family. Together. Yet now, with those simple, damning words, all that had suddenly been snatched away from him and smashed at his feet. For a second he said nothing. Then a voice he hardly recognized as his own said, 'Whose is it?'

Quietly, almost under her breath, she answered him: 'It's Hugo's.'

89

NUMB. THAT WAS how Luke felt. And quietly angry. Turning it over again and again in his mind as he revved the engine of his Land Rover and ran an amber light on the drive in to the MI6 building in Vauxhall. How could he have been so blind? Why hadn't he seen this coming? Of course. Every single time he had had to be away on a trip it was always Hugo bloody Squires who managed to be there for Elise when he wasn't. Always ready to escort her to one of her art-gallery openings or some other diary event. Yet somehow he couldn't bring himself to blame her. Not after what he had done with Tannaz in Iran. Maybe this was some kind of divine punishment.

He was passing the US Embassy building now at Nine Elms, and a pedestrian had suddenly decided to cross the road in front of him, seemingly oblivious to the traffic. Luke slammed on the brakes, wound down the window and swore at him. The man flicked him the finger and walked on.

So what now? Chuck in this whole MI6 gig and ask Elise for a second chance? Well, it was a bit bloody late for that, wasn't it? Luke stifled the thought the instant it entered his head. No, he'd blown this one. Elise, fatherhood, their shared little life in that flat, all built on sand, as it turned out, all gone now. He had walked out on her in silence almost as soon as she had delivered that news. He simply didn't trust himself not to say something he would always regret.

Turning off Albert Embankment and watching the green metal gates open, he hit the accelerator too early and nearly ran over one of the security staff. He took a deep breath and gave himself a silent reprimand. This wouldn't do. He needed to suppress his dark thoughts, control his temper and stay professional.

Angela Scott was waiting for him in the ground-floor lobby of the Vauxhall Cross building, cradling a cup of coffee to her chest. Catching sight of her as he keyed himself in through security, Luke did something of a double take. Instead of her habitual, sometimes dowdy, business wear, Angela was dressed in a dark blue boiler suit with the sleeves rolled up. There would be a reason for this, he guessed, but he decided, on balance, it was probably best not to comment on it.

'Jesus, Luke, you look terrible!' she told him, as she walked over to a tall, circular bin next to the big MI6 plaque and dropped her empty cup into it.

'Thanks.' He ran his hand through his hair. He couldn't remember when he'd last washed it.

'No, really,' she said seriously. 'Maybe you'd better go straight home and get some sleep as soon as we've set this thing up.'

Home. The word cut him like a blade. Because where was 'home' now? Certainly not in the Battersea riverside flat any more. An orphan since the age of ten, Luke had almost no family to fall back on. So if he was not going to return there where was he going to sleep tonight – at the Battersea Travelodge? Bedding down in a lonely bachelor's room for one while the traffic sped past beneath his window? His spirits sank lower still.

'I'm fine,' he lied. 'Let's get on with this, shall we? What's the update on Jenny?'

Angela grimaced. 'Everyone's taken it pretty badly,' she said, as they walked together towards the lifts, 'but Jenny's a fighter. She's out of the induced coma, and they're saying she'll pull through. We're still trying to find out what actually happened at the Ivanovsky. It does look like it might have been an accident, but you can imagine how C feels about this.' She stood back as the lift doors pinged open and two people got out. 'Right now we're just trying to make sure one of our people is keeping an eye on her around the clock. Let's not forget that the FSB tried to finish off Navalny with Novichok when he was in Omsk Hospital in the summer of 2020.'

She pressed a lift button and turned to face him. 'Right. Down we go.'

They took the lift, not up to the operations room but to a part of the building Luke had never been to before, a place two floors below the ground. He reckoned they must be about on a level with the surface of the Thames at low tide, right beneath Vauxhall Bridge, not that you could tell in this soundproofed, windowless corridor. For an instant he experienced an unwelcome flashback to a lockup garage in a Moscow suburb, to a place where a man had agreed to cooperate under great duress. Hell, Luke still hadn't come to terms with that one and there were no excuses for it. If this ever got out he'd find himself in court before he knew it, and he couldn't expect any top cover from this lot.

'I don't believe,' said Angela, 'you've been into Area D before.' She indicated the featureless corridor they were walking down. 'Well, this is it. There are rooms down here that you and I will never, ever visit, right up to the day we hand in our passes.'

'Why are we here, Angela?' He tried to keep the tiredness and exasperation out of his voice, but realized he must have sounded quite irritable. 'Sorry, you were probably just about to tell me.'

'I was. I'm taking you to the Stage.' They had stopped in front of a plain steel door with a cardkey access system.

'The Stage?' He looked at her questioningly.

'Yes – at least that's what we call it. Officially it's Room 13.2 or something suitably anodyne, but nobody calls it that. Think of it as our own in-house theatre production studio, if you will. It's where we set up certain . . . scenarios for critical missions. Like this one.'

310

She took out a cardkey from a pocket in her boiler suit, held it against the reader and keyed in a code. 'I should warn you, Luke,' she said, as the lock released with a soft click, 'that most of the Service doesn't even know this place exists so you won't be able to talk about it upstairs. Is that clear?'

'Crystal.'

The room they walked into looked nothing like an office space. Instead, Luke found himself inside what seemed to be some sort of garage, and a filthy, unkempt one at that. Blackened, oily car parts lay against the wall and on shelves that seemed in serious danger of collapsing. A peeling poster of a Mazda MX5 car was pinned to the wall above a moth-eaten beige armchair, and the whole place was lit by a flickering neon striplight on the ceiling. An old fridge stood in the corner with a crate of Corona beer balanced on top. The only other furniture was a worn-out workbench and a chair on casters. Three people, whom he had never seen before, stood in front of it. The woman in the middle of the group nodded to acknowledge Angela, then stepped forward to greet Luke.

'Welcome to the Stage,' she said. 'I'm Dextra and I'll be supervising your transformation.' She looked to be in her early thirties, with designer glasses, jeans, T-shirt, clipboard and, he couldn't help noticing, immaculate white teeth. She took off her glasses and took a pace closer to him. 'From now on,' she said softly, as if this were a secret to be shared with no one else in the room, 'you're no longer Luke Carlton. You're Steve Keane. I want you to become him, to think like him, scratch, fart, pick your nose like him. In short, I want you to crawl inside his character and *be* him. Think you can do that?'

No one had spoken to Luke quite like that since basic training, but he didn't mind one bit. 'Got it,' he replied. He could feel his pulse quickening. This was going to be intense, he could tell, and that suited him just fine.

'So,' she said, rubbing her hands together in anticipation, 'you're ours for the next three days while we prep you for this mission. Technically, as this is UK soil you're going to be operating on, it now becomes an MI5 lead. But this place . . .' she swept her arm around the mocked-up garage they stood in '. . . the Stage, is unique to the Service. There's nothing like it in either Thames House or Cheltenham.'

She walked over to the workbench, turned around and jumped up so she was sitting on it, facing him. Other people in the room seemed to be busy making adjustments to the props in the room. 'This is where we've conducted some of our most sensitive video calls with individuals in organizations that we need to penetrate overseas.' She turned back to Angela. 'I think this is the first time this year this place has been used for a domestic target, though, isn't it, Angela?'

'That's correct,' Angela replied, standing close by with her hands thrust deep into the pockets of her boiler suit.

'So,' continued Dextra, 'once you leave here you'll be run out of the IOC across the river, which means—'

'Wait, what? The IOC? The International Olympic Committee?' Luke frowned at her. This made no sense to him.

She smiled as she replied. 'No, not in this context. The IOC is the Intel Ops Centre inside Thames House. It's where MI5 run the final stages of all their live ops from.'

She stepped back a pace and gave him an appraising look. 'Right, let's get you started. Hope you're well rested because we've got an awful lot to get through in a very short time.'

90

FOR SIX HOURS straight they were at it, down there in the surreal, hermetically sealed world of the Stage, deep beneath the MI6 headquarters building, getting him ready for the role he was to play. Luke felt like a weapon being prepped for battle, and he loved every minute of it. It wasn't just that all this was taking his mind off the slow-motion car crash of his personal life; this was 'training' like he'd never experienced before. He was the receptacle and they were pouring the knowledge into him. Techies from GCHQ in Cheltenham, voice and drama coaches, experts on Europe's extremist groups brought over from across the river in Thames House, a recently retired member of the Special Reconnaissance Regiment and – from behind a screen – an operational German informant inside an active neo-Nazi group from Dresden.

Time was desperately, worryingly short, but by the end of this weekend Luke needed not just to know everything about his adopted character, Steve Keane, he needed to *be* Steve Keane, the Jew-hating, BAME-despising, racial supremacist, with a history of punching people whose colour he viscerally disliked. The temporary tattoo of a swastika on the side of his neck was convincing – 'It won't wash off in the shower for a good two weeks,' they told him. And his back story was all there for anyone to see if they cared to trawl through his social-media profile, carefully crafted by the people from upstairs who did this stuff for a living. There were the eulogizing tributes to Anders Breivik in his Norwegian island prison, then the Berlin gunman, the Christchurch mosque attacker, Gary Sloane from Kansas, and so it went on, the trail of verifiable online digital vitriol.

Life had not treated 'Steve Keane' well since he had been supposedly 'dishonourably discharged' from the Regiment. He had, apparently, drifted from one badly paid security job to another, eventually ending up as an unsuccessful mechanic here in this 'garage' at Cowley, on the edge of Oxford. But the man being presented as Steve Keane had something that could be very valuable to the movement. After all those years in the SRR he was a consummate expert at covert surveillance, counter-surveillance, detection and evasion. In fact, it was said, there was not a system in operation throughout the UK that, given the right opportunity, Steve Keane did not know how to evade or disable. And that, right now, made him a very marketable commodity to certain individuals.

It also meant that if Luke was to stand any chance at all of convincing the fanatics in this movement, this cult of extremists, of his usefulness to them, he needed to know his stuff. In the Corps he had done a stint in Brigade Reconnaissance, he had mastered the art of the CTR, the close-target recce, and while at Poole with the SBS he had even done a beginners' course in covert breaking-and-entering. Plus various types of surveillance in Belfast and the Province that he would never be able to talk about. But nothing had prepared him for what he needed now. This was a whole different game. A very large part of Luke's day was spent ensconced with the lock-breakers, the counter-surveillance experts and even one retired burglar, all willingly supplied by MI5.

91

Battersea, London
Friday, 18 March, 1901hrs GMT

'I AM A heartless bitch.' There. She wrote the words out for her-self on a piece of paper and stared at them for several seconds before crumpling it up and tossing it towards the bin. It missed. Elise got up from the table and arched her back, then instinct-ively stroked her belly. Nothing showing there yet, but it would soon.

This was awful. Six times she had tried phoning Luke and each time his phone had gone straight to voicemail. She knew he was probably still at work, but that didn't stop her worrying. What if he had taken it so badly that he went and 'did something stupid'? That misleadingly harmless-sounding euphemism for taking your own life. No, she couldn't see Luke doing that, but, still, his silence worried her. They needed to talk: there was the flat to discuss, their joint bank account, all their shared posses-sions that would need divvying up. Oh, God, she couldn't bear this. None of it was what she wanted. It was just that it had all gone wrong after her mother died. Luke never made it to her funeral, he was still away in Iran, and that had really hurt, espe-cially now he'd told her what he'd been getting up to over there. Hugo Squires, on the other hand, had been at her side, a shoulder

315

to cry on. Dependable. Reliable. A rock of support. From that moment on, she supposed, things had just taken their natural course.

On which note, where was Hugo? She had tried calling him the moment Luke left that morning, leaving her forlorn in the emptiness of their doomed flat. She had rung him twice then remembered him saying he was going to be busy for the next few days. Doing what? He hadn't said. Damn, this was all such a mess and she hadn't even told Hugo about the baby. That was a conversation they needed to have very soon. She tried his phone again now. Another voicemail, but different this time. Hugo had erased his own message and left an automated one, a female one with a robotic twang. Odd. Elise shook her head as if to clear it of all the negative thoughts crowding in. She went to the sink, put the kettle on and texted her friend Susie: *Need some company and a heart-to-heart. Battersea Square? When suits? Looks like I'm going to be free all weekend.*

92

BY MID-AFTERNOON ON the third day they were ready, deep beneath Vauxhall Cross in the Stage. Ready for 'the insertion'. To Luke, this was starting to feel like he imagined a full-blown Hollywood production would be. There were just so many moving parts to this piece. While teams of people worked on his Steve Keane alias, putting in the finishing touches, the first approach to WaffenKrieg90 had been made online by the team from GCHQ, using the contact details Luke had brought back with him from Moscow.

He had slept surprisingly well both nights, kipping down in the windowless, one-bed overnight room with its grey airline-style washbag and towel laid out on the bed, ready for use at short notice. The place was so small as to be almost monastic, and the shower room was miles away down a corridor, but none of this bothered Luke. Angela had asked him for the keys to his flat, then sent someone round to collect a change of clothes. Elise had not been there when they'd called.

Luke was glad the mission was finally getting into gear. It was the distraction he needed. It meant he had successfully managed to avoid thinking about Elise for almost the entire weekend. But not quite. At one point, just past 3 a.m. on the Sunday morning, he woke up in an agony of self-recrimination as his thoughts crowded in on him. Why hadn't he made more of an effort to get back from Iran for her mother's funeral? Because it was obvious to him now: that glaring omission, even more than his unforgivable transgression over there, had been the single most destructive element in the slow-motion breakdown of their relationship. It was not just that he, Luke, had let her down in her hour of need. His absence at that crucial juncture had provided Hugo Squires with exactly the entrée he so craved. And Luke had no one to blame but himself.

He had lain awake for an hour, processing what had happened, what had gone wrong. On top of that, there was Jenny Li to worry about. True, he had been given no choice but to return home without her, but it still felt wrong, very wrong. And then, just after 4 a.m., he'd got a grip and reminded himself of the need to focus on the mission, the op. This was no time to be jogging backwards over all the things in his private life that could have been.

In the morning, just after breakfast, he had got straight back into character, transforming himself into the imaginary Steve Keane. Wardrobe arrived first, dressing him in black jeans with turn-ups above laced boots, thick belt with a large buckle, and a grease-stained T-shirt tight enough to show off his muscles.

'Any update on Jenny?' he'd asked Angela, as he sat in a chair that morning, feeling somewhat self-conscious as he was fussed over by the plastics people. They were giving his face a different look, just in case anyone on the other end of the video call should identify the real Luke Carlton from his recent trip to Lithuania.

Angela was still in the boiler suit, but she'd pulled on a sweatshirt with a big NYU logo over the top.

'Yes! I meant to tell you,' she replied brightly. 'She's out of hospital and on her way home. They've run some tests and whatever it was she went down with it was not Agent X, thankfully. They reckon she'll make a full recovery.'

'Thank God for that. So do we think this was just Petrov

yanking our chain?' Things had moved so fast since Moscow that Luke had yet to file his operational report. There were details about his trip that the Service had still to hear about.

'It looks that way, yes,' Angela said, her head tilted slightly to one side. 'But we're letting it go. Now is not the time for a bust-up with the Russians, not when they've helped us get inside this group. And you, Luke, have got much bigger things to worry about right now, so we all need to park it.'

At midday the Chief himself had come down to observe their progress. He had arrived just as the techies from GCHQ were going back over the format, the phrases, the jargon, everything Luke would need, to avoid arousing suspicion that this was what it really was: a sting. Fitted to the base of his throat, concealed by his T-shirt, was a small device: a VC, a voice corruptor. His voice would not sound radically different, but if anyone was checking and they chose to compare it to a recording of his real voice they would find that the sound waves simply did not match.

At 4.14 p.m. they were all set to go live with the Viber call, that being WaffenKrieg90's preferred means of communication, according to Petrov's prisoner. Luke sat hunched over the workbench, wearing a T-shirt that listed provincial British venues from some long-forgotten tour by a rock band almost no one would remember. His hands were blackened with engine grease, and just visible on his left bicep was a tattoo of a skull. Where his missing finger had been, the plastics team had attached a lifelike replica; his hand now looked like anyone else's. Just in case. The earpiece was so tiny you would have had to be right up next to him to detect it.

On the workbench in front of him lay the key to success or failure of this whole enterprise: his mobile phone. Except it was not really his mobile phone, it was a highly specialized piece of digital engineering, devised with input from all three intelligence agencies. If anyone cared to trace his location – and they had to assume that would happen – then it would reveal it as a private residence next to a Big Yellow Self Storage facility in Cowley, on the south-east edge of Oxford. The phone was loaded with

319

all the apps you would expect – WhatsApp, Instagram, Facebook, Twitter – but additional functions had been built in. Like the 'panic button' that simulated the noise of a doorbell in the background if Luke needed to abort a difficult conversation or avoid an awkward question. Meanwhile the techies from GCHQ would be trying to zero in with their scanners on the location of the people at the other end.

'Well, I think we're ready.' Dextra was standing in front of him; her clipboard was gone, but now she was wearing a headset and mike. He thought she looked tense, which was hardly surprising. He was feeling pretty wound up himself. She glanced at her watch. 'They're expecting you to call any minute now. Operations,' she spoke into her mike, 'are we good to go?'

She listened, looking at Luke, and nodded. 'They're all set. That just leaves you, "Steve". Any last-minute questions before I disappear behind that screen over there? Anything you're unhappy with?'

Luke felt his head was fit to burst with everything that had been crammed into it over the last three days. He knew there were 101 things that could go wrong, that just one misplaced word could torpedo the whole operation. But he couldn't afford to think like that. He could do this. He was ready.

'Nope,' he replied. 'Let's do it.'

93

LUKE WAS ALONE in the room. The only sound came from the artificially generated traffic noises from 'outside' – noises that emanated from the 3D surround-sound speakers embedded in the walls of the Stage. Yet he was very far from alone. He knew he was being observed by a dozen cameras and a dozen people, with every word, every syllable, every keystroke monitored and recorded.

A male voice spoke gently into his earpiece. The operational director. As calm and as measured as a Radio 4 announcer. 'All right, Steve. I want you to take your phone and open the contacts screen. You should see a list of contacts there. Now scroll down to the one that says Methuen.'

This was hardly rocket science, and they had rehearsed it only that morning, but, still, they were taking no chances.

'You've found it?' the voice continued in his ear. 'Just nod if you have . . . Okay, good. Now select that and tap the link that says free video call.'

A half-second pause, then a face swam into focus on his screen. He had not expected it to be a woman at the other end, especially not someone like this. Bespectacled, articulate and well-spoken, she introduced herself as Niamh. To Luke, she looked like a sales director for a multinational corporation, and for a moment he wondered if the boffins had blundered and given him the wrong number. But she didn't hesitate: she got straight down to business.

'Don't get any ideas just yet,' she said, in a crisp, businesslike tone. Not aggressive, just icy and to the point. 'We need to know a lot more about you.' Luke couldn't remember the last time he'd found himself in an interview situation like this, but he was primed for it.

'You got my 23andMe genetic test results I sent you, yes?' he replied.

'We did. Nobody's perfect, Steve.' Was this a joke? It was hard to tell, but no, she wasn't smiling. 'So your origins are four per cent Turkish,' she continued. 'How do you feel about that?'

Time for drama school. Luke adopted an expression of concentrated disgust. 'Sick as a parrot, to be honest. I hadn't expected that.'

Infinitesimally, he saw her expression soften. 'It's okay, Steve. Like I said, nobody's perfect. You're ninety per cent plus Aryan and not a trace of Yid in you, so that's a start. And Moscow have vouched for you.' Then, just like that, the icy stare was back. 'But right now we don't give a shit about any of that. We're having this conversation because there are things in your head that we need to know.'

Luke scratched an imaginary itch on his temple, just below his hairline, but said nothing.

'Can you still hear me?' Niamh asked. He nodded. 'Good. So before we agree to meet I've got some questions for you . . .'

And so it began. Interrogation by remote connection. A flurry of questions, some genuine, some not, all designed to throw him off-guard. Who was your commanding officer in SRR? What date was your court martial? When did you first log on to 8Chan? When did you start following White Power?

Luke never blinked. They had prepared him well for this and there was always the voice in his ear, feeding him all the right answers. Then came the one that floored him: a deliberate bear trap.

'What did you make of the ideas in Craig Stephens's manifesto?'

'Craig Stephens?' he'd repeated, playing for time.

'Yes. That's what I said,' she snapped, scowling now. 'Craig Stephens. Don't tell me you haven't even read his manifesto, *The Burning Towers*?'

Silence in his ear. Shit. Was the circuit broken? Or were the team behind him just as stumped by this as he was? Great. So, with no help coming from that direction, he'd have to take a command decision on this one and go with his gut.

Luke shook his head. 'Must have missed it.' He shrugged his shoulders in a gesture of nonchalance. There was a long pause. Had he blown it?

For the first time in their conversation, Niamh smiled. 'You missed it,' she said, 'because Craig Stephens doesn't exist. That was the correct answer, Steve.' She took off her glasses and leaned closer to the camera, her face looming unnaturally large and foreshortened on his phone's screen. 'Stand by and don't go away,' she said. 'We'll call you back in fifteen minutes.' Her image disappeared.

Luke breathed out slowly and sat back in his chair.

'Nice going,' said the voice in his earpiece. Luke opened his mouth to say something in reply, but the ops director cut him off.

'Ssh! Don't say a word to me until this is over. We'll need to purge your phone. Got to check they haven't sent you spyware on that call. It could remotely activate the mike. Apart from that, keep it up, you're doing great.'

It was a long fifteen minutes. When a further four minutes elapsed and there was no call back, Luke started drumming his fingers on the workbench. A delay could mean only one thing: they were having second thoughts about trusting him. Or someone in their group must be. Luke started to over-analyse all the answers he'd given, going back over them in his head, one by one. Then his phone lit up. They were back.

'Okay, Steve. We'd like to meet you. Tonight. You said you weren't far from London, right?'

Luke nodded.

'So we'll send you an exact address in a moment. Be there at eight thirty p.m. Don't be early, don't be late, and do NOT bring anyone else. Is that clear? And, Steve?'

'Yes?'

'Don't fuck about with us. Or it will go very badly for you. D'you understand?'

She didn't wait for his answer. The connection clicked off and the call went dead. Suddenly the room was full of people as the technicians surged in, taking his phone away for analysis while others disconnected his earpiece and mike. Then Angela came up to him, before he'd had a chance to get up from the prop workbench.

'Good job, Luke,' she said, placing a maternal hand on his shoulder. 'You're in.'

94

'WHERE THE HELL is Great Notley?' demanded the SIO, the senior investigating officer, as they clustered round the message on the screen. The communication was curt; it gave the rendez-vous Luke was to attend as a pub car park off the A131, just up from Chelmsford racecourse.

The Stage part of Operation Methuen was over, the mocked-up garage had served its purpose. Direction had now moved across the river to Thames House, the stolid 1920s building that served as headquarters for the Security Service. The entire joint 'fusion' team from MI6, MI5 and GCHQ had moved into the building's Intel Ops Centre. When a fast-paced investigation reached its crit-ical stage, as everyone now believed they were at, it was always here that an operation was run from, in close coordination with the Metropolitan Police.

'Great Notley?' repeated one of the surveillance analysts. 'My wife comes from there. It's just south of Braintree in Essex.' Within seconds a rolling map of the area was up on the wall screen and a route was being mapped out for Luke.

'Options,' someone said. 'It looks like he'd best take the Tube. Quickest way to get across London at this time on a Sunday.

Okay, here we are,' he said. 'He can get the Victoria Line from Vauxhall, change at Oxford Circus, then take the Central Line all the way up to Epping.' Luke was standing right next to the SIO yet somehow he was getting the old familiar feeling of being swept along by forces bigger than himself. The plastics team had made some final adjustments to his face, giving him a fuller, rounder jaw. Enough to pass scrutiny for twenty-four hours they'd told him, but don't get too close to anyone. Now, as the tactical details of his mission were being discussed around him, his hand kept reaching up and touching the unfamiliar contours of his face.

'Make sure we have one of our drivers ready and waiting to pick him up in a "random" minicab the moment he steps off the Tube at Epping,' said the SIO, adding, 'Is the jacket ready?'

The jacket. They'd already briefed Luke about this. It would be a tattered leather flying jacket with an inbuilt GPS and voice transmitter embedded and disguised as part of the zip. One of several options for field ops that the Security Service kept hanging on a rail in a long wardrobe on the ground floor. This would not only allow them to track him all the way to the source: it should, barring any jamming counter-measures, enable both MI5 and the Met to listen in on every conversation and judge exactly the right moment to move in. Luke was to be their human homing beacon.

'So it's ready? Good. Then we're all set.' The SIO was repeatedly driving one clenched fist into the palm of his other hand. 'Let's nail this, then. Oh, wait – Angela, you wanted to say something?'

Angela Scott, one of only three people seconded from across the river for this, walked over to stand next to Luke. She was still wearing her NYU sweatshirt but it hardly looked out of place: no one in that room was wearing business attire on a Sunday evening when the op was about to go critical.

'Can I borrow him for a moment?' She led Luke gently away by the elbow to a corner of the room.

'Listen, Luke,' she said, in a hushed almost-whisper while the others busied themselves with the final preparations. 'As your manager, I'm duty-bound to tell you it's not too late for you to back out of all this.' She waved a hand in the direction of the screens, the maps and the people behind them in the room. He noticed she was still holding on to his elbow. 'Okay, so I know that's not your style.' Her shoulders slumped slightly as she looked him in the eyes, searching in vain for some sort of reaction. 'That's why my Service recruited you in the first place. But, Luke, you know as well as I do, we've been at this point before, haven't we? Colombia. Armenia. Iran. Now this. You've had some really close calls and your luck can't hold out for ever.'

Luke gave her a questioning look. He was already tensed inside, like a coiled spring. The last thing he needed was someone trying to talk him out of it. 'Thanks, Angela. But I'd like to think it's a bit more than luck that got me through those encounters.'

'Oh, come on, Luke!' she said. 'This is no time to come over all macho. You're not invincible, none of us is. And these are not amateurs we're up against here. Their ideas may be abhorrent to you and me – to all of us – but some of these people are highly educated scientists. They've got enough know-how to develop this horrific bio-weapon. You slip up for one moment and they'll be on to you. And never mind what the SIO says.' She nodded towards him. 'The fact is, if the proverbial hits the fan, there's no guarantee we can get to you in time.'

'All right,' Luke replied calmly. 'So that's Angela the manager talking – and I appreciate your concern. But what I'd like to know is, what does Angela the person think?'

She took a step back from him, pursing her lips, and shook her head. 'Luke, you know I can't tell you that. What I can say is that I'm offering you an off-ramp here. This is a highly dangerous situation we're sending you into and, to put it bluntly, this is your last chance to pull out. No one will think the worse of you if you do.'

Luke glanced over her shoulder, to where they were carrying out a final comms check on the bug embedded in the jacket. The whole great machine was up and running. The cogs were whirring into place. Svalbard, Vilnius, Moscow: this was what they had worked so hard for. He returned her stare and smiled back at her. 'Maybe not, but *I* would, Angela. Look, I committed to this thing right from the start and I'm going to see it through. I do know the risks, I can assure you, and, yes, I accept them . . . There. Does that work for you?'

Angela reached out and squeezed his shoulder. 'Good luck, then,' she said. 'Let's finish this thing and close these bastards down.'

Luke put his hand over hers and squeezed it back. He turned away and shrugged himself into the leather flying jacket. Nothing more needed to be said.

95

Great Notley, Essex
Sunday, 20 March, 2024hrs GMT

SIX MINUTES. SIX minutes exactly remaining before he had to open the door of the minicab, walk out into the rain-splashed car park of the Crown and Anchor and take his life into his own hands. Luke sat on the back seat and looked out of the window, scanning the immediate area. The rain had turned to a light drizzle and the whole scene had a dank, dreary feel to it. He was finding the sheer Sunday-evening normality of it completely at odds with the seriousness of the mission. Nothing, even in Luke's four adrenalin-fuelled years with the Special Boat Service, had resembled anything like this. Back then he would be giving the final once-over to his personal weapons, his kit, his comms. His team would be buddy-buddy checking each other over and they would each know that if it did all go to rat shit they could always call for back-up. But not tonight. Not here. Where Luke was going, he was on his own, unarmed, at reach and at risk. And that both scared and excited him.

'Good to go, boss? Got everything you need?' The 'minicab driver' was ex-forces, now on semi-permanent contract to the Security Service. In the forty-five-minute drive from Epping Tube station they had exchanged a few brief words and established they had both done 'Herrick', operational tours in Afghanistan.

'See you on the other side, then,' Luke said, as he closed the door and walked out into the car park. The drizzle felt cool and fresh against his face, except where the plastics team had added extra roundness. There, he couldn't feel a thing.

'Comms check,' he spoke softly into the hidden mike. He had no earpiece: they had decided it was simply too risky, so this was a one-way conversation with the Intel Ops Centre. 'Centurion,' he added. 'I say again, Centurion.' It was the pre-arranged code word to tell them he was going active.

There were fewer than a dozen cars parked up outside the Crown and Anchor. Everything was bathed in the sickly yellow light given off by the sodium streetlamps nearby. It was enough for him to see that no one else was there. Except a solitary figure leaning up against the outside wall of the pub. It looked like he was having a pee. Classy, Luke thought, as he walked past and froze mid-step. Almost inaudibly, the man had uttered two words just as Luke came into earshot. 'Sieg Heil.'

'Sieg Heil,' Luke repeated the Nazi greeting, and turned to face him, making sure the swastika tattoo on his neck would be visible, even in the dim yellow light.

'Follow me,' the man said, retrieving a small duffel bag and slinging it over his shoulder, then leading them inside the pub. That's it? No ID check? No secondary questioning? Was Luke about to be introduced to the very people with their hands on one of the most hideous viruses ever concocted over a round of drinks in an Essex pub? This didn't seem real. And it wasn't.

The pub was only half full but it had a warm, cosy glow to it on this Sunday evening. One look at the clientele told Luke they were probably all locals and all regulars; no one here looked like a fanatic of any kind. But his contact led him past the drinkers and off down a passageway to the Gents.

'Wait here,' the man told him. He was shorter than average, late thirties, with a shaven scalp and a piece of shiny black onyx embedded in his right earlobe. Seconds later he emerged from the toilets and beckoned Luke to follow him. The moment they were inside the man slammed the door behind them and threw the duffel bag at Luke's feet.

'Change,' he ordered. 'Take off everything, including your kecks. There's a set of clothes for you in the bag.'

'Really? But I'm clean,' Luke lied, while at the same time he had to admire their opsec.

'Boss's orders,' came the reply. 'Don't hang about. We've still got a way to drive. And I'll need your phone off you too. Just hand it over.'

Right. So this wasn't the final rendezvous after all. Well, that made sense. These people were taking no chances.

They walked back out into the car park, the man carrying Luke's clothes stuffed into the duffel bag, the precious GPS and transmitter now lost to him and concealed inside. Without warning, he stopped and hurled it high into the air where it sailed over a hedge and into the wood the pub backed on to. Luke watched it go, noting the exact spot, but what use was that to him? Now he was without comms, cut off from back-up, operating blind and alone.

'It'll still be there when this is over,' said the man. 'You can go and fetch it then.' This? What exactly was 'this'? Luke hoped he was about to find out because all this had better be worth it.

The man took out a fob as they walked and the lights flashed once on a parked black Toyota Prius. They got in and buckled up. Then he spoke quietly into his mobile. 'POB.' Passenger on board. There it was again, that unsettling confluence of the harmless and familiar with something altogether far more sinister.

They drove off in silence. Clearly this was not the time for small talk. The road followed the edge of a large wood. They passed a Toby Carvery restaurant, a roundabout with streetlamps that lit up the fine drizzle still falling, and then they were turning down a tiny country lane marked 'Pod's Brook Road'. The man had made no attempt to conceal where they were going. No 'Put this on over your head', no 'Stay low in the back and keep your head down.' This could mean only one of two things. Either these people were so sure of 'Steve's' loyalty to the movement

331

that it wasn't in question or, more ominously, they had plans for him for when it was all over.

A sign appeared, looming up ahead in the Prius's headlights. 'Springwood Industrial Estate'. On the periphery of the headlights, in the darkened space on either side of the road, Luke snatched glimpses of blank, high-sided metal walls on row after row of windowless warehouses. They were alone on the road, the estate appeared to be deserted, yet Luke was making a mental note of everything he saw: the speedbumps, the number of streetlamps, the CCTV cameras.

With no warning, the man beside him braked hard and turned down a deserted road that ran alongside a chain-link fence, lit by more sodium lights. In silence he pulled up at a set of gates where a hooded figure emerged from the dark and shone a torch into his face before walking round to the passenger side and doing the same to Luke.

'It's him,' the driver told him and the hooded figure moved off to unlock the gates.

They drove around the back of a large, steel-grey warehouse, Luke counting the number of parked-up vehicles they passed on the way. When they stopped, the driver got out without a word, jerked his head towards a door with a red frame and beckoned him to follow. Luke couldn't help thinking there was something portentous about that door. By the time I come back out, he thought, I will have either succeeded in uncovering their plan or I will be in extreme danger. But now was not the time to hesitate. Squinting against the brightness of a neon striplight on the ceiling, he found himself standing in a rudimentary office. Three people were facing him, a woman and two men, and they seemed to be expecting him. He recognized one immediately. Short hair, glasses, no make-up, wearing a faded, military-style jacket and a tie-dyed scarf. It was 'Niamh', the woman who had interrogated him on the Viber call just a few hours earlier, and it was immediately obvious that she was in charge.

'Thank you for coming, Steve,' she said, with unexpected courtesy. 'We all appreciate your time and your commitment to the movement. Have a seat.' There were no handshakes, no offers of refreshments: it was straight to business. He noted that all three remained standing while the driver took up a position right behind Luke's shoulders.

'We just need to make sure you're as good at counter-surveillance as we're told you are,' she began. 'Can't afford any mistakes, can we?' She gave him a bleak smile. 'Got to make sure we've got the right person for the job.'

Luke said nothing.

'So, tell us, Steve. How many vehicles did you pass outside since we let you through the gates?'

'Four.'

'It's five. But one's under tarpaulin so maybe you didn't see it in the dark.'

Luke shrugged.

Niamh cleared her throat. 'Since Max here' – she nodded towards the driver – 'turned off the main road back there, how many CCTV cameras did you pass?'

'Since the roundabout, you mean?' Playing for time while he tried to remember.

'Yes, the roundabout.'

'Three.' But was it three? It might have been four. He really wasn't sure. Damn. He'd better not make a hash of this or his credibility as a covert counter-surveillance 'expert' would collapse like a house of cards. She looked at him for what seemed like a long time, then moved straight on to another question.

'And what were they? What make?'

Luke snorted derisively. He wasn't going to make this too easy for them. 'It's dark outside, for fuck's sake!' he replied.

'So you're saying you don't know?'

'No, I didn't say that,' Luke parried. He put his head on one side and scratched an imaginary itch beneath his ear, taking his time. 'Right, so you've got both dome and bullet cameras,' he resumed. 'That's a dome design above the door we just walked through. It's also called a turretcam. That'll give you a 360-degree view. Model looked like an Axis to me, but I'd need another look up close to be sure.'

All three of them were gazing at him intently now, but Luke was into his stride. All those hours of prep back in the Stage had readied him for exactly this.

'Then along the fence back there,' he said, 'you've got a couple of the older bullet designs. All of these have zoom lenses and they'll all give you five-megapixel resolution. Want me to go on?'

Niamh turned to the other two and gave them the faintest of nods. They all took their seats. So that was one reason why they hadn't made him put on a blindfold.

'Okay, Steve,' she told him. 'It seems like you do know your shit.' He could tell that all three were still scrutinizing him, but now the initial frisson of tension had evaporated. Niamh smiled at him encouragingly. 'So this is where you're going to make a difference to the movement,' she said, her tone noticeably warmer. 'It's where you add your name to the roll of honour of all those who are about to "do the right thing" to save everything we all believe in. We're going to show you the plan.'

96

ANGELA SCOTT STOOD in front of the rolling digital map that filled the screen covering nearly half of the wall in the Intel Ops Centre. It was a large-scale high-resolution map of an area of Essex that centred around the town of Braintree, spanning from Great Notley in the south up to the village of Beazley End in the north. A single red LED dot blinked forlornly on and off from a location just beside the A131. It was the GPS tracker inside Luke's discarded flying jacket. That part of the operation was already marked down as a fail and there was not a single face in the room that didn't look worried.

Angela had been a field operative, and a station chief in Mexico City, so she knew all about risk and betrayal. She knew from bitter experience exactly what it meant when an agent's identity was revealed or when a case officer's cover was blown. And she recognized this situation now as one that her Service would euphemistically call 'highly unstable'. The tech team from GCHQ had been unable to pinpoint Niamh's location on the other end of the Viber call because her people had been savvy enough to use a succession of proxy servers and firewalls. The team in Thames House were effectively blind.

'So our driver dropped Luke Carlton off here.' One of the case officers was using her laser pointer to indicate the car park of the Crown and Anchor pub. 'He managed to squeeze off a couple of low-res photos of the man who made the RV in the car park, then watched them leave. He got the licence plate, but he couldn't risk tailing them after that in case the Bravo spotted it was the same minicab that dropped Luke off and got spooked.'

'And the vehicle?' someone asked. Angela looked from one person to another in the room. She knew almost no one there. Yes, they were all professionals, but she would have felt a lot more comfortable sending Luke out there if she knew the team who were running this op.

'We've done the checks on the plate,' the case officer replied. 'It's a black Toyota Prius registered to a Mr Jankauskas, a Lithuanian. We've housed him as living on the outskirts of Reading. But that's where the lead goes cold. We've pulled up Border Force records and they show Jankauskas as having left the UK two months ago on a flight to Vilnius. So either he's slipped back into the country illegally or that's not his real name. All of which means . . .' she let out a short sigh '. . . that right now Luke is in the hands of these people and he could be anywhere in these grid squares.' She gestured towards the digital map on the screen behind her. 'For all we know he could be drinking tea with them . . . or face down in a ditch with his hands tied behind his back.'

Angela let out an involuntary gasp. This was Luke Carlton being discussed here, her own protégé whom she had nurtured and promoted up the ranks of the SIS career ladder. And she did not appreciate the cavalier way they were referring to his current status.

The SIO had clocked her reaction and waded in. 'Yes, right, thank you, Patricia. Let's not get too morbid here. Luke is in-play and that's what matters. He'll make contact as soon as he can.'

'Sorry, I shouldn't have said that,' the case officer apologized. 'I guess we're all running on empty here.'

The SIO glanced up at the digital clock on the wall. 'Right.

Movements. Met Police Counter-Terrorism have set up their own ops room at Cobalt Square and we're feeding whatever intel we have into them. The CT commander in the hot seat there is . . .' he stopped to check his notes '. . . Simon Bradshaw. Meanwhile, CTSFO are on their way over to Braintree—' He stopped as a hand went up.

'CTSFO?' someone questioned.

'Counter-terrorism specialist firearms officers. The operators in the grey ninja suits with all the Gucci kit. This is exactly what they train for. We've also got Cheltenham setting up a SIGINT listening envelope around the area as we speak. They're looking at sending up a drone, but apparently the weather state might be a problem.'

The SIO pressed the palms of his hands together, frowning. 'But that's all going to take time and they're not in place yet. So what does that mean?' He spread his hands and paused for a second. 'It means that for now we're effectively both deaf *and* blind. Luke Carlton remains our best hope – our only hope – of cracking this thing before it's too late.'

97

'PINCH POINTS. THAT'S what we call them.' Luke leaned forward across the workbench where the floor plan lay spread out in the little office inside the warehouse with the four of them hunched over it. 'Bottom of the escalator here, bottom of the stairs,' he jabbed a finger at the plan, 'and over here, where everyone comes out past the shops and on to the concourse. That's where most of the CCTV coverage will be focused. And it's where the British Transport Police spend most of their time watching. These are the spots where you're at maximum risk of detection.'

Luke's voice filled the small room. He was speaking in a calm, authoritative tone. He was Steve Keane, with years of experience in specialized reconnaissance and a man totally dedicated to their cause. And yet inside, his heart – and his mind – had gone into overdrive. They had just revealed the target: a mainline station, somewhere in Britain, he didn't know where yet – the floor plan had its title covered with masking tape. Jesus Christ. That meant these people were planning to release Agent X in a mainline railway station.

This was barbaric, sick, depraved. Yet he couldn't betray the slightest emotion. He had to remain in character, couldn't drop his guard for one second.

'Weapons?' Niamh asked him. So far, she seemed to be the only one doing the talking. She certainly seemed to be the brains of the operation. 'Are they armed, the BTP?'

'They can be,' Luke replied. 'But not always.'

'That's not helpful. We can't be dealing with maybes and might-bes. We need to know for certain. Can't you be more precise than that?' She exchanged a look of disapproval with the others.

'Look, I don't work for them,' Luke protested. 'I was in the forces, not the Old Bill, remember? But what I can tell you is that back in 2010, after the Mumbai attack, the mainline stations asked the Met for a twenty-four-hour armed response. The Met said they couldn't guarantee it so the Transport Police got given two million quid for their own firearms unit.' Just a little snippet he'd learned during his prep session down at the Stage.

'Right,' Niamh said. 'So we must assume they're armed, then.' She looked at the man next to her. 'Sven, can you take care of that?' She turned back to Luke. 'What about timings? Is the station staffed twenty-four/seven?'

Luke looked up from the floor plan and studied her face for a moment. Niamh had perfect, blemish-free skin and she looked so, well, normal. But behind those glasses was a look of frightening intensity: he could read the determination in her eyes. This was someone who had set her heart on a course of action from which nothing could dissuade her. When it came to the crunch, someone would have to take her down or this would never be over.

'Is the station staffed twenty-four/seven?' Luke repeated her question to himself out loud. 'Hard to say when you haven't told me which station it is.' There. He'd said it. First attempt to get the location out of her. Would she bite? He desperately needed her to take the bait.

Niamh did not respond straight away. She thought for a moment, squinting behind her glasses. When she did answer, it sent his pulse racing even faster.

'Would you leave us and step outside for a moment.' Not a

question, but an instruction. 'I need to discuss something in private. Max, stay with him.'

They stood outside in the dark, beneath the dome camera just above the door with the red frame. The one that Luke had correctly identified as an Axis model. 'Max', the driver who had delivered him to this bleak warehouse on the outer edge of an Essex town, sparked up a cigarette but kept his silence. He looked long and hard at Luke as he drew on it. Luke returned the stare. This guy's just a bit player in all this, he reminded himself. He's trying to act the tough guy, but he's obviously just a minor cog in the bigger machine.

The only thing that mattered now was finding out the exact target and the intended time of attack. Again, Luke asked himself the awkward question: if they've decided to share the plan with me, what are my chances of getting out of this alive? It was little comfort that Petrov's prisoner in Moscow had vouched for him: these people here barely knew him. Once he had performed his task he knew he'd be expendable. He looked across at Max, the driver, as he took another long drag on his cigarette. So far, Luke had only encountered four people at this warehouse, but there would be others inside, he was certain of it, and any number of them could be armed.

The red door to the warehouse opened, spilling light from the little office out on to the gravel forecourt. A figure appeared silhouetted in the frame, a man, the light behind him forming an incongruous halo around his head. He jerked his head towards the room inside. Max dropped his half-finished cigarette to the ground and crushed it with the heel of his shoe. They went in.

The three were standing facing him like a firing squad. No one was smiling. Shit! This didn't look good. Were they on to him? A last-minute spot check perhaps, revealing the holes in his hastily built cover story. Or maybe they'd simply decided he was expendable right now.

'Come here, Steve,' Niamh said gently. Luke kept his face expressionless, but to him the sound of his heart pounding in his ears was almost deafening.

'Are you committed?' she asked. He could see those cold eyes behind the glasses boring into his.

340

'I wouldn't be here if I wasn't, would I?' he retorted.

'And you're prepared to do whatever it takes?'

'I just told you, I'm committed.'

'That's good,' Niamh said. 'Because we've decided we need you in on the operation. You'll be riding in the front vehicle with the van following. Oh, and Steve, you'll want to get out of London after this.'

'That's great,' Luke replied, painting on a smile. 'I'm chuffed, I really am. But you still haven't told me what the target is.' And there it was, his second attempt. He waited for the answer, heart in his mouth. Was it too much? Too soon? Had he blown it?

'We're going to tell you now,' Niamh replied. 'You're among friends here so we know we can trust you. And once we do tell you . . .' she paused to give her words impact '. . . there is no going back, Steve. Not for you, not for any of us. Because this is a war, Steve, and we're striking the first blow for the sake of your children and your grandchildren. You want them to live in a better country, don't you? A cleaner, purer place, without all these scum polluting our nation, right?'

Luke nodded vigorously. *Play the part, learn everything, then get the hell out and raise the alarm as fast as you can.*

Niamh was still speaking, flanked by the two men who looked at Luke, their faces set in grim determination.

'So when we began to plan this we looked at a lot of different targets. A mosque, a synagogue, a shelter for migrants. Our friends in Moscow and Vilnius preferred the last one. But that's all old-school, right?' Luke nodded, not wishing to interrupt her at this critical moment. 'And we're looking for impact. Real impact. Something that will change the course of history. You see, Steve, everything up until now – Christchurch, Oslo, all the other small victories on the journey we're taking – these are just warm-ups for the final act. This . . .' again, the dramatic pause '. . . this is going to be the big one.'

Enough preamble. Just tell me the bloody target.

'The target,' Niamh said slowly, 'is King's Cross station. At 0830 hours tomorrow we're releasing the virus, right in the middle of rush hour.'

98

Great Notley Country Park, Essex
Sunday, 20 March, 2140hrs GMT

FOUR VANS, TWO teams and some extra muscle and firepower provided by the Directorate of Special Forces in Regent's Park Barracks. Metropolitan Police Gold Command were throwing everything at this one, deploying two of the UK's full-time operational teams of Counter-Terrorism's specialist firearms officers. Lines were being kept open with constant running updates provided to the home secretary, the director of the Office of Security and Counter-Terrorism, the Met Police commissioner, the director of Special Forces and the director-general of MI5.

It had already been dark for some three hours when the convoy of unmarked vehicles drove through the entrance of the deserted park just off the A131. Armed with an assortment of MCX carbines, Glock 17 pistols and Benelli M3 shotguns, the thirty-one grey-uniformed men and women were parked up next to the deserted children's discovery park, engines running, ready to move at a moment's notice. With Luke's last-known location being the Crown and Anchor pub at Great Notley, this site had been chosen as their forward operating base, a springboard from which they could pounce the moment they got a bead on the people he was with.

In the front of the lead vehicle sat Firearms Inspector Gwyneth Newbold, her earpiece linking her to Gold Command in Cobalt Square, just south of Vauxhall Cross. Next to her was a man with an open laptop and headphones, a comms specialist on attachment from GCHQ in Cheltenham.

'Anything yet?' asked Inspector Newbold.

'Nothing,' he answered, with a slight shake of the head. 'These people are not stupid. They're staying off-air.' He removed his headphones and turned towards her. 'But we've got the triangulation sorted on all the mobile phone masts in the area.' He tapped the laptop that was resting on his knees and showed her the screen where a signal pulsed from each of the transmission masts. 'So if any of the numbers on MI5's database for this case go live, we should be able to zero in on a location within seconds.'

'Okay. Tell me the moment you get anything.'

'Ma'am?' One of her team was knocking at the window, helmet on, goggles pushed up.

'What is it?'

'We've tagged a suspect vehicle a mile out that's just shot a red light going through Braintree. It's doing well over eighty and it's heading west towards London. Could be nothing, but—'

She didn't hesitate. Yes, it could be nothing. But at the same time it could be a van loaded with canisters of Agent X, driven by the very people they were trying to stop and neutralize.

'Get after it!' she ordered, then got straight on the net to Gold Command to order Essex Constabulary to set up immediate snap roadblocks.

For Inspector Gwyneth Newbold, staying behind in the darkened car park of Great Notley Country Park while half her team raced off in hot pursuit, it was a nail-biting nine minutes. When the call came through her shoulders visibly slumped. 'Fuck it,' she swore. 'It was just some pissed-up boy racer who's had a bust-up with his girlfriend. I want everyone back on-station now! It was a false alarm.'

343

99

Near Braintree, Essex
Sunday, 20 March, 2158hrs GMT

THE WORDS SEEMED to explode inside Luke's head as she spoke them.

'King's Cross station, 0830 hours, middle of rush hour. A chosen few of us, including you, of course, will be safe up at the farm.' As the details of Waffenkrieg90's target were finally revealed to him, he felt a rising sense of horror. This was so utterly, gut-churningly horrific that he didn't know what he could say. But all three were looking at him, as they stood there in the warehouse office, and they were clearly expecting a reaction.

'That,' Luke said, 'is pure genius.' He let a smile spread slowly over his face while inside he was feeling so repulsed he was worried he might actually throw up on the spot.

'I know!' Niamh brightened. 'It's brilliant, isn't it? Twenty-five thousand commuters coming into King's Cross at that time and trains heading off to Birmingham, Manchester and Edinburgh, all taking the virus with them. Everyone's very excited. Right . . .' She spread out her arms, welcoming him into the fold. 'Come and meet the rest of the team.'

One by one, they filed out through the inner door leading from the office into the cavernous interior of the warehouse, Luke following next to last. Once he'd gone through the door, Max clanged it shut behind them, with a metallic bang that made Luke flinch. His nerves were already screaming at him and a voice of reason was shouting, *Get out now while you can!* But outwardly Luke was projecting an image of quiet competence: the surveillance expert, come to help steer them through this final phase.

Blue plastic industrial barrels. Those were the first things he noticed. He counted about twenty as they walked past, lined up against the wall. Black carrying handles, black lids, grey seals, no markings. He would need to remember those details. Nobody commented on them.

King's Cross station . . . 0830 hours . . . Those words kept ringing in his head like an alarm bell, growing ever louder. Got to get word to the team at Thames House. But how? His phone had been taken from him back at the pub in Great Notley. Luke was now on hyper-alert for any opportunity to slip away unseen, but would it ever come?

And their plan was insane. Releasing a lethal, lab-manufactured biological weapon into a crowded transport hub like King's Cross? Did these people not realize what a blunt instrument that was? Agent X was not going to distinguish between race, colour or creed. It killed everyone. Horribly. After Svalbard that should have been obvious. And yet here they were now in this Essex warehouse, so desperate to make their mark on the world they were preparing to unleash untold misery in the name of 'changing the course of history'. All to suit their batshit-crazy doomsday worldview.

'This will be your vehicle,' Niamh was saying, as they approached a white Ford Transit van parked up inside the interior of the warehouse. The rear doors were open and two men were loading duffel bags into it. They carried on with their task, not pausing to acknowledge the newcomer. If he was with Niamh he needed no introduction. 'You'll be travelling up front next to the driver and Klaus here.' She indicated a tall, thin man with piercing blue eyes and a shaven scalp. 'He's one of the decoys.'

Luke adopted an expression of eager anticipation. 'Decoys?' he asked.

'Yes, of course.' She sounded surprised that he should even be asking the question. 'We have to cover our bases. Klaus will be setting off a distraction next to the taxi rank outside. That will draw attention away from the target while the canisters are being delivered in place. And we have another trick ready, don't we, Klaus? You can tell him.'

'That is correct,' Klaus answered, in a pronounced German accent. 'At seven in the morning we will be alerting the media that an explosive device has been planted inside the NEC conference centre in Birmingham.' He seemed to be looking at Luke as if waiting for a sign of approval.

'Good call,' Luke said. 'That'll keep them busy.'

'There is no such device in Birmingham,' Klaus added. 'But now we can show you the real devices. I must ask you not to approach too closely. Our science people are still making final checks inside the cabin over here.'

It was a cabin about the size of a caravan inside the main warehouse – a shed within a shed – with a flight of three metal steps leading up to the door. Niamh went up first, signalling for him to follow. Once inside, the four of them stood against a wall at a respectful distance, and Luke caught his breath. He had just seen the canisters for the first time: the instruments of death, laid out neatly in a row beside their backpacks. They were shiny and silver, about the same size as a Thermos. A man and a woman, both wearing goggles and neoprene gloves, were fussing over them. From where Luke was standing he could just make out that each one had a spray nozzle at the top and some sort of timer device taped to it. He strained to see past the pair with the goggles to try to count them all. Seven. Those were just the ones he could see. But what if they had more in reserve?

'I know what you're thinking,' Niamh said, turning to him with a strange glint in her eyes.

'What's that?'

'Are we safe in this room with these?' She waved towards the silver canisters. 'Well, don't worry, Steve. We've got some of the most committed scientists in the business working for us. We've taken every possible precaution.'

No, you haven't, Luke thought, *or we'd all be wearing PPE and gas masks right now.* And then there was the incident in Svalbard where they had accidentally infected one of their own. No, this was not good. He wanted to get out of the cabin, but he couldn't because Niamh was still talking to him, that strange light in her eyes again.

'Once the timers have been activated there's enough virus in each of those containers to kill thousands. Slowly and painfully.' She then surprised Luke by touching his arm. 'We're making history tomorrow, Steve.' This was something they kept on repeating. She looked at him meaningfully. 'And you're a part of it now.'

The door of the cabin swung open. A short, squat man stepped inside, walked up to Niamh and spoke quietly in her ear.

'Now? Already?' Luke heard her say. He saw her look at her watch. 'Okay, take them to the side office. We'll be there in a moment.'

And just as she spoke those words Luke spotted it, out of the corner of his eye: a mobile phone. Still lit up and unlocked. One of the two 'scientists' must have just put it on the corner of the table, so very nearly within his reach. Was this a test? Luke's eyes swept the cabin like a radar scanner. No one was watching him: all eyes were on the pair working on the canisters. He edged closer to the table, his heart beating faster, a plan forming in his head in double-quick time. If he could only lift it, conceal it inside his jacket, press a couple of digits to stop it relocking itself, then tell them he needed the loo, he would lock himself inside and alert Angela and the team at Thames House. It would take seconds, that's all. He began to reach out, pulse racing. Suddenly a hand was on his shoulder. Someone was behind him.

'Steve.' He turned to see Niamh's earnest face. 'We have visitors,' she said casually. 'They're early. It's the money people. They financed all of this.' She nodded towards the row of deadly canisters. 'They've been part of the movement since the start. Now they want to see it through. They've come to witness the final preparations. That's a nice touch, don't you think? Come, I'll introduce you.'

Luke felt both relief and frustration as they stepped out of the cabin. He hadn't felt safe for a second in there, knowing what those canisters contained and what it could do to the human body. But he had also missed his chance to grab the phone and knew he might not get another. They walked back through the warehouse in silence to the cramped little side office with its noisy metal door, the space where only a few minutes earlier Luke had passed his final entry test. He was the last to go through, but already he could hear the clamour of voices on the other side of the door and even laughter. The money people.

Luke squeezed into the office, feeling self-conscious. He had passed both of Niamh's interrogations and he'd been vouched for by Moscow, but he knew he would still be on probation with this organization. He took the opportunity to get a look at some of the people in the room. They were a strange collection, quite different in their own ways: Niamh, Klaus and Max, plus a fourth, silent figure in a denim jacket and an old Status Quo T-shirt. But there were smarter people too. A couple of them were wearing expensive waxed Barbour jackets. One, the shorter of the two, had his back to him. Luke was about to look past him when the man began to turn in his direction.

In a moment of sheer, gut-punching horror, Luke stood frozen to the spot as he recognized the face.

He knew this man.

It was Hugo Squires.

100

Battersea High Street, London
Sunday, 20 March, 2217hrs GMT

ELISE MAYHEW FELT deliciously naughty. She also felt guilty, and sad. In fact, right now she could feel her emotions turning over like washing in a tumble dryer. It was only supposed to be the one glass of wine with her friend Susie.

'Should you be . . . you know?' Susie had cautioned, gesturing towards Elise's midriff.

'Sod it,' Elise had replied, as they settled into a corner seat in the bar off Battersea Square. 'I'll just have the one. What harm can that do?'

It was now approaching last orders and between them they had finished off a bottle of Chardonnay, Elise drinking rather more than her half-share.

'He was just never there for me.' She sighed, taking another sip. 'All these years I thought Luke was the man I would marry, you know, have kids with, grow old with.' She put down the glass and looked around the bar as if searching for answers as to how it had all gone so wrong.

Susie gave Elise's shoulder a comforting rub. 'Well, you've certainly jumped in with both feet now, haven't you?' she said, with a smile. 'So forget about Luke. Is this Hugo going to make an honest woman of you, then?'

Susie had always been very direct, no beating about the bush for her. It was one of the reasons Elise liked her. She regarded her friend with a slightly guilty expression. 'Um . . .'

'Oh, bloody hell, Lise.' Susie slapped the palm of her hand down theatrically on the wooden surface of the table. People nearby turned to look at them. 'Don't tell me. You haven't told him yet, have you?'

'I haven't had a chance!' Elise protested. 'I only found out a few days ago and this isn't something you just tell someone over the phone. I don't even know how he's going to react.'

'I don't want to be indiscreet,' Susie said, toying with the empty packet of crisps they had just shared, 'but how can you be so sure the baby is his and not Luke's?'

'Well, that's an easy one,' Elise replied. 'Because Luke and I haven't had sex for God knows how long. All right? And before you say what I know you're going to ask, no, it was just the once with Hugo. We got carried away one night and it was never supposed to happen.'

Susie shook her head in mock disapproval. 'You're going to have to let him know, Lise.'

'Yes, thanks for telling me the bleeding obvious.'

'Go and see him, then, for goodness' sake. It's not like we're still living in lockdown or something. Just do it. What are you waiting for?'

Elise took a long sip of wine, almost a gulp, and put down the glass rather too quickly, then twirled her finger in the drops that had spilled on the table.

'The truth is, Susie, I don't actually know where Hugo is right now. I can't get hold of him. He's changed his voicemail message and he's not returning my calls.' She looked up in despair. 'I don't know what to do. He seems to have vanished off the face of the Earth.'

101

Near Braintree, Essex
Sunday, 20 March, 2219hrs GMT

FOR ALL OF four seconds neither of them spoke. Luke stared hard at the man across the room, this ordinary-looking individual in a Barbour jacket and scarf. Hugo Squires. His nemesis. Now in more ways than one. This was the man who had stolen his girl from right under his nose, not just stolen her but fathered her child. This uber-confident investment banker who always seemed to pop up in Elise's life every time that he, Luke, was away on a mission. But as he regarded him now, Luke knew he was so, so much more dangerous than that. Christ, how could he have underestimated the man so badly? All this time he had considered Hugo Squires to be little more than an irritation, an almost comical figure with his flash car, his monogrammed shirts, his house in the country, and his occasional bursts of intolerance bordering on fascism. Not any more. For whatever fucked-up reason, Squires was part of this movement, this doomsday death cult, and now Luke was just seconds away from being exposed for who he really was. Squires might not have known exactly who Luke worked for, but he knew it was something to do with the government and that was enough.

Hugo Squires broke off the stare and pushed his way quickly

through the throng of people to where Niamh was standing. Luke saw him say something in her ear and her expression change to shock and anger as she turned sharply towards him. It was almost like watching a film he'd already seen, a film with a very bad ending. In those few seconds, that tiny precious interlude between being 'made' by Hugo Squires and the moment when they would overpower him, the possible scenarios raced through Luke's mind. Make a run out of the door into the warehouse? No chance. A bulky figure was standing with his back to it, blocking the exit. Take him down and race out of the door all the same? No, they'd catch up with him in the warehouse before he could even find the exit. Make a break for the outer door of the office? No dice. Between him and that outer door stood at least four more people and then there was the hooded figure on the locked gate outside. He would never make it. Luke just had to face it: his only way out of this was to play for time until rescue came. If it came.

Niamh moved fast. She shouted something he didn't catch and the next moment three people had rushed him, pinning his arms behind him. Luke had to use every ounce of self-restraint not to fight back, because he reckoned he could have taken them. But one of them was holding something that looked very much like a Taser. The odds were not good.

The blow to his face came hard and fast. Niamh's own face was just centimetres way from his as she pulled back her fist to hit him a second time.

'You piece of SHIT!' she hissed venomously. She was so close he even felt a drop of her spittle land on his cheek. 'We trusted you! We let you in – people vouched for you! We thought you were one of us! But you're not, are you? Turns out you belong to the enemy. You're part of the whole Judaeo-liberal conspiracy that's sending this country down the drain!'

He sensed her preparing to lash out again and this time he was ready for it. He managed to twist his body to one side to protect his groin just before she brought her knee up hard between his legs.

She poked her finger against his cheekbone, just below his left eye. 'Bastard's got nothing to say, has he? Because we'll get the answers out of you – *Steve.*' She spoke his cover name sarcastically. 'And it's going to hurt, believe you me.'

As she was speaking, Luke could feel his arms being pulled tighter behind his back and some sort of cord being tied around his wrists. *Never get caught.* That's what the instructors had always told him, over and over. He would have to do some very fast talking now if he was going to get out of this alive.

'This man,' Luke told her, jerking his head towards Hugo Squires, 'is the one full of shit. Whatever bollocks story he's just told you has got nothing to do with me or the movement. I told you I was committed and—'

Luke didn't get to finish his sentence. Someone behind him shouted, 'Shut it, bitch!' then a blow to the back of his head plunged his world into darkness.

102

Thames House, London
Sunday, 20 March, 2242hrs GMT

THE EMPTY TAKEAWAY pizza boxes sat, upended, in a waste-paper bin in the corner of the Intel Ops Centre. Someone had made an unsuccessful attempt to fold them in half and given up so they sat there, exuding their stale odour, along with the empty Diet Coke cans, the dregs of a hastily snatched meal on the go. It was often like this when a live op was up and running and when it was nearing the endgame. Everyone on the team just put their lives on hold: evenings got cancelled, date nights blown out, mealtimes ignored. The mission demanded total focus from everyone involved. It was one of the sacrifices of the job.

Angela Scott was used to this. She remembered her stint as head of station in Mexico City when she'd kept a stash of take-away menus taped to the wall by the door for the times when an op was under way and normal life had simply ground to a stop. Now she sat hunched over her workstation, earpieces dangling down her neck, nervously tapping the end of a biro on the desk. She had lost count of when she had last had what anyone could call a 'normal day', a day that wasn't completely dominated and subsumed by the crisis that had erupted out of an Arctic blizzard in Svalbard. That was only thirteen days ago, but to Angela,

354

and everyone else working on this op, it felt like months. She could feel the fatigue building behind her eyes as she concentrated hard on what the person at the other end of the phone was saying.

'I'm telling you,' the voice said, 'they had input from Moscow. I can say that with a high degree of probability. It's not RIM, but it's people very similar. Angela, we're getting ourselves caught up in the middle of a Russian turf war here.'

The voice was Jenny Li's. She was back from Moscow, her temperature normal, but still recuperating in the Service's country house in Sussex, where a medical team was monitoring her. She was clearly itching to be in on the action. Jenny had insisted on being patched through to the IOC at this late hour and Angela had taken the call immediately.

'RIM?' Angela replied. 'You mean the Russian Imperial movement, that ultra-nationalist outfit based in St Petersburg?'

'Similar, but it's not them. It's another group altogether. They're in Moscow and they've got people inside state security. I had some interesting conversations while I was over there.'

Angela ran her fingers through her hair, swept it back off her forehead and sighed. Right now, more than ever, she craved a cigarette, but she had given up and that was that: she wasn't going back. 'I'm sorry, Jenny,' she said, 'but this makes no sense whatsoever. If that was the case then why would Colonel Petrov have given Luke this valid lead into the group over here?'

'Listen to what I'm saying,' Jenny replied abruptly. 'It's a turf war. Petrov is GRU. And these people are tied in to their rival agency, the FSB. Look, we've known for some time there's been an inter-agency rivalry between those two. The GRU's been making a lot of waves recently on the international scene – Salisbury, Montenegro, Ukraine, the downing of Malaysian airliner MH17 – and that's obviously pissing off people in the FSB.'

'And so? What's your conclusion?' Angela could be abrupt herself at times, but the two women had worked together long enough that neither took offence.

'Let me give you what I think,' Jenny Li said. She went quiet for a moment and Angela thought the line had dropped out.

'Sorry,' Jenny resumed, 'just had to wait for someone to go past.' She sounded none the worse for her recent ordeal in Moscow – in fact, the Service's foremost expert on CBRN seemed more alert than ever. 'So, it may well be that Agent X was originally intended for a specific target on Moscow's hit list – Chechen separatists, jihadists in Idlib, who knows? It's hard to see a biological weapon this sophisticated getting developed without the use of a state laboratory. But—'

'I thought there was a "but" coming,' interjected Angela.

'But it's ended up in the hands of this far-right transnational group and it looks very much like someone in the FSB is trying to exploit Russia's inter-service rivalry.'

'How exactly?'

'Isn't it obvious? By helping an ultra-nationalist group acquire the pathogen, then dumping all the blame on to the GRU. They actually *want* Petrov and his people to take the rap for this. They want to bring him down, to clip the GRU's wings, as it were.'

Angela was still frantically tapping her biro on the desk as she listened to this. She took her time before answering. 'Jesus, Jenny, that's a lot to take in. I suppose it's plausible. Have you written it up in your report?'

'Well, do you have another explanation? Because I don't. And, yes, it is in my report. I'm about to send it to the Chief and the DG.'

'Okay. Good work, Jenny. Look, I have to go. We've got a situation here. We've managed to run Luke inside the target group in Essex, but they've taken his comms off him and he's gone dark on us.'

'Not the first time he's done that.' Jenny and Angela had once spent an entire lunchbreak in the Service canteen comparing notes about how bloody exasperating Luke could be to work with.

'This is different,' Angela replied. 'It's mission-critical. If we can't re-establish comms with him, we've no hope of stopping these people before it's too late.'

'How long has it been?'

Angela glanced up at the digital clock on the wall. It was nearly 11 p.m. 'It's coming up to two and a half hours now. That's since the Thames House driver dropped him off to meet the contact. Luke had a GPS tracker sewn into his jacket. They didn't find it, as far as we know, but they made him do a complete change of clothes.'

'Shit. That's not good. These people are ruthless, Angela. God knows what they'll do to him if they see through his cover.'

'Yes, thank you for that. You think we don't know this? We're all worried witless about him.'

103

Near Braintree, Essex
Sunday, 20 March, 2255hrs GMT

SWIMMING. LUKE WAS swimming. At least, that was what it felt like. He was back at Poole on the Dorset coast, at the SBS base, doing his underwater lengths of the indoor pool in boots and kit. He was holding his breath and kicking out. Up above him the surface wobbled and shimmered, but there was something bad up there, something dangerous, something he desperately needed to keep away from. He tried to stay down, but it was no good, he had to come up for air, rising slowly to the top. And at that moment, breaching the surface of that imaginary swimming pool, Luke Carlton regained consciousness.

The back of his head throbbed with pain from where they'd hit him. His arms were pinned back, spread eagled, straining the muscles in his shoulders almost to breaking point. He tried to crane his neck round to one side to see what was restraining them. And it was only then, in that awful moment, that he saw what they had done to him while he was unconscious.

They had put him in the cabin and tied him to the canisters of live Agent X.

Turning his head from left to right, Luke could just see the bindings that lashed his wrists to a metal cage holding the silver

358

canisters with their aerosol nozzles and their timers. He was in about the most dangerous place on the planet.

'Bet you wished you'd stayed at home now.' The voice came from somewhere he couldn't see. It was familiar. He'd heard it before. But, still dizzy from the blow, he couldn't place it at first.

Hugo Squires walked slowly round until he was in Luke's field of vision. He pulled up a chair, turned it around and sat on it, resting his arms on the back, regarding Luke with a contemptuous sneer. He was still wearing his waxed green jacket with the baggy pockets. It looked utterly out of place in this functional warehouse with its vile contents and its sociopathic occupants.

'Fucked up royally, didn't you, Carlton?' he said. 'You thought you could stop this thing single-handed, did you?' He shook his head slowly. 'Always got to play the hero, haven't you? Mr Bloody SAS or whatever *Boy's Own* outfit it was you were in. Don't you think Elise has had enough of all that nonsense, hmm? Don't you think she got tired of you running off to play Action Man and leaving her on her own the whole time?' Luke stayed silent, just eyed him coldly, without emotion.

Squires got up from his chair and walked over to where Luke was pinioned to the cage. He grabbed Luke's jaw and yanked it to one side. A large piece of synthetic flesh came away in his hand, part of the work done by the plastics team in the Stage earlier that day.

'Pathetic,' he said, flinging the lump of gelatine prosthetic make-up on to the floor. 'What sort of half-arsed disguise was that supposed to be?' He held up his hand. 'You know what? Don't even bother telling me. Because these people know exactly who you are now that I've told them.'

Luke stayed silent, waiting for the right opportunity. He reckoned he still had one ace up his sleeve and he would only get one chance to play it.

'You work for MI6,' Squires continued, 'or should I say the Secret Intelligence Service?' He spoke the words slowly and with sarcasm. 'Well, it's not so secret now, is it?' He gave out a short, bitter laugh. 'They had you tagged in Vilnius. You had a lucky escape there. Still, you're here now and the others will want to get started on you soon.'

'All right, Squires, let's cut the bullshit,' Luke said.

'Ooh, fighting talk! From the man who's about to be in a whole world of pain.'

'Look,' continued Luke, 'I don't like you, you don't like me. We never have done. But come on! These aren't your people, Squires. You've got way too much to lose. You've got a good life, a place in the country. Why would you want to get mixed up in this death cult?'

Hugo Squires had returned to his chair and he sat there, shaking his head in mock sadness. 'You really don't know a damn thing, do you, Carlton? I bet you don't even know what "puts" and "calls" are. Well, do you?'

'Enlighten me.'

Squires glanced at his watch. 'They'll be coming through that door any moment now so we haven't got time for me to give you the full lecture. But I'll make it easy for you. If you think the market is going to fall, you buy a contract called a "put option". That gives you the right to sell an underlying stock at a certain price, the price it was before the market fell.'

Luke watched him explaining this with a rising sense of incredulity. There they were, sharing a room with canisters of a lethal pathogen, inside a warehouse peopled by fanatical, possibly suicidal far-right extremists. And this man in a Barbour jacket was calmly talking about the stock market.

'A "call option",' explained Squires, really warming to his subject now, 'is the reverse. If you think a stock or a sector is going up you buy a call option.'

Luke's mouth fell open a fraction. Suddenly he got it. So that was why Squires was here. His motive wasn't ideological at all. It was nothing of the kind. It was sheer, naked greed.

Squires picked up on his facial expression. 'So you get it now, do you? That's good. Elise always said you were smarter than you look.'

'Let me get this right,' said Luke, still wincing from the strain on his arms and wrists. 'You've financed all this just to make money out of thousands of people dying from a virus?'

Squires looked positively pleased with himself. It made Luke sick to his stomach.

'Not just me, Carlton. I really can't take all the credit. There's a small consortium of like-minded people who have . . . Well, let's just say we've invested wisely. When this thing goes off it's not hard to guess which stocks are going to plummet like a stone. In fact, even you could probably work that out, soldier boy.'

Now it was Luke's turn to sneer.

'You're off your head,' he told him. 'You don't honestly think no one's going to notice your trades?'

'No one,' Squires replied, his monobrow crinkling in a frown, 'is going to notice our trades because we've concealed them far and wide in multiple offshore accounts. Brass-plate addresses in hot countries that most people in the FCA have never even heard of.' He looked at Luke with mock concern. 'Oh, and if you're worried about the virus on our account that's really very sweet of you, but we've got enough provisions stocked up to last us until it burns itself out. Anyway,' he said, standing up, 'when they bring in the blowtorch and the pliers – oops, I wasn't supposed to tell you what's coming – you can console yourself that someone you knew – me – is going to be very, very rich from all of this.'

Luke felt his anger boiling over in abject fury. Every sinew in his body wanted to leap up from where he lay, bound, and tear into this man. Instead, he kept his cool. It was time to play that last card.

'All right, Squires, you win,' he said, trying to sound calm and collected when all he really wanted to do, more than anything in the world, was to rip Squires's head off and stamp it into the ground. 'But what if I were to tell you that your son will grow up knowing his father had murdered countless people in cold blood?'

'What the hell are you talking about?' Squires was standing over him now, frowning down at his captive. 'I haven't got a son.

Jesus, Carlton, you're getting more desperate with every minute. Just accept it. You'll be dead soon and it will all be over.'

I knew it! This was exactly what Luke had suspected. Elise hadn't told Hugo Squires about the baby. 'You still don't know, do you?' Luke said evenly. 'Well, maybe it's time you did. You're going to be a father, Squires. Elise is carrying your baby.'

For a second Squires stood stock-still and speechless. Then he gave a short, derisive snort of laughter. 'Pathetic, Carlton. That is truly pathetic. Is that really your best shot?' He began walking towards the door. 'Oh, wait, I nearly forgot. I've always wanted to do this.'

He strolled back, deliberately slowly, and launched a kick at Luke's trapped body. It struck him in the ribs, painfully, but at least it was on his right side, not the one still recovering from the knuckle-duster in Vilnius.

'I've had enough of this pantomime now,' Squires said, walking briskly towards the door of the cabin. 'It's time I told them you're ready for your appointment.'

104

Near Braintree, Essex
Sunday, 20 March, 2322hrs GMT

ONE OF THE golden rules of E and E – escape and evasion –
Luke knew all too well was that your best chance of getting away,
your best 'window of escape', was during the early minutes of
captivity. That was before your captors secured your bindings
and moved you to a more permanent location. After that, your
odds of a successful escape fell off rapidly. Luke knew he'd
missed an opportunity – the moment when Hugo Squires spotted him. He wouldn't have made it, but he couldn't let another
chance like that go. He silently cursed himself. It seemed all that
training had come to nothing now and his immediate future was
looking very grim indeed.

Luke knew he had only a few minutes before they came for
him and he doubted he could work his hands free in time. He
needed to focus, to think like a professional, to assess the situation calmly despite everything. These people may be fanatical
sociopaths, but they wouldn't be so stupid as to fire up a blowtorch next to the canisters of deadly agent. They'll have to untie
me before they can move me, he thought. And that may be my
one and only window. He needed a weapon, something to even
up the odds. He looked around for something, anything, he could

use. Nothing. The floor was bare. And then there it was: a glimmer of metal protruding over the edge of the workbench. It looked like a wrench or a spanner and it would have to do. Now all he had to do was get to it in time.

And then the door opened. There were three of them. First through the door was Niamh, followed by two heavily built men he hadn't seen before. Shaven skulls, beards, black leather jackets, one carrying a knife, the other a length of cord. Luke braced himself. This was about to get very ugly.

Niamh squatted in front of him and regarded him coldly for several seconds before she spoke. He could see nothing human in those eyes: they looked completely dead to him. And that, for the first time, left him seriously scared.

'You're going to be quite a piece of art, Luke Carlton, once we're done with you. They might just put what's left of you in the Tate. You see Sean here?' She indicated the man next to her, his fist curled around the handle of the knife. 'He's pretty handy with that thing. You could even call him an artist in his own way.' The man grinned and licked his lips in anticipation. 'We had a little discussion next door. We thought we'd begin on your forehead. A nice, neat swastika. It'll hurt, but I expect you're used to that. Then we'll turn you on your front so he can work on your back. That'll take a little longer so you'll have to be patient with us.'

Luke said nothing. Angela had been right. His luck had had to run out one day and now it had. He tried to focus instead on what he needed to do when the moment came.

'It'll just be the two letters,' Niamh went on. 'WP. White Power. But Sean's going to make them nice and thick, so that'll be quite a bit of flesh coming off you. Of course you might not be conscious by then, but, hey, don't worry, we'll wake you up. Right, then.' She rubbed her hands together. 'Let's get you laid out flat on that workbench over there.'

Luke was trying desperately not to show his fear even as he heard these words. He knew he needed to keep his nerves under control and focus on his one chance. And he saw they had made a mistake. They had tied his hands separately to the metal cage holding the canisters, spreadeagling him. If they were to move him now his hands would both have to be untied.

Sean came towards him with the knife, the light from the neon striplight above glinting off the blade. He waved it right under Luke's nose, so close he could smell his bad breath. 'Don't even think about it,' he warned, in a low, gravelly voice, then moved past him to cut the restraints that tied him to the cage. Luke felt a brief surge of relief as his hands were freed, but he didn't act, not yet. He didn't resist as Sean and the other man reached down to lift him off the floor, propelling him towards the workbench, the tip of the knife nudging him just close to his kidneys.

The bench was just feet away. Now – it had to be now. What he did, in this split second, would decide whether he lived or died in this room. Too late they spotted the spanner and Niamh let out a shout. 'Watch out! Stop him!' But Luke was ahead of them. With an explosion of speed and a surge of anger, he catapulted himself forward to where the spanner lay, his right hand shot out to grasp it and, knowing Sean would be behind him, he whirled round. Using the momentum of the knifeman's charge, Luke drove the spanner hard into his windpipe. There was a sickening gurgle as Sean dropped the knife and began feverishly scrabbling at his throat. Eyes bulging in shock and terror, he swayed on his feet. Luke didn't wait to watch the result of his deadly handiwork. Propelling himself forward, he snatched up the knife and hurled himself at the second man, slashing and stabbing in a frenzied blur, his survival instincts driving him forward in an ecstasy of pent-up violence. Blood spurted from the man's neck in a crimson arc, but Luke wasn't done yet. His senses were alive and on fire, ignited by all the bottled-up fear and tension of the last hour.

He spotted Niamh scrambling to reach the door. He had to stop her. Everything depended on him covering the distance between them. He hurled himself across the room and threw his weight hard against the door just as she was prising it open. Grabbing her hair, he heard her gasp as he dragged her head back, exposing her throat. He brought the knife up in one swift, fluid motion.

105

Near Braintree, Essex
Sunday, 20 March, 2336hrs GMT

NIAMH'S STRENGTH SURPRISED him. He could feel her muscles flexing as she twisted and turned, struggling to escape. Luke's voice rasped as he spoke into her ear. 'Stop moving, Niamh,' he commanded, 'or I *will* cut you.' He pressed the tip of the knife against her neck, enough to draw a bead of blood. He felt her gasp and her struggling stopped. He needed her alive if he was to stand any chance of getting out of there.

'So, listen up,' he growled. 'This is what's going to happen. We're going to walk out of here, you and me, through the warehouse and out of the gate I came through. Got it?' Her breath was coming in heavy wheezes and it was a while before she grunted her consent. 'You're going to order your people to back off and if you – or anyone – try to stop me, I'll use the knife.' Luke swung her round, forcing her to look at her two accomplices. Both lay still. Sean's expression was a frozen rictus of pain while the other man lay face down in a widening pool of blood. 'I'm not pissing about here,' he told her.

Luke knew he was still in extreme danger and far from being free. His best chance – his only chance – of getting clear was to take Niamh with him as a hostage. She appeared to be the brains and the driving force behind what these psychos were planning to unleash.

Awkwardly, clumsily, they stumbled through the door and out into the main body of the warehouse, Luke pushing Niamh ahead of him, the blade of the knife still held against her throat, while he gripped the collar of her jacket with his other hand. For two or three seconds, nothing happened, no one moved. Then it was as if an electric shock ripped through everyone in the room and stunned silence changed to uproar. Looking left and right, Luke saw several steroid-pumped, tattooed thugs moving in on him. He had to stop them in their tracks.

'Back the fuck off!' he roared. 'Anyone comes within ten metres of me and I cut her throat!' He hissed quietly in her ear, 'Tell them.'

Through gritted teeth, Niamh called to the gathering crowd surrounding them: 'Do as he says.'

Now Luke moved fast. He hadn't seen any firearms yet, but some of them must be tooled up. Gripping Niamh close to him and the knife to her neck, he kept moving forward, swivelling his captive from one side to another as they made their way to the door that led to the outside world and freedom. He needed eyes in the back of his head.

The moment they reached the door things fell apart for Luke. Releasing his grip on his hostage so he could open the door, he felt her trying to twist free. And a roar of rage rose behind him as they rushed him. With no time to think, instinct kicked in. He whirled Niamh round so she was facing her followers and, with near-surgical precision, he stabbed the knife just once between her shoulder blades. He felt it cut through the material of her jacket and she screamed as it pierced her flesh. Not a killing blow, but it worked. Luke's pursuers stopped in their tracks. As Niamh slumped to her knees, clutching behind her, trying to reach the wound, Luke let her go, pushed his way through the door and ran. He sucked in great gulps of cool night air as he sprinted for the gates up ahead, his booted feet pounding on the wet, uneven tarmac. Even in the dark, he could see they were closed, guarded

367

by the man in the hoodie. Luke swore and tightened his grip on the knife.

Someone behind him shouted, 'Don't let him out!' and the hooded man stood blocking his path, legs astride, a long club in his right hand. Luke didn't break step, he ran right up to him, slashing the knife through the air in front of his face. 'Open the fucking gates!' Luke roared, as he ran. The guard jumped back from the blade and fumbled with the keys to the padlock. Luke could hear boots running on tarmac in the darkness behind him. They were catching up. He jabbed the tip of the knife into the man's side causing him nearly to drop the keys. 'Hurry up!' he yelled. He had only seconds left. The adrenalin was coursing through him, his mind racing, his body primed for both fight and flight.

The padlock sprang open, the chain fell away and Luke was through the gate, racing down the road back towards the town of Braintree. But now, from behind him, came another sound, the noise of vehicle engines starting up, roaring into gear as they set off after him. If he didn't change course he knew it would be just seconds before they had him. And he really didn't want to think what they would do to him this time.

106

LUKE WAS 'HARD-TARGETING'. In a desperate effort to get away down that darkened lane, he was zigzagging left and right, dodging the bullet he feared might come at any second. From close behind he could hear shouts, yells and revving car engines as his pursuers gained on him. He searched frantically as he ran, looking for an escape route.

To his left, the chain-link fence, far too high to scale. To his right, a steep grassy bank topped by a hedge, thick and impenetrable. He was trapped, hemmed in on both sides.

A stinging pain erupted in his left shoulder, followed by a loud bang. He knew he'd been hit. It sounded like a shotgun. It hurt like hell, but he kept running. The next time he wouldn't be so lucky. He needed to get off the road. And then he saw. A metre-wide break in the hedge. His pulse roaring in his ears, his arm throbbing, Luke veered off at a right angle, leaving the road as the sound of the vehicles grew ever louder. He was up the grassy bank, through the gap and on to the edge of a muddy ploughed field. His night vision was kicking in now as he made a snap judgement on which way to go. *Think, Luke. Think outside the box. They'll be expecting you to keep going, away from the warehouse and back towards Braintree. So do the opposite.*

Luke turned right, doubling back along the edge of the field, running in the same direction he'd just come from, but with the hedge now separating him from the people intent on killing him. He ran on, his breath coming in short rasps, his boots sticking to the cloying mud. He was reaching the end of the field and he could hear shouts not far behind him. It hadn't taken them long to work out where he'd gone. He could see torch beams reaching towards him as they searched him out. Luke dropped to the ground and tried to control his breathing, keeping his face away from the light as the pain from the pellet wounds in his shoulder grew worse. He reached up with his right hand and touched the wound. It stung and his jacket was wet with blood. But there was nothing else for it: he had to keep going. Luke got up and ran. A torch beam found him and suddenly there was a sharp crack as a high-velocity bullet snapped past his shoulder. Shit. Someone back there had a hunting rifle, and they might even be using night-vision goggles. He had to get out of sight or he was going to die out here, alone in a cold, muddy field in Essex at midnight.

He could see the distant orange glow of a village on the horizon. Too far. He'd never make it. But to his right lay the velvet blackness of an expanse of water. A lake. Water was good, water was his friend. He'd spent half his adult life in it. He flexed the fingers of his left hand and pain lanced up his arm. But he could still swim, and he knew he could hold his breath under water for much longer than most. Pushing his way through a low thicket of brambles, he reached the water's edge and waded straight in, silently gasping as the cold clutched at him. He was in up to his thighs, then his groin and now his chest. He glanced behind him as the sound of his pursuers reached him. Turning to face the other side, he took a long, deep breath and sank beneath the surface. It was numbingly cold and he couldn't see a thing, but he could do this, he told himself. It wasn't the first time water had saved him: he had done it before in Armenia on an earlier mission. He was going to give these bastards the slip and he was going to see this thing through to the end.

107

Near Braintree, Essex
Monday, 21 March, 0039hrs GMT

LUKE WAS SHIVERING uncontrollably as he hauled himself out of the lake. His pursuers had gone. He'd watched the beams of their torches recede into the night. They had come close, but not close enough to get him. Now the race was on and he needed to move. And fast.

A quick glance at his watch told him it was already well past midnight. Less than eight hours to go before WaffenKrieg90 were due to execute their plan. And he expected them to bring it forward now. He had to find a phone. Soaked through, teeth chattering and with a searing pain in his shoulder from the shotgun pellets, Luke stumbled towards the distant lights of the nearest village. His head still throbbed from being knocked unconscious, but he was spurred on by the crushing responsibility of what he knew, and what he had to tell, before it was too late.

The outline of roofs and telegraph wires started to appear, dimly visible in the weak sodium light of the streetlamps. 'Panfield Lane', a sign read, as Luke emerged on to an empty road. Two cars, parked in a driveway, and a welcome mat on the doorstep. He walked quickly up to the first house he came to and rang the doorbell. A motion-sensitive light blinked on above his head in the

371

doorway, and as he stood there, waiting for someone to answer, he realized he must make a hell of a sight. Dripping wet, covered with mud, blood oozing from his shoulder, his face swollen and bruised. He could hear footsteps approaching on the other side of the frosted-glass door, then a pause as the person peered at him through the peephole.

'Go away!' a man's voice called out.

'I need to use your phone,' Luke replied. 'It's urgent. I'm with the government.'

'Yeah, and I'm Brad Pitt. Now fuck off, before I call the police!'

For a moment Luke considered whether that might not be such a bad idea, but, no, there would be hours of explaining to do and by then it would all be too late. His precious window of opportunity was already closing by the minute.

'Okay, never mind,' Luke said, and moved off. Damn. Now what? If I keep trying houses in this street, he thought, someone *will* call the cops on me.

Car lights, approaching from the east. What if this was Niamh's people? But he had to chance it. He stepped out into the middle of the road and stood there, frantically waving his arms. The car swerved, braked, and came to a stop yards in front of him, then started to reverse.

'No, wait!' he shouted, sprinting forward until he caught up with the driver's side window. It was a girl, twenty-something, and she looked terrified.

'Please!' he begged, through the window. 'It's an emergency. I need your help.' She stopped the car just before it reversed into a large plastic dustbin. 'Here, look,' he said, hurriedly taking off his watch and handing it to her. 'Have this if you think I'm trying to rob you. I'm not. I just need to use your phone.' She ignored the offered watch and he saw her press the central-locking button beside her. Can't blame her for that. There were specks of glitter in her hair and she looked like she might have had a drink or two. The girl took out her phone, still eyeing him suspiciously, and lowered the window a fraction.

'You're injured,' she said, stating the obvious. 'So what's the number, then?' She shook her head at him to pre-empt his next question. 'No, I'm not going to give you my phone,' she added, the fear clearly audible in her voice, 'I wasn't born yesterday. Now what's the number you want me to call?'

Luke gave her Angela's mobile number, committed to memory long ago and now tripping off his tongue for just such a moment as this.

'Tell the person who answers that you've got Luke Carlton with you.' There. He'd probably broken the Official Secrets Act right there by giving her his full name, but he didn't care. *Pick up the phone, Angela. You have to take this call.* For several seconds he stood beside the car window, starting to shiver again now as the girl watched him with narrowed eyes and a concentrated frown, her phone ringing unanswered in her ear. She started to put it down when a woman's voice answered. The girl spoke briefly then listened, her eyes widening.

Moments later she handed her phone through the window to Luke.

108

Near Braintree, Essex
Monday, 21 March, 0114hrs GMT

FIVE MINUTES AND forty-nine seconds precisely. Luke timed it. That was all it took between his phone call to Angela in the Intel Ops Centre and the armed police team arriving to scoop him up on Panfield Lane. He stood there alone on the kerb, wrapping his arms around himself, shivering with cold, as the two CTSFO vehicles came screeching to a halt beside him. He recognized them both for what they were: a dark blue Land Rover in front – the command vehicle – then a black Jankel Tactical Intervention Vehicle behind.

A door swung open on the passenger side of the Land Rover and Luke didn't wait to be asked. He leaped inside, shuffling up on the passenger seat next to the team commander, who had her helmet on her lap. Two sensations hit him at once. He was in a warm place, for the first time since escaping from the warehouse, and he was safe. The relief was overwhelming, but he knew he couldn't rest for a moment. Not now. He introduced himself and looked around as they drove off. The Land Rover's interior was full of radio equipment, weapons, and men and women, armed to the teeth, dressed in the grey-and-black uniform of Britain's Counter-Terrorism specialist firearms officers. On the phone

Luke had already given a clear description of the warehouse and the road leading to it; the second team had been dispatched while Essex Constabulary raced to set up snap roadblocks on all the exits leading from the Springwood Industrial Estate.

'You're bleeding.' Inspector Newbold had just noticed his shoulder wound as they lurched round a bend. 'Jerry, pass us that blue towel up front,' she called over her shoulder to someone in the back. 'We'll get that looked at, but not right now.'

'It's fine,' Luke lied, turning to her. She was young, maybe ten years younger than him, he reckoned, but Inspector Newbold exuded a quiet professionalism.

'Okay, I need you to give me everything you've got on them,' she said, as Luke used the towel to dry off the icy water that was still trickling down his back. 'I need numbers, weapons, dispositions. Are they going to resist? How many devices do we need to disarm and how many are guarding them?'

Luke started to fill her in, the details of what was in that warehouse still all too real in his mind. He stopped as she held up her hand to take a call. She looked at Luke as she listened.

'Yes, he's right beside me.' She passed him her phone. 'It's for you,' she said. 'Your office.'

Luke sat bolt upright as he put the policewoman's mobile to his ear and heard the voice. 'Jenny!' Four days had passed since they had parted ways in GRU headquarters in Moscow. Four days during which she had survived a mystery illness, and Luke had worried about her every single day. 'You made it!' he said, genuinely pleased to hear from her.

'I did.' Her voice was brisk and businesslike. Good. This was the Jenny he knew. 'We can talk about that later,' she said, 'but right now I need to brief you on what you're up against here. Porton Down say the virus inside those canisters you saw in that room is beyond lethal. It's a genetically modified pathogen made with help from a Russian lab. And, Luke, there is no cure.'

He winced, not from what she was saying – he was only too aware of the gravity of the situation – but because the Land Rover was taking a corner at speed and his left shoulder was suddenly thrown against the side of the vehicle. Christ, that hurt. He pressed the towel to his wounds. It was starting to become saturated with his blood.

'Why are you telling me what I already know, Jenny?' he asked, through gritted teeth, as the Land Rover lurched round another bend.

'Because I know you, Luke. You're going to want to go in there at the front, firing from the hip, and be the first through that door. Well, not this time, okay? Leave the rough stuff to the CT team. It's what they've trained for. We need your eyes and ears on this one and we need you feeding everything back to the Intel Ops Centre in real time. Can you do that?'

'Sure.'

Too much, way too much, had happened for Luke to hang back on this one. He was going in with the teams and taking those bastards down. He was going to do whatever it took to finish this. He ended the call and handed the phone back to Inspector Newbold. The driver was hitting the brakes.

'Listen up!' she called to her team. 'We're here.'

They had reached the outer gate to the warehouse, the same place Luke had hard-targeted away from just ninety minutes earlier. But from his vantage point, sitting up front next to the commander, he could immediately see something was wrong. There should have been police marksmen taking up positions, officers using the available cover to move forward, helicopters hovering overhead, all the tense activity of a developing siege situation. There was none of that.

Inspector Newbold was listening on her headset beside him. Without warning she ripped it off her head and flung it at her feet. 'Fuck it!' she shouted. 'We're too late. We've missed them.'

109

RED RIMS HAD formed around Angela Scott's eyes. Like most of those around her in the Intel Ops Centre, she was running on empty. She was on her third or fourth cup of coffee since they had moved across the river, her nerves on edge, her concentration in overdrive.

'*Noo!*' she exclaimed. 'How is this possible?' She threw her hands into the air and clamped them on her head, squeezing her eyes shut. The news had just come in from the warehouse at Braintree and it was a blow to everyone on the team.

'I mean, we had Luke inside that place, what, less than two hours ago? How could they have cleaned up and shipped out in under that time?' she said.

'But that's exactly what's happened,' an analyst replied, in a morose voice. 'Just take a look at that.' Angela glanced up at one of the screens where the grainy, black-and-white live feed was coming in from one of the CTSFO's chestcams. It said it all. It showed an empty, deserted warehouse, an empty side office and, most troubling of all, the canisters were gone. There was no one around, not a soul. It was a *Mary Celeste* moment.

The senior investigating officer stood in the centre of the room and clapped his hands to gather everyone's attention. 'Listen up,' he said, his voice grave and authoritative, 'there's no point moping over missed opportunities. We don't have that luxury. We need to pin down where they're heading, get blue lights to close off their exits, then let Counter-Terrorism deal with them.'

'But what about the virus?' Angela asked. She had a terrifyingly clear vision of a team of fanatical extremists driving along the darkened roads of southern Britain with a lethal pathogen onboard. The implications were almost too awful to consider. 'Surely we need to—'

'Yes, we do,' he cut her off, the impatience showing in his voice. 'We're alerting the Joint Biosecurity Centre of the risk to the public. Now, King's Cross station,' the SIO continued. 'We have to assume that's still their destination although . . .' he paused to grimace '. . . they might be tempted to release it anywhere now. Carlton mentioned they'd considered other targets: a centre for migrants and so on. And let's not forget there's Stansted Airport just down the road. Met and Essex Police are putting in protective security. But this is where you analysts play your part.' He was looking at three specific people in the room now. 'Your assumption – and I concur with it – is that WaffenKrieg90 have invested too much planning and preparation in this to want to switch locations at the last minute. But in case they do,' the SIO held up his index finger, 'teams have also been dispatched to every mainline station in London. We're taking no chances.'

'And Tube stations?' asked a case officer.

'Becky, it's nearly two in the morning,' he retorted, giving her a tired look. 'The Tubes don't start running again till five.'

'Still,' persisted the case officer, 'shouldn't we be sealing them off? What if they're looking to plant the devices on timers in a ticket hall? Or set them off remotely?' She looked round the room for support, but the SIO chose to ignore her question and, instead, he clapped his hands again.

'Look,' he said, 'I think we're getting distracted by the prepare element here. That's the job of the police. *Ours* is to focus on the pursue element and right now the clock is ticking.' He bent over a keyboard, typed in some figures and up came a road map on the wall screen behind him. It showed all the possible routes between Essex and central London.

'Right, let's break this down,' he said, picking up a laser penlight. 'On a normal day, avoiding rush hour, the fastest journey time by road from Braintree to King's Cross takes an hour and ten minutes, give or take. That's using the most obvious route: the A120 from Bishop's Stortford.' He shone the green laser to indicate the Essex town on the screen. 'Then the M11 gets you into London from the north-east.' He stopped and wagged a finger. 'But are they really going to take the most obvious route? I doubt it. They're going to be looking to evade the police roadblocks and they're certainly not going to risk attracting attention by breaking the speed limit. So,' he clicked off the penlight, 'that should buy us a little more time while the police get the cordons in place around the mainline stations.'

He paused as someone came into the room wheeling a trolley bearing two silver pots of coffee and tea and a plate of Digestive biscuits wrapped in cellophane. The banal, everyday business of refuelling the human body during a massive live counter-terrorism operation.

'In the meantime,' the senior investigating officer continued, once the door was closed, 'this team needs to be zeroing in on the individuals in possession of the canisters. Now, we've had a bit of a breakthrough on the ringleader, this woman Niamh. Well done to Jonathan and his team.' He nodded at a fair-haired man in a green jersey. 'Her true ID is Charlotte James, aka Lotti James. She's a biochemist from Cambridge. Trained in Germany. VX reports her cropping up on the periphery of a German intelligence-service investigation into far-right extremist groups in Saxony. She's a one hundred per cent fanatic, totally committed to their cause.'

Listening to this, Angela had a sickening feeling she had forgotten something so important it should have been mentioned right up front. The stress and exhaustion of the last few days must have been catching up with her. How else could she have neglected to tell them this? She raised her hand.

'Our guy Luke Carlton has a lead on one of the Bravos in the warehouse. He told me he's met him before.'

'Sorry, *what*?' The SIO sounded incredulous. All eyes turned to look at Angela and she could feel herself blushing under their gaze. 'I should have been told this, Angela.'

'I know,' she replied. 'My bad, I'm sorry. Anyway, he's called Hugo Squires. A UK national. He's some sort of finance guy. Part of a "consortium", he called it, that have financed all this. Apparently they've shorted the market hoping to make a fortune.'

'Right. I want everything on him, all his contacts, where he lives, what he drives, what he ate for breakfast. We need to get into his comms, so let's get going with prepping that warrant. Has Luke given us his mobile phone number? That'll save us a bit of time.'

'No,' Angela replied, 'he doesn't have it, but apparently his girlfriend does.'

'Well, what's he waiting for?' The SIO looked nonplussed. 'Tell him to ring her at once and get the number off her.'

'He says she's not answering.'

'Oh, for fuck's sake!' The tension in the room was starting to spill over into exasperation, but the senior investigating officer apologized at once. 'Sorry, Angela, that wasn't directed at you. Look, can we get someone round to the girlfriend's place and bang on the door until she answers it?'

Angela sat down at the workstation she'd been assigned and blinked several times, staring at the screen in front of her. It was so unlike her to overlook something as important as that. But now another thing was troubling her. What was Luke doing 'knowing' someone inside WaffenKrieg90? There would have to be an internal investigation after this; Luke would be facing some probing questions from Security Branch. She looked up as someone was frantically signalling from another of the workstations: a young man in a polo neck, who looked shocked as he relayed the message.

'It's SO15 on the line from Cobalt Square. There's been an explosion. In the warehouse at Braintree. They're saying there are casualties. They think Luke Carlton could be one of them.'

110

DUST, SMOKE AND a persistent ringing in his ears. Yet everything else was silent. Those were the first things Luke registered as he picked himself slowly up off the floor and checked himself for injuries. Nothing broken, no new puncture wounds: he seemed to be no worse off than before. The blast had been enough to blow him several metres backwards and knock him clean off his feet. Damn. How the hell had they missed that? The bastards must have left it on a timer, hidden behind where that cupboard had been.

Luke's nose and throat were full of the smell of burned-off explosive, dust and plaster. And there was something else he couldn't quite place at first. Something he remembered from Afghanistan. It was the smell of singed human flesh. As the smoke cleared he looked across the floor of the warehouse and swallowed hard. He had seen more than his share of injuries in his time: in Kandahar he had helped staunch a man's arterial bleeding after one of his patrol got hit by an IED. But this was different. This was an industrial estate in Essex, it was supposed to be peacetime, and Luke had never expected to witness the sight in front of him now. The CTSFO was still alive – at least, half of him was. His legs, severed just above the knees, were blasted apart and lay some distance off, inanimate objects, still in their wolf-grey fatigue trousers, the black Salomon boots still attached. In the near-silent seconds following the blast, Luke heard him call out in distress and confusion.

'I'm okay!' the man cried, as Luke rushed over to him. 'Tell Ginny I'm fine. I'll see her tonight,' he kept repeating. Luke held his hand and tried to reassure him as other officers rushed up to help, desperately racing to stem the bleeding and get tourniquets on to the stumps of his thighs before he bled out. But they were too late. He was still looking up at Luke's face when his eyes rolled and his head flopped to one side.

'He's gone,' Luke said. 'I'm so sorry, guys.'

He got to his feet, brushing the dust and plaster off his clothes, and walked quickly back to the Land Rover. He felt the anger rising in him once more. He had never doubted that this organization was ruthless, but watching that policeman die right beside him had left him shocked and more determined than ever. And Jenny Li had been right: it had been a mistake to join in the search. He should have left it all to the CTSFO team. As he made his way back to the command vehicle he shook his head in sympathy as he passed the other officers. They had lost one of their own, and he knew what that felt like. First blood had been drawn on UK soil. It was the dead of night, the targets had escaped them and were on the loose. This op was going about as badly as it possibly could.

For a brief moment the thought flashed through his mind that since the people who had left that bomb on a timer had access to a viral pathogen, could there have been more to it than high explosive? He dismissed the thought. Explosives and biological agents did not mix well: one tended to cancel out the other. Still, he had better get himself checked out when this was over.

111

Springwood Industrial Estate, Essex
Monday, 21 March, 0221hrs GMT

LUKE FOUND INSPECTOR Newbold standing beside the open door of her Land Rover, dressed in full Kevlar body armour and helmet. Up close, she looked pale and drawn: an officer had been lost on her watch. She handed him her phone. 'It's your people at Thames House again,' she said. 'Make it brief, can you? I need to keep this line clear. We're heading straight to King's Cross.' She motioned for him to get back in and they set off immediately, driving at speed, racing westwards down the A120 towards Bishop's Stortford to hit the M11 into London.

Luke looked at his watch as he took the call. God, he was tired. Only three hours since he'd been at the mercy of those fanatics, but already that felt like a lifetime ago.

It was Angela on the line, but they were travelling so fast he could only just hear her. 'Don't worry about me,' he told her. 'I'm all in one piece. Really shit about the other guy, though.'

Angela didn't waste time on small talk. 'Listen, Luke, we've got a situation here, one that involves you. Personally.'

It was then that Luke noticed his hands. He saw they were stained dark red with the dead policeman's blood. Glancing around in his seat to make sure no one was watching, he wiped them discreetly on his trousers. It felt somehow disrespectful and he regretted doing it. 'Okay, tell me,' he replied. 'We're coming up to the motorway now,' he told her. 'We should be on location well inside the hour. Angela, is this something I need to know now or can it wait?'

Outside the window he could see blue motorway signs and lampposts flashing past in the dark as they overtook what little traffic was on the road.

'Luke, just shut up and listen. There's going to be an inquest here into how you know Hugo Squires. A lot of people are asking questions. But right now we're tracking him through his phone. It looks like he's heading into London. We think Charlotte James – Niamh as you know her – and her people have taken him with them.'

'I doubt that,' Luke said. 'He's a coward at heart.'

'He might not have had much choice. Anyway, your partner, Miss Mayhew, has given us his number and the Security Service have done a trace on it—'

'Wait,' he interrupted. 'You're getting Elise involved in this? She's got nothing to do with these fuckwits.'

Luke was aware that Inspector Newbold was getting increasingly impatient beside him. She had her hand out, waiting for her phone back, but he held up a finger. He needed just one more minute.

'Never mind about that,' Angela said. 'They've triangulated his last position as close to Brentwood. It's heading towards London but the signal keeps dropping out. Thames have got inside his comms,' she continued. 'Turns out he's been on some nasty chat forums. Some really sick extreme-racist stuff. Squires has been part of the far-right movement for nearly two years.'

'Hang on, Angela.'

Inspector Newbold was tapping his arm quite forcefully. 'I really need my phone back,' she insisted. 'Here.' She handed him another. 'Call them back on this.'

It took several attempts to get through to Angela. Precious time wasted, Luke thought, as they sped past Epping doing 92mph.

'Listen, Luke,' she sounded breathless now, 'there's no time to waste in case we get cut off again. You need to speak to Elise – she's awake. Our people are with her in your flat.' Luke frowned. This wasn't supposed to happen. He wanted his private life to stay private. But it was a bit late for that now. 'Get her to persuade Squires and the people he's with to give themselves up. It's the only option left to them.'

Except it isn't, Luke thought. As long as they're on the loose they're going to go ahead and plant the canisters wherever they can do the maximum damage. He pinched the bridge of his nose and squeezed his eyes shut. 'That's not true, though, is it, Angela?' he said. 'Because I'm telling you, they're going to go through with this. The more we close in on them the more they'll go for an immediate release of the pathogen.'

Even as he said this, Luke remembered the baby. Elise's baby. Whose father was now in a van loaded with lethal germs, driving into the capital for some deranged, fucked-up purpose. Hugo Squires had thought Luke was bluffing when he'd told him he was to be a father. Maybe, just maybe, he would listen to Elise. 'Okay, Angela, we can try,' Luke said abruptly, and hung up.

He turned to Inspector Newbold, who was just finishing her own call. 'Really sorry about that with the phone,' he said. 'So what's the plan when we reach King's Cross? A hard stop? Overwhelming use of force?'

She gave him a look. Gwyneth Newbold may have been nearly a decade younger than Luke, but her face spoke of a career spent at the sharp end; he noticed crow's feet beginning to show at the corners of her eyes. 'Think about it,' she said wearily. 'The Bravos are travelling with canisters of a deadly pathogen. We cannot risk an accidental release. So, no, we're not going to use overwhelming force.' She looked down at the phone in her hand. 'I've just had Cobalt Square on the line. The unit already in place has been authorized to deploy Lomatin.'

'Lomatin?'

'Yes. It's an incapacitant. A knockout gas.'

'Does it work?' he asked.

'In training, yes. Most of the time.'

'Right,' Luke said hesitantly. 'It sounds like something the Russians used in the Moscow theatre siege.'

'That was before my time, but something like that, yes.'

'Which killed at least a hundred and thirty people, mostly hostages.'

'Well, the Bravos had best give themselves up, hadn't they?' She shrugged and went back to her phone.

112

ELISE FELT AS if she was trapped in one of her dreams, a really, really bad one this time. This couldn't be happening, could it? She had gone to bed three hours earlier feeling guilty on so many counts. She knew she should not have drunk all that Chardonnay with Susie, not with the baby growing quietly inside her, but she'd needed something to calm her nerves. Because Elise Mayhew knew she was not in a good place. The man she'd thought she would spend the rest of her life with had walked out of their flat, she was carrying another man's child, and now the baby's father wasn't taking her calls. That was bad enough. But just before two thirty in the morning she'd been woken by a frantic buzzing at the door. It must be Hugo, she thought, come to make amends for his prolonged silence. Or maybe it was Luke, back to ask for a second chance. It was neither. It was a man and a woman with government security ID badges and, after only the briefest of apologies, they had asked her to get dressed as fast as possible while they waited in the living room.

In jeans, trainers and a pullover she sat on the edge of the armchair, a cushion hugged to her midriff, and listened, open-mouthed, as they told her what was going on, right now, on the other side of

387

the capital. Elise hardly registered it when the woman, who had introduced herself as being 'from the Foreign Office', reached out and squeezed her hand as she, Elise, tried to take it all in. And she couldn't: it was just too much. Hugo Squires? The harmless, cuddly banker with bushy eyebrows who had been her rock of support every time Luke was away, the man who had wined and dined her, been there for her when her mother died, the man who had fathered— no, sorry, she simply didn't believe it. Okay, so he'd made some pretty offensive remarks from time to time, usually when he'd been drinking, and she'd had to pick him up on the stuff he was saying about the BLM movement, but Hugo, a bioterrorist? Come *on*. Mixed up with a group of far-right extremists? No, sorry, she simply didn't buy it.

It was the photograph they showed her that did it. It was taken in Alabama the previous year, they explained. And, yes, it was unmistakably Hugo Squires, no question about that, but it was so shocking she'd had to look away. Gone were the clubbable blazer and chinos: in their place he wore a tight white T-shirt emblazoned with just two words in large capitals. One was 'KILL' and the other – well, she had to look at it again to believe it. It was the N-word. On either side of him stood two tall figures draped in white and wearing pointed white hoods with sinister slits for the eyes. Elise recognized the uniform immediately. It was the Ku Klux Klan.

Elise leaned forward and dry-retched into her cushion. She felt like vomiting, but nothing came up. This man's baby was growing inside her, right at this moment. Mentally she kicked herself. How could she have missed this? She looked up at the pair 'from the government' who were still standing in her front room, the pair who had just brought this horrible news into her home. All tiredness was gone now, replaced by a burning anger.

'All right,' she told them, 'I believe you. How can I help?'

'The car's downstairs, ma'am. We need you to come with us right away.'

113

York Way, King's Cross, London
Monday, 21 March, 0328hrs GMT

IN THE DEAD of night York Way was deserted. Just a cold, damp expanse of empty road stretching from the junction with Euston Road north to Regent's Canal. To the west lay the silent railway tracks of King's Cross and the cavernous steel awning of the station.

But parked up in a side street at right angles were four very specialized vehicles, in dark blue and black livery. The Counter-Terrorism specialist firearms team was in position. Luke Carlton sat in the lead vehicle, now wearing a borrowed Kevlar jacket and helmet, still squeezed up next to Inspector Newbold as she listened intently on the command net through her earpiece. The pain from the shotgun pellets in his shoulder was coming in pulsing waves and he was fighting periodic bouts of nausea from the explosion in the warehouse. He touched his temples with his fingertips – he might even have concussion. But Luke was not going to show any of this, not when they were so close. He hadn't survived Svalbard, Lithuania, Moscow and his brush with Waffenkrieg90 just to sit this one out on the sidelines. Luke wanted closure and he was damn well going to get it.

Inspector Newbold suddenly nudged him and took off her

389

earpiece. 'You'd better hear this, Carlton,' she said, putting her radio on to speaker mode. 'I think your partner's on the line now. She's in one of our vehicles three blocks south of here.' The connection was crackly with static but Elise's crystal-clear syllables sliced right through it. Luke sucked in his breath as he listened to the woman he had loved and lived with. Elise was speaking directly to Hugo Squires.

'. . . and I've been trying to tell you this, Hugo,' she was saying, her words taut with emotion. 'You're going to be the father of our child. Look, I've even thought of some names . . . So, PLEASE,' she was raising her voice now, 'you *must* do what's right for our baby. Stop this craziness and give yourself up. Hugo? . . . Hugo, are you there?'

Silence. Then a long bleep. Her message had gone straight to voicemail.

Luke let out a sigh. The attempt had failed. He glanced out of the Land Rover window at the street. They had parked in a cycle lane in Wharfdale Road beneath a line of bare trees, sandwiched between the closed and darkened premises of a Pret a Manger and a Franco Manca restaurant. His door was next to a 20mph traffic sign. It was an unobtrusive setting for an ambush.

'We've tracked Squires using the GPS in his phone,' Inspector Newbold told him. 'Looks like your friend got careless.'

'He's not my friend,' Luke corrected her. 'How far off are they?'

She checked the rolling map on the laptop beside her just as her earpiece crackled into life once more. 'Shit. They're getting close.' She clicked the pressel switch of her mike to address her teams. 'Stand by, all teams. Bravos are inbound from the north. Two vehicles, two minutes from our location. On my command, execute the takedown.'

Luke's pulse was racing as he rubbed the knuckle of his missing finger. Right now he wanted to be checking his weapon, taking out the magazine, ensuring none of the rounds were loose, slotting it back in, preparing to issue the commands. But he was a civilian now, unarmed and reporting back to Vauxhall, not about to lead his troop into action. He felt a sudden, brief pang of longing for the world he'd left behind.

He heard Inspector Newbold issue a terse command and suddenly car doors were springing open, everyone was dismounting, fanning out across the street in a staccato rush of rubber-soled boots on tarmac, taking up positions on either side of York Way. The empty side street was suddenly full of grey uniforms and weapons. Luke stayed close behind Inspector Newbold, who was dressed identically to her team in Pro-tec ballistic helmet, goggles and black gloves. He could see little natural cover, just a long, low brick wall on the left, stained black with years of London grime, a line of transparent barriers that ran down the central divide in the road and some large bins beneath the red canopies of Franco Manca. They positioned themselves behind the bins, squatting on one knee as they faced northwards, staring up the length of York Way. Waiting.

It was a white van in front, moving slowly, doing a cautious 20mph, drawing level with the green glass cube of the Guardian News building. Behind that, another vehicle, too far off for Luke to make out what it was but possibly a pick-up truck. Had he seen either of them at the warehouse? He couldn't recall. Maybe he'd been too busy trying to stay alive at the time. But now he was picking up a familiar noise: the approaching thud of rotor blades, clearly audible above the perpetual London soundtrack of distant sirens. A black-and-yellow police helicopter swung into view from the north, behind the oncoming vehicles. Luke recognized it as a Eurocopter, part of the Met's emergency back-up for CTSFO operations. The cut-off group for the ambush.

The two vehicles stopped abruptly. He guessed their occupants must have heard the chopper. Still squatting next to him, Inspector Newbold was listening intently to something in her earpiece, her fingertips pressed against it. Then she leaped to her feet. 'All call signs,' she said into her mike, 'confirmed. It's them. Execute.'

Grey uniformed figures surged forward towards the vans, the

black muzzles of their Swiss-made SIG Sauer SG516 assault rifles jutting out in front of them. Luke could see that the helicopter had gone into a hover, low to the ground and just beyond the *Guardian* building. Lit by the streetlamps, a stream of tiny figures was fast-roping down on to York Way. The targets in the vans were trapped. Luke scrabbled for his phone and sent a single curt message to Angela at Thames House: *Contact. We're engaging.*

114

York Way, King's Cross, London
Monday, 21 March, 0349hrs GMT

INSPECTOR NEWBOLD WAS standing in the dark, beneath the red canvas awning of Franco Manca, her goggles pushed on to her helmet, frantically signalling to someone behind them. An officer ran up and handed her the megaphone. She grabbed it without a word and began walking down the pavement towards the two vans, past a South East Asian food outlet and a barber's shop. Then she stopped.

'Armed police!' she shouted into the megaphone. 'Get out of the vehicles now! Hands in the air! Do not make any sudden movements.' Five seconds elapsed, then ten. Luke was a few metres behind her and, despite his Kevlar vest and helmet, he felt horribly exposed out there on the pavement. There was simply no cover. He saw Newbold raise the megaphone once more.

'You have just ten seconds to comply!' she called out. 'This is your final—'

Gwyneth Newbold, qualified firearms officer with the Metropolitan Police, and mother of one, did not get to finish her sentence. Luke watched in horror as she appeared to spin round 180 degrees, followed almost instantly by the crack of a bullet he recognized as a high-velocity round.

393

'Officer down!' he shouted, and sprinted forward to pull her to safety. Ducking low, expecting at any second to hear the crack of a second bullet, he grabbed the collar on her Kevlar vest and dragged her behind the nearest cover he could find. It was a grey electrical junction box, just a metre high, but it would have to do. Leaning over to examine her, he could see she was still breathing and conscious, but the bullet had torn into her shoulder where it wasn't protected by the Kevlar armour. Blood was still pouring from the wound and he searched desperately for something to staunch it with.

'Front . . . pocket,' she gasped, managing to nod down at her chest. Luke ripped open the Velcro fastening on her vest and retrieved a field dressing. In less than ten seconds he had it open, unwrapped and pressed to her wound, just as others were rushing up to help. There wasn't room for all of them to hide safely behind the junction box so Luke sprinted fast and low to a spot behind a parked car.

The air was still full of the rhythmic *thwock* of rotor blades and he expected at any moment to hear the ear-splitting fusillade of automatic weapons in response to the shot fired at Inspector Newbold. Those inside the vans clearly had no intention of giving themselves up.

Instead he heard a succession of low reports, like those from a shotgun being fired, followed by the tinkling of glass. And then an eerier silence, broken only by the distant hum of night-time traffic on Euston Road.

Lomatin. The knockout gas. That must be the incapacitant being fired through the vans' windscreens, he guessed. Luke waited a further ten seconds, then peered around the side of the parked car. He saw three officers, dressed in full chem-bio protective gear and respirators, holding shields in front of them as they advanced towards the two vehicles. Quickly extracting his phone, he called Angela and gave her a brief, breathless running commentary on what was happening.

'Look, I'm not leaving this location until I've sent you visuals on all of the Bravos, okay? That's what I'm here for.'

'Vehicle One!' someone shouted. 'Clear!' Followed almost immediately by 'Vehicle Two! Clear!'

Luke moved forward, just behind a phalanx of CTSFOs, all armed to the teeth. They formed a cordon around the two vehicles as a man in protective gear came towards them, his boots crunching on the broken glass. Luke could see a neat hole in the windscreen where the first gas grenade must have penetrated the glass, then knocked out everyone inside. It must have been the same for the next vehicle. He could hear sirens behind them now, drawing closer from Euston Way. It was about to get very busy here so he'd need to work fast.

'They're all out cold,' announced one of the officers in protective gear after removing his respirator and wiping the sweat off his face. 'But you can't go in there yet. There'll still be traces of Lomatin. We'll bring them out to you.'

'The canisters,' Luke called. 'Have you secured the canisters?'

The officer gave him a sceptical look. Luke realized he was the only one not dressed in grey. He probably thinks I'm from the media, for God's sake. But the policeman answered him anyway. 'We've secured all the canisters onboard, yes. Porton Down are sending a team to pick them up. When this lot come round we'll make sure we've accounted for every single one of them.' He turned away and began addressing the other CTSFOs.

For a long moment Luke stood there, immobile, taking in the significance of this. It was over. They had stopped WaffenKrieg90 in their tracks. Prevented a man-made biological weapon from being released on the British public. Two weeks of intense, frenetic work and extreme danger across four countries, all leading up to this moment. And yet what did he feel? Exhaustion, yes – he was ready to sleep for a week. But there was something else, a sense of a job not over. Luke couldn't relax until he'd made sure they'd really caught these people, that no one had slipped through the cracks. He needed to look into the faces of Niamh, Klaus and, yes, Hugo Squires to know that it was over.

They brought out the occupants one by one, laying them like corpses on the pavement even though they were just unconscious.

A long-barrelled hunting rifle was also being brought out, carefully handled by officers with forensic gloves. Two officers stood over prone figures on the pavement, fingers on the trigger guards of their SIG Sauers. Further down York Way the police were putting up barriers, throwing up a cordon, and beyond that Luke was pretty sure he could see a satvan with antennae on top. The media were arriving. That meant cameras and long lenses, and the last thing he wanted was to find himself on breakfast news.

Luke borrowed a pencil torch from one of the team and now he stepped forward, shining it on to the first face he came to in the row. As he did so the moon appeared from behind a cloud, bathing everything in a ghostly, silver glow. These people laid out at his feet, these monsters, he thought, looked almost beatific in this light.

He recognized the first man immediately. It was Max, the taciturn driver who'd been sent to pick him up from the pub car park just a few hours and half a lifetime ago. He moved on to the next. A man he didn't recognize. Then another. Then Klaus, the tall German he was supposed to ride with. His heart jumped. Because the next one he came to after that was Niamh, or whatever her real name was. Her scarf was still half wrapped around her face and suddenly he saw her eyelids were fluttering. She was conscious, just. The scarf must have somehow reduced how much Lomatin she'd inhaled. So it wasn't 100 per cent effective after all. He called to the team and moved aside to give them the space to search and cuff her. Then he took her photo with his phone and sent it straight to the Intel Ops Centre.

They had caught the ringleader alive.

But something still wasn't right. He had reached the end of the line and someone was missing. He called to one of the three in protective gear, 'Is that all of them? Are there any more in the vehicles?'

'No. That's the lot. Forensics are on their way.'

Luke went back and rechecked every member of WaffenKrieg90

who'd been laid out on the pavement. His heart was beating faster now as his fears were confirmed. Shit. He had been right the first time.

'Fuck!' he exclaimed, slamming his fist against the Kevlar armour of his vest in frustration. Hugo Squires had vanished.

115

York Way, King's Cross, London
Monday, 21 March, 0414hrs GMT

MINUTES. MAYBE JUST seconds. Luke knew that was all they had before Squires was lost in the darkened streets of the capital and racing towards a little-known harbour or a private airstrip.

He called it in at once to Thames House, getting Angela to check the location of Squires's phone. If he still had it on him, this would be easy. It wasn't. The answer came back while he was still on the line.

'It's showing up as where you're standing,' she told him. Damn. That could mean only one thing: Squires had realized his mistake and dumped it in the van before he ran. How the hell had he managed to get away unnoticed? And where could he have gone? Luke scanned the street, looking for exits, the phone still clamped to his ear. The place was rapidly filling now with police officers, many in plain clothes. Then something caught his eye. On the other side of the street there was a black-and-white bollard. Someone had chained a bicycle to it and it was missing its front wheel. But just beyond that, easily overlooked, was the entrance to a passageway that sloped down off York Way towards the platforms and tracks of King's Cross station. Would Squires have . . . ?

Could he . . . ? Luke did a rapid 360-degree scan of the street. Yes. There was nowhere else he could have gone.

'I'm going after him,' he told Angela.

'Wait!' he heard her say, but Luke was already hanging up and crossing the street.

He broke into a run immediately, ignoring the pain in his shoulder, setting off down the sloping passageway, searching for exits. It was quieter here, off the street, but the London night still seemed to resound to the noise of endless sirens, rising and falling, the soundtrack to the city. He stopped at the bottom, listening. A corrugated-iron fence, brown with rust and overgrown with weeds, blocked access to the platforms. He moved closer for a better view, and there, between two vertical panels, was a space just wide enough for a person to slip through. How many minutes had it been since the police stopped those two vans in their tracks? Five? Ten at most? Could Squires have made it down here in that time, unseen? Yes, had to be the answer.

The phone in his pocket was vibrating – it was the one they had lent him in the Land Rover, but Angela must have logged the number and now she was calling him back.

'Luke!' she said sharply. 'You *must* wait for back-up. I'm ordering you to—' He killed the call and pressed both side buttons at the same time to switch it off. He would do it his way, because this was personal now.

Luke was well aware that he was still wearing his heavy Kevlar vest and ballistic helmet. He was never going to squeeze through the gap with those on, so he peeled them both off and dumped them at his feet. Through the gap in the fence, out the other side, and the only sound was the soft ripping of his jacket as it caught on a jagged piece of metal. He found himself standing on an empty stretch of concrete, not a platform exactly, more an abandoned siding. A sudden gust of wind sent an empty Coke can rolling noisily towards him, coming to rest against his feet. Was Squires hiding down here among the deserted railway tracks? Or was he making a run for it? Squires was certainly no athlete so, no, Luke was sure of it, he would have gone into hiding, somewhere close. Hell, he might even be watching *him* right at this moment.

Luke raised his eyes beyond the nearest platform. A blue sign read 'Welcome to London's King's Cross'. A train sat silent and brooding on the other side and he could just make out the words on its silver-grey livery: 'East Coast'. Beyond that, the great curved awning of the station and then a sprawl of ugly urban development reaching up into the pink night sky. Out of the corner of his eye Luke caught movement. He turned slowly. And exhaled. Just a rat.

He looked towards the train. It was the only available cover. Squires wouldn't have headed there, would he? The thought of the pampered, privileged investment banker crouching amid the grime and spilled oil of a railway siding seemed utterly absurd. But then nothing about WaffenKrieg90 and its repugnant followers had made sense. And if Squires had fled to this railway yard there was simply nowhere else for him to hide.

Luke crept forward on silent footsteps, reaching the edge of the concrete siding and gingerly lowering himself over it, making barely a sound as his feet touched the stony aggregate. Speed had given way to stealth. He listened again for any movement. From behind him, in York Way, the siren of an approaching ambulance. A grisly reminder of what had happened to Inspector Newbold, felled by that high-velocity bullet. Her wound wasn't fatal, but a few millimetres to one side and it would have been very different.

Treading carefully, Luke reached the first carriage. Squires, if he had come this way, must have followed the same route. It was too late to think about back-up: there was no time for that. If he stopped now, Squires would be gone before they got here, out of sight and then out of the country, with all that money in the bank and all that blood on his hands.

Luke moved along the side of the carriage's blackened, spring-loaded bogey until he came to the first gap big enough for a man to crawl through. The doors to the carriages above would be locked, he was sure of it, but down here in the darkness there was plenty of space to hide. Luke took out the pencil torch the police had lent him, held it against his sleeve to muffle the sudden light, and switched it on. He crouched and squeezed through the space between the wheels, hearing his breath coming in short gasps. Very slowly, avoiding any sudden movements, he swept the space beneath the carriage, playing the torch beam across every surface, probing into every recess and crevice.

It took him nearly two minutes to search the length of the undercarriage and that was just one car. He moved on to the next, noticing his hands and arms were already black with grime. After searching below six carriages with no sign of Squires, Luke began to feel failure creeping up on him. He was deep inside the station now and he just didn't think Squires would have come this far. Perhaps he had misjudged him after all. Maybe the bastard had indeed made a run for it and was already flagging down a cab and heading out of London right at this minute. He crawled out from under the carriage, scraping his knee painfully on the stones, and stood still, listening to the sound of his own breathing and trying to ignore the throbbing pain in his shoulder from the shotgun blast. It had grown worse in the last hour and if he didn't do something about it soon then the wounds would become infected. He was running out of time.

Retracing his steps, Luke paused by the first carriage, barely daring to breathe. *You bloody idiot, Carlton.* You forgot to search beneath the locomotive. But if Squires was down there, he was cornered. And that made him desperate and dangerous. Unarmed, Luke would have to improvise. It took him a few seconds to find what he was looking for: a stone with a sharp point. Crude but effective. With this in his right hand and the torch in his left, he ducked down beside the engine and squatted beneath it. He had the torch switched off and now he almost held his breath, keeping deathly still, waiting, watching and listening.

And that was when he heard it.

It was just the softest clink of stone against stone, barely audible above the growing hum of pre-dawn traffic from Euston Road. But it was a noise unmistakably made by a human. Someone was down there.

401

Luke felt a surge of adrenalin course through him. This was what he'd come here to do: confront Hugo Squires and finish this once and for all. A voice in his head was telling him to hang back, use his phone to call for back-up, wait for reinforcements and surround the locomotive with so many people Squires would have no hope of escape. But that wasn't his way. *Fuck it*, he thought, *let's do this*. He slipped beneath the engine, bending himself double in the cramped space, and flicked on the torch once more. Crouching and peering, he probed the darkness. Nothing. And then he heard it again, the unmistakable sound of a boot moving against stones. Someone was shifting their weight and they were right behind him.

Every muscle in his body was tensed for action as Luke half turned to face the source of the noise. In that moment he felt a searing pain lance into his thigh. Crying out, he staggered back, twisting round to shine the torch on his assailant. There, lit up in the white beam, was the crouching figure of Hugo Squires. His eyes were wild and staring, his face and arms blackened with engine dirt, and in his right hand he brandished a penknife that glinted wetly with Luke's blood. But it was what he was holding in his left hand that terrified Luke. It was a silver canister with a timer attached.

Luke gritted his teeth against the pain as he felt the blood seeping down his leg. But he willed himself to block it out. *Focus, Carlton, you need to finish this*. He called into the dark, 'Give it up, Squires. It's over.'

No reply, just heavy breathing. Suddenly Squires lashed out again. Luke saw the glint of the blade and recoiled just in time. He let go of the torch and shot out his left hand, grabbing a fistful of dirt and stones. In one fluid movement he flung them into his opponent's face. Momentarily blinded, Squires howled and Luke made his move. He reached out in the dark to locate Squires's leg with one hand and slammed the stone down hard on his kneecap with the other. There was a sickening crunch as the bone shattered and Squires let out a high-pitched scream, dropping both the knife and the canister. Luke sprang forward, his own pain forgotten, his arm poised to slam home the pointed stone once more, this time into the man's skull. Everything Luke had been through with this mission boiled down to this supercharged moment as he held a human life in his hand.

And then, suddenly, there were lights and shouts and shadows and figures running. 'Armed police!' he heard someone yell.

Luke lowered his arm and dropped the stone, exhaustion washing over him. God, he felt tired. Lifting his head, he called back, 'It's Luke Carlton. I've got him, and the last canister.' And then he put his face up close to Squires's. The man's eyes were squeezed tight shut in pain. Luke grasped his adversary's chin in a vice-like grip to get his attention. 'You useless piece of shit, Squires,' he hissed. 'Your insane plan is finished and so are you.'

Epilogue

Monday, 21 March, 0914hrs GMT

IN A REMOTE and secluded farmhouse some way off the A6 dual carriageway between Stockport and Derby, a transistor radio stood on the slatted wooden kitchen table. It was tuned to Radio 4 and the only sound in the room came from *Start the Week*. News of what had happened at King's Cross had played big that morning, dominating the *Today* programme and every news bulletin on the hour. By 8 a.m. a collective decision had been taken at Abbot's Farm: there were to be no exceptions, no exemptions. It had to be a collective action by everyone.

The bodies were slumped everywhere: over chairs, on the rough-tiled floor, out in the yard, in the armoury and on top of the industrial freezers. No exceptions. Everyone at Abbot's Farm had played their part: at the appointed time they had all swallowed the death pill.

*

It was just after midday in Vilnius when the line of armoured vehicles drew up outside the offices of Matulis ChemExport. They didn't press the bell or wait for an invitation to come in. Instead the lead vehicle revved its engine and accelerated towards the gates, smashing them down in a screech of metal on metal. Once inside the inner courtyard, the men of Lithuania's elite ARAS counter-terrorism police spilled out of the vehicles and filtered into the corridors and offices of the Soviet-era building. Minutes later, a heavily built, middle-aged man was escorted out in handcuffs, bewildered and protesting. Sergei Kadunov, sales director at Matulis ChemExport, had just been charged with assisting an international terrorist organization. He was facing up to thirty years in the notorious Pravieniškės House of Correction.

At the exact moment that Kadunov was being placed under arrest in Vilnius, five hundred miles to the east, Colonel Arkady Petrov was having an encounter of a very different kind. Summoned at short notice to the second-floor offices of the Kremlin, he was not entirely sure which way this meeting would go until he stepped through the door. Then came the smiles and the handshakes, the slaps on the back and the clink of multiple vodka glasses. The GRU and his unit had distinguished themselves, they told him. He was to be congratulated. There would be a promotion after this, and medals for all of his team. The intelligence gleaned from Jenny Li on the UK's chemical and biological weapons research, during those precious few hours while they had her under artificial sedation at the Ivanovsky Institute, had been most instructive. And the best of it? They laughed at this one. She would remember nothing of what she had told them. Nothing at all.

*

Luke was back in the flat, the one he shared with Elise in Battersea. For a long time they simply held each other and said nothing. Around his shoulder and upper arm there was a neat new bandage where all the shotgun pellets had been safely removed and they had taken the precaution of pumping him full of antibiotics. His other hand rested lightly, almost protectively, on Elise's midriff. There was still an awful lot they needed to talk about, but

405

now was not the time. Luke had been through hell and so had she and this, in a way, had brought them back together.

He glanced out of the window at the river traffic going past and a dark thought crossed his mind. They still had not discovered who the mole was, the informant, the secret source giving tip-offs to WaffenKrieg90.

But now he was beyond tired, exhausted in fact, and he could feel an aching in his glands. It was only later that morning, just as he went to take that well-earned nap, that Luke Carlton felt the beginnings of a real killer headache coming on.

Acknowledgements

My thanks to my tireless and meticulous editor, Simon Taylor, and the team at Transworld/PenguinRandomHouse. This is the fifth book of mine that Simon has had to read through and yet miraculously we are still friends.

To my calm, clever and well-connected literary agent, Julian Alexander at TheSohoAgency. We have come a long way together since I first waved a manuscript at him from my hospital bed in 2004.

To my lovely Elizabeth, for listening so patiently while I read out numerous passages, and for offering me advice and encouragement throughout.

To my daughter Sasha for all her help, hard work and advice with the proofreading. Nothing, it seems, escapes her notice.

To the brilliant Dr Nigel Lightfoot, for all his professional advice on virology, Russia and the crisis machinery of Whitehall.

To 'E', for pin-sharp advice on professional jargon.

To Richard Walton, for sharing his expert knowledge of counter-terrorism policing.

To the Norwegian Arctic guides Stian Aker and Inge Solheim, for showing me the pristine beauty of Svalbard archipelago.

Frank Gardner has been the BBC's Security Correspondent since 2002. He holds a degree in Arabic and Islamic Studies. In 2004, while filming in Saudi Arabia, he was ambushed by terrorists, shot multiple times and left for dead. He survived and returned to active news reporting within a year. He still travels extensively. Awarded an OBE in 2005 for services to journalism, Frank published his bestselling memoir, *Blood and Sand*, in 2006. His first novel, *Crisis*, which introduced readers to SIS operative Luke Carlton, was a No. 1 bestseller. The second Luke Carlton thriller, *Ultimatum*, was also a *Sunday Times* top 10 bestseller. He lives in London.

You can follow him on Facebook and Twitter @FrankRGardner